Cover

Stephen Hunter, film critic for the *Washington Post* and winner of the Pulitzer Prize and the American Society of Newspaper Editors Award for criticism, is the author of twelve novels. He lives in Baltimore, Maryland.

HAVANA

Havana, Cuba, in 1953 is flush with booming casinos, sex and drugs. The city is a lucrative paradise for everyone from the Mafia to pimps, porn-makers and anyone looking to grab a piece of the action — including the Cuban government, which naturally honours the interests of its old ally, the United States of America. Of course, where there's paradise, trouble can't be far behind. Trouble, in this case, is in the charismatic form of a young revolutionary named Fidel Castro. The Caribbean is fast becoming a strategic Cold War hub, and Soviet intelligence has taken Castro under its wing. The CIA's response is to send the one man capable of eliminating Castro: the legendary gunfighter and ex-Marine hero Earl Swagger . . .

STEPHEN HUNTER

HAVANA

Complete and Unabridged

CHARNWOOD
Leicester

First published in Great Britain in 2004 by
Century

First Charnwood Edition
published 2005
by arrangement with
Century, a division of
The Random House Group Limited, London

British Library CIP Data

Hunter, Stephen, 1946 –
   Havana.—Large print ed.—
   Charnwood library series
   1. Castro, Fidel, 1926 – —Fiction 2. Havana
   (Cuba)—History—Fiction 3. Cuba—Politics and
   government—1933 – 1959 —Fiction 4. Suspense
   fiction 5. Large type books
   I. Title
   813.5'4 [F]

   ISBN 1–84395–869–4

Published by
F. A. Thorpe (Publishing)
Anstey, Leicestershire

Set by Words & Graphics Ltd.
Anstey, Leicestershire
Printed and bound in Great Britain by
T. J. International Ltd., Padstow, Cornwall

This book is printed on acid-free paper

For Hannah Mark and Wenkel's little boy
in hopes that they meet as friends

RICKY: Oh, Lucy!
LUCY: Oh, Ricky!

— Lucille Ball, Desi Arnaz
I Love Lucy, CBS, 1953

1

It was a perfect O.

It floated from the smoker's mouth, an amazing confabulation, and then caught a small charge of wind and began to drift, widening, bending a little, until at last, high among the buildings, it atomized to wisps, and then nothing.

'How the fug they do that, Lenny?' Frankie Carbine asked.

'It's a machine, Frankie. They have machines for everything now'days. You got a machine there too, Frankie.'

It was true. Inside his overcoat was a machine from across the seas, Denmark, a place so far away Frankie couldn't begin to imagine it. Not that he would have tried. Frankie didn't care much for stuff like that.

Anyway, this machine was a gun, just an assortment of tubes and housings and plastic handles and prongs and things that slid in and out. It was a Danish Model 46 9mm submachine gun with a thirty-two-round magazine, though Frankie, not interested either in the technical, didn't know that. Someone who knew guns somewhere in the thing said this was the best gun made for the kind of work the thing did. Frankie had no imagination for the theoretical: he just knew that it was much lighter and more concealable than the old-fashioned tommy guns because its stock was a bent metal shape on hinges — which meant it could be folded and made smaller — and that it fired faster, kicked less and was easier to use. You pointed it, you sprayed, you walked away. That was his job.

Frankie — born Franco Caribinieri forty-three years earlier in Salerno, moved to Brooklyn when four, a common enough trajectory for a midlevel soldier — idly watched as another vaporous O was manufactured and dispatched into the loud air near Times Square, courtesy of the R. J. Reynolds Tobacco Company. CAMELS, said the launching platform, a billboard that sheathed the entire front of the building between 44th and 45th right on Broadway, NO. 1 FOR SMOKING PLEASURE. The hole that belched the ring was cleverly situated at the mouth of the painted face of a movie-star handsome fellow, while over his shoulder some classy blonde dame with lips like roses looked seductively out upon the anonymous masses who hastened by foot, automobile, bus and cab through the great metropolitan space. The air was almost blue with smoke, the people were gray with exhaustion, worry or hurry, the cars were still mostly black except for the cabs which were yellow, and everybody was in a hurry. It was also loud. Honks, squeals, yells, the roar of engines, all of it pounding away. It gave you a headache. Frankie loved it.

He sat in the back seat of a freshly stolen '47 DeSoto, black; he shared the cushion with a teddy bear, a doll and a Lone Ranger comic book. He wore a blue serge pinstriped suit, a black wool overcoat (to keep the gun hidden, not to keep him warm; it was spring and in the sixties) and, because everyone he knew and respected did, a black fedora pulled low over his eyes.

'I wonder, I got time for an Orange Julius?' asked Lenny.

It was an easy reach; the OJ stand was just across the sidewalk from the parked car, sandwiched between two theaters (*Roman Holiday* at one and *Target Zero* at the other), a souvenir shop, an entrance to the commercial floors above, and then a shabby bookstore with FRENCH BOOKS in big letters above it.

'No,' said Frankie. 'You can get an OJ another fuggin' time. I don't want to come out of that place and find you wit' an OJ in your hand and the car turned off.'

'Frankie, it's an easy one. You get close, you squeeze, you see brains, you turn, we drive away.'

'It's always easy, until it's hard,' said Frankie.

Someone tapped on the farside window. It was a kid, Dominic's boy, fifteen, and he'd spotted the mark coming down the street. He made brief eye contact with Frankie, who repaid the gesture with a wink and a smile — the boy loved Frankie, seeing him as one of the coolest guys in New York — and departed.

'Yeah, I got him too,' said Lenny. 'You see him, Frankie?'

'Yeah, yeah, I got him.'

The mark was a tall sprig of a guy in a raincoat. He had two salesman's bags under his arms and two black bags of approximately the same size under his eyes. His name was unimportant, his background meaningless, his identity unworthy of attention. He was hawking California wares in New York territory and he'd found a clown dumb enough to consider buying at quite a discount for being first, only he didn't know that someone in his own little fiefdom had already ratted him out.

It was nothing a great one would be involved in. All that was finished now. Those had been great days, but somehow Frankie never got close to the action; he was just a mechanic on the outskirts, a gun toter for a crew that was affiliated to a mob that was affiliated to a bigger mob. He went, he did, he managed. But once at a club he'd seen them: the great Bennie Siegel, now dead, the great Meyer Lansky, now exiled, the great Lucky Luciano, with the one dead eye, now deported, such movie-star men, men of charisma and grace and beauty, the center of the universe.

There was the romance of the life he loved: the power, the women, the way men made room, the respect, the way people acknowledged your importance. He loved that. He'd never had a fuggin' taste of it, not even a smell; he was just a cheap fug with a gun. So he was waiting outside a dirty-pix store to do a quickie, and get out. Five hundred bucks in the till, a yard for Lenny the driver, that's all.

They watched as the mark slipped into the door beneath the FRENCH BOOKS sign and disappeared.

'I'll smoke a ciggie, Lenny. Let 'em get comfy, get set up, get cool. Then Frankie Carbine

4

transacts his business and we're home by noon.'

'A great plan, Frankie.'

So Frankie lit another cigarette, and tried to blow smoke rings for a few minutes, and his never quite cohered like the giant masterpieces floating above: another frustration, and the perfect illustration of the life he had as opposed to the life he wanted.

'Okay,' he finally said.

'Good luck, killer,' said Lenny.

Frankie left the car and walked swiftly to the store, making eye contact with no one. No one noticed him, which was not a bad thing, for he was, he knew, an odd customer: a fellow in a heavy overcoat on a warm day, with one hand deep in his pocket, where it actually slid through the slash in his coat so it could grasp the grip of the Danish submachine gun. His coat hung too straight, because in the other pocket were two more thirty-two-round magazines, each weighing a pound and a half. His hat was too low, like Georgie Raft's in a picture. His suit was dark, he was a glowering death figure, a movie gangster, come to call. But no one noticed. It was New York, after all; who notices such things, when there is so much else to notice?

Frankie evaded a popcorn cart, slipped behind a nigger working a three-card-monte con on stiffs, smelled hot dogs from another vendor on the street, wished he had time for a chocolate Yoo-Hoo, a favorite of his, and turned into the store.

He had been in such places before and so nothing shocked him, except that every week it seemed they were getting more and more bold in what they sold. The windows had been painted black for privacy, and the interior lit by fluorescent glow, which cast a dead-bone color on everything and dazzled off the cellophane. There was a lot of cellophane, and behind it, flesh, everywhere, saggy and pale and raw, things you could see nowhere else. This broad had oval-shaped nipples, that one bad teeth and stretch marks, this one was a hot piece, the next your mother's mother's sister. Packets of cards lay on tables, sealed but promising whores showing off butts or coochies. The nudist camp stuff occupied its own tables, most of it from Germany, where dumpy blonde dames stood with towels covering their hair-pies, smiling as if photographed at a church picnic. Over on that wall men's magazines sold war atrocity laced with sex, where Japs were torturing busty American nurses behind screaming red headlines like BUNA BLOOD BATH! Behind the counter, reels of 16mm stag movies in boxes blank but for numbers had been filed, and maybe they gave you a glimpse of something you never saw anyplace except Havana, but you had to pay big for it. The smell of disinfectant hung in the air, and a bruiser cruised the aisles looking for dirty boys who were jigging themselves under their clothes; that was never permitted. They had to be tossed.

But Frankie knew the big kid wouldn't stand in his way, not once the fun started. That was the point of a subgun, even a Danish one: it spoke so loud and powerfully, Joes just melted into

6

puddles of nothingness in its presence.

Quickly, Frankie checked the place out, seeing only furtive men locked on what they were considering buying and sneaking home in lunch buckets or briefcases. Nobody would ever admit to being in such a place so no witnesses would come forth and no statements would be signed. That was what was so great.

Frankie edged through the throng, bumping into a guy gazing yearningly at *Black Garters* magazine, and another, a homo, in the homo section where *Male Call* seemed to be the big item. At the cash register a surly creep reigned supreme and guarded access to the stag movies; behind that was the window of the office. Frankie might have to pop the creep first before he had a clear shot at the two in the office. He could see them, bent over the new product line from the sample cases. Shit, color! These California pricks had gotten so well established they could print out in color. Frankie's understanding of the business — any business — was limited, but he understood that color was the next big thing in nudie books and pix.

No wonder the big boys were so interested in sending a message to California: deal through us or stay off our turf.

'Hey,' said the clerk. 'You here to buy or just to poke your pud? Get your goddamned mitts out of your pockets, pally, or take a hike.'

Frankie decided the man's fate in a second. It pissed him off to be dismissed so roughly. This fug thinks he's *tough?*

'Yeah, here's your hike,' said Frankie.

7

He shrugged to spread his coat and raised the muzzle of the gun, his left hand coming around to grab the magazine, clamping down a safety lever behind the magazine housing. The clerk's face went numb and he just froze up, like a guy who sees the car coming and knows there's no point. There wasn't one, either.

Frankie fired. Three shots, but they ripped out in a millionth of a second or so it seemed, that's how fast the fuggin' gun fired. The light — not much was there to begin with, but there was maybe a little — left the clerk's eyes as the bullets speared him, and he said 'Thelma!' to Frankie as he slid down.

The moment froze. It was dead silent. Nobody moved, nobody looked, nobody even farted. The echo of the three shots seemed to clang through the smoke and the only noise was the light metallic grind of the spent casings rolling on the floor. The acrid smell of the burned powder overpowered and dissolved the disinfectant stench. The two men at the desk through the window looked at Frankie, who now transacted his day's labor.

He fired through the glass, and watched it fracture into sleet, like the glinty spray of a Flatbush trolley through new snow on a winter afternoon in a long-lost childhood, all chaos and sparkle; and the bullets were like the arrival of a tornado, for as they dissolved the glass, they dissolved what lay behind the glass. The desk erupted in a riot of splinters and dust and smoke and nudie books flew into the air as if seized by a whirlwind.

8

You couldn't say the two stiffs didn't know what hit them, because Frankie knew they did, in that split second when they'd looked over to him and seen their deaths in his eye. But in another second they were gone, for the bullets bullied them relentlessly, causing them to jerk and twist and lurch. One fell back into his chair and went limp, the other rose, twisted as if on fire, and beat with his hands at the things that tore him up, but then he slid to the ground, his skull hitting the linoleum with a thud.

Again, silence. Each man lay still. Then not still: as if dams had been burst, a sudden torrent of blood began to empty from each penetrated man, from a dozen new orifices. So much, so fast; it soaked them, running from broken face to burned shirt to twisted arm to splayed fingers to hard floor, spreading in a satiny pool. Frankie squirted them again, to make sure.

He turned, realizing the gun was empty, and hit a little lever to drop the one mag. Neatly he fitted another one in, felt it snap in place. Then he looked up.

This was not working out.

There before him, with a stunned look on his face and a copy of *Gal Leg* in his hand, a uniformed New York City policeman stood in stupefaction equal to Frankie's. The two armed men faced each other.

'NO!' Frankie screamed, imploring the cop to cooperate as he knew clipping cops led to career difficulties, but the cop refused to cooperate, and his hand went inside his double-breasted coat and tugged the cop Colt out, and Frankie

9

watched, as it seemed to be taking forever. He should have smacked him hard in the head with the gun barrel, but he didn't think fast enough, and about an hour later the cop got the revolver unlimbered, actually paused to cock the hammer with his thumb, and raised it onto Frankie, who again screamed 'NO!' except that the word was lost in the thunder of the gun. It fired so fast, it slithered and twitched like a snake in his hands, desperate to escape.

The cop fell sideways and back, the revolver clattering to the ground. He too immediately began to issue copious amounts of liquid from new openings.

This was the one that unlocked the frozen customers. Now, frantically, they broke for the door, fighting each other to escape the madman's bullets. Someone broke the black painted window and rolled out, admitting a sudden piercing blaze of fresh light, which in turn caught the smoke and dust heaving in the air, glinted off of tits and coochies. The panic was contagious, for now it struck Frankie, and he too lost control and ran, as if fleeing a mad gunman, utterly forgetting the fact that he was the mad gunman.

Again, it took a while. But eventually, the passage cleared and Frankie stepped out.

He saw two things immediately.

The first is that there was no Lenny and no car and the second was that there was a horse.

It wasn't a cowboy horse at all, though for just a second that's what he thought, because cowboys were all over the place on the television now. It was a police horse, and on its back was a policeman and it cantered through traffic down Broadway, right at him, amid a screech of horns, and the screams of people who dived this way and that.

Fug, thought Frankie.

The officer on horseback had possibly himself seen a lot of television, for he had his gun drawn and he leaned over the neck of the plunging horse and began to fire at Frankie. Of course on the television or in the movies, somebody always falls, usually shot in the arm or shoulder, when this one is pulled off, but in real life nothing at all happened as the bullets went wild, though Frankie had a impression in his peripheral vision of a window breaking.

Onward, onward rode the horseman, though nobody knew the reason why. Possibly it was stupidity, possibly heroic will, possibly an accident, he just rode right at Frankie through the traffic, cut between cars to the sidewalk and cantered on as if to crush Frankie to the pavement.

Frankie watched in horror, seeing the wide red eyes of the animal, filled with fear, the lather of foamy sweat, hearing the clatter of the iron-shod hooves against the pavement, and the heavy, labored breathing of the animal which was, he now saw, immense compared to him, and just about to squish him like a bug.

He never made the decision because there wasn't a decision to be made, but Frankie found himself the sole proprietor of a rather angry Danish machine gun, which in about two seconds flat emptied itself into the raging animal. He himself heard nothing, for shooters in battle conditions rarely do. He felt the gun, however, shivering as it devoured its magazine, and sensed the spray of spent cartridges as they were spat from the breech this way and that, hot like pieces of fresh popcorn.

The animal was hit across the chest, and, opened up in the process of the slaughter, it reared back in pain and panic, flipping its tiny rider to the pavement with a shudder. Then, huge and whinnying piteously, it fell to its forelegs, awash in blood from the sundered chest, and from its mouth and nose where blood from its lungs had overwhelmed its throat and nasal tubes. It thrashed, tried to rise because it had no clear concept of the death that now stalked through its body, and then its great head slid forward and it was still.

'Fungola!' cursed Frankie, tossing the empty gun. He looked and prayed for Lenny but Lenny had long since quit the field. Sirens arose and it seemed that several brave citizens were pointing at him.

'You killed a horse!' a lady spat.

Frankie did not think it the right time to offer explanations, and turned toward an alley and began to run like holy hell.

2

In the early spring of 1953, a big noise from Winnetka dominated the diplomatic tennis circuit in Havana. That was what they called him, after the famous hit tune from the '30s. It summed him up: big, powerful, American, unbeatable. And it didn't matter that he actually came from Kenilworth, a whole swank town down the North Shore from Winnetka. He was close enough to Winnetka. His name was Roger St. John Evans, and to make him all the more glamorous, it was rumored he was a spy.

He was in demand that season. He played at least three or four times a week, on his own courts or at some other embassy out in leafy Vedado or, even more frequently, at the Havana Country Club, or even occasionally on the private courts of the big Miramar houses out La Quinta owned by Domino Sugar executives or United Fruit Company bigwigs. In all those venues, the embassies, the big northward-facing houses in Miramar and Buena Vista, the courts behind the Vedado embassies, out as far as La Playa and the Yacht Club, the country club, his beauty, power and smoothness made him many a wealthy young lady's dreamboat, a sought-after dinner guest, a real catch.

So on a certain late spring day — the sky was so blue, the summer heat had yet not attacked the Pearl of the Antilles, a breeze floated across

13

Havana, just enough to lift flags and palms and young girls' hearts — Roger tossed the ball upward for service, felt his long body coil as pure instinct took over, and the strength traveled like a wave up and through his body and the complex computations of hand/eye circuitry functioned at a rate far more efficient than most men's. As the ball was released he tightened, then unleashed and his arm ripped through an arc, bringing the racket loosely with it in the backhand grip for a bit of English. He caught the ball full swat at its apogee — the nearly musical *pong!* signifying solid contact was so satisfying! — hit through it at a slight cant, and nailed a bending screamer that seemed to spiral toward the chalked line on the other side of the net. It hit that target square, blasting up a sheet of white mist, and spun away, far beyond his poor opponent's lunge.

Game, set, match.

His two opponents, a Bill and a Ted, executives for United Fruit, accepted the inevitable.

'That's it, boys,' sang Roger, allowing himself a taste of raptor's glee.

'Well done, old man,' said Bill, who though not an Ivy had picked up certain Eastern affectations from the many who dominated the island's American business culture.

Roger's doubles partner, his eager young assistant Walter, who played a spunky if uninspired game of tennis and always seemed a bit behind, gave a little leap and clapped a hand against the base of his racket face, in salute to his partner's brilliance and victory.

14

'Way to go, Big Winnetka! Boola-boola!' he chanted, in a voice clotted with affection and admiration.

The players gathered at the net, to shake hands, exchange respects and towel off.

'A drink, I think,' said Ted. 'Pedro, mojitos please. At the pool. And tell Manuelo not to spare the rum. I think we can afford it.' He winked at Roger. 'I have an in at Bacardi.'

'Si, señor,' said Ted's senior servant, who trotted off to fetch.

'Walter, help him, will you,' said Roger.

'Sure,' said Walter cheerily.

'No, no,' said Ted, 'it seems compassionate, but you spoil them and there's problems later. Let's go to the pool.'

They walked through the garden to the shimmering blue reservoir behind the great house. The men sat at a table under an ancient pruned palm, close to flowers, hedges, tropical bouquets and recently turned earth, in the shade of a vast umbrella, and Pedro brought the drinks. They were expertly made, the rum soaked in dense sugar, the mint sprigs crushed to loosen that herb's magic, the gassy water aboil with bubbles, all mixed to swirl and the ice cubes giving the whole an intense chill. The pleasing ritual of men drinking: the booze took the sting from the losers' loss and spread the glow of the winners' win. Cigars, Havana Perfectos in fact, came out, were lit and sucked and a warm fog settled upon the four.

Blah blah blah and more blah blah blah, all pleasant if pointless: a little embassy gossip, a

15

little business climate analysis, a little on current politics and what a good job the new president Batista was doing, he was really on the team, and on and on —

But then it seemed a shadow passed over the sun. No, it was Pedro. He whispered something to Ted, who nodded.

'Well,' he said, 'this is so pleasant I wish it would never end. But now it must. There's someone you have to see. Will you follow me please? He's just arrived.'

Roger shot Walter a look. What's *this?* it seemed to say. Who are these boys to be playing so mysterioso? Being mysterioso: that was Roger and Walter's profession. And the locution was so strange: someone you *have* to see, as if it were a professional situation, not a post-match social obligation.

But, of course, they both rose with their host and followed him into the big house with its gleaming floors and up marble stairs. United Fruit knew how to impress. Not even El Presidente, as Batista was mocked by the Americans behind his back, lived quite so grandly as United Fruit's most important executive.

'That way. The library. I'd hurry. He's expecting you.'

Roger led the way through French doors and into a vast room, lined with books that had never been opened, and furniture from somebody's empire, and silk and damask and the usual gewgaws of conquest, a bronze telescope on a tripod, a Brown Bess hung on the wall, lancers

16

pennants tripoded in the corner. Both men blinked, for the doors to the balcony were open and the light of day blazed in unrepentant and powerful.

'Well hello, boys. My, aren't you a sight? Sweaty but unbowed, athletes of the moment.'

Roger recognized the voice, thought *no, no, it can't be*, and squinted as from a dark corner a man came into the light. He was not remarkable in any way and wore a simple khaki suit and a white shirt and black tie. He wore black plastic-framed glasses, was quite bald, if a little tall and rangy. No charisma, no attraction, no drama. The face so regular as to instantly vanish from memory. He looked like a salesman or possibly a minor attorney. His name was known but to a few, though to those few it had acquired legendary status. Roger was one of the few. That name, however, was not spoken, and had never appeared in print. Instead he was called Plans, for he ran the Directorate of Plans, on the Agency's clandestine side. He didn't fight the Cold War, he *was* the Cold War. To his face he was called . . . well, nothing. It was awkward, but nothing could be done about it. *Sir*, uttered by the subjects of his attention, clumsily facilitated his face-to-face transactions.

This was a highly unlikely situation. Plans normally functioned out of the station, as the slang had it, in the embassy. He never just, er, showed up like this, in some private house miles from the embassy, unless something really interesting was about to happen.

'Sir, do you know my assistant, Walter Short?'

17

Walter bowed nervously; he could not have known himself who this fellow was, but as a quick study had intuited from pal and supervisor's gravity that he was important.

'Hello, sir, I — '

'Yes, yes, Short. China, no? Some military stuff, advising Chiang. Is that right?'

'Yes, sir, I — '

'Well, Roger, and, uh, Short, sit down, we must have a chat.'

And so they sat.

'How are your parents, Roger? Is your father still prospering?'

'Sir, Dad's fine. The heart attack slowed him down, but Mom says he's back at work now. Nothing can stop that man.'

'Yes, I know. I crewed with him at Harvard. But I was never an athlete like him. I wonder if he remembers me. He was a fine athlete.'

'Yes, sir. Dad was. He still has a three handicap.'

'That's remarkable. Now, anyway, Roger, I am here — '

'Roger, should I take notes?' whispered Walter.

'No, no, we don't want any of this on paper,' said Plans.

'Yes, sir, I — '

'That's all right. Now, Roger, I just looked through your OSS record. Very impressive. Then there's your medal citation. Silver Star. Very impressive. You were part of a team that hunted down a German sniper in Switzerland. You killed him. I like the finality in that. No ambiguity to it at all. You blew the bastard out of his boots, you

18

recovered some advanced technology that was very helpful. Short, did you realize you were working for a genuine war hero?'

'I knew — '

'So, Roger, you were, in a sense, a manhunter.'

Roger swallowed, ever so gently. It was all true, but just barely. He'd been a child. An officer named Leets did all the work. At the end, when they killed the German, Roger was aware that most of his burst of .45s had missed. He had just hosed the tommy gun away, running through thirty rounds in three seconds, the only bullets he fired in the entire Second World War.

'I suppose,' said Roger.

'Good. A taste for it? Like it dark and dangerous? Like the guns, the excitement? Like the thrill of the hunt, the satisfaction of the kill? That's what we're looking for.'

'It was necessary,' was all Roger could think to say.

'Like to run another operation like that, Roger?'

Well . . . here it was. Roger knew that if he said no, it would be a dark mark against him. Plans didn't come this far, enter through the back door, and fly home tourist class to hear a rejection. But if Roger said yes, well, that had its problems too: one didn't want to get caught up in something sticky and illegal that couldn't be controlled. He smiled, and said, 'Of course I — '

'Oh, I don't want *you* doing anything violent. We are not gangsters, after all. We plan, we make sure things happen, we liaise, we coordinate, we administer. But you know how to put something

19

like this together? You've done it. Part of it, of course, would be finding a man to do the actual work. Someone from outside our organization, but someone who could be trusted. Someone reliable. We both know there are elements in Cuba who would do such a thing for money or self-interest or a dozen other motives. But they are not reliable and we don't want anything coming back to haunt us, do we? That's why I rely on your discretion. You could find a man, no? You could supervise the operation. You could make it happen?'

'Yes, sir.'

'*Good show!* I knew you'd say that. Short, you aboard? You can play this sort of game under Roger's supervision, can't you? You won't let us down?'

'Yes, sir,' said Walter, 'and I — '

'Excellent,' said Plans. 'Now, you are wondering, who is all this about? Well, it's a young Cuban lawyer,' said Plans. He pushed a manila envelope over, and Short opened it to find the usual run of documents, plus a photo of a young man with an oval young face, a Spanish darkness, an intensity to eyes that could not yet have seen very much.

He turned it over, said the name aloud, feeling its newness on his tongue: 'Castro.'

'That's him. Very charismatic, an orator. He might be a problem.'

'A problem?' said Roger.

'A problem,' said Plans. 'People are talking already. I'm getting serious inquiries from our own Caribbean Desk, from all sorts of people at

State, from the Brits and the French, from the Mexicans and the Canadians. He was involved in anti-American demonstrations against John Foster in '48 in Colombia. When the Ortodoxo party founder Chiba killed himself, this fellow astutely put himself at the center of the mourning process and got on the radio.'

'There are so many of them,' said Roger.

'But this one is different. He may be a problem.'

He paused.

'Everybody wants this island to stay just the way it is, now that we've reinstated Batista. We don't want any applecarts upset, and we don't want our Red friends taking an interest in this sort of fellow. He's exactly their kind of man; they could play him like a Stradivarius. Too much money has been invested, and too much time has been spent. We can't let this get out of control. If we're not on top of it, it could be on top of us.'

'Sir — ah, I — '

'Yes, Roger, go on.'

'It's just that, well, isn't this a bit, you know, *radical?* I mean, there might be other methods: we could give him money, I suppose, or recruit him in some way. We could, you know, leverage him with photographs of some sort or other, we could acquire influence with one of his close associates so that we'd always have tabs on him and in some way could control him, why, there must be — '

'You know, that's what some said in Langley. It's worked in the past, it'll work in the future.

That's the *American* way and everybody's comfortable with it. You're comfortable with it.'

'Yes, sir, I — '

'But maybe just this once, as a kind of test case, we ought to not do the American thing. We ought to make a statement. Nothing bold, nothing flamboyant, nothing cruel, nothing attention-getting. But the right folks would notice: this fellow, he was about to upset applecarts, and then suddenly he was dead. Who? Why, not the Americans, they don't do that . . . do they? Maybe it's time to add that *do they?* to the equation.'

'Yes, sir.'

'That's why I want to go ahead on this thing. I'm approving a budget and it gets tucked into a National Security Working Group, and a senior case officer will run interference at Langley and I'll supervise closely. We'll code-name it Big Noise. I like that. I love thinking up the right code names. I don't think an op can go unless it's got the right damn name. Anyhow, I'm clearing the decks for you on other assignments. You don't have to troll for sources at the country club any more. Though of course you should continue with the damned tennis. You can't just walk away from it and huddle in the office.'

'Does this mean I can start winning faster? I'm very tired of throwing a couple of games to keep these people happy.'

'Yes, it should get you in the right mood. Kill them, crush them, stamp them out. In the meantime, I want to see you put together a scenario, find the personnel, develop it plausibly,

22

set up a timetable, and we'll run it by the Director and see if we can make it happen. I don't need to tell you how top secret the operation is. That's, of course, why I'm not operating out of the embassy station. You can't keep anything secret in an embassy. Are we together on this? Roger, you're with me now?'

'I'm just concerned about finding a fellow,' said Roger. 'The whole thing would hinge on that. The wrong fellow, the wrong result. It has to be someone you can trust, who is heroic, capable, and patriotic. Where do you find such men?'

'Well, Roger,' said Plans, 'the Agency has resources. We will — '

Walter Short interrupted.

'Excuse me,' he said, louder than Roger had ever heard him speak before. 'I know where you can find such a man.'

They looked at him.

'There's a man in Arkansas,' he said finally. 'Strong, tough, smart, capable. A real hero. A genius with guns and in fights. A man who's killed, who's good at it, but who hasn't been made crazy by it and doesn't need to do it. And a man who knows how to get anything done. If you could get Earl working for you, you'd have something. I mean, *something*.'

3

Sautéed *en beurre*, then served with a complex red, possibly a St. Emilion, a '34 or a '35, the cockroach would have tasted delicious. Why red? Because red goes with meat. A cockroach certainly isn't fish, of that you may be sure.

But Zek 4715 did not have a St. Emilion, a '34 or a '35, or a pan or any butter, or anything much at all, except the cockroach.

It was not even much of a cockroach. But cockroaches were hard to come by, and so this one, as runty and pitiful a specimen as it was, would nevertheless have to do, and the zek held it between his long and elegant fingers and considered it carefully.

Little bug, he thought, you and I, we are brothers. So it is entirely appropriate that you nourish me with your little pinch of protein. I salute you. I admire you.

'Just eat it, damn you,' said Zek 5891, known to be Latkowsky, the Polish saboteur and wrecker. 'Don't torture us with your exquisite manners.'

It seemed rude to consume a sibling so quickly, however. Zek 4715 and the bug: both were held squirming against their will in the grasp of a larger organism, and would live or die according to the dictates, no, the whimsies, of that organism.

So be it.

24

Outside, a wind howled. This was not remarkable, as outside a wind always howled. It was Siberia, after all, where the wind was supposed to howl. It was Gulag No. 432, some twenty miles south of the arctic circle, not far — say 150 kilometers — from the big town of Verbansk, with its cosmopolitan population of thirty-five, and a railhead.

'Gentlemen,' said 4715, raising the bug, 'to you, the living, I dedicate this kindred soul.'

The living included Latkowsky; Zek 0567, one Rubel, an oppositionist; Zek 9835, Menshov, the famous careerist who had murdered hundreds for Beria only to be sent just as far north as anyone else; Zek 6854, Tulov, the spy for the Zionists; Zek 4511, Barabia, the spy for the French and Americans; Zek 2378, Krakov, the deviationist and wrecker; and . . . well, on and on, a barracks full of former intelligence officers, diplomats and soldiers who had in one way or another disappointed the regime or, more likely, its boss, and were turned magically into zeks, sentenced to die out here amid howling winds, nourished on beet soup and the odd potato or bug.

'Eat it, damn you!' someone called.

4715 did. There had never been any doubt about that. The bug squirmed against his teeth, then went still as it was halved, then quartered, then ground by forces beyond its comprehension. A weird prick of flavor, extremely odd, flew to 4715's brain, reminding him of something. What, possibly? The paella in Spain in '36, full of crackly shrimp and squid and zesty tomato? Or

25

the leek soup at Stalingrad, so delicious after a day's battle in the snowy wreckage? Or possibly the veal sausage and sauerkraut he'd had in a German city, ruined though it was, in '45, before his final arrest.

The bug vanished, leaving an aftertaste on his tongue to be savored for hours.

Applause rose, for the diversion of 4715 and the cockroach had been more entertainment than the barracks had seen since Zek 2098 died spitting blood and cursing the Boss several months or possibly years ago.

'Thank you, my friends,' 4715 said, and it was true: these were his friends, with their hollow faces and shaven scalps, cheekbones like bedknobs, eyes black and deep and exquisite with suffering. Tomorrow, the road, the eternal road on which they labored in the cold, a road that would kill them. It was being built against the possibility that the Boss would someday want to drive to the North Pole. Although the Boss had died recently, and would never drive to the North Pole, that hadn't seemed to affect the roadbuilders of Gulag No. 432, not even a little bit. Onward, to the North Pole, in salute to triumphant socialism!

So resigned were they, in fact, that when Senior Sergeant Koblisky entered the barracks with a loud thump and a bump, escorted by three men with rifles, it was an astonishment to all. The guards pretty much left the zeks alone on the one Sunday afternoon of the month they were not required to build the road to the North Pole, in case the Boss should come back from the dead and demand to be driven there. The guards didn't want to be at 432 any more than the zeks did. Only one person wanted all these humans to be out here at 432 and he was dead now and it still didn't matter.

'Easy now, move back, you bastards, or I'll have the corporal run a bayonet through you.' That was Senior Sergeant Koblisky in a good mood.

It was so unfortunate that the Senior Sergeant, once a tank ace with Marshal Konshavsky's Fifth Shock Army at Kursk, had uttered a sentence of compassion for the poor German bastards he'd just machine-gunned as they surrendered (under NKVD orders of the day). That was enough to transfer him to 432 after war's end, a chestful of medals and twenty-eight Nazi Panzers destroyed or not.

'Let's see, where is he? I know you're here, damn you. You didn't die yet. I saw you yesterday, I saw you this morning, I — oh, there you are. 4715, get your ratty little ass over here.'

'What?' 4715 said. 'Why, I — '

'Goddammit, get over here. It's cold out, I want this over with so I can get back to my bottle. Wrap yourself up and let's go.'

4715 blinked, stunned. In fact this event was unprecedented in living memory. Men came, men died, men cried, men were buried, but men were never summoned. There was no point. It was almost incomprehensible.

'Yes, Senior Sergeant, I — '

'Here, wear this, dammit, it'll save time.'

He tossed the spindly 4715 a guard's wool

27

coat, something that weighed so much it almost crushed the poor man, who was used to rags stuffed with newspapers as a barrier against the cold. 4715 found the strength to wrap it about himself, wished he had shoes of leather instead of wood, and, escorted by his protectors, stepped out.

Cold of course. The eternal wind, the eternal pelting of pieces of grit and ice and sand and vegetation; a gloom that was endless, a landscape that, beyond the wire, was itself an eternal flatness of snow and scrub vegetation giving way in a distance too far to be measured to leaden, lowering skies.

It was spring in Siberia.

The party trudged against the blistering wind across the compound to its one well-constructed building, a headquarters house, of stout timber, with actual smoke escaping a chimney to signify the presence of fire and warmth within. Immediately the clever 4715 spied the anomaly.

Camp 432's motley of vehicles, consisting mainly of old trucks that had somehow survived the war, were drawn up in formation outside the headquarters building. These were the ancient contrivances that hauled the prisoners' food out to them, and brought back the bodies, as the road headed farther and farther toward the Pole, a foot or so a day. Success was expected in 2056. But parked immediately before the building was something astonishing: a black, gleaming Zil limousine, well-waxed and showing only mud spatters on the fenders and a thin adhesive of dust after the drive from the railhead.

But 4715 hadn't time to conjecture on the meaning of this strangeness; he was inside and felt absolute, pure, quite beautiful warmth for the first time in many a month, or year, whatever.

'This way. You must be clean, of course. Important men can't be offended by your stink and filth. Really, it's sad how you've let yourself go.'

'True, I missed the morning bath. I decided on a second glass of tea instead, and a strawberry blintz with cream,' said 4715.

'See, men, how 4715 has kept his wit? Not like some I know. All right, 4715, there it is. Have fun and be quick.'

4715 stood before a shower stall in the guards' quarters. He stripped quickly, stepped inside and turned on the blast of hot water. It scalded blissfully, grinding off years of filth. He shivered in pleasure, found a rough bar of soap and lathered. Possibly they were readying him for his own hanging; it didn't matter. This was worth dying for.

★   ★   ★

'Speshnev, Speshnev, Speshnev,' came a voice familiar to 4715 from a thousand or so years ago. 4715 blinked hard in the newness of it all; yes, his name. His name spoken publicly, loudly, affectionately, when to utter it had been forbidden for so long. It was a weirdness so profound he had no idea how to comprehend it, but that drama was dwarfed by the next, when he encountered the speaker himself, large and blustery, but with shrewd eyes and glossy hair that only partially softened the brutality of his features.

It was his mentor, his teacher, his sponsor, his betrayer, his interrogator, his most reluctant torturer, his sentencer, the famous wizard of the service, one P. Pushkin, once a university professor and chess champion, then a secret soldier in the wars of Red conquest. P. Pushkin was the warrior incarnate, a kind of natural cossack who saw all opponents as manifestations of pure evil, fit only for obliteration. Though brilliant and even charming, his flaw and his genius was that he was without moderation in all things. He wore the dress uniform of a senior general of NKVD, and a chestful of ribbons that dwarfed even Senior Sergeant Koblisky's.

'How are you, my good man?' Pushkin inquired warmly, giving the spindly prisoner a bearish hug, as if Speshnev had just returned from a week in the country.

'Well, I am fine,' said the man named Speshnev. 'I just ate a delicious cockroach. I won it at cards from a Polish saboteur named 6732.'

'I see you've lost none of your edge. That's Speshnev, always at the top of his game, no matter the circumstance. Come, sit down, have some tea. A cigarette? No, cigarettes are probably meaningless to you at this stage of your socialist evolution. I'm hearing now they may even be bad for your health, so you were probably lucky to find them unavailable.'

He smiled, flipped a ciggie from a pack of

American Luckies, and made a show of putting the pack away. Then he smiled, the cigarette wobbling in the tightening of his lips in that broad smile, and handed the package to Speshnev, who quite naturally adored cigarettes even if he hadn't had one in years.

Speshnev internally cursed himself for his weakness of character, but he could no more turn down a cigarette than the shower, or the fresh clothes and the actual leather shoes he now wore.

The lighter flared. It came to the cigarette Speshnev had inserted in his own lips; he drew the fire to himself, through the vessel of the tobacco, and his lungs flooded with the pure drug of pleasure. His head buzzed, his senses blurred, and for a second, he was happy.

Was this some plot? Make him see the things he had disciplined himself to forget. Get him to taste pleasure, comfort, warmth, which had all but ceased to exist except in the zone of the theoretical? Then to plunge him back to the bitter nothingness of the barracks? To return him to zekness? That would be beyond endurance. He would hang himself, there could be no other way.

'I know you may have some resentments, Speshnev,' said Pushkin. 'It can't have been pleasant out here, no indeed. And though no official apology will ever be uttered, I think you will begin to see people who will admit that mistakes were made. A shake-up now and then is good, of course, but the Boss went too far. I told him myself, yes, I did. Boss, I said, I'm all for discipline and commitment and keeping the fellows on their toes, but don't you think you've sent too many away? Well, you know the Boss, he always played his cards close to his chest. He just smiled in that mysterious way and went about his program.'

This, of course, was apostasy; it would have earned any speaker a trip to the cellars instantly and a committee meeting with a Tokarev bullet behind the ear by dinnertime. But the Boss was dead; new things were in the works.

So Speshnev merely enjoyed his fabulous cigarette, feeling its smoke in his lungs, and drank the tea and felt the warmth everywhere.

Pushkin leaned forward conspiratorially. It was as if he were afraid men were listening and reports would be made, when in fact, if he so wished, he could order all the men in the camp shot.

'I will tell you this, Speshnev,' he said in a whisper. 'You may even have been luckier to be out here, though it can't have been fun. No, but Moscow in the last years of the Boss's madness was a *terrible* place. The fear, the paranoia, the betrayal, the burning out of whole bureaucracies, sometime three and four times, the brutal whimsy of the Black Marias as they took this one and left that one. No, it wasn't fun. A fellow hardly knew what to do. Here at least things were clear.'

Pushkin could not have believed this even for a second: he was a man without illusions, a practical man in all habits of mind. It pleased him, however, to utter the absurd and know that it would be accepted without argument.

But Speshnev could not help himself. Merrily he said, 'Yes, many a time, General, I woke at four in the morning for the long trudge across the snowy plains to work on that infernal road to the North Pole, telling myself, 'I am the luckiest man on the face of the earth, and thank the stars I have General Pushkin in my corner, looking out for me!' '

Pushkin ignored the irony, as was his whimsy of the morning.

'Speshnev, it's with great pleasure I have come all this way to announce your rehabilitation! Speshnev, so hard have I fought for justice in your case, so fiercely have I waged a campaign! I never forgot you, Speshnev, when all the others did. It is to me, Pushkin, that you should genuflect in thanks. I, Pushkin, give you your life back!'

'Does this mean — unlimited access to cockroaches?'

'Absolutely. Now listen. There is a country, Speshnev, that has long been oppressed. Its trajectory is toward chaos, crime, filth, degradation. It is owned lock, stock and barrel by American criminal and business interests, who use it as their whorehouse, shitter, and sugar factory.'

'Actually, it sounds delightful.'

'It is. Quite. The señoritas! *Muchas bonitas!*'

'I take it this is a Latin country?'

'The island paradise known as Cuba.'

'Excellent señoritas.'

'As there were in Spain. Same stock, actually,

though with a tinge of negro blood for that extra paprika in bed.'

'In my mind, I'm there already.'

'Speshnev, there is a boy. We have him spotted. He is clever, committed, ambitious, unbearably courageous. He could be the leader.'

'I see.'

'You will study the documents on the train back to Moscow with me. But you already see where this is going.'

'I see where I am going.'

'This boy. He must be seduced, smoothed, trained, aimed, disciplined, taught to expect success. As he is currently situated, well, it's that Latin temperament. Romantic, unrealistic, too quick to act, too slow to think. He needs a mentor, a senior fellow of wisdom and experience. Speshnev, with your magic ways, your charm, your ruthlessness, I think this is a task for you. It was made to order. It is your redemption, your future, your rehabilitation.'

'So I'm to help the regime that imprisoned me twice. Eagerly, willingly, aggressively?'

'Of course. There's only a paradox if you build it yourself. You can have a model contradiction in which we punish you unjustly, almost to the point of death, certainly to the point of misery, then we demand heroic service of you. A lesser man might find a source of resentment somewhere in the equation. It takes a great man to make the contradiction irrelevant on the strength of his will alone. Speshnev, I won't even ask you. Because of course I know the answer.'

34

'There's really not an alternative, is there? Not after tea and showers and American tobacco. Who could say no?'

'No one, little 4715. No one.'

4

The deer hovered between shadow and light. It was almost not there. The boy blinked, to make certain again that he had it fixed. There was a magical quality to it: the way it seemed to disappear, lose its lines among the blend of darkness and illumination, then to materialize, then again vanish.

He felt his heart pound. He was eight. He had worked his father's deer camp for three years now and had seen them many times before, in the trees, or thrashing in fury as they were hit, just a second of rebellion against the steel message of the bullet, shot above the shoulder, or gutted skinless and hanging to bleed out from a rack. Nothing about it frightened him, except that he himself had not killed a deer yet. But he was ready.

He had hunted squirrel with a Remington single-shot .22 until he hit what he aimed at every time. He had learned stillness. He had learned to sink to nothingness, until only the animal in him breathed, but only barely, yet at the same time he saw and heard so clearly.

Now, cradled in his arms was a 94 Winchester, the .30–30, which he had just grown strong enough to shoot. He was eager, he was ready, the hunter's bloodsong pounded in his ears.

'Let him come out into the light, Bob Lee,' his father said.

His father's presence loomed behind him, calm and imperturbable. That was his father. Whatever he was, no one could take that from him ever: he was a man among men. Bob Lee had begun to pick up the signs, the subtle ways others deferred to him, the coming of silence when he walked into a room. It wasn't just that his father was a state policeman or something they called a hero in the war. There was another thing. Something, well, hard to know what to call it. Just something else.

Now the animal moved fully into the light. It turned. It seemed to look right at Bob Lee, with dark eyes as calm and intense as anything he'd ever seen. He looked right into Bob Lee's eyes.

Or that's the way it seemed. They were like that: watchful for a bit, concentrated, and then forgetful. The entire animal tensed, its ears pricked, its nose sampled the air. It was about seventy-five yards away.

'Are you ready?'

'Yes, sir.'

Soon the animal forgot that something hunting it could be out there. The thought vanished and, without a care, the deer returned to its eating, picking at the tender shoots in the shadow of a pine tree at the edge of the cornfield.

'All right, Bob Lee,' his father whispered. 'Easy up, hold that breath, see that front sight, head down and steady, tip of the finger against the trigger and then the squeeze. The gun will fire when it wants to fire.'

'Make your daddy proud,' came the voice of

Sam Vincent, his daddy's best and possibly only friend.

Bob Lee took a breath.

He was nestled against the trunk of an elm. It supported him and absorbed his trembling. He drew the rifle to his shoulder, let it point naturally to the animal, and the sight, steady as a brick, went to the beast's tawny shoulder where the bullet would strike and take its life.

He knew the rifle. It was cocked, but he'd thumb-lowered the hammer for safety. Now his thumb flew back to that hammer, and notched it back where with an almost inaudible click it seated itself. His thumb returned to the rifle's grip, locked on, steadily, and his trigger finger went to that instrument, and began ever so gently to press against it.

Steady now, just easy pressure, without disturbing the stillness of the sight, not a problem, something he had done in the fields and in his dreams for years.

But —

Maybe it was the sun, the way it lit the deer's white withers. Maybe it was the spring smell of flowers alight in blossom. Maybe it was the buzz of some kind of insect life, or the chirping of some dim bird or other.

He could not say. It wasn't that he could not kill. The boy had killed before, understood that it was somehow man's work, necessary, and it was what a fellow did, without complaint or doubt.

But today, in the sunlight, in the warmth?

'Daddy?'

'Yes, Bob Lee.'

'I don't know. I just — I don't know.'

'It is your call. You are the hunter. You may take the shot, and we will eat good tonight. But I cannot make the decision for you, Bob Lee. It's a serious thing to take the life of something so beautiful. So you must decide.'

The boy decided.

'Maybe not this time. Maybe in the fall again, when it's cold. It's spring now. It's all green, everywhere. Maybe not when it's green.'

'If that's what you've decided.'

'It is.'

'Then that's what it shall be. We'll let Mr. Deer have his summer and his fun. Then we'll come back for him in the fall.'

★   ★   ★

'You know what?' Sam whispered to him, on the long trudge back, 'I think you did make your daddy proud. You felt it, you did what was right. You didn't do what someone said, and your daddy respects that.'

'Yes, sir,' said Bob Lee. His father was a bit ahead of them, broad across the shoulders, bristly across the head where his hair had gone iron gray with age and been forced back with a stout brush. He still carried the marine discipline with him.

The father was a man with scars. His son had seen them: streaks, where something long and sinewy had bit him, puckered clusters from bullet holes, more ragged ridges of dead tissue where the Japanese shrapnel had torn through him. His fists, too, were a latticework of dead white. A bitter mark or two also flecked his jawline. He was a man who'd seen a lot of what the world can do to flesh.

'Come on, you two,' he turned now and called. 'If we don't get back by supper, Junie's going to be plenty teed off.'

They reached his brand-new used pickup, with the gray fender and the cracked rear glass, but still an upstanding vehicle, if cheap after much bargaining.

'Daddy, what we gon' tell Mr. Nelson?'

'The truth, Bob Lee. That's all. He can handle it.'

'Best way,' confirmed Sam.

Mr. Nelson, who farmed a spread seven miles the other side of Blue Eye, had a deer problem. The young bucks had grown brazen as they nibbled his corn. He was a man of law, and so didn't shoot, as so many might have, out of season. But he'd applied for a special dispensation from the state game agency, had gotten it, and asked Earl, the best shot in the county, to handle his problem in exchange for the meat to be harvested. It was a generous offer. Earl, who was not rich, could use the free meat. But that was before Bob Lee had decided not to shoot.

Another father might have ordered the son to shoot, or shot himself. But Earl wanted his son making up his own mind about things, and tried never to order him toward conclusions. He alone in Polk County would not permit his son to call him sir, as all the other boys did to their dads on pain of a mighty licking. Earl in fact could not

40

bring himself to strike the boy, even when he was bad. Why was a mystery that he never communicated to anybody; it's just the way he was, and when Earl Swagger was set in certain ways, then those were the ways they would remain.

'I'll call him and explain,' Sam said.

'No, I will,' said Earl. 'Actually, I know a fine hunter named Hitchens, a colored fellow, who could come out and take the deer, and that meat'd do him and his'n right fine in the months to come.'

'If I know Ed Nelson, he'll not want colored shooting on his property.'

'I'll make him understand.'

The drive was not long, though they stopped and bought the boy an RC Cola. But when they got home to Earl's place off Route 7 this side of Board Camp, and saw the house that had been his own daddy's set a mile off the road, on a bit of a hill, painted freshly white and nice looking in the now failing light, they were amazed at what they beheld, as it was so completely unexpected: three state police cruisers and a Cadillac Fleetwood limousine, black and big and gleaming in the sun from somebody's fresh labor that very morning.

'Oh, Lord,' said Earl. 'I do wonder what's up.'

'Can't be much,' said Sam. 'We drove on through Blue Eye, and there was no sign of a commotion.'

They approached.

'I'll be damned,' said Earl. 'Lookie that.'

41

What he gestured toward was the white-and-black license plate on the Caddy, not green and tan like Arkansas's; this one bore a low number with no letters and the identifying inscription UNITED STATES CONGRESS.

They pulled in, climbed from the pickup, and went quickly to the steps. Through the windows, Earl could see Junie inside, slightly nonplussed, and Colonel Jenks, who was his commanding officer, two or three other state police sergeants known to him as the sort that hung close to headquarters in Little Rock and thereby prospered, and two men in black suits.

'Good lord, Earl,' said Sam, 'what does this mean?'

'Daddy, what is — '

'You just no never-mind, Bob Lee. It ain't a thing to worry about.'

He picked up his son, for the boy's fear upset him, and meant to give him a hug of reassurance, because he himself had never been hugged as a child. But immediately they were discovered on the porch, and en masse, the visiting party rose, abandoning poor Junie, and headed eagerly to him.

Earl knew in a second this was no lynching party.

'Well, Earl, by god, *there* you are,' said Colonel Jenks in a way far heartier than his normal dour style. 'Why, Junie said you and the boy and Lawyer Vincent had gone hunting south of Blue Eye.'

'We came back early.'

'No luck? I don't see no animal on the fender.'

'The best luck. It worked out fine.'

He put his son down.

'You run off, Bob Lee. Seems these boys come to talk to Daddy. Junie, can you get the boy some lemonade?'

'You come, Bob Lee,' sang Junie, taking the boy in her sheltering presence.

Earl turned to face whatever this would be. They stood, all of them, on the porch, in the pale twilight. 'Now what is going on here, sir? You don't come to call with a Cadillac every day.'

'Earl, may I introduce Phil Mackey of Governor Becker's office and Lane Brodgins, on the staff of Congressman Harry Etheridge himself.'

The two men stepped forward behind large smiles and pushed hands at him; Earl shook each numbly. He looked behind them to see that Junie had been pressed to prepare for whatever this would be: A suitcase, the nice one he'd bought for her when she went on a trip to Cape Girardeau for her mother's funeral last year, lay on a table. In it he saw neatly folded clothes: shirts, socks, slacks — his own. He also saw his new Super .38 Colt, wrapped in a cotton cloth, nested in his undercover shoulder holster. It was the right gun to pack, whatever was coming up. Junie knew.

'Earl — may I call you Earl, Earl?' said the governor's man. 'Earl, you know how highly Fred Becker thinks of you. We all know you may have put him in the governor's mansion.'

'That was some years ago,' said Earl.

'Yes, sir, it was. Now — well, you tell him, Lane.'

This Brodgins, the Washington version of the slickster of which Mackey was only a rural prototype, stepped forward now, and put a well-manicured hand on Earl's shoulder.

'Earl, you know how Congressman Etheridge — hell, Harry — how highly Harry thinks of you, too. You're one of three Arkansas Medal of Honor winners. Harry thinks of you as his boys.'

Earl just nodded. He knew enough of Boss Harry to go on edge, for he didn't trust the man: a speechifying, dealmaking politician who rose to power through old Ray Bama's organization in Fort Smith. But Boss Harry — who came originally from Polk, moved up to Fort Smith, and made his way from gofer to secretary of the Democratic party to city legislator to mayor to congressman — had far exceeded his mentor. He was a man who, getting to Washington in record time, and quite young, had mastered its lessons, solved its system, and learned how to get himself into key positions. He'd been there so long he was a power, now especially, as chairman of some big moneybags committee.

'The governor always says, 'That Earl, he's the most capable man in Arkansas,' ' said Phil.

'Earl,' said Sam, 'I'd keep my hand on my wallet. These boys are reaching for something.'

'Now, Mr. Sam,' said Phil, 'you may be Polk County's prosecuting attorney, but you are still Earl's best friend, so you advise him to listen to us, because we come with some damned good news.'

'Let's hear it,' said Earl.

'Earl,' said Phil, 'you've seen gangsters. You've seen how they take over, how they make things their own, how they kill what gets in their way. You know that truth well,' said Phil.

'The point is,' Lane said, 'as Senator Kefauver has exposed, crime ain't just home-grown no more. It's national. You saw the hearings, Earl. They're everywhere.'

'It was on the television, Earl.'

Earl didn't watch television much.

'I see where this one is going,' said Sam. 'Harry's seen how much ink old Estes is getting and wants a big bite of gangster pie, too. They're saying Estes might run against General Ike in '56, that's how famous he is. Well, not if Harry has his way.'

'Mr. Vincent, Harry's commitment is to the people of his district, and his state. He's not anxious to give up representing Arkansas. *But* — '

'Here it comes, Earl. You watch yourself.'

'*But*,' continued Lane, 'Harry ain't content to sit back and let the gangsters do what they want. Now it happens they're at their boldest on a little island just off of Florida called Cuba.'

'Woooieee,' said Sam. 'Earl, Cuba's so hot it makes Hot Springs seem like a Baptist church picnic.'

'We can't hold hearings in Cuba,' said Lane. 'It's not our country, though we cooperate closely with its government. But there is a large naval base called Guantanamo. Marines are there, too. Now there are allegations that the gangsters from New York might be muscling in on the contracts for all the service to Guantanamo: you know, garbage, laundry, that sort of thing. We can't have gangsters living off our servicemen, can we, Earl? So the congressman proposes an investigation.'

'Where do I fit in?' Earl asked.

'Well, sir, the congressman needs a bodyguard. It's a dangerous town, Havana. He needs someone who can talk to the military, whom the military respects. He needs someone who's been out and about in the world, someone who's been the world over, say, in the Marine Corps. He needs someone who's been up against gangsters, beaten them down, knows how they operate. Any of these seem like anybody you know, Earl?'

'What does Colonel Jenks say?' asked Earl.

'Well, Earl,' said Colonel Jenks, 'the governor wants us to cooperate with the congressman, and so it seems we could easily enough detach you on special assignment to the congressional party that's headed to Cuba. You'd go down there with the congressman, help him in any way you can, report to Mr. Brodgins here, and of course the state of Arkansas will continue your pay, and you'd be back in a few weeks. It's a great opportunity, Earl. You could do well for yourself.'

'You've noticed, Earl, how them who help the congressman get helped themselves? It can happen to you, Earl.'

'Sounds to me,' said Sam, winking at Junie, 'like this deal's been signed, sealed and delivered for a month. These here fellows are just bringing the word.'

5

'That's *him?*' Roger asked.

'Yep,' Walter Short replied.

'Hmmmm. Somehow, from your descriptions, I was expecting Superman.'

'Don't get him mad. Then you'll see Superman.'

The two of them were huddled like junior G-men behind a sofa on the balcony above the foyer in the ambassador's residence in the American embassy complex in the posh precinct just west of Centro Havana called Vedado. It was an old sugar millionaire's place converted from opulence to mere luxury, and down below candles glinted, potted palms waved and a warm sea breeze cascaded in through the open marble atrium. A three-piece combo beat out one of Desi Arnaz's softer rhythms.

The reception for the Honorable Congressman Harrison J. Etheridge and staff was well lubricated by ample rum from the folks at Bacardi, which bought so much of the sugar Domino milled from the Cuban cane. But all that labor against the good earth was far from view. Men in dinner jackets swirled about; women, brown and quivery, laughed gaily. Congressman Etheridge could even be glimpsed — that is, when he slowed down: a heavyset man with great, carefully tended mounds of white hair. But his dinner jacket was bespoke, from a fine Savile Row firm, and he cut a surprisingly dapper figure for a man whose Arkansas accent, amplified theatrically, seemed to come from a radio humor hour hosted by Lum and Abner. That mighty, booming voice cut through the air above the laughter and the music.

But neither Roger nor Walter watched the congressman. The congressman wasn't nearly as interesting as he thought he was. They watched instead the congressman's bodyguard, the large, dour, flattopped man in the khaki summer suit standing near a pillar, almost at parade rest, his piercing eyes glancing around the large room.

'He doesn't look capable of making the Big Noise we need. He's so banal,' said Roger.

'He won the Medal of Honor.'

'Not banal, admittedly. But he could be any cop. He looks so cop. The brush haircut, the size, the wariness, the solitude.'

'He was a marine sergeant.'

'Well, yes, a sergeant. I do see that. Not the college polish of your typical officer. Walter, really, this isn't a mistake, is it? A state cop with a good war record? We've bet a lot on this fellow, and engineered our butts off to get him down here.'

'Take it from me, he's not just a cop. Put a gun in his hand and he's something you would not believe. Ask the Japs at Iwo, they found out the hard way. Ask the thugs of Hot Springs, if you can find any above the ground. He made plenty of Big Noise in those places.'

'Well, I hope you're right. Let's go start the dance.'

But Roger immediately sensed something from his younger assistant: reluctance, possibly fear. At least awkwardness. It was odd coming from a perfect no. 2 like Walter Short.

'Well? You're the one who knows him. It's your job to smooth this thing out, facilitate, make it happen.'

'Yes, but . . . '

'But what?'

'Well, we parted under ambiguous circumstances.'

'Now is a fine time to tell me.'

'I did tell you, Roger. Possibly you weren't listening.'

'Oh Christ, of course it's *my* fault. So you were sacked?'

'Sort of. A long story. Not worth retelling. Then, a few days later, that outfit had a catastrophe and some men were killed. I had nothing to do with it, of course, but you don't know how some people may see things.'

'So suddenly you're frightened? Excellent timing. My compliments.'

'I just feel a little off tonight. If I'm there, you won't get a sense of who he is and how to handle him. My presence will throw the dynamic off. I'll make myself known sometime later.'

'God. You sound like a schoolboy with a crush afraid to ask the girl out.'

'It's complicated. Don't stare at him.'

'We're way up here — '

But down below, it was as if Earl Swagger sensed that he was being examined, and from what angle. He immediately flicked his eyes up to them, and they were barely fast enough to recede into shadow before he locked on them.

'See? He has incredible reflexes. He *feels* things. It's the predator's sense of danger. It's his natural aggression. You stare at him, he feels it. It's what kept him alive in the Pacific.'

'You are so ridiculous,' Roger said. 'All right, Walter, hide up here from your love object. You be Cyrano, I'll be Christian.'

'Go, Big Winnetka,' said Walter.

★ ★ ★

'Good lord, Sergeant Swagger, you don't have to stand at attention,' said Roger heartily, turning on his best and most blazing Indian Hill Country Club charm. It had served him well there and at Harvard, in the army even, and most certainly in the Agency. He had no doubt that it would help him here, too.

'Sir?' said Swagger, turning his direct gaze upon the younger, thinner, far more glamorous man.

Roger saw less a face than some kind of Spartan shield with eyes: bronze, bone and leather, baked in the sun until brown, dented, battered, hooding gray eyes almost serene. Roger hurried onward. 'I mean, the place is guarded by U.S. Marines. And it's Cuba, for God's sake, the forty-ninth state. It's practically Miami.'

'Sir, I'm just trying to pay attention,' said the state policeman.

'Let me introduce myself. I'm Roger Evans, I

50

do a little something in the codes department upstairs.'

'Yes, sir. I guess you'd be the spy.'

Roger laughed.

'Say, I *wish* it was that exciting. No, I just make sure the private messages to Washington stay private. I button things up for later unbuttoning. That's all. It's easy work, and it leaves me a lot of time to work on my tennis. You don't play?'

'No, sir.'

'Please. A man with your combat record should not be calling a man with *mine* sir. It should be the other way around.'

'Sure, but don't *you* know a lot about me.'

'Sergeant, you can't keep a secret in an embassy, let me warn you of that right now. So everyone knows about the medal on Iwo Jima, the five battle stars. Why, I only have *one* — '

'All that was a long time ago. I hardly ever think of it.'

Great! Roger had played what he assumed would be his best shot, the brotherhood-of-arms angle, and this Arkansas guy hadn't even noticed. But Roger wouldn't let it go without a struggle.

'Well, I think of it all the damned time,' he responded. 'Nothing that big ever happened to me before or since. I'm no hero, Sergeant, not like you, but I tried to do the right thing. I even got shot at a little, over in Europe. I was a sergeant, too. Look, if you feel you must stand here, let me get you a drink or something. You look so damned rigid.'

'I don't drink no more. I'm fine. I'm not a man for parties, that's all. I just stand around like a dumb ox and maybe sneak a peek at a gal now and then. The congressman seems to be enjoying himself.'

Damn! Roger was disappointed that the man hadn't picked up on his war-service gambit.

'Yes, well, if certain people are to be believed, he has a *history* of enjoying himself. Anyhow, you'll be happy to know that this is just the warm-up. The ambassador likes these intimate gatherings to show the staff and his millionaire pals how important he is. But next Monday, he's got the whole island coming in for a more formal thing. Oh, it'll be something. Movie stars, some athletes, Hemingway, newspaper joes, probably some actors, lots of corporation big boys, and the best kind of beautiful women: those of dubious morality. Some mobsters, some gamblers. They call themselves 'sportsmen'. If you don't like *this*, you'll hate *that*.'

'Thanks for the warning.'

'You sure I can't get you anything?'

'I'm just fine.'

There was no contact at all. Earl Swagger wasn't particularly interested in Roger St. John Evans, and Roger felt his coldness totally, despite the net of charm the young man had flung out. It secretly enflamed him. He was, after all, the celebrity of the station: handsome, debonair, a superb athlete, a war hero, the one everybody picked as the best boy, the fellow who'd go far.

But Earl just stood, in his centurion's stillness, his face wary but untroubled, his eyes steadily on

52

the move, flicking this way and that, but nowhere near anxiety. He just watched.

He was completely ill-dressed for the dinner-jacketed formality of the evening, and if he'd noticed it — unlikely — it clearly didn't bother him a bit. His khaki suit was rack-bought, new, rather baggy and shiny at once, and too tight through the shoulders. Roger had to fight the temptation to give the man his tailor's name.

But then Roger noticed something, a lump under the coat, left side, under the arm where it oughtn't to be.

'You're *armed?*'

'Yes, sir. Today and every day.'

Roger sort of slid around and, looking across the chest, he could see the grip of a pistol protruding just half an inch from the shoulder holster that contained it. He brightened, because he recognized it.

'Oh,' he said, 'your old .45? I carried one, too.'

'Close enough,' Earl said. 'Yeah, it's a Government Model, but not a .45. It's what's called a Super .38.'

Roger knew just a little about guns.

'Super? It must kick?'

'Much less than a .45. The point is, it holds two more rounds. Nine. It shoots a little small bullet, about half the weight of a .45, but much faster. It'll go through most anything. I figured down here if I'm shooting — and I hope to hell I'm not — I'm shooting through or at a car. Sometimes a .45 won't even get through a car door.'

Roger suddenly lit up. He had it!

53

'*Say*,' he said, 'I know! You're a shooter, a hunter. Would you like to shoot pigeons while you're down here? You know what, I'd like to put you together with Hemingway. He's a great shotgunner. Damn, that would really be something. You're a hero, he's a hero, he'd love you. I'll bet you're a great shotgunner.'

'I've shot ducks. In Arkansas, we flood the rice fields in the fall, and the mallards come in. Many a fine morning I've spent there with a good friend. I hope to take my boy duck hunting soon.'

'Hemingway,' said Roger, from his reverie. 'Let me work on that! A little shooting party. You, Hem, possibly the ambassador, down at Finca Vigia. We'll hunt, then roast the ducks, drink wine, or rum punch or vodka. I've known him since the war. You'll love Hemingway. He's a man's man. Wait till you see his place, his trophies. He has a buff you simply *would not* believe. Oh, say, won't this be something?'

'Uh,' said Earl, 'who's this . . . Hemingway?'

Before Roger could register incredulity at the fact the state policeman had never heard of America's most famous writer, a new presence swirled in on them. It was Lane Brodgins, a little drunk, clearly on a mission from Harry.

'Evans, Sergeant Earl, howdy. Great party, Evans. You boys know how to throw a hoedown and damn if Harry doesn't appreciate it.'

'Ah, yes,' said Roger. 'Well, as I was telling Sergeant Swagger, this is just the warm-up. Next Monday, the stars come out.'

'Say, that's a great idea! Harry will like that

one, he will. Earl, you should relax. You're off duty now.'

'I'm fine.'

'I have a feeling Sergeant Swagger will only relax in his grave, if there,' said Roger.

Swagger, for the first time, let a crease of a smile play across his face. Roger had been flattering him hard, not easy work but he was good at it, and finally the effort was beginning to tell.

'Tell you what,' he said, 'maybe I'll have a Coca-Cola.'

'That's the spirit, old man!' said Roger. He snapped his fingers, a waiter appeared. 'El Coca-Cola, por favor,' he said, sending the man off on his mission.

'I was just telling Sergeant Swagger I thought I could put an afternoon of pigeon shooting together. He's a great sporting shot, I hear. It happens I know Hemingway a bit and we could all go down to Finca Vigia and shoot pigeons. Hem's a shotgun man.'

'Who's Hemingway?' asked Lane Brodgins. Then he turned to Earl.

'Sergeant Earl, you'd better finish that Coke and then head back to quarters for your beauty sleep. The congressman has decided he has to see the Cuban criminality firsthand, for himself. So that means tomorrow we've arranged for a tour of certain areas. Who knows what we'll run into.'

'Good God, where are you going?' asked Roger.

'Zanja Street,' said Brodgins. 'You know, in

Centro, where the whores and the Shanghai Theater and the — '

'Zanja,' said Roger, with a shudder that indicated how tasteless he considered the mention. 'Sergeant, you'd better bring *two* Super .38s.'

6

The Soviet Trade Legation was located on the upper floor of the new Missiones Building, nos. 25 and 27, in a section of Centro Havana formerly known as Las Murallas — the Walls. At one time the old city's walls had been the dominant feature, but they were now being dwarfed in the building boom as American-financed and -designed skyscrapers were taking off like rocketships all over the landscape, as Havana transfigured into Miami. The Missiones Building, however, had been designed by a Frenchman, and so it lacked the bold, soaring modernism of the New Havana of Batista's second regime; it looked, in fact, like something out of Barcelona or Madrid in the twenties, rather than something out of Las Vegas in the fifties.

And so it was that Speshnev, in espadrilles and loose-fitting peasant's trousers and shirt, found himself sitting across from a rather intense young man in a suit, with hair brilliantined back glossily, who looked more like an American investment banker than a Soviet spymaster. Young Arkady Pashin was brilliant, feared, despised, connected, vigorous, tireless, ruthless, ambitious and oh such a pain in the ass.

'Speshnev, you were supposed to be here at 10 A.M. It is 10:05 A.M. This is not acceptable, it is not permissible, it is not desirable. We must

57

maintain tight discipline here. We are out-manned, underbudgeted and without adequate resources. Only discipline and dedication will see us through here, through these difficult times. Do you see?'

'Pashin, they told me you would be a monster. But, young man, I had no idea that you would also be such a little prick.' He smiled warmly.

'Look, old goat,' said bloodless Pashin through thin lips, 'this was not my idea. I have a number of very promising projects going on here. This came from some doddering genius at Moscow Control who knows nothing of the complexities of the situation. I don't need a hoary old myth who's disobedient and insubordinate, eating up my time and budget for nothing.'

'It was a nice day in the spring sunshine. An old man wandered a bit on the way over, to smell some flowers, to smell the warm sea. The Boss would have sent me back to the gulag for such treason, but at least for now, Pashin, you lack the power. You have to play along. It has been ordered. So any shit you give me is unsanctioned, pure sport on your part.'

'And they said you'd be a proud one. Still the Comintern movie star. The vanity, the narcissism, the love of self. That is why you'll never be a true Soviet man. You can't let the love affair you have with your mirror go; you're too used to being special.'

'I am a humble servant of the people. Just make certain you get the name right. It's Zek 4715.'

'All right, all right. This is getting us nowhere.

You have a job to do, that is why you are here. I'm assuming you're already on it.'

'I don't report to you, Pashin.'

'No, but my reports will help you or hurt you. Wouldn't it be nice if mine helped you and yours helped me.'

'Both our reports should help the revolution, that's all. But to get through the business, yes, I've nosed around. I've seen our young prince. Did you know he has a nickname? I assume he was initially your discovery? So you have a lot riding on this and are probably annoyed I was brought in to handle him, because you were not considered experienced enough. Well, his nickname speaks of his power, his promise, his grand possibilities and your excellent nose for such matters. Do you know what it is?'

'I am not interested in — '

'It's 'Greaseball'. Evidently, he's so anxious to hurtle into the socialist future, he periodically forgets to bathe. Ugh. Did you smell him before you saw him? I can't stand a dirty fellow when there's no excuse for it. I have quite recently gone nine years without a bath. Not pleasant. I will bathe every day of what little life I have left.'

'Forget his odor. Concentrate on his potential. Have you heard him speak? It's magnificent.'

'I have heard accounts. He likes long ones, or so I hear. And I hear also he likes the spotlight.'

'He is ruthless; he has already killed in the gangsterismo politics of the forties; he is dedicated; he believes, if in nothing else, in change. He has that thing you have, Speshnev, that most of us lack. The magnetism.'

'It's called charisma. Yes, I have it. Yes, you don't. Yes, he does. Yes, I suppose he has some potential. If only he learns to trim his fingernails.'

'This may not be as easy as you think. There has been a development.'

'And that is?'

'Batista's secret police aren't a threat, at least as long as Castro is benign and an orator, not a fighter. The time for fighting is still some years off, and it is your job not merely to recruit him and train him and prepare him, but possibly also to protect him.'

'From what? His wife's wrath at his mistress? Or his mistress's wrath at his wife?'

'No,' Pashin said, sliding a photograph across the desk toward Speshnev, 'this man's commitment to his duty.'

The photo had been snapped at the Havana airport. It was of a group of men leaving the Air Cubana Constellation's stairway and heading to the terminal. One was flashy in his white hair and two or three others clearly bowed to him in body posture, factotums or assistants or eunuchs or whatever.

'This one?' Speshnev asked, pointing to the member of the group who was also not a member of the group.

'That one.'

It was a large square-headed American, with a jutting jaw and a crewcut.

'A soldier?'

'According to embassy gossip, a killer. He killed in the war, many, many times.'

'Oh, yes, there's a word for that. I think it's 'hero'. Why is he here?'

'Ostensibly as the bodyguard of that showy one there. That's a famous politician in their country. But this man for some reason was recruited to accompany the politician to Cuba. Our Washington people have noted it and alerted me. They find it curious.'

'And . . . '

'And we don't know why. Maybe just because. Or maybe it's that if you had to kill someone, this is the man you'd want to do the killing. He's not like the rest of them. Give him a job, he does it.'

'Hmmm. That doesn't sound like them.'

'No, but maybe they're thinking of changing their ways. They want to get the attention of certain people in certain countries and this would be a very good way to do it, wouldn't you say?'

'Possibly.'

'So I think you should look about carefully. See what this fellow is up to. And . . . '

'And?'

'And if he's here to cut short the career of the prince of all our dreams, Zek 4715, then it's simple. You must be the faster, the better man. You must kill him.'

7

The old men were not pleased. They made him hide in a warehouse on the East Side, among rats and spiders, where it was cold. No one brought him coffee, no one commiserated with him, no one asked him how he was doing.

He felt their displeasure, but he could not truly gauge its fullness because he saw no newspapers for three days, saw no television, heard no radio. It was just him in the darkness of the warehouse, and every ten hours or so some greasy food was brought: cold hamburgers wrapped in wax paper from a diner, warm soda in a Dixie cup, a dried-out Danish. For a shitter he had a bucket; for wad he had old newspaper left around; for a mattress he had nothing except a wall to doze against, his butt on the hard cement floor.

Then he was summoned. He traveled by garbage truck from his warehouse, across the boroughs of the city, at last to Brooklyn and there, at night, shadowy figures smelling of cologne took him in through an alley. He found himself in a social club from Garibaldi's day, where the old men sat at single tables, drank bitter coffee from tiny cups, and smoked gigantic cigars. Most wore glasses, all looked creaky and wrinkly, but he understood that he was among the powerful and the legendary.

'Frankie, Frankie, Frankie,' said one. 'A cop,

maybe. Two cops, at the limits. But . . . you clipped a horsie?'

'It's the fuggin' horse, Frankie, you understand?' said another. 'Our people have never whacked a horse. It don't look good.'

'On the television, Frankie, the horses with the cowboys. Little kids love the horses. Now one of our people machine-guns a horse in Times Square in broad daylight.'

'I didn't have no choice,' said Frankie. 'If you want to know, wasn't Lenny supposed to handle lookout? He's responsible. I can't do everything. I'm coming out of the place and there's no Lenny and just the cop galloping my way on a horse. Lone Ranger or whatever, he's about to pound me into the sidewalk. I just did what I have to. Fuggin' cop, what's he doin' there anyhow?'

'Frankie, he works there. It's his *job*, goddammit. They can't eat donuts all day long. Frankie, some, some even in this little room, they'd like to see Frankie the horsekiller floating in the river with a stevedore's hook through his throat, so as to say to the newspapers and the people, see, we don't kill horses. We only kill our own kind. Frankie, is that what you'd like to see?'

'No, it ain't.'

'Frankie, what we gonna do with you? You want to go for a swim inna river with a hook?'

'No, sir.'

'Miami don't want you, Tampa don't want you, Cleveland, Boston, they don't want you. You are hot as Catholic hell. We can't send you to

63

Vegas 'cause they'd snitch you out to butter up Washington. They'd find a way to let certain people know you were available, and next thing you know, you're sitting in front of a television camera and you're talking 'bout us and you're famous.'

'I wouldn't never do that.'

'We can't let that happen. Frankie, my friend, you are now a pawn in a game you couldn't possibly understand.'

'I could go back to Italy.'

'Italy! I wouldn't wish you on Italy. In Italy, they expect results, not chaos, scandal, shame and newspapers.'

'They *like* horses in the old country, Frankie.

'Frankie Horsekiller, I can only think of one town where you can go and not be noticed. A man of importance has agreed to take you in, as a special favor and because we have arrangements with him over long time. You must be good and obey him and work hard for him before you can ever begin to think of coming back to your home.'

'Yes, sir.'

'Frankie, the Jew Meyer, that's Mr. L to you, he will take you in. He may have some enforcement problems and you might fit in to his plans. Frankie, don't embarrass us again, do you understand?'

'Yes, sir,' said Frankie.

'And, Frankie,' said one, 'say hello to Desi for me.'

8

The boss and his man Lane stayed in the embassy itself, in VIP quarters; Earl had been dumped at an old joint called the Plaza, facing a beauty of a park square, right at the border of Old Havana. It didn't make much sense for the bodyguard to be that far apart from the body he was supposed to guard, but it was clear that Lane didn't want Earl getting too close to the action.

So he took a cab in on that first morning and found the whole shebang starting with a briefing, put on by one of the ambassador's brightest boys, which laid out the realities of organized crime in Cuba for the Right Honorable United States Congressman Harry J. Etheridge (2nd, Democrat, Ark.), chairman of the Defense Appropriations Committee, winner of the American Legion of Merit, awardee of the Hearst empire's 'Proud to Be an American' contest, 1951.

It was a familiar story. With the big American gambling spas like Saratoga and Hot Springs and, worst of all, Coral Gables, being closed down by reformers, the boys, the fellas, the mob, whatever you wanted to call them, they looked south to Cuba ninety miles away. Somehow Fulgencio Batista was coaxed out of retirement (suspiciously, he had retired to Coral Gables), and in 1952, in a bloodless coup, re-took the

65

government. And so the mob moved in, and with its know-how at the gaming tables, soon took over the big houses. Muscles Martin, of Pittsburgh, ran the Sans Souci; Billy Bloom ran the games at the Tropicana; the old S. and G. wire syndicate, closed down in Coral Gables, moved over and operated the Casino Nacional. Meyer Lansky bought a share of the Montmartre and was the unofficial boss of American criminal interests in Cuba. So well set-up was the outfit here, the functionary explained, that a courier took off every night for Miami with the checks of the losers, to clear them that very night. If they didn't clear, the managers could confront the check-bouncers the very next day.

Boss Harry appeared to listen during this explanation, but he asked no questions and he took no notes. Earl, with his police brain, wrote it down in the interior of his mind; that was the way he worked, filing the data away. A quick rundown of what the young man called 'risque' spots followed, with admonitions to avoid them all, but Earl did note that Lane took this down: the Bambu on Zanja Street, the Panchin at Fifth Avenue and C, the South Club at San Rafael and Prado, the Taberna San Roman at San Pedro and Ovicios, the El Colmao on Araburu, the Tasca Espanola at Carcel and Prado — all spots of colorful reputation and possible organized crime ownership. The mob probably hadn't taken over Johnny's Dream Club out on Almendares River, or Mes Amis or El Mirador, and it certainly hadn't taken over the Shanghai Theater, also on Zanja Street, where naked

66

women and dirty movies could actually be seen. The Palette Club and the Colonial were two other dives the congressman and his intrepid investigators were advised to avoid. And that was it for the official American presentation to the congressman, as if the government itself had made peace with the idea that some of its nastiest boys had set up a government in Cuba. It made everything easier on everyone, and, what the hell, it was only Cuba after all.

Then the investigation itself commenced, and Earl was surprised to learn that despite Lane's prediction and Roger's warning, a stop on Zanja Street didn't turn up the first day, or the second, or even the third. What happened instead proved less an investigation than a sightseeing tour, well-fortified by huge rum drinks with little American flags on toothpicks stuck in pieces of pickled pineapple, melon or whatever. The boss had several of these an hour at this spot or that, and his face turned redder and his hair whiter. Other than that it was cruising. The boss was driven about slowly, seeing the sights, admiring the women, checking out the casinos.

They did the big downtown joints first, old and distinguished, the pleasure palaces that made Cuba in the twenties and the thirties and the forties and now, in the fifties, such a destination. In Old Havana the Hotel Sevilla-Biltmore on the Prado, then over to La Rampa, where the Hotel Nacional, the Hotel Lincoln, the Hotel Capri all clustered, like Spanish castles, usually white and tall and flanked by trees and elaborate gardens just off the broad avenues of the most modern section of the city. The casinos themselves followed, such as the Tropicana, the world's biggest and most beautiful nightclub, and the less imposing but still beautiful Sans Souci, all in the section called Centro, clustered in the same modern downtown that could have been Cleveland with gambling. In these joints, the layouts were the same: the gaming room with its busy sense of drama, the wide esplanade where a pool of aquamarine water glinted in the sun and waiters plied the bathers with elaborate fruit-and-rum concoctions, the nightclub and bar, with a stage and always a vast bar.

Boss Harry was always expected. A senior executive waited, and an attending staff. There were many pretty women, flashy and fleshy, as if that too, were a coinage all knew the boss to enjoy. Usually, a tour ensued, and the boss and his party were taken from the big gaming rooms to the nightclub to the backstage area, where in the day the behind-the-scenes theater world seemed stale and filled with sad odors. Then they moved to the pool, usually overlooking the sea, where hundreds of vacationers lay out cooking in the sun, trying to turn brown in a basting of cocoa butter or Coppertone. When recognized, as happened more than a few times, the boss generously mixed with the common or not-so-common men, shaking hands, posing for pictures, holding babies. You'd have thought the man was running for office of mayor of Havana or something.

Another day there'd been a long, larky drive

out La Quinta, as the broad Fifth Avenue was called, as it ran along the North Coast, a two lane road with parklands between the lanes, where lights gleamed and trees rose. They passed through the section called Miramar, and went to the famous resort at La Playa, next to a Cuban version of Coney Island, complete with rides and freak shows, as if the city itself weren't already a freak show. At La Playa, a big do was thrown. A later stop took them to the Havana Yacht Club, the greyhound races nearby and then even further inland to the Oriental Park, a racecourse where in season the swells went in straw boaters and white linen suits to throw money away on the ponies. Now, however, it was not in season, and only a skeleton crew of lackeys awaited the great man, to show him what he wanted to see.

'Noticed any gangsters, Earl?' Lane said at one point.

'There seem to be some slick fellas watching us,' said Earl. 'If they're gunmen or pimps or hooligans or grifters, I couldn't say. But in places like these, they watch hard.'

'Well, what I see,' said Lane, 'is people having a good time, having some fun. I don't see no gangsters. Earl, I think you've been reading Dick Tracy in the funny papers.'

Lane in all matters seemed to know a little better than Earl, as if he were afraid anything Earl might say could impress Boss Harry and in that way damage his own position as the boss's no. 1 boy.

'Now, Lane, you listen to Earl,' said Harry.

'He's fought gangsters toe to toe, isn't that right? He cleaned up Hot Springs. Didn't stay clean long, but he did the job up fine, as my friend Fred Becker tells the story. Ain't that so, Earl?'

'We fought 'em but it did seem they got that town up and running again fast after the shooting stopped,' was all Earl could admit, for he had dark superstitions that moneys were paid and that some of Arkansas's most distinguished sons — like the heroic Hot Springs reformer Fred Becker, who rode his victory to the governor's mansion, and the wise and compassionate Harry Etheridge, congressman and Washington kingmaker — all somehow turned out the richer for it.

And now finally, on the night of the fourth day, they had descended to the lowest of the low, to the lower end of the seventeen blocks of Zanja Street, where everything was cheap and easy. The long byway carved a streak through Centro, aiming toward the far more elegant Prado, but where the Prado made many think of Paris, Zanja made men think only of sex. It was lined with bodegas, fruit stands, old women rolling cigars at card tables along the street, lottery agencies — the town seemed washed in numbers, testament to the greed that lay everywhere — bars and tabernas, nightclubs of smoky reputation, a mess of open-air Chinese restaurants just off the main drag, the mysterious doors in which a single square hatch opened, a man was examined, then admitted — and of course the Shanghai Theater.

They pulled the big Cadillac slowly over the

cobblestones and the building itself came into view.

'I do believe we ought to take a look-see,' said the boss. 'Might never get a chance like this again.'

'Driver, did you hear?' Lane, sitting next to Harry, asked.

'Si, Señor Brodgins,' said Pepe, a sergeant in the police seconded to chauffeur's duty. He pulled the car over not far from the destination.

'Earl, you go on in and make sure it's safe, now, you hear?' said Lane.

Earl looked at 205 Zanja on the shabby whore street whose washing of pastels only emphasized its crummy squalor, and saw just a big theater marquee with TEATRO SHANGHAI lit by orange lamps so that it had a lurid blood glow to it. Chinese symbols ran down the wall flanking the ratty entrance on either side, also orange in the lamplight. One of the lamps, however, was somehow miswired, and it flickered and crackled and nobody had gotten around to fixing it yet. Like a broken radio, it leaked hiss and sputter into the night, while it pulsed orange weirdness across the land.

Earl looked at Lane, bathed in the orange light so that he seemed to be an ice cream treat. Lane nudged him forward with a little shooing motion of his eyes. Earl got out, slipped toward the theater, and stepped in. It was shabby inside as out, and seemingly deserted, and a small box office under a sign in Spanish (but with $1.25 clearly marked) stood toward the rear. But it smelled not of popcorn but of disinfectant, and soon enough a fat Cuban came to him with a hand out for the buck-two-bits, and Earl just flashed the big automatic in his shoulder holster, as if to say, I am here to see what I will see. The man melted away, smiling broadly and insincerely.

Earl stepped through a curtain and into a darkness. He was aware of other men in there, an immensity of them, row after row after row, silent and transfixed, and the smell of more disinfectant, and in the glare of the screen he could see the men staring, unmoving, unbelieving. He looked up. In bold black and white a woman in a mask seemed to have something in her mouth and be working it easily, and it took a little while for Earl to put the details together and then he realized what she had in her mouth and that she herself wore only stockings and heels and that flabby immensity to the left of the screen was her big butt, inelegantly parted, revealing in its flaccidity that which should not be revealed. He recoiled, stepped back, and looked away from the screen.

Jesus Christ, don't this take it all! This old coot come a thousand miles from Washington, D.C., to look at a smoker on a movie screen in a theater.

He looked around and realized the place was full and the other watchers in the dark wouldn't be paying any attention to anything except what was on screen.

He slipped back out to the car.

'It's okay. The boys are watching the movies and the movies aren't like nothing playing in

Washington, D.C. Mr. Congressman, you sure you want to go into this place? It don't smell very clean.'

'Why, Earl, I must go where duty takes me.' And with that he rose into the orange electrical glow, and with Lane hustled into 205 Zanja.

Earl smoked an orange cigarette and blew orange smoke while the boys had their fun. They were in there for almost an hour while he lounged on the fender of the Cadillac, and eventually, they came out.

'Ain't never seen a thing like that. Where do you suppose they find the gals? Earl, you are a po-liceman. You would know such things. Where would they find the gals?'

'Them gals looked pretty broke-down to me,' Earl said. 'Old whores, can't walk the streets no more, don't know nothing else, that's what I'm betting.'

'Whoo-ee,' said the boss, 'that was a thing to do, and now I am all up and ready for the next step. Shall we see what other adventures we might get into?'

Earl knew: he was looking for a woman. He said nothing to express his discomfort, but kept looking back, his eyes flicking quickly to the rear as he examined what lay back there.

'We being followed, Earl?' Lane wanted to know.

Earl wanted to say yes, for he felt something. A presence, an attention, something somehow *concentrating* on them. But it was only that feeling and that alone; nothing emerged to his vision to confirm the suspicion.

'I don't think so,' said Earl. 'But if we are, he's a damn better man than I am.'

'Didn't think there were no better men than you, Earl.'

'There's plenty. But no, I don't think there's anyone back there. Maybe it's just my old imagination heating up.'

'Earl, have a drink, relax. A little drink wouldn't harm you a bit.'

Actually, Earl knew it would. He be back on the bottle full-time.

'No thank you, sir,' he said to Lane.

Earl checked the rearview mirror again just in case. No, nothing. Here, in this human tide of hustlers and grifters, whores and low-rent crime dogs, it was the bottom of the Havana pool. It reminded Earl a little of Hot Springs in 1946, that sense of a town gone mad for pleasures; but the Spanish twist to it also called up Panama City and its whores' paradise from 1938 when he'd done a tour down there, and every weekend the boys would head off for cheap beer and cheap women. Earl was no saint; he'd had a big share of each on the principle that if war came he'd not survive it and so he should take what he could buy now. He had no regrets, but now, married, with several wars under his belt, he somehow couldn't connect with it. He didn't need it.

'Now there,' said the boss, 'goes a right fine piece of pootie.'

She was a right fine piece of pootie, too.

'She sure is,' said Lane. 'Yes, sir, that she is.'

'Si, señor,' said Pepe, who immediately got

74

what was going on.

'Is she a nigra, do you suppose, Lane?' asked the boss.

'Well, sir, she does have a caramelly skin and that be-hind of hers shakes just like a negro gal's. I'll bet she rattles around in bed like a negro gal, too. Don't you, Earl?'

Earl had examined the flowing clothes of the señorita only briefly, pausing not at the quivering abundance of the flesh of shoulders and rather awesome breasts, nor at the undulations of high, proud buttocks, nor at the firm, luscious legs held just so tensely atop a pair of spindly black heels, for he had ascertained that so dressed, she probably didn't conceal a machete or a hand grenade, and had passed on to other concerns.

'Yes, sir,' said Earl, in his dullest cop voice.

'Let's see where she goes,' said the boss, still consumed by the presence of the undulating brown woman. 'Just, you know, for the damned heck of it.'

'Yes, boss.'

The car oozed down the narrow street, over ancient cobblestones laid by slaves in the previous century or two. Lights danced or sparkled, illuminating the brown flesh.

The woman, all ajiggle on staked heels and thongs that cut into her ankles, at last found her destination, and saucily halted. She turned to confront the men in the close-by Cadillac, and threw a lascivious wink right at the boss. Then she opened a door bathed in red light, and slipped inside.

'Boss, I think she likes you.'

'I think she do, too. Don't you, Earl?'

Earl thought: she's a whore. She's paid to like you. That's what whores do. That's why they're whores.

'She looks available,' was all Earl could think to say.

'Pepe, you pull over here. You follow her up, Pepe, and see what's what. You give me a good report.'

Pepe started to get out.

'Now hold on, sir,' said Earl. 'Mr. Congressman, this is not a good idea. This here is a very tough part of town, that I know. That gal is a whore, sure as rain and heat. You don't know who's up there, some pimp fellow with a knife, some robbers, it's all the kind of thing a man in your position cannot be involved in, let me tell you that. Nothing here for you but bad trouble, sir.'

'Now, Earl,' began Boss Harry, but it was Lane Brodgins who took over.

'Damn, Swagger, it ain't up to you to judge and call shots. This here is a United States congressman and he will go and do as he pleases and your job isn't to second-guess him but to make goddamn clear and sure he is safe. That is your only job, goddammit.'

'Earl, you go with Pepe and you see what's what. We'll wait here. Pepe, come here a second.'

The tough little Cuban leaned close, and Harry whispered something in his ear. Pepe nodded sagely.

Earl didn't say a thing. Didn't seem like there was much to say. His hand fled to the big Colt

Super .38 resting in the holster hung under his left shoulder, to remind himself, yep, it was there. Then he went along with Pepe, under the glow of the red bulb, and watched as Pepe knocked. In time, a small square hatch in the door opened at eye level, and someone examined them from within, up and down. Then the hatch snapped shut, the door opened, and in they went.

9

Speshnev never followed directly. He had learned that lesson the hard way, in Barcelona, in 1937, when two members of the Anarcho-Syndicalists had observed him, counter-ambushed, and sent him crawling through the alleys with a Luger bullet in his belly.

So he ran his operation carefully using classic technique, drawing on a hundred years of tsarist and Cheka-NKVD collective espionage experience. He still did the small things well. He never went out of town. It was impossible to follow on the dusty Cuban roads. But in Havana, it was different. He trailed by taxicab, but never directly. Sometimes he paralleled, other times, if streets were busy, he crosscut and switched back. He had a bagful of hats and changed them every hour, from the white straw boater so popular in the streets to the more elegant felt fedora, to a shapeless straw rural head cover, to, finally, a red bandanna, knotted tightly about his head. He never wanted to stay in the same profile. He had two ties and a bolo, which came on or off as circumstances warranted; his jacket too was on or off, buttoned or unbuttoned, collar up, collar down. Then, at random hours determined by predesignated unpredictables — like the appearance of a pigeon with gray wings, or of a rare woman seller of *bolita* tickets (as the unofficial lottery was called) — he'd abandon the cab he was in, or he'd make a guess as to destination based on good professional instincts, and zip ahead, not to follow them but to foreshadow them.

It was expensive, of course; too expensive for the annoying Pashin, who would not cover the taxi expenses, would not hire a car and driver, yet would not alter the nature of his assignment either. Make do, Speshnev. You are supposed to be so good, simply make do.

So early in the mornings, when the congressman and his more interesting companions had tired out, he went to a smallish casino, lost a little money playing blackjack, and then, when the decks were charged with face cards, made a swift big hit, pocketed the excess and left. He never hit the same place twice, he never wore the same hat twice, he never won too much to get himself beaten or robbed. He just knew the numbers and held them in his mind with an eerie concentration, made his profit, and retreated quickly, before he became known, before his card-counting could be classified a professional's skill as opposed to luck. He'd already made $10,000 that way, in a few nights. It was a shame he didn't defect, he thought, and make the numbers work for him in the world's gambling spots.

But fool that he was, he did his duty, for men who despised him, for a system that had almost murdered him, for cynics and scoundrels and sociopaths that ran the intelligence service. His duty: it was all he had.

He followed them for the better part of a week

and had reached some kind of provisional judgments already. The first was that the American congressman, showy and vain about his hair, was a man of great strengths but equally great weaknesses. The man was a drinker and if Speshnev still had instincts for such things, a whoremonger as well. He loved to dominate and to be obeyed and he sat back and watched people scurry, enjoying every second of the theater of fear. Of those around him, most were of the sort familiar in political circumstances: little factotums who did what the Great Man ordered and sought to acquire his favor and avoid his rage whenever possible. An assistant seemed to be the chief of these pathetic creatures, and he never ventured far from the Great Man's elbow, which made him the prime subject of those compliments and those terrible rages.

There were a few others, a Cuban driver, an embassy babysitter, a secretary, who at various times accompanied them. But mainly, there was the bodyguard. This was Speshnev's true quarry, the first American he'd ever been assigned to evaluate from a professional point of view, and the man whom he might in fact have to eliminate.

Speshnev knew the type. He had something. Some tankers had it, some ace aviators. Old infantry sergeants had it, and the snipers, the really good ones, who scored kills in the hundreds, they had it. He'd seen a lot of it in Spain too, in some of the crazier advisors who had to go on every attack, so burning were they with fervor. Death truly meant nothing to such men. It was courage and cunning, but those alone weren't it.

Speshnev picked it up at once. No word really existed in English; the Russians had one however, *tiltsis*, expressing a certain unmalleability of character. This chap could not be bent, influenced, seduced, tempted. He simply was what he was.

Speshnev read body language. In the separation, the isolation, of the bodyguard he saw the man's bull-pride. He would not be one of them, 'them' being political operatives of a parasitical nature. He had a quality of stillness to him. His body was under discipline at all times, his arms always held in. He carried some kind of big American automatic in a shoulder holster. Through opera glasses, Speshnev studied his hands, and saw that they were huge. Typical: the good pistol people always seemed to have large hands, and manipulated the guns so much more surely than the rest.

But mainly it was his shrewd eyes. It wasn't that the fellow craned his head this way and that, and made an extravagant show of checking things out at every opportunity; rather, it was that the eyes, disciplined by battle, were always moving. They roamed, probed, pierced, incised. They made quick discriminations and quick judgments. His face never changed, his emotions never showed, but he was watching everything, always on the scout.

Speshnev knew from the first and his further observations only convinced him further: this man is dangerous.

Kill him now.

There were no other options.

He would slide closer. He had a .25 caliber Spanish automatic in his left sock. He would meander close, never approach on a line, he'd fall back in a second if detected. The man had a natural radar for aggression, fear and turmoil. You had to approach under camouflage. You had to believe in the benevolence of yourself and sell that message through every pore in your body as you floated ever closer, ever more slowly, ever more gently, and then, at the very last second, only then commit to murder. The gun would come out swiftly, for to hesitate was to die. The gun would come out, cupped in the hand, and with extravagant nonchalance, the nonchalance of a confident lover, sweep upward until the unseen muzzle touched the base of the neck. The small pistol would fire its small bullet into spine or brain, he would melt away, and the American bodyguard would topple, not even aware that he had been stalked and murdered.

That is what I must do, Speshnev said. I must do that, and prevent the complications this sort of man can bring to my mission and in that way guarantee myself a freedom from the gulag. It is a simple proposition: I kill him, I am free forever of the gulag.

He sat at a sidewalk table outside the Bambu on Zanja Street. It was late, but not so late. The street still seethed with action, the lights blared garishly from the enticements along Havana's most notorious boulevard. He sipped a coffee, so

82

strong and black it would kill the unprepared. He saw them.

The Cadillac had been halted now for some time. Other cars maneuvered wretchedly to get around it, and people yelled and cursed and honked. But the Cadillac, like the great American empire it represented, refused to acknowledge an outside world. Speshnev could see there was an argument of some sort with the bodyguard holding forth against the no. 1 assistant, who was clearly out of control. Obviously, this no. 1 fellow had a problem with the bodyguard, for the bodyguard, by his body language and head placement, refused to accept the no. 1's authority and clearly, by a thousand subtle clues, let his contempt be known.

Speshnev had a laugh. As he himself had, the no. 1 assistant had discerned how dangerous the bodyguard was, and was now moving to kill him. Unlike Speshnev, he hadn't the courage, the decisiveness, the ruthlessness to kill him literally, but he was trying to do the deed bureaucratically, symbolically. What a fool.

Speshnev took another sip of the black sweet Cuban coffee. The Spaniards and their bean artistry! The brew was so thick and powerful and relentless it would keep him awake for another thirty hours, which is exactly what he needed. The sugar would keep him jacked and primed.

And now at last, some movement. The bodyguard and the driver got out of the car, endured the ritual of examination at the door in the red glow, then headed inside. Speshnev knew negotiations were being made. And soon

83

enough, the bodyguard came back down, and leaned into the car. The congressman, his white hair pinkish in the glare of the red lamp, rose from the car, looked about nervously, slicked back his hair, and headed inside. The bodyguard, his eyes ever watchful, his hand never far from his automatic, his movements lightfooted and prepared, shadowed him in.

Another ten minutes passed.

Speshnev had another cup of coffee and a Cuban sweet roll. It was delicious.

And then, the door of the brothel flew open and a bleeding man crab-walked out groggily, holding an arm atilt from breakage.

Oh, my, thought Speshnev. Somebody tried to get tough with the wrong fellow.

Then, its sirens bleating savagely, its red lights pumping illumination into the night, the first police car arrived. And then another and another. The no. 1 assistant rose to intercede from his place in the car, but was rudely pushed aside by the Cuban coppers as they assaulted the stairs, clubs and guns at the ready.

10

Why are they always green? But they are, and he should know, having been in whorehouses in Shanghai and Panama City and Nicaragua and Pearl Harbor and San Diego and Hot Springs. They were always green, but a thin wash of green, pale and sloppy enough so that the grain of stucco or stone or drywall shone through. The Asian ones were smokey and sedate and dark, as if sex were a form of narcotic. The Spanish ones all had crucifixes, gaudy and wracked, hanging on the walls, while in America the tendency was toward calendar art, with preposterous hourglasses of womanflesh showing garters and thighs and a hint of pink-tipped breasts. This one had the crucifixes, the candles, the stench, the beaded curtains, the dark corridor leading back to small rooms, a toilet somewhere — you could smell it — and a mama and her girls.

Earl checked it out, wondering if there was a bouncer somewhere. If so, he wasn't visible. He poked a look down the dark hall and saw nothing, and peered into a small kitchen and again saw nothing. Maybe he was downstairs, maybe he was on the roof. But he would be there.

Meanwhile, Pepe negotiated. It was brief and intense and it turned out that Pepe had talents along these lines, suggesting that he'd done this ten or possibly fifteen thousand times before. It was all done in advance, so that when the boss arrived, all the embarrassing financial details would be worked out, all questions settled, all bills paid in full, and only the pleasure remained.

There were three girls, the one the boss had chosen and two others. Mamasita told the two others to take a hike and they disappeared down the dark hall, leaving Esmeralda, as she was called, to face her fate, which was Boss Harry the American humanitarian politician. The yellow negress had rolling shoulders, breasts and buttocks; in fact everything about her was somehow rolly and quivery, fleshy and powdery and sweaty meat, and dankness and moisture. A sheen of wet glittered on her forehead. She looked nervous and forlorn. But the boss wouldn't notice.

Earl heard Pepe, after some lengthy hassles in Spanish, divert to English.

'Drink the Coca-Cola bottle, no? *El Coca, si?* That's what he wants.'

'He pays the extra, he gets.'

'Then it's done, Mama?'

'It is done.'

He turned to Earl and just nodded. No expression at all lit his eyes, the mark of a professional.

Earl went down the dark stairs, opened the door and went to the car, its engine still running to provide the power for air conditioning. A window wound down under the power of a miraculous modern pushbutton.

'He says it's set,' Earl said to Lane.

'You sure, Swagger?' asked Lane.

86

'I'm sure that's what he said. What that means, I don't know and can't say. This ain't a good idea.'

'Just do the job, Swagger.'

The window clamped shut.

Earl looked about and around. It was a familiar whoretown scene: when a customer came to call, it was as if he entered a bubble. The commerce was sacred and invisible, and the Cuban throngs massing along the sidewalks of Zanja walked blankly on, watching nothing. Earl looked about for photogs — you never knew — and saw none, saw no sailors from Gitmo or the Merchant Marine, no American college students out raising rum-soaked hell. Just Cubans, who lived here, and, down and across the street, a few late drinkers at a cafe, maybe some diners headed down to the Pacifico in Chinatown, the best Chinese eatery in town.

'Okay,' he said.

The door of the Cadillac opened and the congressman stepped out, wobbled slightly under the influence of his own rum consumption, ran his hands through his magnificent white hair, tightened his tie as if the Duke and Duchess of Windsor awaited upstairs, and started unsteadily forward.

Earl thought he might fall, even pass out, which would make things easier all around, but no, he was set in his course and he made it to the red-lit portal, Earl opening the door to admit the man, nervously following and scanning. Both headed up the stairs.

The congressman's brogue-shod feet pounded

heavily on the ancient stone, as they rose a story under the illumination of a single bare bulb at the top. Up, up, up they went, until at last he stopped.

He turned to Earl.

'Now don't judge me harshly, Earl,' he said.

'I have been in a cathouse or two myself, sir,' said Earl.

'I know I have a beautiful wife, a handsome young son and a blossoming career. But sometimes a fellow has to have what he wants, and gol-dang it, here is such a time.'

'Yes, sir.'

'I have an idea about a certain thing, Earl, God help me. It's a thing you can't get no white woman to do. I've had a few girls in my day, but there's a thing I've never had. Tonight I will have it, by God.'

'Many a man feels the same way, sir, and don't you think nothing about it. Now I am on your six o'clock, and will keep a watch.'

'Good work, son. You are a true man of Arkansas, I can tell. All that stuff about how hardheaded you was — no, sir, you are a fine young man.'

The congressman smiled, seemed almost to pass out, and Earl made to catch him, but he got hold of himself in the instant before his knees buckled, then turned to continue his advance on paradise.

Earl waited a second or five, or even ten. He didn't want to see the man's exchange with the woman. He heard muttering, her nervous laughter, the madam's admonitions in harsh

Spanish, and the swish and tinkle of the beaded curtains as john and whore sought privacy for their commerce. Only then did Earl enter, finding a bored Pepe lounging on a couch, the mamasita sitting at a table working on financial accounts, and a radio blaring from a shelf, chronicling the narrative of some mambo-rama or other, with excitement from the male and female hosts but nothing he could pick up, though he knew a form of brothel Spanish from his years before the war.

Pepe made no room for Earl, who in any case didn't want to be on his butt, but on foot, ready. So Earl leaned, arms crossed, the interior hand not far from the Colt hanging under his shoulder. Time passed, one mambo became another and then another, Pepe said nothing, Earl saw nothing, mamasita added columns and columns of numbers and then —

'AIEEEEEEEEE! No, please, no!'

It was Esmerelda, screaming as if the devil himself had forced himself upon her, and then came the unmistakable thud of a hand hitting a face with considerable velocity.

'Damn you, you thief! Damn you, damn you, damn you to hell's fires!' There was the sound of another slap, and another. 'Do you know who I am! *Do you know who I am?*'

Earl was there in an instant. The congressman was atop her in the flickering candlelight, slapping her hard in her bloody face. Earl grabbed him in a bear's iron grip and hoisted him from her, aware that his pants were bunched around his knees absurdly, that his stiffened member was jousting crazily, his face as wet with sweat as hers was with her own blood, his fabulous hair a nest of silver thorns and curls.

Earl heaved him into space but not against the wall, and put himself between him and the sobbing woman, who had gathered herself up in bedclothes and was shivering violently, her blood filling the fibers of the sheets and turning them purple in the flickering light.

'I paid,' the congressman was screaming. 'She wouldn't, she wouldn't, but I paid, *I paid!*'

Earl spread his arms like a crossing guard to keep the congressman away without hurting him.

'Now, now,' he counseled, 'now, now, now. You don't want to be doing something you will regret. It ain't worth it, sir. You just settle on down and we'll get you to the embassy and you can have a nice shower and — '

Pepe was beside him now, saying, 'But, señor, she is only a nigger whore, is no matter, the whore must do what — '

And mamasita went over as if to comfort Esmerelda but in the inverted madness of the moment didn't hug her at all. Instead — WHAP! — she hit poor Esmerelda harder than the boss ever had, and with a fistful of rings.

Earl grabbed the madam, threw her hard aiming for the wall, so that when she hit her arms flung wide and her mouth and eyes popped. Then he shoved Pepe for good measure too, just because he was in a shoving mood.

Then, finally, he turned to the congressman and somehow gathered him without actually

90

touching him, as if to get him out of there with a minimum of damage, and if Pepe's back were broken from the way he went over and through that table, so be it; he, Earl, would drive the big Cadillac and get the congressman back to the embassy.

It seemed to be going quite well, at least for a moment or so, and he actually had the congressman under control, his pants up if not yet belted, as they headed to the door — and that's when Earl saw the man with the knife.

Where had he come from? Earl would never know. And worse, behind him was another, also with a knife, a Spanish thing with bone handle that had just flashed outward, spring driven, from its concealment.

'Hey, hey,' said Earl.

'Oh, Jesus,' said Boss Harry, and commenced to slide pitifully to the floor, as if that was a form of escape.

'Motherfucker,' said the first knifeman. 'Going to cut choo bad, *cabrone*.'

Well, Earl didn't think so, and he hit the fellow square up in the nose with a shot so fast and hard no camera could possibly have caught it. He felt the satisfaction of the perfect impact. That man's head jerked back and his eyes rolled up even as his nose, now squashed, began to spritz blood. He wheezed wetly and large numbers of shattered teeth came out of a suddenly slack mouth. He turned ash gray, his knees melting, his eyes rolling skyward. Then he went with a thud, landing next to the balled-up congressman, and then the other man came around and jabbed at Earl with his knife.

You can't fight a man with a knife and not get cut and when you get cut you can't let the sight of your own blood scatter your mind. The man, clearly a knife expert from his balance and precision and the backwards grip with which he clenched his weapon, got a good two-inch diagonal gash across Earl's parrying left arm, which began oozing its own red through the cheap suit, a garment that offered no stanching qualities at all.

Pleased at what damage he had wrought on one pass, the man stepped back to admire his work and accept the plaudits of the audience, a mistake, because Earl caught the bottom of his wrist with his good hand, twisted and pivoted, stepped under the raised arm with a nifty jujitsu thing he'd picked up somewhere eastern, and brought his man under control, though his cut had begun to hurt like hell. Now, what to do with him? That was the question. The stairs: that was the answer.

Earl, controlling him roughly, though he squirmed like a fish on a line, monitored him to the head of the stairs and without giving it a second thought pitched him down. He yelled and clattered as he went. He limbs went this way and that and his head hit stone stair or wall several terrible times, each with its own particular thunk.

He came to rest at the bottom, arms akimbo, eyes closed, small patches of blood from the abrasions of the fall beginning to seep through his clothes and mark his face.

Oh, shit, thought Earl, thinking he had killed him and wouldn't that be a pretty pickle. But the men who guard whorehouses as a profession tend to be a hardy lot, and this one opened his eyes, shook his head and rose unsteadily. He looked up the steps at his conqueror, gripping his own now weirdly twisted arm, screamed a Spanish blasphemy, pushed open the door and headed out into the night.

Earl turned, gripping his arm to hold the bleeding in. Now it really stung.

From the floor, Boss Harry looked agape at him with eyes full of love.

'Sir, get yourself dressed and we will git the hell out of this place. You, goddammit — ' this to hapless Pepe, still stupefied on the sofa, ' — you help him and get him out of here. I have to get this cut stitched before I bleed out.'

'Oh, *si señor*, yes, sir,' said Pepe, jumping into action.

And suddenly, like three goddesses from some old Greek story, Esmerelda and her two colleagues were on Earl, one cleaning, one pressing, one wrapping tightly. They gazed at him with adoration too, and were nattering away in Spanish at a mile a minute.

'They say *mucho hombre*, much man. You have defeated two of El Colorado's worst fellows, Scarface and the little one you tossed down the steps, he was Mulatto Sam. They beat these girls and so many of the girls often and on Zanja Street are very well known as the Dark Angels of El Colorado.'

El Colorado. Now who the hell could *that* be?

93

It didn't sound promising.

'Just help the congressman, you,' said Earl. 'Ladies, thank you for your help, but this will hold me fine till I get to a hospital. You are very sweet and kind and — '

The clambering on the stone steps announced the arrival of the local constabulary, and come to think of it, Earl had heard sirens, he just hadn't affiliated them with his current situation.

He turned, and began to smile at his rescuers, but it was the madam who dominated the action. She suddenly stepped from behind the curtains and began pointing at Earl, and shrieking. Behind them, rushing to the fallen congressman who Pepe now had more or less dressed, came Lane Brodgins, the color of dry leaves, and he bent, screaming hysterically, 'Oh my god, oh my god, sir, *sir!* Harry, dear God, what has happened? Oh it is so *awful.*'

This was fine and good and spoke of Lane's love, devotion and admiration to his boss, but it did Earl no good whatsoever, for evidently on the instructions of the madam, the two beefy policemen advanced on Earl and began to beat him.

Taken by surprise, he covered up and had a brief respite when the three whores ran to the cops to implore them on Earl's behalf in their own form of hysterical Spanish. But mamasita had the stronger will, the louder voice and presumably paid the biggest bribes, so the two coppers — now three, now four, now a whole mob — closed on Earl and the blows rained down.

As he fell, he saw Lane and Pepe gently guiding Congressman Etheridge to the steps, but at that point someone hit him expertly on the elbow and the pain was so intense, he uncovered to rub the spot of the blow. The next one hit him flush to the jaw, the knockout punch, and down he went, into swirling darkness.

11

Earl's head felt like Esmeralda had it between her thighs and was crushing it to pulp. The place stank of piss and shit and sweat, and Esmeralda — he thought she had liked him! — just crushed away, squeezing his temples toward nothingness, while meanwhile the other whores rifled his pockets.

He fought to be free, and only upon opening his eyes did he realize he was in a holding tank in some Centro police station, and Esmeralda and her two pals were nowhere near. The crushing sensation was just the residue of the cosh's solid thump against his jaw.

He shivered, and the magpies scattered. They had been looting him, not that the cops hadn't already picked him clean. His shirt was gone, his jacket and tie, the gun and holster of course, and his shoes and socks. Only his pants remained, though not the belt. But his cellmates were searching him for what few remaining dollars they thought he might have. He had none.

'Get out of here!' he screamed, kicking one away, shoving several others. They scampered to the other side of the room, where they joined the larger night's haul of street scum, pimps, grifters, pickpockets, strong-arm men and what have you that the Havana cops had rounded up that night on Zanja Street or other dark corridors of the city. They watched him suspiciously, muttering among themselves.

Earl's head hurt bad. It hurt extremely bad. This had to be concussion ten or so. A few more and he'd start to go punchy, like some old fighters he'd seen. He touched where the hardest blow had landed and found that someone had taped a grapefruit to his face. But it wasn't a grapefruit on his face, it was the grapefruit *of* his face. It hurt also to the touch.

He touched the gash on his arm, found it secured tightly by a linen strip. The blood had blackened on his skin where it congealed. He could hardly move it. He needed stitches bad; it could reopen at any moment.

He pulled himself upright. He was in the back of the biggest cell in the back of the biggest cop shop in the town, him and twenty or so of his best friends. They eyed him ominously. These boys didn't appear to care for Earl. Perhaps word had gotten out that he'd whacked the shit out of two bad boys and these fellows in here thought they'd score some points with bossman El Colorado, whoever that nightmare might be, by giving Earl a little taste of same. But that's what the cops had already done. He spit something on the floor and saw that it landed and splattered red. Somewhere in the night's squalors he'd cut open his tongue on a tooth. He reached in, and felt, and all the teeth remained, but the jaw was swollen on the left side and crowded the choppers, and several teeth wiggled loosely even as they jacked in pain. He drew his hand smartly away, and the fingertip too was red. He needed three weeks leave at the beach somewhere, and a diet of Jell-O and Coca-Cola.

'Hey!' he screamed, and there was no answer from wherever officialdom concealed itself. Outside the bars was only a deserted stone corridor and way down it some light, where perhaps the office was. He knew this was the tank. Every city had a tank. You dump the shit in the tank: that's how it worked. In the morning you flush it out and let all the scum that are still alive run free, knowing they'll be back in the evening, or if not them, then their twin brothers. Nobody cared what happened back here.

'*I demand you call the American embassy!*' he tried again.

No answer and then, 'Eeeye deman choo call Americana eeem-buzzy,' a not-bad imitation of himself from one of the concealed comedians, and everybody laughed.

'Hey, Charlie,' someone said, 'choo inna lotta shit, man.'

Earl said nothing. What was there to say? His head hurt too much to think, it was so dark he could hardly see a thing, and the boys were roiling themselves toward violence. Not good. He drew back. He'd been in a prison before but there he'd had the righteous wrath of hating it and what it stood for and the dream of its destruction to impel him onward. He had none of that now. He felt tired and old, and his wife and son were oh so far away in Arkansas, as were his friends, his hopes, his ambitions.

Fuck, he thought. I am going to die in a prison.

Maybe the cavalry would get here in time,

maybe it wouldn't. But for now he could do nothing but wait and ache and pray.

★ ★ ★

Some time passed, though here in the Centro tank no sense of a concept called 'time' truly existed. He may have passed out. Possibly it was near dawn. He wasn't sure. He felt human warmth, and blinked.

He looked up. Three men loomed over him. They dangled shivs from hands, blades formed from spoons or screwdrivers or whatever. Their eyes had the blank look of killers. The pride they had in what they were capable of doing — anything — radiated off them. Two of the three had scars, which meant that the one without was really dangerous.

Earl was flat against the wall, on a bench that passed for a bed. He had no room to maneuver. They towered over him, pressing in, all advantage to them, none to him. If he rose, they'd gut him quickly enough. If he stayed down and balled up, they could cut him bad enough that he'd lose his strength, then pry his limbs away in that fashion, longer but going the same inevitable destination, and get their blades into his guts.

'Hey, Joe,' said the scarless one, 'choo got money?'

'I don't have nothing, friend,' said Earl.

'Oh, that is very bad. I want to help you, but my friends here, they want to cut you now.'

'They can cut me all they want, but they're

99

not going to get any money, because I don't have any money.'

'Then maybe they cut you for fun.'

'I ain't done nothing to you. Please leave me alone.'

He had decided on the balled-up defense. It wasn't much but it was all he had. Now it was a question of how quick he could get his knees up to his chest and bury his face and throat in them and lock his arms around his legs.

'We don't like Yankees. El Colorado tells us choo people come here and fuck our women and steal our crops and make us your monkeys, and we don't like it nohow. *Cuba libre*, mother-fucker.'

'Just leave me alone,' said Earl. 'I ain't done a thing to you.'

'I think we have to teach *norteamericano* a lesson. Charlie, you are the history lesson of the evening.'

Suddenly a fourth party joined the exchange.

He said, 'Excuse me, gentlemen, but would any of you be interested in purchasing a very fine vacuum cleaner?'

★ ★ ★

'He's *where?*' said Walter Short.

'The police took him,' said Lane Brodgins. 'I don't know — '

'You idiot! You moron! Who the hell gave you authorization to head to Zanja Street?'

'Congressman Etheridge doesn't need autho-rization, Short. Who the deuces do you think — '

'You moron! If anything happens to Earl, I will personally see that your career is so completely destroyed you won't even be able to get a listing in the phone book!'

'You cannot — '

'You were to get him here so we could develop him. That was the *point*. That was the *only* point. This wasn't a let's-get-Boss-Harry-laid mission.'

'You try and tell a United States — '

'*You* had an obligation to us. We put money into this, we are picking up the tab, we are getting you great press, you had one job to do — '

But it was pointless.

He slammed down the phone. Then he deslammed it and quickly called Roger, who answered groggily. He explained.

'Oh, Christ,' said Roger.

'We can handle this. I have friends in the Cuban State Police.'

'You would, Short.'

'Roger, I have to do the shit so you can be the golden boy at the Yacht Club tennis tournament. Now please get dressed, get a cab, get over here. Meanwhile, I have to think.'

He hung up, then started dialing.

★ ★ ★

There was a moment of dumbfoundment.

All eyes — the three thugs', Earl's — went to the vacuum representative, to discover a scrawny scarecrow of a man with a bristle of gray hair,

101

wearing a baggy linen suit. His face looked as if history itself had marched across it several times in several climates. He spoke with some indeterminate European accent and had the palest eyes Earl had ever seen.

Then he smiled.

'Hey, you, get the fuck outta here!' screamed one of the assailants, drawing himself up to full power and stepping forward to thrust his bull-chest against the skinny man. 'You, go, I cut your — '

That assertion was halted by the evening's biggest surprise: what could only be the sound of a small pistol firing.

Everyone looked down to discover that the European vacuum salesman had just shot out the knee of the knife-wielder, who collapsed. As he fell, the European caught him, twisted an arm behind his back, and stuck the muzzle of the small gun into his throat.

He spoke in a commanding Spanish of such intensity it was amazing, not only in fluency, blasphemy and eloquence but also force, for the seriousness of his argument was instantly recognized, and the others backed off.

The wounded man crawled away, howling.

Earl, astounded, watched them go.

The man sat next to him.

'As I was saying, I have a very nice upright model, superpowered, what we call the Atomvac 12. It's not atomic-powered of course, but you know how sales brochures love to exaggerate. Anyhow, it's new to the island, has a thirty-foot extension cord and — '

'Who the hell are you?'

'Ah, yes. Of course. Vurmoldt, Acme Vacuums. This is my territory. I don't seem to have a card on me. Perhaps you have one on you and I could call and make a more formal presentation.'

'A vacuum salesman with a gun?'

'It comes in handy.'

'I'll say, bub.'

Earl stared at him in the darkness. What astounded him was the utter finality with which the vacuum salesman had just shot a man, then forgotten about it. That was the first mark of a professional. Shooting a human being isn't an easy thing and some people never come back from it and you see it in their eyes forever. Yet this Vurmoldt, of Acme Vacuums, had done it precisely, even scientifically, and had not wasted a single breath on it. It was necessary, he did it, and now he had moved on to other arguments.

'You seem to have been in some scrapes, if you don't mind my saying so,' Earl told him.

'The recent ugliness. Oh, it was quite unpleasant. I was shot at in France by French, in Russia by Russians, in Italy, then France again, and finally in Germany itself, all by Americans. Quite annoying, you know. Possibly you and I exchanged shots at Normandy or the Ardennes offensive?'

'I was in the Pacific killing Japanese. Though I'd have been happy to shoot you too, if you'd given me the chance.'

The man's face lit in laughter.

'Say, you are a scamp!'

'My name is Swagger, Mr. uh — '

'Vurmoldt. Lower Silesian. An old family of mercantile disposition. The vacuums, by the way, really are quite an excellent product. You would be pleased.'

'*Earl!*'

Earl looked up. It was Roger St. John Evans, rushing down the corridor, flanked by nervous-looking Cuban policemen and various embassy assistants. Keys rattled, men bustled with urgency. It was a little war party come to rescue Earl. They weren't as quick as the vacuum salesman, but they had finally gotten there.

'Earl, Jesus, I had no idea until that idiot Brodgins called the embassy to complain about the Cubans. Good god, are you all right?'

The doors were flung open.

'I'm fine, I'm fine. This here fella saved me. I — '

But Vurmoldt had disappeared into the dark mob of Cubans gathered in the corner, away from the husky guards with their clubs and automatic pistols.

'Hell, he was just here. Sir, I — '

But then Earl looked at the man next to Roger.

'Hi, Earl,' said Frenchy Short. 'Long time no see.'

12

The old men met in an impoverished mountain state so foreign to all the things they knew it seemed like a trip to someone else's old country. The site was an air-conditioned house that had once belonged to a mine manager and looked down across the coaled-out ridges, the abandoned and rusting steam shovels, the scars in the earth. It was like a mansion in a battlefield.

They arrived by Cadillac, each with two or three bodyguards. The huge cars dominated the roads up from Miami and New Orleans, over from Cleveland and Pittsburgh, down from Boston and New York. When they reached the small town that was their destination, it was almost like a funeral parade: black Caddy after black Caddy, negotiating the hairpin turns, crawling through ruined, desolate, misty villages, past knots of curious, slat-ribbed children with hollow faces, lank hair and deep eyes.

And the men in the cars were famous too, at least in their worlds. They were the wisest of the wise, the toughest of the tough, the meanest of the mean, the fastest of the fast. What stories they could tell if storytelling were permitted, though of course it was not. What those old eyes had seen, what those old brains had calculated, what those old, still-strong hands had crushed.

They were lumpy, dark men, set in their ways, in black suits and ties and white shirts, and fallen

105

socks over big black shoes. The lenses of their glasses were thick. Their veins showed, their eyes were rheumy and bloodshot, their hands large, their jowls fallen, their faces swaddled in fat and unsmiling, drawn, serious. They spat a lot, smoked a lot, cursed a lot. They wore pomade in their thinning hair. They looked as if they'd never laughed in their lives, or had a drink with a girl or gone to a dance or a ball game or a party. Their faces had the gray pallor of indoors at night, the waft and stench of cigarettes, the glow of neon. They were old men of the city.

They drank Sambuca or Frangelico or Amaretto from small glasses and sat listlessly around the living room, not at a single grand table like medieval potentates — there was no nobility in their world, only practicality — but like old peasants at a coffeehouse in Salerno, too frail to toil in the fields. The subject was not who was there, but who was not there.

Chicago was not there.

'These Chicago people, I don't know,' said one. 'They get more arrogant all the time. They think their thing is such a great thing.'

'What is to be done? Our thing must be protected, but I am not eager for a return to the old days.'

'Me neither. I've been shot enough already, six times, cut twice, beaten a dozen.'

'If I'm to be stabbed in the back,' one joked, 'I want it to be by friends, not enemies!'

Everybody laughed.

'The Chicago thing could become a problem,' said the eldest of the equals. 'The Chicago thing grows mighty on the river of money that flows to it from this Las Vegas, the city in the desert. Who would have dreamed such a thing? A city in a desert!'

'Sometimes even the longest shots come in. Someone picks the number.'

'The Chicago thing owns Las Vegas, so Chicago now sees itself first among equals. Soon, possibly, it will see itself as first without equals. It will be the only thing. Our things will be nothing.'

'Ben Siegel would be horrified if he knew how his dream had turned out because he was always, in his heart, an East Coast boy,' someone said.

'He was a great man, a seer — '

'He was also a nutbin jaybird whose eyes were bigger than his brain and he never had no judgment at all. He starts a fight in a train station with a fellow turns out to be a professional boxer. Goes urp all over his fancy clothes. He ends up like all the hot ones, with his face blown off on his sofa. His eye, I understand, is on the floor.'

'But Ben was committed, rest in peace and a slow death to whoever done the deed on him, to a fair shake for all the things. His idea was that Vegas would be for us all, we'd all have a piece. Not this Chicago thing, as these greedy bastards have established, and now it teeters dangerously toward what nobody wise and old wants.'

Though unsaid, all acknowledged privately the theory of mutually assured destruction that kept the peace, fragile as it was, in their tough little world of things. All knew that if any thing grew

107

too powerful, it would wage war on the others. Alliances would be formed, treaties broken, it would be city against city, thing against thing. Worst of all, of course, it would embolden the class of men these men feared the most: The FBI? Not a chance: No, far worse: their own children and grandchildren, eager to take over, eager to drink from the river and to strut their strength and to push the old bastards aside. These people really frightened the old men. The kids: they wanted their thing.

But at last the one from New York, the wisest of them all, spoke, and all listened.

'The Chicago thing has Las Vegas. We have Cuba. As long as we have Cuba, we need not fear Chicago. Chicago needs to fear us. Next to Cuba, Las Vegas is nothing but an annoyance.'

'This is very true,' someone said.

'He speaks what is real.'

He continued.

'We have our best man down there. He is clever, oh so clever with the numbers — '

'The Jew? He is not one of us.'

'He is in cunning. Only he lacks our will to do what is necessary. He has not killed, I believe.'

'No, he has not. He is an arguer, a fixer. With the guns, the boomboom, the flying blood, the puddles all sticky and black, the faces blown off, the hair mussed, the newspaper shots of what happens in alleys to men who have transgressed. No, not for him.'

'That is a shame. Sometimes that is where it must end. In an alley, with a pool of blood and the face gone.'

An amen chorus agreed. That was where it had to end some time. Nothing else would satisfy.

'This is why I have made an arrangement, which I now put before you, for your approval,' said the New York thing representative. 'I have done this already. It can be undone, if you demand, but I think you will see some wisdom in it.'

'So, go ahead.'

'What is needed down there is someone with our kind of hot blood. The balls to get close with knives or guns. Fists even. Sometimes necessary as we have said.'

'It is not in the Jew to be that way. Any Jew. They have been beaten on too many times for them to take pleasure in that.'

'It was in Ben, at least a little. It was in Lepke Buchalter, rest in peace. It was in Murder, Inc. and in Barney Ross, the boxer. They were all Jews. Now in this Israel. These Jews are fighters, too. With the machine guns, what have you.'

'They are a new kind of Jew. Our kind of Jew is like our man in Havana. Or Abbadabba Berman: the numbers, the quickness, the sureness with the figures. That is your typical Jew. Certainly, yes, in certain times, it changes. You cannot, I think you will agree, count on it to be that way. You have to count on the typical, not the extraordinary.'

'So what have you done?'

'I have sent him a man.'

'One man would make such a difference?'

'One man, yes. *This* man.'

'And who is this man.'

'Frankie Carbine.'

'Frankie Horsekiller? Frankie of Times Square? Frankie of the two policemen? That Frankie?'

'That Frankie, exactly.'

'Oh, my god!'

The amen chorus rumbled nervously, then the wise man spoke again.

'He is crazy. He has no judgment. He likes too much to shoot. All his problems he solves with a gun. He wants to be big but he hasn't the vision. He just has his gun and his craziness. But sometimes you need craziness. You need that thing where there is no fear. Some of the old-timers had it. We had to move on, but there are throwbacks, and Frankie Carbine is such a man. We may have need of the crazed down there. Cuba is the lynchpin of all our things; we may have to defend it with crazy. Sometimes, crazy is necessary.'

All amened in honor of crazy.

13

'It's obvious,' said Roger. 'You were set up.'

But Earl couldn't concentrate on what Roger was saying. He kept looking into the front seat at Frenchy Short and images returned of the young man in Hot Springs in 1946, his talent, his ambition, his anger, his hurry, his inability to fit in.

There'd always been something funny about it. They'd had to dump Frenchy because he was difficult to control and a politician couldn't stand having him around. And a week after, somehow the unit had been ambushed and so many other young men killed. All for nothing, as it turned out. It was as sorry a thing as Earl had ever been involved with.

And Frenchy? What of Frenchy? What had he known, who had he talked to, what was he capable of? To look at him, you'd never think he was capable of a thing. He looked, if anything, younger today than that first day in Hot Springs. Like Roger, he was blond and had a square, almost pretty face. He was dressed just like Roger too, in khakis, a white shirt, some kind of striped tie and a blue blazer with an insignia on the pocket. It was like the duty uniform with these guys. You'd look at him and you'd think, gee, this kid, he's probably a big man on some leafy campus somewhere. His eyes were guileless; he hardly shaved; he had freckles.

'Really, Earl,' Roger was saying, 'it seems so sleepy and tropical down here, but there's a war going on. It's the same war that's going on everywhere. The Reds sneak in and call it 'liberation' and get the brown people all heated up thinking they can have Cadillacs and freezers and televisions if only they overthrow the governments and take over, under communist supervision. That's the new war, Earl. Korea is an anomaly, because it's direct and involves actual combat. But we've studied the phenomenon and we know the wars of the future will be guerilla things, low-key dramas of assassination, subversion, sabotage and propaganda. Getting a congressman's dick in a wringer is exactly their kind of operation.'

Maybe Roger meant it as a joke, but still, Earl had not laughed.

'They have to make us look ridiculous and weak. So along comes an idiot like Harry Etheridge and with his appetites and lack of judgment, he's an incident waiting to happen. And it happens.'

They were driving an embassy car back from the Centro Havana jail after a stop at the emergency room, where Earl's wounds were tended, he was given shots and painkillers, and his knife cut was stitched. He was back in his suit even if it was a little bloodied; the Colt Super .38 had been restored to the Lawrence holster held by leather halter under his left shoulder.

It was early. The old city was coming awake. Gray dawn splashed across the white streets and a cool wind ruffled the trees. They seemed to have found the Malecon, that great Havana roadway that girded the waterfront, and a gray sheet of as yet unlit Caribbean spread off to one side, while a row of bricky-bracky pink and pale-blue colonnaded buildings dominated the other. Frenchy, who was driving, had rolled down the windows. All the smells of Havana — the sea, the fish, the fruit, the meat, the poultry, the tobacco, all of it rawly ripped from where it had been the day before — rode in on breezes, propelled by the smell of very hot, strong, sweet coffee.

'But, Earl,' continued this talky Roger, 'Earl, you stopped them, you stopped them cold. Walter said you were the sort of man for this kind of work and he was right.'

'Who's Walter?' said Earl, then realized Roger was talking about the boy in the front seat. 'Frenchy,' he said, leaning forward, 'what the hell is going on here?'

'Earl, we needed a good man. The best. I knew you. Whoever's been in Arkansas knows Earl Swagger. So I made a suggestion. That's all.'

'It was a good suggestion,' said Roger. 'Walter, or should I say *Frenchy*, made a good suggestion. You handled the knuckleball they threw us, so Congressman Harry isn't on the cover of *Life* magazine beating up a whore in a blow job dispute and making the United States look like two cents worth of garbage.'

'So is that why I'm here? I wondered.'

'Earl, this is nothing formal. Just think about things. You have several futures ahead of you. You can stay in Arkansas and be a state cop and probably, given your skill and integrity, end up in command. But again, some wiseguy politician or newspaper joe may cut you off at the knees if it earns him three extra votes or some kind of prize.'

Earl said nothing.

'Or . . . well, you just think about the *or*. The *or* could be something you never dreamed of. Someone has noticed your talent, your skill, and there's no reason you should waste it in Arkansas. Nobody ever made it in Arkansas. Look at Boss Harry and Fred C. Becker: they're the best Arkansas has managed. No need for you to be a big fish in a microscopic pond like Arkansas.'

'I like Arkansas.'

'Buy a summer house there.'

They turned up the Prado and navigated its leafy broadness, sliding by the mock-Paris cafes, the heavily ornamental central strip with its stone benches, palms and statues, passed the Sevilla-Biltmore where the gangsters lived, then turned left to the Plaza.

'Just think about it,' said Roger.

'What was your name again, son?' Earl said to Roger.

Roger let out a long sigh of exasperation. 'All right, show the Ivy League hotshot how little you think of him because he never fought on Iwo Jima. Let me tell you, though, I seem harmless and silly because I'm supposed to seem harmless and silly. It's called cover. It's what we do. For the record, my name is Roger St. John Evans. Roger Evans. I told you I was in codes? That was cover, too. I'm a senior case officer of the Central Intelligence Agency, head of Havana station, reporting directly to the Caribbean Desk in Langley, Virginia, directly to Plans, directly to the Director of Central Intelligence. That makes me important. I am important, take it from me. Walter — Frenchy — is my no. 2.'

'Well, I'm sure you're very important, sonny. Now I want you to take a hike, because I have to have a talk with young Walter here and what he says and how he explains some things between us has a lot to do with whether I'm staying or whether I'm on the next plane home.'

'Sure,' said Roger. He leaned forward to Walter and said, 'Don't blow it!'

★   ★   ★

Time ticked away as the two men sat in the car next to the pie-shaped, five-story building that was the Plaza. Across from them the Parque Central began to fill up; Havana was an exceptionally busy town and today would be no different. Cubans in straw hats and white suits came and went along the street and on to jobs in Old Havana, in the buildings along the Prado, here, there everywhere. Old ladies set up their tables and began the day's work of rolling cigars for the touristas. It was a little early yet for pimps and touts, but they would be there, you could be sure.

Finally Frenchy said, 'Well, Earl, I'm up front, but you're in the driver's seat. They want you. It's something, let me tell you.'

115

Between Earl and the young man lay a whole gulf of mistrust. Frenchy had been a member of Earl's raid team in Hot Springs some years earlier, in an ugly little war against mobsters, supposedly for the moral betterment of mankind. But Frenchy was wild then, and made mistakes, some innocent people were killed, and it was decreed by frightened higher authorities that he should be let go. Off he went, spewing fury and screaming betrayal.

A week later, the team was mysteriously ambushed in a rail yard, after being set up by someone with an unusual sense of its weaknesses and vanities. Seven good men died that night and only Earl and one other made it out. Within six months, the tables and wheels of Hot Springs were up and running, so it had all been for nothing. It still left a dark, rancid taste on Earl's tongue. He hated to think on it; it got him riled in ways unnecessary for a calm life.

'You don't tell me nothing. You understand? Was a time when I thought I might come looking for you so's we'd have a little talk, get some things straightened out.'

'Earl, there's nothing to be straightened out.'

Earl looked at him and Frenchy held the gaze square and hard. There was no evasion, no furtiveness of the eyes, none of the things you saw when you had a crook before you, as Earl had had before him now a thousand or so times. Earl watched: the boy didn't breathe hard and shallow, his eyes didn't flutter left to recall or right to make something up, his throat didn't dry or crank up a quart or two of liar's phlegm. He held steady, maybe even a little too steady. That was the thing about Frenchy, damn his skills, he could look anybody square in the eye and tell him anything and say it with such passion he made you believe it.

'Does this Roger kid know what a little snake he has working for him?'

'Earl, I never did you or any of them any harm. I heard about it when I got back from China. I looked for you, because I wanted to know what happened, too. When I heard that Bugsy Siegel got pasted, I figured Mr. Earl paid him a call.'

'Like as if I'd waste my time on city trash like that. No, he wasn't part of what happened in Hot Springs.'

'Neither was I. Ask me any question. I'll go over it with you day by day, I'll cite time, date, location. I'll account for it all. You try your hardest to trip me up, but you won't be able to do it, because there's nothing for me to trip up on.'

'What I know is you got canned, and both the old man and I fought as hard as we could against that. Some fights with some assholes you just don't win. Next, you disappear. A week later we are turned inside out by someone who knew us so well he played it straight to our weaknesses, to that old man's silly vanity, to his memories. Only two of us walked away.'

'You and Carlo Henderson.'

'That left seven good men and one great one to die in a railyard.'

'I'd bet he didn't go unavenged.'

'There was justice paid out, and I'd do it again in a second, even if it was evil killing work. But that ain't got nothing to do with you. We were talking about the great D. A. Henderson and seven good men.'

'I remember D.A. He was a good hand. Earl, I had not a thing to do with it. I left town, I drifted to Washington, I went to work in a small unimportant department of the government, I had a lucky break and met some people — through a girl, actually — and got a small, unimportant job in the Agency. A nothing job. In there, I worked hard and met some more people and got some training and got the China assignment. I saw some things, but you know we lost China, and some men were stained by it. Their careers are finished. I just barely survived and I'm still at it. Going nowhere except fetching coffee for this Harvard asshole Roger who thinks he's the next Director. Anyhow, that's the story, the whole story.'

Earl just studied him.

'Truth is, you could be spinning a lie or saying the word of God and I wouldn't know. Some — very damned few — criminals have that gift. But most don't. Not hardly nobody does. I never saw it in fifteen years in the Marine Corps. But it exists, I have learned that as a cop.'

'Earl, I'll take a polygraph.'

'You could beat that.'

'Earl, you just watch and wait and make up your own mind. You belong in the major leagues, not out on some lousy Arkansas state route, handing out tickets. You'll see.'

Earl shook his head.

'I need some sleep,' he finally said.

'Earl, tonight there's the big party. You'll see it's the world you belong in. I know you, Earl. I know where you belong.'

14

'I must say, Speshnev, you've quite a queer notion of doing business,' said Pashin.

'How so?' asked Speshnev. They sat at a disagreeable cafe in Centro, just off Zanja Street, just down from the Barrio Chino, for their weekly. The coffee was strong and sweet, the smell of tobacco stronger. All about them throbbed the Cuban working classes, in whose cause they so energetically labored.

'You were assigned to shadow a man who could be an opponent. And, if necessary, kill him. You establish surveillance, you penetrate the target, you even manage to enter the zone with an automatic. Then, astonishingly, you save his life when fate is about to give you exactly what we needed and expected of you. I wonder what the meaning of that decision is?'

'Oh, that. Yes, well, he seemed rather too impressive a man to end up with his gizzard cut in a Havana drunk tank. The theater of the moment demanded that I intercede. One has to have a feel for such things.'

'His records have been found. We have sources in Washington, you know. Here, take a look.'

Pashin slid the documents over. They were photoed copies of the Marine service record of Earl Lee Swagger. They told of many wars, much battle experience, many wounds, many lost friends, and a few moments of insane heroism.

The list of medals was impressive.

'As you see,' said Pashin, 'a man of great talent. A formidable opponent, one they could not easily replace. And so . . . you *save* him?'

'I thought he had a salty look to him. Like one of the old zeks sent to the camps to perish who instead flourish. Zeks are one thing I know all about.'

'Yes, well, if you fail, it's a zek you'll know about again, 4715.'

'Ah, yes, the magic number, 4715. Why, how sweet to hear its rhythms again.'

'If he determines to move in a certain way, how will we stop him? It would have been so much better to deal with this now.'

'He doesn't know Cuba well enough to do us any harm yet. And the men with him, they are idiots. So I will watch him, while I become an intimate of this Castro, and all things will develop as we hope. I will perform magnificently.'

'You know, Speshnev,' said the younger man, leaning forward, his face empty of humor or irony but filled simply with aggression, 'I grow tired with your whimsy, your poetics. I'm sure all your Comintern colleagues at the Hotel Luxe in Moscow found them amusing, but out here, we've no room for romantic gestures. This is a war, and we must win it.'

'Little Pashin, I do believe I know more about wars than you do. After all, I have fought in all the ones you only read about.'

15

'Cigar, Marine?'

It was the fifth one he'd been offered tonight, a huge, dense thing, expertly woven into the perfect tube.

The offer came from a little man in a dinner jacket, his tanned face alight with pleasure. He had to be Somebody Important. Everybody here was Somebody Important.

'Damn fine,' he continued. 'These people know their goddamned tobacco, I'll say.'

'No, thank you, sir,' said Earl. 'I'm pretty much a Camel man.'

'Fine smoke, a Camel. But these Cubano torpedoes, they're sweet and dense, like a great whiskey.'

'All the same — '

'Well, no matter. Hell of a job, I hear. These politicians, children in my experience. Glad a fellow like you was along to handle things. That's my line of work too, by the way. Son, if you're ever looking for a job, I'm always in the market for a certain kind of talent. Here, take my card, and think about it. We pay top dollar for the right man.'

The card gave a name and said underneath 'Director of Security, United Fruit, Caribbean Division.'

Earl was a star as he stood there in a new dinner jacket himself, courtesy of Congressman

Etheridge; it fit tight and beautifully, the black striped trousers perfect, the shoes a marine-bright shine. He sipped a rumless Coca-Cola, now and then lighting a Camel. He could hardly move, because people kept coming by to see him and say nice things. He wasn't sure how this had happened, but happened it had: in the American community, the word had gotten round.

It was the most fabulous party ever thrown at the embassy in Havana. It had been less smokey on Iwo, an island made of ash. The vapors rose but didn't dissipate; they hung in the vault over the merriment, seething, dense, caught in the light. It was a party in a dramatic fog, men in white dinner jackets, tan women with sleek white breasts peeking out of tight-cut dresses, the tinkle of glass and ice, the pulsations of a mambo combo beating Desi at his own game, the closeness of the tropical night and whatever it concealed just beyond the swimming pool. Even the congressman seemed to get it.

'Well, I must say, Earl, I am used to being the center of attention but it does my heart good to see that I'm just a footnote tonight. You done me a good turn and saved me a bad one, and so I am in your debt, now and forever. That's a card you can cash in on, and when I'm gone, my boy Hollis'll pay off on it too, that I swear. You have a son, don't you, Earl?'

'Yes, sir.'

'What's his name?'

'Bob Lee.'

'Well, I'd be happy to see Bob Lee and Hollis grow up together and go to fine private schools

123

in Washington, D.C., and have lives of significance together. That's something for you to think on, Earl, you hear me?'

'Yes, sir.'

'Good, Earl. You have been discovered. Not many are, and it's a sometime thing, but a smart fellow takes advantage. You be smart now, Earl. Don't you be stupid and bullheaded. Look, enjoy, partake, and you can move up.'

With that, the distinguished southern gentleman was gone, off pressing flesh, bumping into women's plush butts, hugging and charming his way across the room. That everyone knew he'd been whoring and almost gotten in a hell of a mess didn't seem to plague him in the least. He was who he was and that was that for Boss Harry Etheridge.

'You know, Earl,' someone whispered to him, 'you belong here.'

It was Frenchy Short, of course.

Earl merely grunted.

'Earl, look around. These are people who matter. These are the cream of the cream. A lot of 'em got here by luck. Roger, for example. Son of wealth going back five generations. All the advantages. Best schools, people looking out for him all the way, connections, mentors, teachers. On top of that, he's handsome as a movie star and a hell of a tennis player. Some guys get all the breaks, huh? But you and me, Earl, we got here on our talent alone. We've earned it.'

Earl looked over at Frenchy, so neat and shiny in his dinner jacket, his crew cut glistening with butch wax so that the hairs all stood up straight, like a platoon at attention.

'You're talking about yourself,' said Earl. 'I never wanted this shit. I just wanted to make an honest living and go to bed tired and honest, on nobody's take. That's enough for me.'

'Earl, don't throw this away. Think of what it could mean to your family.'

Earl had a laugh at that one. He imagined poor Junie trying to fit into this crowd, or Bob Lee hitting a tennis ball around in short white pants with Roger the Big Noise from Winnetka.

'Earl, you — '

'Excuse me, sonny.'

Earl pulled away from the grasping young man, and somehow negotiated his way across the crowded room. He needed some air. This was getting him down. He stopped at the bar for another Coca-Cola, spied an opening to a porch, and slipped out.

The night was cool. There was no moon. Even with the backwash of light, he could see a spray of stars across the dark. He tried to breathe cool air and relax. He checked his Bulova, saw that it was after eleven, and felt that by midnight he could be in bed to catch some sleep for whatever else this trip had in store for him.

He reconstituted a bit, then figured he ought not to lose contact with his employers for much longer and turned to head back inside.

There was a man standing there.

'I know you,' he said.

'Beg pardon?' said Earl, stepping forward.

He looked at the fellow. His face was bunched in a dog's feral aggression. His hair was slicked

125

back and the dinner jacket looked alien on a body so bursting with physical vitality. He needed a shave but he'd be the type that somehow always needed a shave. There wasn't a single thing tropical about him, and nothing smooth, nothing slick, nothing disciplined. His eyes were tiny and dark and fierce, his nose a vertical blade beneath them, his mouth a horizontal blade beneath it. Eyetie in spades, city in aces, tough in queens and kings. He was pure-D mob, down to the bone level, exactly the kind of gangster gun boy so prominent in Hot Springs.

'They're saying you were in Hot Springs,' the man demanded, and Earl was not surprised.

'What's it to you?'

The man smiled, but it wasn't a smile of love or friendship. It was a smile of release as a man tries to relax his face just before the shit begins.

'I heard about a guy there. They're still talking about him. He supposedly punched out a big famous mob gun down there and got free lunches for years on the story. Yeah, I don't believe it for a second. Ben Siegel was tough as they come, and if anybody laid him out, he must have sucker-punched him, that's what I think. You know anything about that, bud?'

Earl said, 'You know what? I don't explain things. That ain't my job around here.'

'You don't know me, but I know you. I been watching you eating all this shit up. Some kind of hero. Yeah, well, heroes go down too, mac, just in case — '

'Hey, let me tell you, bud. If someone takes a

whack at me, I put him flat faster than a ghost's boo. If some hooligan face-boy thinks he's tough and wants to take a cold shot, I'm the man who shows him he ain't much but average. And I don't like it when some bunny rabbit in a dancing-lesson jacket sticks his nose in mine and tells me some business. You got that?'

'Oh, well, say, ain't we got us a hero here, but ever notice how outside the movies heroes end up cold and still? Why — '

But then another man was on the porch, slicker, older, comforting, smoother.

'Frankie, Frankie, there you are. Oh, sorry, sir, Frankie's been drinking too much and he gets cranky. He doesn't mean a thing by it, don't pay any attention to him.'

He pulled Frankie away but Frankie broke free, not to assault Earl but to whisper.

'Somebody killed Ben Siegel on his own sofa. Shot down while reading a newspaper. If I get my hands on that guy . . . '

But the older man reined him in with surprising force, and sent him on his way. It was as if the younger suddenly realized the power of the old, and slumped and dejected, he exited.

Earl looked at the old man: he saw sadness, wisdom, smart eyes, a nose both huge and beautiful at once. He saw something he recognized, if not by name, by instinct.

'Mr. Swagger, please don't pay any attention to my associate. He's in his cups, he has dreams of glory, he spent too much time at lousy tables in New York nightclubs. He plays the gangster when he's the assistant to the assistant. Sober and free of his fantasies, he means you no harm at all, believe me.'

'He's way out of line.'

'He gets that way when he drinks. I'll have words with him. By the way, I run a casino. It's called Montmartre. Come on by and spend a night gambling on my tab, just to show there's no hard feelings. You can't lose and what you win is yours to take. It's owed you. You're quite a hero. My name is Meyer Lansky.'

A king gangster! A big gangster! The biggest of the big!

'I'm not a gambler, but thanks anyhow.'

'Whatever makes you happy, my friend. The house will always be open to you and I think you'll find the cards run your direction.'

He smiled, and slid back, and with that smooth way of his seemed to vaporize into invisibility.

16

The young man studied the board. Now this was interesting. It seemed that the force was setting itself up to the left, where the queen commanded doughty pawns, clever rooks, heroic knights and even the bishop, while the king languished, as was his wont, far away, shielded by a few disengaged pieces. The old lady did the work.

But the more he studied, the more he concluded that his opponent was lulling him. He was engineering what seemed to be an aggression on the right, but the real action would come suddenly from the left, and it would be blinding and clever and swift. He knew a possibility lurked here. In his mind, he struggled to unlock it, but no epiphany arrived for assistance.

Yet his faith was deep: he was convinced the right was a ruse, the left a trap. He knew he had to decide, to countermove, to show aggression and tenacity. So he —

'*No, no, no!*' the older man screamed at him. 'Have you learned nothing these days? Have you been sleeping? Have you been daydreaming! Ach, such an idiot you are!'

'But, sir,' said the twenty-six-year-old Castro, 'it appeared to me that — '

'Go ahead, make your move, this is becoming boring.'

Castro moved, the older man countermoved

insolently, a performance of abject contempt, and in the countermove Castro saw a seam open, an unexpected thrust of aggression rupture his defenses, and felt the steam go out of him.

'Damn!' he said. 'Again.'

'Play it out, idiot.'

It was quick: three moves and for the sixth straight time and the ninth time in ten days, he was checkmated. He had but a solitary, lucky draw to show for his efforts.

'You have to have a feel for these things,' said the chess master. 'Maybe chess is not the game for you. There's no opportunity to give speeches or go on the radio. Perhaps that is what you are really good at. It's a tawdry talent, but I suppose it is what one has, and one must make the best of it. Let the smarter fellows make the decisions and figure things out.'

'No, no,' whined the young man, 'I am smart. You will see that — ' But then he stopped. He said, 'That was last year. How did you know I was on the radio? You are not from Cuba.'

'I know some things. One thing I know: You need a better head for chess. That would be a wiser place to start than speeches, where you get paid in plaudits and end up the day with nothing tangible. What have I been telling you? Don't be so hasty. It gets you massacred every time.'

'At least it's a glorious massacre,' said the young man.

'Have you ever seen a massacre?' the older fellow asked.

'No,' Castro admitted.

'Well, I have. Not pretty. Certainly not

glorious. Ugly, bloody, pitiful, pathetic, squalid. So all great crusades end up, if they are not carefully managed.'

'Who are you?' Castro asked. 'You show up and suddenly we are playing chess every day. You speak our language too well, and with a European accent. You learned your Spanish in Spain.'

'Spain, it's true.'

'Thirty-six to thirty-nine? Where also you saw the massacre?'

'I have, alas, seen many massacres. Too many. I hope not to see another.'

The two sat in the park called San Francisco under palm trees in Old Havana, not far from a coffee stand, a shoeshine man, a fleet of *bolita* salesmen, two whores taking a time off from a busy morning, a woman rolling cigars, and many relaxing seagulls. The sun was hot, but a fresh sea breeze from the nearby harbor made the palms dance and kept the sweat from collecting.

'I think you've come a long way to see me,' said Castro. 'You were interested in me from the start, that I could tell. I understood that.'

'I have some practical experience. Possibly you'd listen to my advice now and then. Sometime in the future, when you are wiser, you might even take it.'

'Where are you from?'

'What does it matter? What matters is that you and I believe in the same things and possibly the same methods.'

The boy began a hoary recitation of what he believed in. Meanwhile, Speshnev looked hard at

131

him and, try as he could, only saw a familiar type, thrown up by revolutions and wars the world over. An opportunist with a lazy streak, and also a violent one. Not smart, but clever enough to get himself in real trouble. A minor gift for gab, but no real character or integrity. No vision beyond the self, but a willingness to use the vernacular of the struggle for his own private careerism.

Speshnev had of course read the documents. The boy Castro was only a third-generation Cuban, his father being the son of a Spanish soldier who, when Spain left in 1899, had decided to stay in the new country rather than move back to the old. The father's family was Galician, from that severe province in the north of Spain whence hailed conquistadors and other men of cruel disposition and rapacious appetite. But there was no evidence the boy was comprised of such fortitude. So far, beside the speeches, there'd only been mischief: he played at organizing demonstrations against the American secretary of state in 1948 and had gone on some mad pretend campaign to liberate the Dominicans from the strongman Trujillo, abandoning the quest when things got tough. No questions had been answered.

This was the sort of boy who — like dozens of others — ended up hanging on a meathook in Secret Police headquarters, or turned, compromised, made a parody of himself, trafficking in betrayal for a few dollars, a few more days of limited freedom.

Did he have the steel will? Was he able to kill

and not die of guilt? Could he spy, torture, intimidate, betray to advance the greater cause? Who knew? Could he yield on the shabby bourgeois 'morality' of his father, a petty landowner in Oriente province who had done well by groveling before American interests?

So the boy bobbed before him, a weird blend of gifts, ambition and vagueness, too romantic for anybody's good, particularly his own. He might have what it took, and Speshnev might be able to help him. But as for now: who could tell?

'Allow me to point out,' Speshnev lectured harshly, delineating another flaw, 'that you lack curiosity. Day in, day out, I beat you. You don't wonder why, you don't try new tactics, you don't do research or make intelligent sacrifices. You attack, attack, attack. You find romance in the attack. That is a way to die young and bitter.'

'I am following my heart.'

'Ach, you're giving me a headache. So much passion, so little accomplished. Work steadily toward a goal that is immediately attainable. A seat in the legislature, a column in the newspaper, an endorsement from an older fellow. Reach out to them, so that they may reach out to you. In the arms of others shall you rise. The great revolutionaries all knew that. Thus far you have demonstrated that you know nothing.'

Castro now took the insults easily. Another man he would have killed for such an insult, but this dry old buzzard knew a thing or two.

'So, think. Think of a man who can help you.'

'Hmmm,' said Castro. 'I know of such a man.

Perhaps I should go to see him and make a strategic alliance.'

'An excellent start.'

'His name is Leon Lemus.'

'And should I know Señor Lemus?'

'He is a leader in the movement. He led the Socialist Revolutionary Movement in the forties, and worked hard to change things. He is still a power.'

'He has retired?'

'Not so much retired as changed paths.'

'And where does his new path take him?'

'Well, many places. But he has power and influence, he pays much in protection money, so the police look with favor upon him. He has gunmen, so they fear him.'

'He is a gangster, I take it. A killer, a robber, a whoremonger.'

'I suppose. He is known as El Colorado. I will go to him; is that a good idea? I will make an alliance and good things will come of it, you shall see.'

'El Colorado,' said Speshnev. 'It sounds ridiculous, but you may have to learn that the hard way.'

17

There were things Frankie accepted. Being yelled at by a screaming old man who told him he was shit, he was nothing, he was so stupid his mother should be ashamed to have opened her legs for his father. That had happened enough times so that Frankie knew how to deal with it, which was just to close down, issue the aspects of contrition that would ultimately bore his punisher, and wait for it to blow over and go away.

But this was new. The little Jew man simply closed him out for the next few days. He, Frankie, ceased to exist. The world went on as if he were a ghost, an invisible man; nobody spoke, nobody acknowledged, nobody even let his shadow touch Frankie's, that's how deep the freeze was.

And the funny part: it hurt Frankie. It hurt him badly, in ways he still didn't know he could be hurt. And so he prayed. Not that he was a religious man, but he did have some notion of something Up There that he would have to answer to, and that cared little for the venal sins he had committed and would burn willingly for. But he wanted to face St. Peter unblemished by treachery. He wanted St. Peter to say, 'Frankie, you've been a bad boy, but you always done what you were told and you never ratted nobody out, so by your lights you were a good man, a good gangster. All else is forgiven; only disloyalty may not be forgiven.' He prayed for another chance, and possibly not much went on in the world that day, for God found time enough for Frankie, and allowed the little Jewish man with the sad face to forgive him.

'I am so sorry, sir.'

'Don't call me sir, Frankie. I am no boss. I am a counselor and a friend and bent under responsibilities. Just call me Meyer.'

'Yes, Meyer.'

'You did so wrong. You were not supposed to drink or speak. You were not supposed to act out.'

'Yes, Meyer.'

'Frankie, these instructions were not pointless, arbitrary. I did not give them to amuse myself, do you realize that?'

'Yes, Meyer.'

'When you say *Meyer* you are thinking *sir*. I can hear it in your voice. Say *Meyer* as if you mean *Meyer*.'

'Yes, Meyer. Yes, *Meyer*.'

'Better, by far. Now listen to me and think. *Think!*'

'Yes, Meyer.'

'We cannot lose Cuba. We cannot. Absolutely. So much depends on Cuba. But Cuba is a strained balancing act. Our partners, though it is unsaid and unvouched for by document, are certain American corporations that also depend upon Cuba for rivers of money in the form of cheap sugar, labor and fruit, as well as real estate ventures and eventually offshore manufacturing.

136

But these men are not our kind. They don't like our ways. The force we use to settle our problems scares them. Yet we need them.'

'Yes, Meyer.'

'They must be comfortable around us. They must see us as slightly comical versions of themselves, as capitalism gone raffish and exotic. We're from Damon Runyon, or out of the movies and played by Georgie Raft or Eddie Robinson or Humphrey Bogart. We're not squalid, violent, profane, quick-tempered. No, no, we're colorful, vivid, amusing rogues. We're stars and crime is our screen, do you see?'

'Yes, Meyer.'

'Ben Siegel, of them all, he understood this. They loved him out there, and had he lived, he would have become a star, I'm convinced. He would have been on the television. Big, handsome, lovable, a lady's man. He would have been such an emissary from us to them. It's a crime he was killed so young.'

Frankie knew God was being merciful today. He blinked back tears of thanks.

'Meyer, I know of Ben. Ben, Ben, Ben, he was my hero,' he said. 'How I loved him. Others loved DiMaggio, or Ted Williams, me, I loved Bennie. I wanted to meet him but he was taken from us before that could happen. I just want to be like him. That's always been my ambition.'

'That pleases me. I loved that boy like a son and lit candles for him for a month in the Catholic church, though both of us are Jews. That's how much I loved him, and I had a need to show it. Someone shot him in the face while he read the papers, and some even say it was me who gave the order.'

'I never believed it. It couldn't have been the great Meyer.'

'It was not one of mine, or one of ours. It was from the outside, do you understand?'

'Meyer?'

'Yes.'

'Not an excuse. But an explanation. Please, just this once.'

Meyer considered. Then he said, 'So explain a little.'

'The man I was yelling at?'

'Yes, the congressman's bodyguard.'

'Don't you know who he is?'

For once, Meyer had no real answer.

'Some thug,' he said, 'with a badge. That's all.'

'Meyer, I heard it from one of the croupiers at Sans Souci, who recognized him. That's what's eating me. That's why I went all hot and cuckoo. He's the man in Hot Springs. Who punched Ben. Who became famous by punching Ben without warning. Ben swears to get him. Yet it's Ben who is shot, in the face, on his sofa. This big guy: he's the one, I tell you.'

This struck Lansky in a curious way. He saw how well it fit together, what perfect sense it made, the Arkansas connection, the political connections, the size and apparent toughness of the bodyguard. A little flare of some passion he had never felt before suddenly coursed in shades of red through his mind.

'Think about it, Meyer. Please. Think about it. I won't mention it again. But the man who killed

Ben Siegel . . . God has put him here, under our noses. What would you do with him?'

But in another second, Meyer was wise again. Something had changed, but he was wise.

'Never follow your feelings. That way is damnation. The business first. Always, the business first, and there's much to do here, and it must be done discreetly, yes, to solidify and indemnify our position.'

'And then?'

'If it's him, if we *know* it's him.'

'Yes.'

'Then we kill the *schmata*. But always, business first. Then vengeance. Or, rather, justice. I could kill for that.'

18

'Oh, the young crusader!' said El Colorado. 'What a fine specimen he is. Come in, boy, let's have a look at you!'

El Colorado was vast and brown, the mahogany of his skin set off by the whiteness of his teeth and his hair and his suit as he sat on the patio at his house, no. 352, on the corner of 23rd Avenue in 15th Street in Vedado.

The old man was enjoying a perfectly hard-boiled egg in a cup. A sea breeze blew in, as the Caribbean was but a few blocks away, yet what Castro could see, as he was brought in to the old man, was flowers: a cascade of them, in the gardens below the patio, invisible from 23rd Avenue.

'The great El Colorado,' he said. 'I come at last to show my respects!'

'*At last* is certainly right, boy. You young ones, you have no respect for those who came before and did the hard work. You think we lived merely as midwives to the birth of your generation.'

This bitter truth, nevertheless, was delivered with a great deal of zest and humor. Whatever had passed before, this day found El Colorado in fabulous humor.

And why not? He lived in one of Havana's most beautiful houses, he had six of the most beautiful mistresses in the city — Castro had eyed them longingly as he was escorted through the house by a factotum, but he could see their tastes were too evolved for a ragamuffin speechifier, as he was — and he ruled the city's vice network, with the exception of the women who worked the big *Americano* hotels and gambling houses. He was rich. Not bad for a socialist.

'It is true,' Castro said humbly. 'In my generation, we think we have invented everything ourselves. That is our shortsightedness. We forget the great Marti, we forget the great El Colorado. Now, with a view toward what is possible in the future, I have come to make introductions, amends, and to seek the advice of the greatest revolutionary fighter of the thirties.'

'Sit, then. Julian, bring the boy some coffee. I see in your face, in its ovals and whiteness, you are not long separated from the motherland.'

'I am only a third generation. My father is a petty *caudillo* in Oriente, and his father a humble soldier who stayed after the debacle of '98.'

'Otherwise, you would have more cocoa in you. I see only lily-white. That is good for your ambitions, I know. It will be yet a time before anyone of chocolate persuasion makes a difference in our homeland.'

'That is one of the things I hope to change.'

The old man laughed hilariously. He found young Castro truly amazing.

'See, Julian, how well he plays. He knows which keys to hit, and exactly when to hit them. This boy has talent.'

'Yes, señor,' said the servant.

'Fetch him more coffee. You, young man, are a pleasure to have around.'

'Thank you, señor.'

'But what exactly do you seek? A favor? A source of income? A strategic consultation?'

'Advice, I suppose. And, I hope, friendship. That you would say good things about me, if asked. And if I am in a position to repay this kindness ever, then I shall do so. We in the struggle must concentrate on our opponents, not each other.'

'Possibly I am too old and used-up for good advice.'

'Yet still I hear of your heroism in the '36 strike against United Fruit, and leading the dockworkers in '42. Those were great days.'

'My best, my favorite, the source still of pride and manhood. But I'll tell you my miscalculation. I believed too much in the strike as a weapon. Now, especially, with all this American money invested and the people getting used to soft living, I doubt the power of them to sustain a strike and of a strike to topple Batista and drive the Americans out.'

'Then it's terror?'

'Terror is messy. The wrong people die, always. The hunger for blood becomes difficult to manage. Killing begets killing. A nightmare of betrayal and recrimination. I am thinking of something new: symbolic terror.'

Castro leaned forward.

'I don't follow you.'

'Suppose something happened that was grand,' El Colorado said, leaning forward, his

142

eyes lit with inspiration. 'Big! Something that had never happened before. Something that gave the people hope and heart and dreams of the future. And yet nobody died. And now I see a greater possibility. What if, furthermore, they ascribed that thing to you. You, young Castro, you had done this wondrous thing. Your name was on everybody's lips. Moreover, upon this occasion, you gave a grand speech. Your words were heard the country over. History, you say, will absolve me! And this speech puts you on the map so powerfully that no force on earth could take you off.'

' 'History will absolve me.' Hmmm,' said the young man, 'yes. Yes, I do like that. I am for that, I agree to that.'

'Excellent. What wondrous instincts you have. Amazing in one so young.'

'And what is this thing?'

'Imagine . . . an American casino. Bandits attack it. But they kill no one. They abscond with millions, yes? They abscond with millions, and before the police can intercede, they have passed it out in the slums. All that American money, gone straight to the poor. And if the agent for this deliverance were seen to be young Castro, can you imagine the impact? Ah . . . ' He paused.

The American gangsters who ran the casinos were by repute men not to be trifled with, Castro thought. Yet the gain would in fact be so enormous it stunned him. And if the connection between himself and the crime were more associational than exact, no charges could be

143

brought, no prison sentence would ensue. He turned it over in his mind.

'Such a thing is going to happen?'

'Exactly as I have described it. It is a thing I have contemplated for many a year, and the planning is immaculate. Come with me.'

The old man stood up. He led young Castro through what seemed countless rooms jammed with treasures both of artistic and fleshly perfection. In most, servants bowed and scraped unctuously, and the grand socialist El Colorado sailed through as though it were beneath him to notice.

But from this heaven on earth, they departed quickly enough by way of stairs to the cellar, and in its darkness discovered a hell on earth — or more precisely, the capacity to bring hell to earth by virtue of violence.

In the deep underground, men labored, shirtless, on machine guns. So many machine guns! Many were broken down, and their parts lay greasy and sparkling under bare bulbs. But some of the guns were being assembled with a surgeon's care, by black men with soldier's graces who knew what they were doing.

'They have just arrived. From friends in Chicago, of all places. Come, look.'

He seized one of the finished guns, held it, admiring its weight and density, its gleaming beauty, the glow of its wood and metal parts, the sleekness of its design, the efficiency of its workings.

'Do you know this weapon, young Castro?'

'You see them everywhere. The police carry

them. The Thompson gun, I believe. And now we have them.'

'Yes. To even the odds. If you fight mobsters, you must have a mobster's gun. He respects the gun. These guns will make my enterprise work smoothly and without damage.'

'I had no idea you had machine guns,' said Castro, deeply impressed.

'These will carry the day,' said El Colorado. 'You may be sure of it! They won't even have to be fired! Now go, young man. You have a speech to write. You have to tell people that the day after tomorrow, big things are coming and that they come owing to your strength and vision. You should profit from this venture in power; I will profit merely in satisfaction.'

'History will absolve us,' said Castro.

19

Earl wondered where the marines were. According to the schedule, the congressman would drive to Guantanamo today for a two-day inspection tour, under escort from armed marines. But when he arrived at the embassy that morning, he could see no marines except for the two young men standing at parade rest at the gate.

He walked inside to find the duty NCO in his embassy security office just down the main hall from the visa section.

'Sergeant,' he asked, 'where're the jeeps? They ain't here yet?'

'Gunny, the escort was canceled. I don't know why. We were alerted when we came on at 0600 there wasn't going to be any escort.'

'Christ. Any idea what smart guy thought that one up?'

'No, Gunny.'

'Tell me, what do y'all keep in the embassy strong room?'

'Mostly shotguns. Them old short-barreled 97 Winchester pumps.'

'Maybe Teddy Roosevelt brought 'em over. Could I check one out?'

'Well, Gunny, there's paperwork. You have to get the ambassador's written permission. Arms are only allowed out of the strong room on his authority. But I guess if the congressman wants something, all he has to do is ask, that's the way it works.'

'You know what? I think you're right about that.'

He went back to the motor pool, where Cuban workers were just finishing a nice wash and wax job on the congressman's black Cadillac, while an American supervisor watched from a chair.

'You check it?' he asked the man, a senior motor pool mechanic.

'I checked it yesterday,' said the man.

'Well, check it again. I don't want no hoses pulling loose or fan belts popping in some goddamned jungle, you hear me?'

'Hey, I don't work for you. I work for the State Department.'

'You must be from the navy at one time.'

'Twenty years. Retired a bosun's mate, as a matter of fact. Say, what's it to you?'

'Figured. Anyhow, check the goddamned car,' said Earl, leaning forward and fixing his own NCO glare on the man, 'or I'll have the congressman ship you off to the North Pole. Check the tires too, and the oil. I want that car shipshape.'

Bitterly, the man set about to do the work, and Earl watched as he ran over the car, digging through the hood, pulling the dipstick, tugging the fan belts, doing a fair once-over, even if his attitude was all nasty and dark.

'Good work, son,' Earl finally said, checking his watch. At last, he saw Lane approaching.

'Mr. Brodgins?'

'Yeah, Earl, what is it?'

147

'Sir, what happened to the marine escort? The plan I saw, we were going to have two jeeps of marines with us the whole way.'

'The congressman changed his mind on that. He thought it was better to keep a low profile and not associate Americans with a military occupational force.'

'Mr. Brodgins, I — '

'Earl, I swear you are a load every single day, aren't you? One thing or another, every single day. Earl, it's the congressman's decision. He makes the decisions, don't you understand?'

'I do understand that. I'd feel safer with some nice young privates in khakis or class A's, all trim and proper looking. It's a deterrent — '

'Earl, you know the boss. He may want to have a stop somewhere. For a rum drink. You know his proclivities, too. You do know them.'

'Yes, sir. Then can you ask the ambassador to sign the paperwork so I can take a shotgun out of the strong room? I'll keep it down low, but that's some firepower it'd be nice to have along, just in case.'

'Earl, I don't think so.'

Earl got all heated up. His temper flared, his breath grew sharp, his eyes went narrow and hard.

'Goddammit, I am not asking, Brodgins. If you want security on this little trip, you let me make the security decisions, you hear? If something happens, I'm stuck with a god-damned handgun and that's it.'

'Earl, what on earth are you expecting? This is a vacationland paradise for God's sake.'

148

'We're going to be miles inland on dusty little roads where no Americans don't hardly go. Why don't we fly?'

'He doesn't want to spend a lot of taxpayers' money on an air trip. The trains here are terrible. A boat would take too long.'

He left Earl standing there. Earl spat in the dust. He looked up and saw the ex-bosun's mate eyeing him, and expected a smirk. But instead the man came over, as if a new page had been turned.

'Okay, I got her squared away, Gunny. Sorry about your run-in. These political guys can be a tear in the rigging.'

'They sure can.'

'Look, I was at Guantanamo for a few years before the war. I'll tell you what's going on here. If this congressman has a hard-on big as everybody says he does, he's going to Gitmo City first. There's more whorehouses there in two blocks than in any two square miles of Havana. It's a navy town, after all.'

'Yeah, I can see that.'

'So you may have to bang some more boss pimp skulls before you're done. I'd be on my toes.'

'I get all the number-one jobs, don't I? Have you traveled the roads down there?'

'Yeah. The roads are okay. No problem. And you should be all right all the way down the island. I'd watch out as you get close to Santiago. It's very mountainous down there. And be careful in Ciego de Avila province. It's mostly empty marshlands. They don't see Americans

149

very often. Dark, jungly, you know. Sort of like the Pacific jungles.'

'I was there for a little while.'

'Then you know what I'm talking about.'

'I got some idea. Thanks, pal. Sorry for the harsh words earlier.'

'Forget it, Sarge. Hey, I know you were in the Pacific. I know what medal you won. But I can tell, it ain't gone to your head.'

'It ain't my way.'

He winked at his new pal and headed back into the main building, to get familiar with the route via maps.

20

Speshnev first began to hear of it in the barber's chair, his face swaddled in towels full of steam heat. He'd come to this place on the morning of every day — one in four, usually — when he'd had to slide by a casino at night, to pick up some of his improvised operational budget at the blackjack tables.

So he wasn't thinking of much except numbers. The numbers had to stick like glue, never falling out, always in place, as if on a big board which he could scan instantaneously if necessary. But it was beyond thought, as most games were to him. He had a game mind; his imagination thrilled at the boundaries, the rules, the strategies, as he sought to know, always, how to crack it.

So he was dillydallying with that so-necessary state when, seemingly from nowhere, he heard a single phrase in Spanish.

'They say it will be big.'

Sometimes he missed these things, as the Spanish he'd learned was pure Castillian, and the Cubans spoke more briskly than anyone in that motherland. They also pronounced their Z's and C's without the Castillian lisp, hard and brisk, like Andalusians. Worse still, their diction was frequently lazy and unclear, as if they had picked up the jangled rhythms of the Americans, particularly in the way they dropped their S's and sometimes even the entire last syllables of words.

But he heard it clearly: 'They say it will be big.'

'What?'

'I don't know.'

'They always say that.'

'No, this time it is real. It is said that young man is associated with it.'

He whispered the name to his companion, and Speshnev could not make it out, but he could tell it was a two-syllable name with the emphasis on the first syllable.

It could be. Possibly, yes, it might be.

But then the conversation stopped, and when the towels came away, the shop was empty. The two had left already.

'Sir,' he asked the barber, as that man lathered him up, then stropped the razor, 'I am provoked. Those two men? Their conversation? Did it have some meaning?'

The barber eyed him suspiciously, even though he came in so often.

'I don't know what you're talking about. I don't listen to what idle gossipers say.'

'Ah, I understand,' Speshnev said, and then endured torture as the man shaved him over the next ten or twelve hours.

Well, of course, it was but ten or twelve minutes, but it dragged so for the Russian he began to shudder with anticipation toward the end.

'Sir, if you don't relax, I will cut you badly.'

'Sorry, sorry,' he muttered.

At last finished, he rose, paid, and exited quickly. Where to now? Possibly the open-air market at Plaza de la Catedral, a gathering spot for other idlers, as well as self-styled radicals and reformers. As he rushed down the crowded narrow crinkle that was the Emperado, he had the ridiculous impression that everywhere people were muttering the same thing.

Finally, he could stand it no longer, and headed into a large cafe, well short of the Catedral. It was crowded and as he bumped along, trying to reach the espresso behind the bar, he heard snippets.

Finding a man who also appeared to be alone and listening, he said to him, 'Have you heard?'

'Heard what?'

'You know . . . about *it*. They say tomorrow.'

'Tomorrow. I heard this afternoon late, if not early in the evening.'

'Possibly such things cannot be planned with precision.'

'I wouldn't know anything about that. But if it doesn't happen today, then the rumors, you know, about the speaker tonight, they will be ridiculous, no?'

'I suppose. I just heard that fellow talks but does nothing.'

'But if he is involved, then maybe it has moved beyond nothing.'

'He is a good speaker.'

'His radio speech when Chiba died' — *Castro!* — 'it was good, but nothing ever came of it. Possibly this time it will be different.'

But Speshnev was already gone.

153

★ ★ ★

Where was the young bastard? Of course, not in any of his usual haunts. He wasn't in the park of San Francisco, where the chess players gathered, indulging in his pastime. He wasn't in any of the coffeehouses around the hill that was crowned by the university, or on its glorious splurge of steps, or among the yakkers in the law school cafeteria. He wasn't anywhere except . . . it was hard to believe, hard to understand, but could he actually be . . . *working?*

So Speshnev rose in the rotten old apartment building, entering through a dark corridor, wending up a dark stairway, following his way around the balcony engulfing the narrow courtyard, reading the numbers on the battered pastel doors, until at last he came to his destination.

He knocked.

After a time, there came rustling noises, the sounds of a baby stirring, and finally, the door cracked but a bit. An exceptionally pretty face glared at him suspiciously. What a beautiful young girl!

'Ah, is he here?'

'Who are you?' she demanded.

'A friend. He knows me. We talk in the park.'

'He is writing his speech.'

'For tomorrow?'

'For tonight, he says. Can you come back?'

'It's important that I see him.'

'And why?'

'Young lady — Maria, isn't that it?'

154

'Mirta. But how could you know? He never takes me anywhere.'

'He talks of you often.'

'Ha! He *never* talks of me. I do not exist for him, except when he is in a certain mood. He — '

Before she sailed off on the seas of inconsolable bitterness, Speshnev reseized the momentum.

'Mirta, you do not want policemen visiting, do you? That would be even worse. Arrests, beatings, the scandal. Think of the parents, the family honor. Therefore it is important that I see him.'

Mirta continued to eye him.

'Where are you from? You speak like a Spaniard.'

'I am of Spanish experience, yes, extensive. That is where I learned the language. I am not one of these excitable Cubans.'

'All right. But if he yells at me, I'll be so mad.'

'He will kiss you.'

'That I doubt.'

He walked through the apartment, not that it was far to go, and heard the baby stirring restively, saw the fight between the woman's tidiness and the man's contempt for tidiness — that is, books in piles and gewgaws in rows, in continual battle.

He arrived at a back bedroom where, in his flaccid, shirtless condition, his eyes shielded by thick glasses, Castro scribbled away furiously by the bald light of a lamp whose shade was somewhere else.

He looked up, saw Speshnev, and did not pause even a second to remark on the incongruity of that man's presence in his home, a phenomenon which had not occurred before and was not remotely conceivable to him.

'Listen to this, and tell me what you think,' he said. He cleared his throat. ' "History will absolve us. Our cause is that just. We seek not profit but freedom, not mastery but equality. Freedom, however, cannot be won without sacrifice." '

'Idiotic,' said Speshnev. 'You are a young fool who will get yourself killed.'

'No, no,' Castro said. 'I think not. This is a very fine opportunity and I must seize it. It will win me followers on a grand scale. In grand scale is power. And so it is that — '

'What are you talking about?'

But the weirdness of the situation suddenly made itself known to the young man.

'What are you doing here? How did you find me? I never told you where I lived. It's supposed to be a secret. I don't even know who you are. I don't know your name.'

'You know perfectly well who I am. You know why I am here, so names are not important. What is important is to get you to the next stage. Now, everywhere I go, I hear big things are coming and that they involve you. I insist that you tell me what all this is about.'

'Opportunity. An alliance — your idea, incidentally — has produced a wondrous chance. Listen to this, and tell me I am not wise to grab this with everything I have.'

He then proceeded to narrate the previous

156

day's adventures, the shrewd council of El Colorado, the raid on the casino, the democracy of giving the people all the money, his own ability to stand forth in the moment and take command and —

'Oh, you fool! You blind, stupid young fool! God, you are so lucky. There might even still be time.' Speshnev looked at his watch, saw that it was nearly eleven.

'I don't . . . Why are you angry? This is a wonderful opportunity to embarrass the Americans and the regime, without any harm being done. It redounds with honor and glory. It speaks to a glorious future. It — '

'Stop with your pap. How many men did you see in Colorado's cellar.'

'Why, four or five. I wasn't really paying attention.'

'Of course you weren't. Lesson number one: *always* pay attention. How many, idiot? Four or five?'

'Does it matter?'

'No, but you don't understand why, do you?'

The young man looked at him. Speshnev could see confusion on his face.

'Well, I — '

'Well you nothing. You could not possibly rob a big American casino with five men. There are too many hidden guns. It would be a slaughter. The American gangsters do not yield on such things easily, and they *always* have their revenge. Their whole culture depends upon revenge. No, El Colorado could not conceive of such a thing.'

'I hadn't thought of that.'

' 'I hadn't thought of that.' Idiot! Fool! Is your brain a raisin?'

He clenched his brow, then hit himself in the head with his fist.

'Think! *Think!*' he ordered himself. 'Five, you say. With machine guns.'

'Thompsons. Like the police.'

'The same. Hmmm. A bank? But he doesn't need money, he has money? What? *What?*'

'I don't — '

'Four or five men, machine guns. What else?'

'Negroes. Possibly foreign.'

'Foreign?'

'Darker than our negroes. Almost black. You never see that here, especially five times over. A dark one, yes, once in a while, but not five of them in one — '

'Did you speak to them?'

'I saluted them. They didn't respond. I thought it odd.'

'They didn't understand you. Of course, now I see. You are right, at last. They *are* foreigners, and can't stay with the quickness of the Cuban tongue and its lazy ways of working. Foreigners. Poor, desperate, dark men, brought in to . . . well, to what?'

'Rob?'

'No.'

'Kill?'

'Yes, you would use such men to handle killing chores. They would be expendable, courageous, nameless. Perfect. But who? El Presidente? No, don't be absurd. He's too well protected. What about some ambassador? But for what reason — '

158

It suddenly dawned on him.

'Of course. *Of course!*'

But if his wisdom illuminated him, it did not animate him. Instead, a terrible weariness set over him. He had so much to do, so little time, so few weapons. Melancholy seeped through him.

'What are you talking about?'

'The American congressman. They'll kill him and his party for violating the inviolate rules of the brothel. Of course; it's pimp's honor at stake. And from his point of view, there's no negative attached. It'll make the government look bad, it'll terrify the American government, but it won't enrage and engage the American crime syndicate.'

'Perhaps it will send a message.'

'Fool. You have no instincts at all. More likely it'll produce invasion.'

'Mother of God,' said Castro. 'And I — '

'And you have gone all over town affiliating yourself with it. Your mission is now to disaffiliate yourself. These stories you have spread must now be denounced as lies and slander. Go even to the police and tell them that El Colorado is the one.'

'I — '

'Meanwhile, I must stop this. Do you have a machine gun?'

'No, of course not.'

'Hmmm, I need a machine gun fast. Now where does one get a machine gun?'

159

21

The sergeant laid his ambush well. He was not without experience, having fought in Argentina, Peru, Colombia and the Dominican Republic at different times in his career, in some cases escaping just ahead of the firing squad. But that was another story.

He did not select the first, or even the second, bend in the road that ran down Ciego de Avila province, about five miles inland from the sea, in the sudden burst of mangrove swamps. He knew that if his target had any security, security would be at its highest at that first bend, and again at the second bend. By the third bend, they would have settled down and grown used to the closeness of the trees, the sudden sense of impinging jungle after so long on sparse scrublands where cattle fed randomly.

He also needed two trees, unusually tall for the vegetation.

One tree was not enough.

It was a question of timing. The car had to slow to round the bend, and as it cleared the turn, but before it began to accelerate, the first tree had to be downed. It would take any driver three seconds to respond. By the time he had braked, and begun to turn around, or back up if he were clever, the second tree would come down, trapping the vehicle.

That's when his gunners would fire. He had

three Thompsons, each with a fifty-round drum, and it was important that all three fire at once and that they lay down continuous fire. The car had to be still. He did not think these men were well enough trained to efficiently engage a moving target, even with the fast-firing Thompsons. He wanted the guns blazing for a good three to five seconds. He wanted the Cadillac ripped by three machine guns. Then he himself, on the other side of the road where the car would almost certainly stop, would raise up and quickly close the distance from the other side. He would pull his Star 9mm from his holster, advance to the automobile, and quickly fire a head shot into each of the four men, living or dead. Then it was only a matter of pulling their own automobile out and heading toward Cabanas Los Pinos, where a boat awaited them with their money aboard and orders to sail to Florida.

The sergeant was pleased. He had five good men besides himself. The innards of the two chickens he had slain last night had revealed by the sacred laws of *Santeria* that prospects were excellent. He had prayed hard to Odudua, mistress of the darkness of that blend of Bantu religion and Catholicism, and knew that she favored him, for she favored all killers. Her mission was to harvest their bounty and take it with her across the river to her dark land. The blood of the chickens, their squawking as their guts were pulled living from them, merely excited her.

The sergeant found his two trees without

difficulty, an exceedingly good omen. He had examined the cuts his men had made in the trees and saw that the trunks had been expertly brought to the brink of collapse and one or two more ax strokes would deposit them exactly where he wanted them. The men with the Thompson guns knew how to shoot them well enough. He knew his Star intimately, and knew it would not fail him.

He checked his watch. It was nearly six; he knew the time was close but that he had a good hour before sundown.

'Sergeanto,' came an excited cry from the man who'd just come sprinting around the bend, 'I can see the big black car with the American flags on its fenders.'

'Be ready, my boys. It is time and then we will be gone from this godforsaken country.'

The men scattered to find their positions.

★   ★   ★

'My, my, my, my,' said the congressman, 'at last we git to look at something *different*. Not better, mind you, but *different*. Trees, or what they might call trees in some primitive place like Mississippi or Alabama.'

'Yes, sir, Harry,' agreed Lane Brodgins. 'That flat land was damned boring. Like Kansas, only no damned cowboys or Indians to make it interesting.'

'Lane, I ever tell you 'bout the time Joe Phillips of Montana's 13th and I got in a hell of a row over a navy typewriter reconditioning

162

installation I had all sewn up for Fort Smith, but he had his heart set on setting up somewhere way the Sam Hill out there?'

'No, sir, don't believe you did,' said poor Lane, whose capacity for eating Boss Harry's shit was beyond legendary and near to entering mythical.

'Well, I don't know how that fella got it in his mind the United States Navy needed to fix up its old typewriters way out yonder in the purple west. But I decided . . . '

Earl tried to close it out and concentrate. He saw the low dark trees suddenly rising up to swallow the Cadillac and nudged his elbow into Pepe's subtly, then with his hand pressing flatly downward signaled the driver to slow down.

'We slowing down, Pepe?' asked Boss Harry.

'Señor, I think is a curve coming up.'

'Let's just take it easy through here,' said Earl. He knew that nothing would happen on a road so straight and open that you could see a man three-hundred yards ahead and there wasn't a stick of cover anywhere. He supposed a sniper could take a long shot but doubted if anybody down here had that skill. He also worried about a mine or a command-detonated bomb of some sort, but again, nothing in Cuba had communicated the possibility of that kind of sophistication.

Darkness didn't swallow them, but it did grip them, as suddenly the trees, though rarely higher than a man, clustered close to the road, and through them, he could see pools of standing water, knotty clusters of tropical vegetation, the

163

occasional bright flare of jungle blossom, the flutter and slither of pink shapes indicating the presence, here as elsewhere close to the sea, of pelicans.

The car slowed as Pepe negotiated the first bend, got around it, and saw a mile of straight road ahead before the road disappeared in blackness.

'You can speed up now, Pepe,' said Lane. 'We want to git there before dark. This here has been a long damned sit.'

'Didn't know your goddamned island was so big,' said Boss Harry. 'I had the idea it was a little old place, and there wouldn't be so many miles between bars and women.'

'In Guantanamo City, señor, is plenty bars and women, I tell you that.'

'Now *that's* the kind of spirit I like!' said Harry. 'I'm going to need a refresher pretty damned soon, and I don't mean no Coca-Cola!'

★ ★ ★

Speshnev had a car and a machine gun. The former he stole, the latter he rented. It took the last of his casino earnings, but he managed, rather quickly, to bribe an NKVD security goon assigned to a Russian freighter moored in the harbor to sneak into the strong room and remove one PPsH submachine gun, and one drum — seventy-one rounds — of 7.63mm ammunition. It was to be returned within twenty-four hours or the goon would come looking for Speshnev. The goon was a former Black Sea

164

Marine, reportedly the toughest of the tough, so Speshnev had no desire to disappoint him. Now the gun lay across the seat awkwardly, its drum precluding easy stowage and causing it to roll about as he accelerated through the gears. Speshnev also had a direction and a route. A source in the American embassy had told the unctuous Pashin that the schedule had the congressman heading north to Guantanamo today, leaving at 9 A.M. With stops for lunch, they should pull in by eight in the evening, time enough for a night of carousing in the low dives of Guantanamo City.

He drove madly, following the big road through Matanzas, Cienfuegos and Villa Clara provinces, honking rudely at lorries, careening around buses, fighting the traffic desperately. Around Sancti Spiritus, the traffic lessened, with the majority of it siphoning off toward the south, toward Santiago. But he knew the Americans would cling to the upper road along the Caribbean coast, through Ciego de Avila and Camaguey, then on to Las Tunas and Holguin, that way avoiding the mess around Santiago. Effectively bypassing it — a faster way, though longer — they would then head south, and veer directly toward Guantanamo. He hoped that the Americans would stop for a nice lunch, would poke about here and there, and wouldn't press on.

Americans are lazy, he told himself. They are addicted to comfort. They're stupid. They're —

But he realized that Swagger wouldn't be stupid. He roared ahead.

165

The damned gun rolled to the left as the car accelerated, down empty roads, surrounded by arid meadows where here and there a cow grazed.

★ ★ ★

'Why are we slowing down?'

'I need to check some things,' said Earl.

'What, Earl,' said Brodgins. 'We've still got a far piece to travel. The congressman is hot and tired.'

Earl didn't say a word. He had commanded Pepe to stop and ahead he saw that the road took an aggressive left-hand crank, which mandated another slowdown, almost to a crawl. Something about it bothered him. So now he climbed from the front seat, hung himself over the open door, and just looked. What he was looking for was — well, he couldn't put a name to it. They had eased through two natural ambush sites without a problem, and according to the map would soon enough be beyond the swamps, and then could take their southern turn and head down to Gitmo.

But he was looking for something: some anomaly, some clue that things weren't as they should be. His eyes scanned, and what he saw was only dusty road disappearing as it bent to the left, low trees on each side, no movement, no wind, nothing at all. It was ungodly hot, and mosquitoes hummed around him, as the sweat crested to his skin and broke free.

'Aren't you being a little melodramatic here,

Earl,' Brodgins called from inside the car, where the air conditioning still pumped out cold, stale air. 'Sir, can't you just tell him to get us there? This ain't easy on any of us.'

'Earl, do you see something?' the congressman called. 'Is that it? Lane, old Earl, he does have pretty good instincts for this sort of thing, I think you'd agree.'

'Yes, sir, but sometimes these folks get an exaggerated sense of their importance.'

Earl ducked back inside the car.

'All right,' he said, bending forward. 'Let's go. But Pepe, when you git around that corner, I want you to punch it. I don't like the fact that we'll be slowing down.'

'Earl,' said Brodgins, 'we are *stopped* now. So what is the big deal about *slowing down* a hundred yards ahead? You have to be consistent in this. It has to make some sense.'

'Well, Mr. Brodgins,' said Earl, 'we are stopped of our own volition. No one could anticipate us stopping here. But when we reach that curve, any idiot could see that's a place where we *have* to slow down. That's the difference.'

'Think Earl scored a point on you there, Lane,' said Harry, merrily. 'Earl, you take your time. Just let's get us through this, so we can head on.'

'Yes, sir,' said Earl. He turned to Pepe. 'You have to slow down, as I say, but once you're clear and you have open road, you punch it, do you understand?'

'Yes, sir,' said the driver.

Speshnev saw before he heard. What he saw was dust, hanging above the trees, like a squall of smoke. Immediately as that perception dawned on him, he jammed his brakes on, stopping fast, skewing to one side.

Then the gunfire broke out.

He heard automatic weapons, a group of them, all ripping away simultaneously. They fired and they struck automobile, for in each percussion came the reverberant *whang!* of a high-speed missile hitting metal hard.

Speshnev knew the action was all taking place just a few hundred yards ahead, right beyond the bend in the road.

He prayed he wasn't too late. He leaned over, seized the PPsH machine gun with its absurdly swollen drum, pulled it out.

They were still shooting as he began to move through the trees, toward the site of the ambush.

★ ★ ★

The car slowly picked its way around the bend. Ahead lay nothing but straight road.

'Is okay, señor,' said Pepe.

'Is fine, Pepe,' said Lane Brodgins. 'Let's get the hell out of here.'

Pepe's foot went to caress the gas pedal but exactly in that moment Earl jabbed his foot over and crushed the brake to the floor.

'BACK!' he commanded and possibly there was a moment, even two, of ridiculous silence, as a sense of unreal confusion filled the automobile, the bodyguard ripping at the gear shift to find reverse, the driver stunned by his sudden action, trying to respond, the two men in back themselves stunned, aware that something unplanned and unwanted was happening, unsure entirely about the bodyguard's sudden speed of movement.

Then the windshield shattered into a quick-silver smear of webbing and punctures as glass bits spewed at painful velocity into the car, and the interior was suddenly full of the presence of alien things among them, hard and cruel and without interest in them except as targets. The car shuddered as gunfire thudded against it, and the sound of metal banging loud arrived in the same second, to overload all senses and drive them toward stupefaction. A bullet struck Pepe in the head, like a fastball, and the sound of that — missile striking and tearing into bone — filled the car with horror, accompanied by the pink steam that blew outward from the horrible wound and the instant sense of destruction as the ruined head slid forward.

But Earl had the car finally in reverse, and moved his foot to the gas, pushing Pepe's dead one — the man was by this time a sack of sloppy weight, his broken head pitched forward — aside. He hammered the pedal and the car shot backwards perhaps twenty-five yards, even as more gunfire came after it, tearing up hood, punching out more glass, ripping tires and engine to shreds. Riding the last gasp of engine power, Earl jacked the car's wheel left, depositing it at an angle in a gully. He slithered out, came up over the hood, pulled his Super .38 from the shoulder holster, thumbed the hammer back from half cock as he did so, and punched out six fast two-handed shots, at a line of gully across the road and fifty yards or so down, where the accumulation of gunsmoke and suspended dust announced the presence of the shooters. The pistol recovered fast with its lessened kick and when he was done shooting he knew he had four rounds left. But still, while he had the chance, he yanked a magazine from his pocket and reloaded another nine. With the round in the chamber, he had ten.

Even as he did this, a tree fell lazily across the road. It was a tree meant to trap them, but it hadn't. They were behind the kill-zone.

Earl swung around and saw the woodchopper bound forward from the tree for cover, but Earl got a shot off fast at the deflection, finding an instinctive lead, knowing to pin the trigger on the stroke, and heard the sound that can only be bullet on meat, knew that he had hit the man.

He slid along the body of the twisted automobile, pulled open the back door. Inside, on the floor, Lane and the congressman lay in a terrified embrace.

'Oh, Jesus, what is — '

'God, why are they — '

Earl grabbed the nearest, Boss Harry, and yanked him brutally out of the car, dumping him hard in the gully. He paused as another fusillade of fire tore into the car, but by the weird physics of the situation, the car was tilted up in such a

170

way that most of it blocked the men from the shooters.

Earl next reached in and pulled out the gibbering assistant.

'You crouch here, goddammit. Behind the wheel well. That is where it is safer.'

'How many are there?' Harry was finally cogent enough to ask.

'I have no fucking idea, but they do mean business, that I guarantee you.'

★   ★   ★

The sergeant cursed. No language has more pathways for blasphemy than Spanish and this was a construction of such horror it would have made even Odudua ashamed, and perhaps disappointed in him, even if he was one of her most favored facilitators, having seen and done so many terrible, evil things.

Why had the car stopped short? What on earth impelled whoever was inside to make such a decision? Had the killers been betrayed?

But now he watched in helpless rage as the car roared backwards. He prayed to Odudua that the car would not swing around the bend and disappear. And Odudua helped out her humble servant. In her magnificence, she guided the shots of his three machine-gunners and they did a great damage to the automobile, so that finally it jerked off the road and like a broken-backed bull wedged itself at a hideous angle, tilted, one ruined tire uplifted, in the gully.

Its occupants could still be killed.

171

He watched as fire lashed against it, tearing it, puncturing it, spewing liquids and shards of metal from it, turning what had been such a shiny emblem of power into shabby wreckage in just a few seconds. As theater it was fabulous; as action, it lacked finality, for from his position on this side of the road, he could see the guard emerge, bring fast fire on his shooters, pull the two very important *norteamericanos* from the vehicle and squish them down where it was safest, and then reload and fire again, with almost astonishing speed.

What an hombre! Oh, this was somebody who knew a thing or two.

For a daffy moment, the sergeant brought up his Star, took a good supported position, and considered firing as he saw the front sight cross the American's solid body. But then he thought better of it, as he was still seventy yards distant from his targets, such a long shot for a man with a pistol, and if he fired, he simply told them where he was.

Instead he saw that he had some advantage still. If the gunners kept their heads, continued to bring fire, didn't lose their nerve, he himself could slither and close the distance and, suddenly, jump out from the rear and kill the guard. The two mewling men, who now crouched behind the wheel well, gripping each other like women, would be easy. He could even kill them with his knife and truly enjoy it, but then that might take too long.

Gripping the pistol, he began to slither ahead through the gully.

172

Earl dropped back to the rear of the car, behind
the tail fin. It was the smart move, for in that
second, two of the tommy-gunners opened up,
trying to pin him where he wasn't, which was at
the front wheel well. Meanwhile, their third
member dashed heroically from cover, firing
from the hip like a movie marine, and, feeling
himself well protected by the oblique raking fire
his friends brought to bear on the car, began to
advance.

He moved fast yet with courageous purpose,
closing steadily, eyes on the move hunting for
targets. Earl thought he was a brave man, even
as he rose from behind the tail fin, put the
front sight of the Super .38 on his throat,
figuring the flat-shooting, fast-as-hell little
bullet would drop only an inch or two at fifty
yards, and p-r-e-s-s-e-d off a shot. The gun
smacked crisply against his hand as it operated
in super-time, flinging a spent shell off to the
right, though in the rage of blood chemicals
and dust and total sensory overload he did not
notice it. What he saw in the split second
before he dove for cover as the fire steered
toward him was eminently satisfying: the man,
stricken, stumbling drunkenly as the big
weapon fell pitifully from his once strong
hands. One hand flew to his mouth, which now
drooled lakes of blood — that's what a lung
shot does — and possibly he sealed some in,
but by that time he was on his knees and a
second later had toppled sacklike, devoid of

173

dignity, forward into the dust. His tommy gun lay atilt in the road.

★ ★ ★

Speshnev, at the end of his run, saw almost nothing. These things are never clear. It was all dust and confusion, the noise was terrifying, and no one unifying vision made any sense of it. A man lay ragamuffin-pitiful in the road, in a pool of blood, so bright in a world drained of color. The car, which had come to rest half in, half out of the gully, looked like the *Titanic* settling into the sea. It was badly torn up, and a puddle of gasoline collected under it from a gas tank so many times punctured. The slightest spark could send a flaming cloud high into the sky.

But he could see no living men. One of those odd moments of gunfight silence prevailed. No one quite knew what to do, all parties were out of communication, blood had been spilled in copious amounts and the terrible thought occluded all minds: When will this be over? This followed close upon: Will I die here? Prayers and curses were mixed in, but the gist is always the same, and the results the same. Luck comes for or avoids bold and meek the same, but still a smart guy, if he's just a little bit lucky, has all the better chance of surviving.

Therefore, Speshnev assumed that somewhere behind the tilted car, the American still breathed. Clearly that was his kill out there in the sun, with that splayed look of beyond-caring the dead always find a way to assume. Possibly men closed

174

in upon him; possibly they were even now about to kill him. Speshnev didn't know; he only knew that he had to get closer still, and do what could be done.

* * *

Someone had beshat himself, but Earl didn't know or particularly care which one.

He crouched beside them.

'When I rise up and fire, y'all break into the jungle. But don't lose sight of the road. Don't get lost back there and drown in the swamp or something. I think they're all on the other side of the road. I will hold them here long as I have ammo.'

'I can't do it,' said Lane Brodgins.

'Yes you can, Mr. Brodgins. You are younger and stronger than Boss Harry and he needs you like he never needed you before. Ain't that right, sir?'

'Actually, no, Earl. In fact, you're completely wrong. I really don't care if Lane comes or goes. I just don't want him holding me back. Plus, he smells. His pants are full of shit. That's how I see it and I always call it the way I see it.'

'Well, in cases like this, teamwork is the best thing.'

'Teaming up with Lane ain't going to do me no good whatsoever. Earl, you hold them here. I will run as you say. As for Lane, I have no idea. Lane, you're fired. You're on your own now.'

'Goddamn you, Harry Etheridge. If I get out of here, I will tell all that I know about your filthy doings and it will — '

'Boys, boys, shut up, I can't think. I am low on ammo, and they're creeping around out there, possibly changing positions. I have killed two but there are at least two more and possibly a goddamned third I don't yet know about.'

'Well, can you kill them all, Earl?'

'I don't think so, sir.'

'Well, what goddamned good are you then, boy? You were hired to do a job and now's a fine time to see you ain't up to it.'

'Sir, there's a goddamned bunch of them. Just shut up, old man. I will try and get your precious Arkansas ass out of here.'

'Did you hear how he talked to me, Lane? The nerve.'

'You fired me, Harry, so I don't give no two shits. Earl, shoot him. They came for him. If he's dead, they'll let us go.'

'Lane, you are showing me no loyalty at all, and I want you to know that I have noticed it.'

The two gunners opened up again, obviously having changed drums. Their fire ripped into the car, raising hell's own worst racket, and the vehicle shuddered as it took so many more hits.

And then — poof! — something somehow lit, and a sudden feathery fountain of flame leaped upward, accompanied by a smeary fog of smoke, black and thick.

'*Go, go!*' screamed Earl, rising not behind front fender or rear tail fin as before, but more or less in the center of the car, where he had not been, to shoot through the shattered windows.

He pumped his nine rounds out fast, and saw a man with a heavy gun sit back and set his gun down. But immediately more bullets came speeding after Earl, and they kicked slivers of metal and glass into his face. He sat back, wincing, and saw that the two old friends had skedaddled, though in which direction he did not know.

He dumped his mag, slammed in his last one — only nine left! — and drew back, to cover the retreat of his charges.

★ ★ ★

The sergeant was very close now. He had seen the two fat ones depart, and thought to shoot at them. But they were not a problem. The problem was this hero here. If he wasn't killed and killed soon, the whole thing went down in defeat.

But still he wasn't quite close enough. He wanted to be close enough to make sure. He wanted to be at muzzle distance and watch the blackness of cloth where the flash burned the clothes of the man he was killing, and burned his flesh, even as it sent bullets into him.

So he paused. Across the way, he saw his last machine-gunner, crouching, moving ever so slowly, trying in his own way to get close to the American.

The sergeant stared hard at him, commanding him mentally to turn and make eye contact for signals.

Of course, not being a wizard, the sergeant was unable to influence his colleague in any way;

177

no such thing happened. But then it did. The man looked directly to him.

The sergeant raised a finger, to halt the man. Their eyes met passionately. The sergeant gave pantomime signals, pointing to the man, then to himself, then raising one, two and three fingers, hoping to communicate the following: on the count of three, we both rise and fire. He cannot cover two points and will retreat and that is when we will have him.

The man nodded.

The sergeant gave the signal.

He nodded at the man, who steeled himself for the final rush.

The sergeant rose, the man rose. The man rushed the car screaming and firing.

The sergeant did not. He was no one's fool. He simply dropped down, and began to slither forward.

The man ran at the car, and the American shooter dropped him with one shot to the head.

The sergeant, creeping around, got close enough. He fired at the man, hitting him. He saw blood spurt, and the gun fly away.

Ha! Amigo, I have you now!

★ ★ ★

Earl saw a man come at him, wildly, and put an easy shot into him, thinking for just a second that this wasn't —

Then he was hit.

He felt the whack of something crashing into his hip, another buzz as something flew by his

178

face as he went down, and then by the crazy laws of these things, his gun hand went numb. He couldn't have pulled a trigger, even if there'd been a trigger to pull, for the simple reason that a wild shot smashed hard into the Colt right above the trigger guard, mashing the gun terribly and blowing it out of his hand in the same instant.

Earl slid to earth, coming to rest next to the tilted Cadillac. Even now he was working. His hand flew to his hip and felt a black, hot welling of blood. But he didn't panic. He would fight to the end, and in a fast second or two, he spied the gun lying a few feet beyond him. He scuttled toward it, picked it up and saw that it had been ruined. The bullet had savaged the slide, bending it so grotesquely it could not operate on its rails. It was totally dead.

He spun around, hunting another weapon, but saw his own slayer standing above him. So this is what the guy would look like. A black, wild negro in khakis, with dusty boots and a lined face that had seen several hundred battles. Dead eyes, no curiosity, no light. Gray shot through the wool of tightly knitted hair. Sweat circles under the arm. A uniform of no army on earth save the universal one of desperate men good with guns, for hire cheap for any work at all.

'Choo fucked, man,' the fellow said to him.

'Fuck you, Jack,' said Earl.

'Yah, fuck *choo*, man, that's who eez fucked, no? I kill you then chase down those fat pigs and kill them. Ha! You so brave, but it comes to this, poor fucker.'

179

The man was too experienced to come close enough for Earl to kick him in the nuts. He had the gun, the advantage and all the time in the world. He would make no foolish mistakes. It wouldn't be like a bad movie, where the hero kicks dust in the bad guy's eyes. He'd just shoot Earl, reload, finish the job and move on. By tomorrow the memory would be vague and by Friday gone forever.

He raised the pistol.

Then he lowered it to study a curious phenomenon.

His chest was spurting blood. Wasn't this an odd development? He couldn't believe it. Where had such a terrible atrocity come from?

He went to his knees, finding the Star pistol immensely heavy, letting it drop to the ground. His ears were filled with pounding, so much so that he did not hear the second burst that cut into him either. A presence loomed suddenly before him. He reached out and touched the face of Odudua, who gathered him to her dark bosom, a former servant and now, alas, just another john.

Earl watched him die. He lay babylike in the mud. His eyes were blank, his shirt red with new blood, lots of it. The smell of gunpowder hung in the air.

Earl thought he'd heard the shots, especially the second burst. He thought they came from the right. He pulled himself up and looked over the car's trunk, then scanned left and right, hoping to spot the shooter. But there was no shooter. Dust hung in the air and a quiet breeze stirred the leaves of the low trees.

'Hey!' Earl called, and there was no answer, no sound, no indication of another human being on the face of the earth.

22

They would not stop screaming. It wasn't that you could blame them. The secret police worked first on the fingernails, with a specialized device, then on the toes, with knives. But it wasn't until the specialist arrived that progress was made.

His name was Captain Ramon Latavistada. He was called Ojos Bellos, 'Beautiful Eyes.' Not that his were beautiful, but that, as a high officer in SIM, the Sevicio de Inteligencia Militar, at the Moncada Barracks in Santiago, he worked on the eyes. He knew that eyes were the key to a man's soul. His reputation was mighty. He worked quickly, with passion and skill; it was never pretty but it was always effective.

The prisoners screamed and screamed and screamed. There were three: the man Earl had shot immediately at the tree; another tommy-gunner he'd wounded across the road; and a third, unwounded, who'd been positioned at the far tree, had never brought fire to bear in the fight, and had escaped only to be tracked down by a dog team.

It was well after dark. A U.S. Navy generator had been unlimbered and lights strung to allow the crime scene to be examined and the dead to be toe-tagged and body-bagged. Pepe, with his queer, deflated head, rested with several of the men who'd killed him and were now in bags themselves.

First the navy had shown up, then a detachment of security police from Guantanamo and some Cuban soldiers from Santiago, who brought the dogs that had tracked the one escapee. Now, a few hours later, the scene bustled with dark purpose and energy, as soldiers guarded, investigators investigated, detectives detected, Americans worked on their earnest looks, and the Cubans smoked and joked and tortured.

Earl still lay on a gurney next to the ambulance, a bottle of plasma hung on a prong above his head. A corpsman had cut his pants away, and now a U.S. Navy doctor worked on him, and told him that he would not die.

'You were lucky, sir,' the young man said. 'He hit you flush in the hipbone with a pistol bullet, but you must have bones like concrete. Or maybe it was the angle. The bullet didn't shatter the bone, it glanced off. It tore up some gluteus maximus but no arteries were hit, and you got the wound stanched right away, so you're going to be okay. I take it you've been shot before?'

'Once or twice,' was all Earl said.

'Well, you are a tough old coot. You get to walk away from another one.'

'I am going to run out of luck sooner or later, though.'

They tried to load him into the navy ambulance, but Earl would not leave until finally the last of his charges was found. This was Lane Brodgins, who had taken off on a tangent from the congressman as they fled through the jungle

183

and gotten himself completely lost, until a squad of marines uncovered him in a bog. Now he was back, wrapped in a blanket, drinking coffee, unseeing and uncaring, trying to fight the shock that warped his brain.

As for Boss Harry, he didn't miss a beat. He'd already shaken hands with each of his rescuers, American naval or Cuban security personnel, glad-handed, backslapped, hee-hawed, guffawed, and managed to find the one PFC — there's one in every squad — with a pint of hooch aboard, and he'd had a few hard swallows and was mellow again. His hair wasn't even mussed.

'Well, Earl,' he said, 'you done fought 'em off and saved my worthless old hide again, this time from killers.'

One of the prisoners screamed.

'Woo,' said the congressman, 'bet he don't like that a bit.'

'No, sir, I don't expect he does.'

'You let them take you to Gitmo, son. You relax and the United States Congress will take care of this one, this one's on us. And I will call Governor Becker myself and demand that the State of Arkansas confer on you the highest damn medal it can. I know you've got every damned medal there is and it's pointless, but still I insist, son. You'da made a lot of Republicans happy if you hadn't gotten us through this.'

'I was just — '

A shot rang out.

'God, what was that?' Harry said, wincing and ducking. 'Are they attacking again?'

'I'd bet the Cuban interrogator made a point

184

for prisoners A and B by shooting prisoner C in the head.'

'Earl!'

It was Roger, rushing over, having just arrived on the long haul from the Havana embassy. 'Good God, are you all right? Lord, we came as soon as we heard. We have been driving like fools. Congressman, you're safe. I heard about the driver. Oh, lord, you're so lucky there's only one dead.'

'It ain't luck, it's old Earl,' said Congressman Etheridge.

Roger closed with Earl, who smoked a cigarette and lay on the gurney.

The congressman drifted away, and Roger leaned close.

'Earl, again — fabulous work. You have any idea what would have happened if they'd managed to kill an American congressman? Jesus, I hate to think. It would scuttle the Cuban economy for months to come, it would get us militarily involved in a way we cannot afford to be, it would have unsettled the whole Caribbean, it would have pissed off the president, and it would have cost a lot of us our careers!'

'Well, thank god nobody's career got wrecked,' Earl said, taking a draw on his Lucky.

'Okay, poke fun at me. That's all right.'

'Mr. Evans — '

'Earl, please, *Roger*, dammit, you saved my career tonight, you should at least call me *Roger*.'

'Roger. I just want to knit up and git out of

here. Every time I end up on an island, I almost get clipped.'

'Well, now, let's not — '

'Sir, I have had it with your damn island. I am too old by far for this kind of thing.'

'Of course, of course. But have you — '

'No. No, don't say a thing. Just send me home, for Christ's sake!'

Roger's eyes clicked through disappointment to hurt to numbness. Then he turned to the corpsmen.

'Okay,' he said, 'load him up, get him to the hospital.'

'Wait,' Earl said, 'is Frenchy here?'

'Yes, I sent him to talk with the Cuban Secret Police. His Spanish is actually pretty good, and he gets on better with — '

A fusillade of shots rang out, and men flinched and ducked, and turned toward the source.

'Well,' said Earl, 'I think that's it for them boys they caught.'

'You can't tell them how to do things,' Roger said.

'I want to talk to Frenchy. I got a job for him. You boys' — he addressed the corpsmen — 'y'all give me another few minutes, okay?'

'Sir, you need bed rest, a dressing change, a more substantial examination, a . . . '

But undirected, Frenchy stepped out of the dark.

'Well, there he is, the man himself,' he said.

'What did you find out?' Roger asked.

'Uh, the Cuban 'specialist' broke the last one. Scalpels, eyes, you don't want to know more. I

186

never saw *anything* like that. Anyway, before they shot him, he told them who's behind all this. He gave them a name. They wouldn't share it with me. Goddammit, I handed out smokes and everything. They just seemed exceedingly happy and somebody got on the radio to *El Presidente*. Somebody's going to get roasted tomorrow!'

'Lord,' said Roger, wincing at the prospect of yet more distasteful violence. He turned and left to go tend to the congressman.

Earl gestured, and Frenchy bent close.

'What is it?'

'I ain't said nothing yet, but somebody else was here. Someone with a burp gun nailed that bastard who was about to finish me.'

'What are you saying, Earl?'

'Listen here. Not tonight, when all these bastards are around, but tomorrow you stop off. Mark a tree or something so you can stay oriented. About forty yards up the road, maybe ten yards in, that's where whoever was shooting set up. I want you to get your Princeton trousers all muddy by getting down on them hands and knees, and don't you get up till you find a cartridge casing. I have to know who this guy is, and why he done what he done.'

187

23

Roger played three hard sets with Lt. Commander Tom Carruthers — not only a Harvard teammate but a member of his same dining club — and only won in the third, six-four. Even he had to admit he was slipping; he had not played singles in some years, he had not lifted a tennis racket since this whole Big Noise thing had started, and he was creaky and slow through the first set — he actually lost it on a double-fault! — and only got a wind up and found his form halfway through the second.

'Good show, old man!' he said, when he drilled Tommy's last service down the line, puffing up dust, to take the match. 'Damn, that felt good.'

'Roge, must say, you've played better. I don't believe I ever took a set off you before.'

'Haven't had a racket in my hand in weeks, you know,' said Roger. 'They keep us hopping in the America house.'

'I imagine it'll get worse, what with these Juan Lopez types now shooting up the U.S. Congress!'

'This may be the last tennis I play this year, Tommy!'

'Come on, let's shower and hit the Officer's Club for mojitos.'

'Actually, yes to the shower but no to the bar. I've got some house-setting-in-order to do. You know. Ugly, but necessary. A certain slippery assistant needs to be straightened out.'

'Ugh, hate that stuff. That's what bosun's mates are for.'

'Unfortunately in our little outfit, there are no sergeants to kick tail when necessary. One must do it oneself. Melancholy work, but character building, I think.'

The two old pals showered and changed, shared a quick Coke out of the nickel machine, and then Roger went off in search of Frenchy.

He had to admit, Guantanamo felt like home. Everywhere you looked, Americans. No Latin chaos and sultriness, no squalor, no pathos, no endless parade of numbers-sellers, whores and cigar-rollers, no pale tropic paints off that whole different sun-soaked palette, no ratty beggars or starving, swollen-bellied children. Instead, order, tidiness, cleanliness, safety, security. The sailors were crisp in their whites, the marines crisp in their olive fatigues, everyone was clean and everyone saluted or nodded. They didn't know him, except that his suit and pressed blue shirt and rep stripe tie proclaimed him, immediately and totally, Important, and as he walked from the tennis courts at the Officer's Club to the Naval Intelligence offices where he was temporarily headquartered, he must have passed a hundred smiling faces, none of them, fortunately, brown.

The trees were well tended, the gardens sharp — oh, yes, the gardeners, he could tell, were all Cuban — and a topiary at the Officer's Club proclaimed the initials USN in dense, immaculately trimmed bushes, under a flagpole, where the American flag waved eternally vigilant against the azure sky. And beyond — he could see, because they were on a slope — he observed a bustling harbor where sleek gray ships under the same proud banner either put out to sea or returned from sea, always on duty, always on the ramparts.

This is what we're offering the world, he thought, adoring the order, the cleanliness, the sense of high purpose everywhere evident, *if only they aren't so stupid as to turn it down.*

He reached the Naval Intelligence offices, in a tempo that seemed to have become a permanto, shaded in palms and guarded by marines. But he was known by this time, and walked by and through the casual security of a place securely American and went upstairs and down halls past rooms of decoders and yeomen typists and WAVE secretaries, and found at last the rooms he had been assigned, stepped in, was saluted by two enlisted men and had his hand shaken by another officer, a lieutenant from Yale, who was his official liaison.

'This way, Roger. He's back now.'

'Excellent.'

'Good match?'

'Tommy still has some moves. My treachery prevailed over his youth and athleticism in the end, however.'

'Not how I hear it, Roge. They say you're the tops.'

'Well — '

'Just a thought, Roge. I'm coming to Havana

190

next weekend, possibly we could get together for a drink? My service is up in a couple of months. Dad wants me in law school and all that crap, but I don't know if I'm cut out for it. I might be thinking about moving laterally in your direction.'

What was the guy's name? Yale, football. Oh, yeah: Dan, Dan Benning, he thought.

'Dan, yes, we must. Yes, with your experience, you could be vital. The only thing is, things are a little hectic with all this.'

'Yes, I know.'

'Let me take care of this, and we *must* get together.'

'I'll count on it.'

At last he entered the last door, his temporary office, formerly belonging to a marine colonel who had been hastily evacuated to make room for the Agency hotshot of whom so many spoke so well, and what he found, sitting at *his* desk, feet up, was Walter — *Frenchy!* — in shirt-sleeves, tie down, soaked in sweat, reading reports.

'Well,' he said.

'Oh, hi, Roge, how are you?'

Frenchy rose — though just a bit slow, Roger thought — and made room, waited for him to sit, then took a seat on the sofa under photos of the marine colonel's fabulous career stops in Okinawa, Seoul and Panama.

'Fine,' Roger said.

'The match?'

'Fine, fine. So what did you find out?'

It had been Frenchy's idea to return to the

191

crime scene this morning to look for whatever had to be looked for, to talk with the Cuban security police who handled the 'investigation', such as it was, while Roge played tennis.

'Well, no new physical evidence has been uncovered. The Cubans are pretty sure, though, that they have their man. I did find out who. Oh, this is rich. It's some gangster named El Colorado. How cowboy-movie is that? I think we'll see something happening very soon.'

'El Colorado? That does sound Republic Pictures.'

'An ex-socialist. Now a pimp master. He owned the brothel where the congressman acted up. Furthermore, it appears he tried to have Earl killed in prison but was mysteriously thwarted. But these Latin types: you play by their rules or the hammer comes down. I believe the Cubans will hammer the hammer very quickly. Certain messages must be sent.'

'And you got the traffic out?'

'Yes, Roge, last night, after we got in. And I checked for incoming, but there was nothing. I put out another report this morning before I left for the site, in your name, of course. I haven't told them about impending action against El Colorado. Should I?'

'It might look good if we're predicting it. You might even tell them we suggested the action.'

'Yes. Yes, that's good.'

'Short-term, but good.'

'Uh? Meaning?'

'Meaning I am worrying about long-term.'

'Long-term?'

'You see, that's your flaw, Walter. You're a good nuts-and-bolts man, I give you that. But you have to see a larger picture, see where it's all going.'

'I can never seem to remember that.'

'It is this Earl. He said last night he just wanted to go home.'

'Well, Roge, I mean, he'd just been in a gunfight, he'd just gotten *shot*. Possibly he was a little, you know, *down*. You know, his pep dipstick was reading a quart low.'

But Roger didn't see a joke.

'Look, I'm worried that this is not shaping up the way we anticipated. We've invested a lot in this man. I want something to happen. This isn't the Big Noise we wanted to make. This was someone else's Big Noise and it will upset a lot of people at United Fruit and Domino Sugar and Bacardi and Hershey's and Curtis. We need to make *our* Big Noise.'

'Roge, I think it's going swell. Look, he's going to be in that hospital another week, he'll rest up, his morale will improve, his sense of duty become clear again. And when he gets out we can put a full-court press on him. We've got this assassination attempt as proof of subversion and guerilla activity. We link it to Castro, we make the case to Earl, and we are all set. It's in the bag and — '

'*Stop it!*'

Roger hated emotional outbursts, loss of control, anger, the quiver in the voice, the tremble in the fingers, the dryness in the lips, the secret thump of an agitated heart. He hated all that. But now he could not stop himself.

193

'I am tired of your con-job answers. You always have an answer. You're never at a loss for words. You always pretend to *know*. I'm tired of it. You assist. You make sure that what policies I set, you make certain they happen.'

'Of course, Roge, I merely — '

'You merely were doing your hustle again. I hate it. I'm sick of it. This Earl thing — it's your hustle. Let me make that clear. We have a responsibility. We have something we have to do and it's got to be done soon, and with Earl, and it has to be a permanent, total solution to our problem, a successful conclusion to our mission. The Big Noise. Do you get it?'

'Of course, Roger.'

'My next ticket is West Berlin. That is the real action. I need a feather in my cap. Now the question is, are you coming, or do you go onto the Langley scrap heap of failed assistants, of young promising fellows who just didn't quite work out and ended up in analysis or training or admin? Which is it, Walter? You can come with me, you can stay behind. It's up to you.'

'Roger, I'll deliver. Earl will deliver.'

There was an urgent rap at the door.

The two men exchanged looks, then Frenchy rose and opened it, to admit Lt. Dan Benning, in an agitated state.

'You really ought to have a radio on.'

'What's going on?'

'The Cuban army has attacked a gangster named El Colorado at his house in Centro Havana. Tanks, armored cars, machine guns. There's a battle going on downtown right now!'

194

24

Speshnev and the young man Castro sat at a sidewalk cafe in Centro, sipping coffee as the tanks rumbled by.

'Pah!' said Speshnev. 'These are not tanks. I have seen tanks. In Spain, there were tanks. The German Panzers were huge and carried immense armor and armament. Now *those* were tanks!'

These tanks were American M4 Shermans, obsolete by a decade and somehow seconded to the Cuban national army for defense of the island against threat of invasion by, er, Haiti. They rumbled down La Rampa before turning onto 23rd, for Vedado, just a block or two away, where the battle still raged.

'It took them long enough to get here,' Speshnev continued in his rant. 'Good heavens, your people are so slow. It is the Spanish disease. Siesta, siesta, always the siesta. That is your curse. It's an abomination.'

The tanks would signify the last phase of the battle. A squad of Batista's prize assault troops had attempted to broach the house several hours earlier, but withering automatic fire killed half and drove the others back. The house was sprayed with machine gun fire — its noise rattled off the windowpanes all over town — and when whoever was in charge decided enough was enough, that everyone inside was

195

dead, he sent in two squads of *asaltos*. Half were killed, half driven away.

So then it was wait and snipe, wait and snipe, for hours, until at last the tanks arrived. Now they were here. It would soon be over.

'Isn't this a little dangerous?' asked Castro. Now and then a ricochet would whine by, loosed by who knew which side and off of how many bounces. Most people were behind cover, but Speshnev insisted on pretending it was a calm summer day. He sat drinking his sweet coffee. The waiter wore a pot on his head and scuttled along the ground like a crab, but continued in his profession, rather heroically.

'No,' said Speshnev, 'it is not a little dangerous. It is in fact very dangerous. You can never tell which freakish way a bullet or a chunk of shrapnel or a wave of concussion will bounce. At any moment, we could die. Waiter! Another coffee, please, *pronto*.'

'Si, señor,' came the meek call from within.

'Then why do we sit here? Is this to test my courage? Are you trying to prove me a coward? I am not a coward, but I see no point in pointless, flamboyant risk for no gain.'

'Well, then, let me explain. All in all, what is happening so close by is an interesting object lesson for a young man who seeks to enter the profession in which you claim such an interest. Far more beneficial for you, I would say, than your awful chess, at which you show no progress and even less aptitude than before.'

'I play Ping-Pong. Do you play Ping-Pong?'

'Of course not,' Speshnev sniffed. 'It's an idiotic game.'

'It's actually rather fast and exciting and — '

'You are trying to change the subject. Shut that mouth and listen and try and learn. What is the moral of the day?'

'Don't fight tanks with machine guns?'

'That is the moral of any day. No, *this* day.'

'I suppose — '

The world ended in noise. Then it came back again, just as it had been.

It was the sound of a Sherman's 75mm cannon firing. It seemed to momentarily suck the atmosphere from the planet and all within the cone of its percussion waves flinched, young Castro especially, for the pain seemed to drive two sharp needles into his ears.

'Eeee-gods!' he said.

'Yes,' Speshnev said, 'war is loud. Battle is tremendous. It is not for the — '

But another explosion followed, as loud, and then the sense of sitting and talking in a cafe was gone totally, as one shell boomed, then another, in steady succession, ever so painfully loud. The Shermans were firing salvos, the shells detonating in the wreckage of the once beautiful house. Dust and smoke filled the air, and the vibrations from each individual blast seemed to linger and mount as yet more shells were fired. The cannonade went on for a solid three minutes. Castro put his fingers in his ears and his face down on the table to avoid dust. The agent simply sipped his strong sweet coffee, seemingly unperturbed.

At last it was over.

'My mother!' said Castro. 'That was something.'

'Yes it was, and back to the subject please.'

'I suppose the lesson is, he struck too soon.'

'Ah,' said Speshnev. 'At last you have said one tiny thing that impresses me. Not much, but a little. Yes, too early, no follow up, no alternative plan, no alibi, nothing.'

'Well, he was outsmarted. His men were captured and I would think tortured and they gave him up. What can be done?'

'What can be done is simple: discipline, patience, coolness, cunning. That is the way wars are won, not by flamboyant stunts.'

Machine gun fire. Lots of it. Then individual shots, as, presumably, troops shot at corpses to make certain they stayed corpses.

'You said we would go look.'

'It's happening faster than I anticipated. Use your ears. This is the radio of failed revolution. He had no need to assassinate the congressman and had he succeeded, the consequences for all of us — except him — would have been tragic. There are always consequences. Nothing occurs without consequences. You must face consequences.'

'I must be realistic in my thinking, you are saying.'

More machine gun fire. A steady, beating roar, then silence.

'Learn this: you must have discipline. You must not strike until you are strong enough. You must withdraw quickly to avoid being caught.

You must bleed them and bleed them and bleed them. It is a question of will. Do you have the will? Colorado did not. He had the means, and that was all, and it got him crushed in the stones of his own house.'

'I see.'

'You were very lucky. You managed to disaffiliate yourself from his plot, and to disconnect yourself from being his pawn. Otherwise you would be in prison now and before the wall tonight. Yet here you sit, drinking coffee.'

'I was lucky to have someone so astute looking after me. I will not be so hasty and foolish in the years to come.'

'I hope not. But I need a promise. You will not do anything stupid or ill-founded, no matter what anger seizes you. Do you understand? If I am to continue, if our sponsorship is to grow, if your movement is to prosper, it has to be well run. You have charisma, but do you have wisdom? The former without the guidance of the latter is pure anarchy. From now on, you must seek approval. If you do that, you'll be surprised how you can be aided by us.'

'I can tell you are experienced.'

A last rattle of machine gun fire echoed down the dusty streets.

'What is next is, you go on vacation.'

'Vacation! Why, I have work to do. We have a plan already in place, I shouldn't tell you this, for Santiago, although, yes, it needs some polish — '

'You have no work. Don't delude yourself. Don't bore me with fantasy. Forget Santiago. For now, you are too famous. I want you gone. And I do mean *gone*. You don't tell your wife, you don't tell your three mistresses — '

'Four, actually. The new one, so beautiful.'

' — your four mistresses, your three, or is it two, followers. Poof! You are vanished, invisible, as of the moment you leave this cafe.'

'But my wife — '

' — will forgive you, as she always has. I am not joking. There will be something like a terror ahead, and some deaths will be whimsical. With your idiocy, you could walk into that in a second. Some people think you have talent, and must be preserved, and that task, melancholy though it be, has fallen to me. So off you go.'

'Where shall I go?'

'Don't even tell me. Think of me as a magician. I count three, and when I reach it . . . you are gone.'

The young man had vanished by two.

25

What a wonderful story. Drunken American congressman goes to whorehouse, gropes, squeezes, requests vague perversions, acts up, strikes the girl, causes a ruckus and insults Cuban hostess. His bodyguard roughs up the local security. The hostess complains to the overboss, and in that fiery Latino way, psychotically obsessed with honor and face, he takes it too seriously and decides to teach a lesson to the congressman and by extension all arrogant grasping Americans, with their money, their new buildings, their disdain for Cuban machismo.

Alas something goes tragically wrong; the assassination attempt is foiled, and the heroic Cuban security services, ever fast on their feet and so professionally agile, track the attack back to its source and decide that's where the lesson must be taught. Thus the military settles the score, though it's a daylong battle not settled until the tanks arrive late in the afternoon, and scores of the innocent and even some of the guilty die. But finally El Presidente's flag flies over No. 353 23rd Street in Vedado, and for days the curious, the bloodthirsty, the horrified come look at the smokey ruins where so many died, and where the story ended in a brilliant explosion of bloodlust, ambition, vengeance, crazed bravado and fabulous theater.

But the serious people understand that there is so much more to it than that, and underneath the gossip and the scandal and the delicious details, they begin to investigate. This includes the expat business community, diplomatic and intelligence circles, even the American military. All must know more and all are eventually satisfied. But chief among the ranks of the intensely curious is the unofficial American crime boss of Havana, Mr. L, who receives many urgent calls from compatriots back in America. These august, elderly gentlemen are suddenly worried about the political stability of the island in which they've invested so heavily. Mr. L is no fool, and understands that these men need an 'inside story,' the true gen, as it were, that conforms to their intuitive sense of conspiracy. He makes calls, he asks favors, he gently twists arms, until something resembling an underplot emerges and though it's not a thing that could ever be proven in a court, it's enough to satisfy the various people he must satisfy. This is done over several days with careful deliberation, for such is Mr. L's way, cautious and painstaking, good with details, ever patient. And of course finally a plan is devised, and like all good plans it not only satisfies its own mandates but also, magically, several others as well. It's too good an idea, really, not to be implemented.

So Frankie is summoned to the Montmartre from his dank exile, ever ready to please, primed to go the extra yard, incredibly happy to be noticed again.

'You've heard it all, I suppose,' said Mr.

Lansky, drinking milk in his office in his linen suit, as always.

'I went down myself to look at the ruins. Man, that wasn't no gunfight, that was a goddamned artillery attack.' Frankie has a black Ban-Lon sports shirt with red piping, white trousers, a pair of expensive Italian loafers. He is holding his sunglasses because his pockets are too tight to accommodate them.

'Frankie, I've told you. Please, no swearing. It's coarse, and other ways can be found to make a particular emphasis.'

'I apologize.'

'It's just a small thing. Anyhow, suppose I tell you there's more.'

'I bet there's more. For one thing, there's twenty-five or more whorehouses completely up for grabs. These houses could be a start. They could be a front for narcotics distribution; they could be a source of talent for color dirty pictures, which I guarantee you is the next big fuck — , uh, next big moneymaker in our business, and already the West Coast is trying to push it; they could be a way to get in with certain business execs who consider themselves too hoity-toity for our kind of action, and politicians too, including, if I hear right, not only congressmen but senators as well.'

'Excellent, Frankie. Your instincts are superior. And I suppose you know just the man for the job and I wouldn't be surprised if he was born Franco Carabinieri in Salerno forty-three years ago.'

Frankie blushed.

'It would be a very tasty deal for everyone, all around the table.'

'It would indeed. Even now the Cubans are jockeying for the strength to make such a grab themselves. There's a certain captain in the military intelligence service named Latavistada, recently of Santiago, where he had a reputation for getting things done, who is most anxious to take over. He owned brothels in that town.'

'I should have a talk with him.'

'You should. And what would you tell him?'

'For 70 percent, I won't kill him.'

'Perhaps he isn't the sort to scare. His nickname is Ojos Bellos, 'Beautiful Eyes', for unpleasant things involving knives and eyes, known to make prisoners sing loud and fast.'

'I will make him sing loud and fast.'

'Now, Frankie, maybe there's another thing, another way of going, which would bring you into intimate contact with Latavistada, even as a buddy, a partner, a pal. And in that way, the two of you could acquire serious property in this town and a franchise for the future. Without bloodshed or rancor. Can you think of such a way?'

Frankie thought hard. Here's what he came up with: nothing.

'I . . . I . . . ' He felt like a fish flopping on a dock, drowning in air.

'Okay, Frankie, that's not your way of thinking. It's all right. It's fine. Just sit back, relax, take a load off, and listen.'

'Yes, sir. Yes, Meyer.'

'Frankie, here's the thing. Maybe this fellow

204

who got himself all blown up, this El Colorado, maybe he was only the muscle end of the show. Maybe there's someone behind him, someone shadowy, who's secretly planning a big takeover and when he gets that done, he kicks us all out, El Presidente at the top and all of us on down, and we are out of luck.'

'Who could do such a thing? Another crew? It would have to be a hell of a crew, that I know.'

'Not a crew, Frankie. Worse than a crew, more powerful than a crew. An idea.'

'An idea?'

'The idea of communism. The idea that nobody owns a thing, that nobody pays for a thing, that it's all free, it's all cooperative, no bosses, no anything. No mobs either. The mobs have to go.'

Frankie blinked.

'It's fucking *evil!*' he finally blurted, and Meyer did not, for once, correct him on his profanity.

'It is evil, Frankie.'

'They could do that?'

'Maybe this is the beginning.'

'Jesus Christ.'

'Frankie, there's a young man in this town whose goal it is to arrange just such a thing. He believes in it. He hides under sweet sayings about freedom and peace and bread, but that's what he wants. A world without ownership. A world without wealth. A world in which no matter how tough you are and how smart you figure and how hard you work, you get just enough and no more. It doesn't matter you're

205

clever and brave. That doesn't matter. You get your few beans every week and that's it. Everybody's the same.'

'Except some guys at the top.'

'*Exactly!* Of course. The guys at the top, they get it all. They've sold everybody on this we-are-all-equal malarkey, but behind closed doors it's party time, with babes and drinks and fancy cars. But for nobody except the big shots. There's no give and take, only take by a few. Under the guise of something called equality. It's the greatest scam in the world.'

'That is so wrong.'

'It is wrong, Frankie. It's anti-American. This young Cuban man, he's a lawyer who doesn't practice, he just roams, giving speeches, collecting followers, making allegiances, looking for ways to advance his program, laying with a girl or two along the way. He's catnip to women. And, as you might imagine, he's exactly the one who'd benefit from the kind of chaos and instability as the day before yesterday.'

'He's gotta be stopped.'

'Frankie, suppose I tell you police snitches saw him *in the house* with Colorado the day before the assassination attempt. He's the thinker behind it. He's the brilliance figuring all this out. He gives the orders, and some other schmoes do the work and take the heat and maybe get burned.'

'The bastard. He needs a bullet in the brain.'

'You could do this?'

'Without blinking an eye. It's what I do best.'

'That's my boy, Frankie. And that's where

Captain Latavistada comes in.'

'Yeah?'

'Yeah. In Military Intelligence, it's his job to keep tabs on this kind of boy. On your own, without contacts, I think he'd prove too slippery. You'd never run him to earth. It's his town, Frankie, not yours. But Latavistada knows this stuff. He can help. You, him, I think you two could get along. Frankie, this is the job you were born to do. Can you concentrate on that and put the business of Bennie Siegel aside? It's called discipline and it's the hardest thing to learn. But I know you can do it, Frankie. I have my faith. There'll come a time when we call in the tab on Bennie's killer, but we've got this job to do, and you are the man to do it, right, Frankie? Then comes the business of the whorehouses and who's to take them over. And naturally it's you, Frankie, under my supervision and with the captain's assistance. You see, Frankie? Sometimes I think all this was planned out by someone with true vision. Are you ready for such a thing?'

'I am your man, Mr. Lansky,' said Frankie, meaning it with every fiber of his being.

26

The eagle soared. Its wingspan was immense, stretching for at least twelve feet, each feather immaculate and precise in the rigidity of the windswept moment. Its beak hooked downward sternly, its eyes were sagacious and farseeing as it observed the horizon for signs of danger, and it looked as if it were on freedom's patrol, ready to slide down and issue destruction from its razor-sharp talons at any indication of threat. It was, somehow, freedom itself. But it also wasn't; it wasn't going anywhere. It was made of brass, and it was tethered to a marble bridge between two marble pillars.

Earl stood below it, watching, supporting himself on a cane, trying to ignore the pain that a thousand aspirin had not mollified. He stood at the foot of some steps thirty feet beneath the ornamental bird, and behind him rushed the busy traffic of the Malecon. If he turned his head just a bit, over his right shoulder he could see the twin, gleaming towers of the Hotel Nacional, Havana's finest, atop a green hill, surrounded by green gardens.

'Do you know what this is, Earl?' asked Roger.

Weren't they supposed to be on the way to the airport? Wasn't there a 6:05 Air Cubana Constellation to New York, which would lead to a 10:15 to Saint Louis which would lead to a night in a hotel and an 8:30 A.M. to Little Rock,

208

which would lead, by three tomorrow, back to Blue Eye, Arkansas, and a home, a wife, a child?

'Of course I know what it is,' said Earl.

What remained of the USS *Maine* was this bird on these two pillars, two cannons embedded in the concrete base of the monument, and some brass words on a plaque, all of it facing empty sea under a hot sun. The ship itself had blown up some half mile out on that sea at this spot, but nothing out there indicated that it had ever existed.

'Do you know how many men died here, Earl?' said Frenchy.

'No. A hundred?'

'Three hundred sixty-two, in a flash. Bang, all gone, just like that.'

'I get the point,' said Earl. He glanced at his watch. 'We have to be going. I have a flight.'

'One more stop, Earl,' said Roger. 'No lectures, no chatter, no rah-rah from men you must think of as boys who haven't done one-tenth as much as you. But one more stop. It's just a bit of a way.'

Roger signaled and the car came and got them, and Earl lumbered into the backseat with his hip throbbing away and now his head and shoulder also racked from the funny tension of walking with the damned cane.

'You let them give you anything for the pain?' asked Frenchy.

'I'm taking aspirin. I didn't want nothing stronger. You get used to feeling too happy. This ain't bad. Been through worse.'

'I'll bet. The stories you could tell,' said Roger.

'I don't tell stories, Mr. Evans.'

'I know, Earl. It was just a figure of speech.'

The car drove through Havana's busy traffic, where the cars all seemed to date from the thirties. The men wore straw boaters and linen suits and the women high heels and bare shoulders. Spanish in its most riotous form filled the air, and the sun slanted through palms and dust and beeps and squawks. Kids sold lottery numbers on the street, bananas, coffee, carvings and their sisters.

But then the car passed through gates, under the dark glade of well-nurtured and -tended trees, and up to a house that had once been a palace or at least a mansion. Earl saw the brass plaque next to the mahogany doors, and knew what he was in for.

They went up steps and of course the place was deserted. It was not a tourist hangout nor of much interest to the Cubans themselves. It spoke only of a kind of national vanity and the nation in question wasn't Cuba.

MUSEUM OF THE SPANISH-AMERICAN WAR

They entered to church-like silence, and the presence of ghosts. Behind glass, manlike forms without faces stood in khaki uniforms, with hats upturned jauntily, speaking of vigor and mission and courage. They wore gold piping and puttees and carried big-flapped cavalry holsters crosswise on huge belts that were marked with cartridge loops.

Earl walked, with the aid of his cane, down the

210

aisles, to more displays: medals, maps, a papier-mâché model of a hill outside Santiago, with forces identified by tiny flags and color-coded: blue for American, red for Spanish. Cooking utensils, newspaper front pages, pocket-knives, compasses, all un-dusty, under glass, which *was* dusty.

'See, Earl? There are other islands where Americans died. Iwo, Saipan, Guadalcanal, Tarawa, terrible islands. But there were other islands.'

Saddles, well-worn and burnished, and other horse gear appropriate to a cavalry unit at the turn of the century. Boots and saddles. A beat-up old bugle. Quirts and whips. Spurs, jingly-jangly tack, saddlebags, rifle scabbards, all preserved under the dusty glass in the darkness, untouched for years.

'Here, Earl. This one should interest you.'

The guns. Colt revolvers, single-action armies, six-shooters, Peacemakers, whatever you wanted to call them. They were familiar to him because his father had buckled one on every single day of his life, and Earl's job had been to clean it. He knew the old man was good with it, because in 1923 he'd shot it out in a Blue Eye bank with three wild brothers, and killed them all, and been a hero. Earl couldn't remember clearly, possibly because he didn't want to.

The guns were beautiful orchestrations of balance and harmony, of circles and curves, of the precise melding of steel and wood in the brilliance of design.

'Ever shoot one of these old Colts, Earl?'

211

'Of course I have,' said Earl.

At least twenty-five of the guns that the Rough Riders had carried up San Juan were displayed in the case, most with long, elegant barrels, the 71/2-inch models that Teddy Roosevelt himself carried. But there were a few others brought in by western lawmen who'd joined the Rough Riders in San Antonio, men who preferred the shorter length of the 45/8 for its quickness in maneuver and deadliness at short range. They were gunfighters, the men who carried those guns, not soldiers.

And ammo. What museum would be complete without the old boxes with their quaint nineteenth-century printing, the cardboard now delicate, the boxes slightly distended for their loads of cartridges inside, huge as robin's eggs, weirdly dense, weirdly serious.

And holsters, too. Of course. Those big flapped things for the cavalry, with the leather over top securing the revolver against the jostle of the animal beneath. But that was not all. Being gunfighters, many of the Rough Riders had their own private rigs, shoulder holsters many of them, to tuck the shorter-barreled Colts away from prying eyes. Earl saw several of fine leather, basketweave-stamped, complex nests of strap and stay and loop and buckle, built to hold the gun just so out of sight that a dexterous man could get it into play in less than a second.

'Okay,' said Earl. 'I see what you're up to.'

'Earl,' said Roger, 'I just want you to know that men came here, American men, with guns, and fought and died and bled to make this island

212

into something. They were young men, they probably didn't want to die, but they did. And I'm not even going to take you into the disease room, the yellow fever room, and that particular horror. We'll stay here, where we don't have to think about all that dying.'

'This ain't right,' Earl said. 'You are fixing it so that if I say no to you, I'm supposed to be saying no to the men that carried these guns and died on this island. But you ain't them. They are them, and you and Frenchy are something entirely different.'

'That is true,' said Roger, 'and I know you don't care for us and would never see us as their inheritors. *You're* their inheritor; we're merely little bureaucrats to whom fate has given a responsibility that we hope to hell we can live up to. Well, maybe we can't. I know we can't without your help, Earl.'

'Time to stop horseshitting around. This ain't a place for doubletalk. You tell me straight out what you want.'

'The island is in play. You've almost gotten killed twice on account of it. Someone sees a destiny for it that isn't free and isn't American. That destiny will grow and grow and maybe sometime down the pike, more American boys with guns will have to land on this island to take it back. You know how many times bigger Cuba is than Iwo Jima?'

'A hell of a lot bigger.'

Now Frenchy spoke.

'We have a lot invested in this place. A lot of men died here. It's our blood in the soil as much

213

as anybody's. So we have a moral right to protect it. Now there's a force on the island that means to steal that away and make it something different and foreign. Suppose now, while it's early, we could stop it. Stop it with the big noise of a single shot. Would you have fired a shot in 1938 to kill Hitler? Or in 1940 to stop Tojo?'

'It's always this way, ain't it,' Earl said. 'Some college kids dream up something and convince themselves it's so right. Then some poor jerk with a gun has to make it happen.'

'It is always that way, Earl,' said Roger. 'That is it entirely. But as annoying as you find us, Earl, you have to admit that we are right.'

'You bastards,' said Earl, knowing that he had no choice but to sign on, for better or worse.

'It's your call, Earl. We can still make the plane.'

'You bastards. Take me to the goddamned hotel. I have to call my wife and make her cry again.'

27

'You see,' explained Ramon Latavistada, 'it's not a question of stuff. I can get stuff. I can get any stuff. This is a talent of mine. Excuse, please.'

With that he turned and inserted the tip of a scalpel into the eyelid of a prisoner named Hector. Hector was chained to a wall in the bowels of the Military Intelligence Service's Havana location, which was the Morro Fortress. He had been picked up on the recommendation of the political section as a well-known agitator, subversive, pamphleteer, speechmaker and confederate of 'Greaseball,' as Fidel Castro was known to the SIM.

But Ramon did not plunge the blade into the eye, thereby blinding Hector. What would that have proven? Nothing. Merely that blades cut, blood flows, eyes are vulnerable to violence and the result is exceedingly messy and painful.

Instead, with a deft flick of his wrist, he incised just deep enough into the eyelid to open a small cut that would nevertheless bleed profusely. Since Hector's eyelid was taped open, he could not blink; the blood would flood his eye, and he would have the sensation of drowning in a pool of his own blood, while at the same time facing, by implication, a forever of blindness.

He commented, in Spanish, '*Aieeeeeeeeeeee!!!!*'

'Hush, hush, my friend,' said Ramon.

'You can get stuff,' said Frankie, oblivious to

215

the scene. 'And by stuff, I suppose you mean contraband. I'm thinking narcotics.'

'Yes, of any sort.'

'In quantity.'

'I have my suppliers, yes.'

'The problem then is distribution.'

'Well, I would think those concerns would be handled on the other end. My more immediate concern would be importation, protection, intelligence, political allies, essentially the whole apparatus. It takes a skilled operator to set up such an organization. This, my friend, is where I thought you and I could have some conversations.'

'*Aieeeeeeeeee!! Please! Please, no more, sir!*'

'Hush,' said the captain. 'We are not ready for you yet.'

'My eyes! O my god, my eyes!'

'Yes,' said the captain in Spanish, 'your eyes. Anyhow,' he returned to his extremely fluent English, 'Señor Carbine, I seem not to get very far with the old men who run your business in America. They have their allies, their connections, their situations all set up. They seem committed to certain groups in Mexico. I suppose the temptation of that long border, so hard to patrol. But if only someone would see: my way is so much better.'

'You could move in quantity?'

'Of course. In time, though. All things in time. It would first be necessary to move small test shipments, to make certain the apparatus was adequate. But even in that small step, you see the genius of this business. The product, shipped in

216

pounds, can then be stepped on and turned into hundreds of pounds. From so little, so much. The profits are astonishing. Once people are exposed, they cannot say no. Another thing: when the women are hooked, they will do anything to satisfy their need. *Anything*. Do you understand what I am saying? I am talking of beautiful women, too. It is amazing, truly.'

He turned back to Hector, reinserted the tip of the blade, and administered the next tiny little flick. The results were as desired and designed. Hector jacked in pain and terror. He had a bowel movement. His muscles stood out like ropes against his arms. He bucked and twisted, beyond degradation.

'Ugh,' Frankie said, 'do they always shit like that? Man, he dumped a ton.'

'It's hard to predict. Some do, some don't; you never can tell. All will talk, though. No one can stand the idea of the eye being sliced away, the pain, the humiliation, the infirmity. It always works. It always works, doesn't it, my friend Hector?'

'Please, sir. Please, please, no more, I beg you. I'll tell you anything.'

'I know that, Hector. But I am not ready for you yet. Contemplate the darkness and the pain more rigorously, if you please. Then I may blind you anyway, simply as punishment for your evil ways. That is, even after you spill the beans.'

He raised the scalpel and Hector, seeing it through the eye not awash in blood, began to cry grotesquely.

'See,' the captain said to Frankie in English.

217

'The power of it. Really, it's amazing.'

'Huh? Oh, yeah, yeah, that. Yeah, that's swell. Anyway, this hold on the beautiful girls? See, there's a big deal coming to America. It would be dirty pictures but in *color*. High quality, great lithography, glossy pages. And not just the melons. You know, all of it, the plumbing, the tunnels, the bush, all that stuff. Maybe eventually the fuck itself. If we could show it, man, the moolah would just roll in. We would have something there, let me tell you.'

'Ah,' said Captain Latavistada, 'yes. Yes, that is very good. I like that. I had not thought of it. But, yes, the drugs, the girls in the brothels, some young and quite lovely, yes, I can see. Yes, there is potential there, too.'

'Good,' said Frankie. 'See, I see a two-pronged thing but only one organization. That's the thing of it. By the same methods that you import, protect and distribute the drugs, you could do the same with the pictures.'

'Yes, that's true. However, the drugs can be destroyed very quickly in a raid, while the pictures, being bulkier, would prove problematic. That's why initially the drugs seem a safer enterprise.'

'We could solve the destruction problem with the pictures, then we'd be in good shape. I'm thinking, well, I'm no expert or nothing, but acid. Some kind of acid. Much faster and more complete than fire. I saw a guy once get a faceful of sulfuric. Man, not even Hector there would change places with that guy. Let me tell you, acid works fast.'

'Hmmm,' said Latavistada. 'You may have something there.' He looked at his watch. 'Mother of god,' he said, 'how late. I have a meeting with a very beautiful young lady. You would excuse me, Señor Carbine.'

'Frankie. You have to call me Frankie.'

'Frankie, then.'

'But what about — '

'Oh, that. Yes, of course.'

He turned, and very quickly sliced through the eyeball of Hector, blinding him forever.

'Hector,' he whispered, 'tell me what I want to know.'

Hector muttered something desperately through tears and snot and tremors and gasps for breath.

Latavistada nodded gravely.

'He says this Castro can be found generally at one of three coffeehouses in the afternoon, and he will give my man Eduardo the addresses of all his known supporters. Tomorrow we may intercept this Castro in any of a dozen places. It's not to be any kind of problem, my friend.'

'You work very professionally.'

'I mean to impress upon you that Cubans are precise and motivated and capable, not lazy, sombrero-wearing peons like the Mexicans. It's our truer, richer, purer Spanish blood. Now, as I say, I must go. I have a date at the country club.'

28

It was a quiet night at the little bar called La Bodeguita del Medio. The first wave of johns had gone off with the first wave of marias, the gamblers hadn't won or lost enough to come to celebrate or drink themselves into oblivion, no marine regiments or naval crews were on liberty, and so Earl sat alone, under a slowly spinning fan that looked like the prop on a Wildcat, and contemplated the bottle.

It lured him.

It beckoned him.

He didn't want to give in.

It sat before him on the bar, in the darkness, glinting magically, promising so much.

Fuck it, he said, and gave in.

He swallowed half with one swig, sucking greedily.

'Doesn't it go down better with something to drink?' asked someone next to him.

Earl set the aspirin bottle down before him, took a long swallow on a concoction he called a ginless-and-tonic and washed the dry, scratchy feel of the tablets from his throat.

'Yes,' he said. 'It does.'

'How's the wound?'

'It hurts like hell.'

'Why don't you take something stronger?'

'Boy, do I want to. But if I do, three weeks later I wake up in Shanghai with a Chinese wife, seven kids, four sets of grandparents and six new tattoos.'

'Ah,' said the man, 'you are such a creature of discipline — the secret, I suppose, of your many excellent accomplishments.'

Earl didn't have to look, but he did anyway. The man was still thin and papery, with dry skin, sharp, hard, bright eyes, a gray crewcut, dressed in a baggy suit.

'The last time I saw you, you was selling vacuum cleaners. What was the name then?'

'Actually, I've forgotten. I sometimes grow hazy on details.'

'I think it was Wormer or Wormhold or Wormgeld.'

'That sounds like something I'd come up with.'

'Vurmoldt. Yeah, Acme Vacuums or some such. Maybe Ajax. Of Nebraska.'

'I wonder where I got the Nebraska from? There can't be any vacuum cleaner companies in Nebraska, can there?'

'Wouldn't know.'

'You're certain you're not drinking anything with alcohol in it? I rather enjoy the blur at the end of a busy day of selling vacuum cleaners. I'd be pleased to buy you one.'

'I'd be pleased to accept one from you tonight and damned tomorrow. That's how it is. Sorry, but I do appreciate the offer. Anyhow, I should buy you one. I think I owe you one.'

'Very well. I will have a mojito. This place is famous for its mojitos. Movie stars come here for the mojitos.'

221

Earl got out a wad of bills, hailed the bartender and ordered another ginless-and-tonic for himself and a mojito for the gent on the next stool.

The two men watched the ritual as the waiter crushed sugar and rum and mint sprigs together, added lots of rum, a little spritz water, a few ice cubes, and, to top it off, still more rum, puncturing it with a straw. Then he added a little American flag on a toothpick before handing it over.

'Why, how patriotic,' the vacuum salesman said. 'Here's to the U.S. of A.!' and he took a nice long draught through the straw.

'I do like a man who enjoys his drinking,' said Earl. 'You know what, I am glad I ran into you. Here, take a look at this.'

Earl reached into his pocket and came out with a brass casing less than an inch long. He set it on the tile of the bar.

'Now what do you suppose that little thing is?' he asked.

'Why, could it be from a gun?'

'You know, I believe it is.'

'Guns are very dangerous, you know.'

'So I've heard. Anyhow, it took some digging, but I finally figured out this came from a Soviet PPsH 41 tommy gun. It's in 7.63mm.'

'A commie tommy! How alarming!'

'Yep. The commiest tommy there is. Anyhow, the other day I was busy getting killed. Seems some feller didn't like me and he was about to part my hair with an automatic. Suddenly he goes all swiss-cheesy. Someone stitched him six times with that commie tommy. Then, before he could fall, he stitched him six times again.'

'Ah! Well, one can hardly miss with those guns, I'd imagine.'

'Actually, it ain't so damned easy. Most folks, they squeeze the trigger and the gun runs away on them. They miss the target but redecorate the room. I had a gun something like that in the war; they're pretty hard to master.'

'Your point is?'

'Whoever saved my bacon knows how to shoot. Has been around a long time. Knows infantry weapons, the way a soldier would. Would that fit you?'

'Ah, well,' said the man. 'One hates to tell stories on oneself. I learned some of those skills recently. If I recall correctly, it was called World War II.'

'Yep, believe I heard of that one. You said you was in the German army.'

'Did I? Well, possibly I meant a European army. There are so many countries over there, one can hardly keep them all straight.'

'But there's a big red one, isn't there? Seems I read about that one. They had lots of commie tommys. Know anything about that one, mister vacuum cleaner salesman?'

'Oh, it all gets so mixed up, you know? And it's late.'

'So I don't reckon I'm getting a straight answer. My question being, who the hell are you, and why have you saved my ass twice? Why do you keep showing up like a movie sidekick? And why did you follow me to this little place? I made you an hour ago as I'm moseying down Emperado, and I'm not even any damned good at this game. I been sitting here waiting. And that's another peculiar thing. I had the distinct impression you *wanted* me to see you, and a smart fellow like you, if you didn't want that, why there's no way I'd have caught on.'

'I'd give you a straight answer if I had one. But I don't. I did, yes, come here for you. Not for questions or answers, but just to tell you something.'

'I'm all ears.'

'It's just this. I mean to warn you, as one ex-soldier to another ex-soldier: this is not your kind of fight. If you want to fight the wicked communists, go to Korea or Cyprus. They have them also in Malaysia, Kenya, Burma and Indochina. They're all over the place. Fight them straight on, in a war, and kill them, or die, if you're finally unlucky. That's something you're so good at. But, Swagger, not here. This is Havana. Things are different here. Duties aren't as clear as they are in a war.'

He smiled, finished his mojito.

'Thanks awfully for the drink. Now I must go.'

'It's the least I can do, friend. And I still owe you and I do prefer to pay off my debts.'

'Swagger, you owe me nothing. I operate at so many levels that what helps you can also be construed to help me. Enjoy the night, my friend.'

He put his Panama on, smiled rakishly, and left.

Earl watched him slide elegantly through the half-empty bar, wondering how the world conjures up a fellow so mysterious and capable at once.

29

The trunk of the black, unmarked 1938 De Soto, parked near the university, was nearly full: a Mexican Mendoza 7mm light machine gun and a thousand 7mm rounds; a Star RU-1935 9mm submachine gun; ten thirty-round magazines, full; three Model 97 Winchester shotguns, riot-gun configuration; three hundred double-ought shells; three Ruby revolvers in .38; seven automatic pistols in 9mm and .45, mostly Stars and Obregons. Also truncheons, bullwhips, hand and leg irons, hand grenades, flares and billy clubs, blindfolds, ropes, chains — the usual duty issue of the Cuban Military Intelligence Service.

In the front of the same car were Ramon Latavistada and Franco 'Frankie Carbine' Carabinieri, both in linen suits, with open white shirts, sunglasses, and panama hats pulled low over their eyes. Though it was night, and much cooler, the two men sweated, and kept running handkerchiefs over their damp foreheads as they sat and waited and smoked and sat and waited and smoked. It never occurred to them to take off their sunglasses.

'He ain't gonna show,' said Frankie.

'I fear you are correct,' said Ramon.

'What the fuck?'

'Exactly. What the fuck?'

'It's like he knew.'

'It is like that. It is like someone is watching over him.'

'And he done gone thataway.'

'What?'

'Oh, something stupid we say in the States. Meaning, he's vamoosed. From the pictures. You ever go to pictures?'

'No picture can compete with the reality of my daily life.'

The crowd was thinning. The speakers had been dreary. First was Ortez, the liberal, with much praise for the paradise of England. Then Lopez, the socialist, with even more praise for Russia. Then the Señora Ramilla, who had been bombed in the Spanish War and was blind in one eye, with colorful remembrances of parades on the Ramblas and the sense of unity among the young people.

Alas, and so disappointingly, the young orator who counted, who could spellbind and inspire, who could make the blood sing and the heart throb as he laid out his vision of a Cuba for Cubans and an end to El Presidente — he did not attend, though he was on the program. And since most of the crowd had come to hear him, there was a palpable air of disillusion. A leader's first obligation was to lead, not to disappoint.

'Man, what a wasted day. My people are not going to be happy.'

'Nobody will be happy till we find this cabrone.'

'What does that mean, 'cabrone'?'

'Homosexual.'

'Is he?'

'No, I call him that because to call him that is to spit on him.'

Latavistada started the car and nudged it rudely into the street, not particularly caring whether or not he hit any members of the dispersing crowd. A few young men raised their fists against their arms to display contempt, one so rudely that the captain nearly got out and beat him senseless with a sap, but instead coolness prevailed, and the two new pals sailed out into the Cuban night.

'I will call the Political Section,' said Latavistada. 'Possibly they have something new on him. If not, we'll go to a fellow named Kubitsky, a newspaper reporter on the *Havana Post* who is known to keep tabs on things. Then we'll swing by Castro's apartment one more time. We may not get him tonight, but we will get him, and soon, I guarantee.'

★　★　★

But the rat had fled. Nothing produced the necessary information: not phone calls, not sightings, not stakeouts, not interviews with witnesses and colleagues, willing or not. Even the man's wife, Mirta, a sullen abused creature with an unruly baby, had no idea where he was when she was approached obliquely in the laundry by a female SIM agent, and drawn out. There was no need to interrogate her more directly, for surely that information would reach the young man with the speed of light, and then he would learn he was being hunted.

'Maybe he went home.'

'Where is home?'

'This is a good question. I have heard he is from the east. But where exactly is not known. Who is this man? We know what he does and what he believes, we do not yet know who he is.'

'This information, would it be tough to come by? You could get it — '

'You could get it many ways,' said Ramon. 'You could torture for it or bribe for it, or spy for it. Alas, I find these ways uncertain as well as slow. You think Cubans are lazy and shiftless, my friend, no?'

'Pal, I never — '

'Well, I will show you the one organization in Cuba that teems with efficiency. We will have this information in — ' he paused, looked at his elegant watch, and continued, ' — two hours. This you will find so amusing, Frankie Carbine.'

★   ★   ★

Frankie watched them go in. They arrived in six black two-ton trucks and poured out, ten men from each vehicle, with clubs and rifles, commanded by sergentos with whistles and pistols, the whole thing working with brutal precision. The soldiers liked to hurt people, that was their secret. As they thundered up the famous hundred marble steps of the University of Havana, atop its green Arcadian hill, so untouched by the tarnish of reality, they flailed at anyone who came within their range, breaking limbs, shattering noses and teeth, sending screaming students bouncing down the way amid a spray of loose papers and flung-aside books. They screamed. They were primitive men, from the country, nurtured in violence, held in monstrous discipline, seething to release themselves in brutality. They never disappointed. Now they reached the top, diverted slightly, and swarmed into the law school building.

By the time Ramon and Frankie reached the administration offices on the third floor of that building, it was pretty much in ruins. Blood splashed everywhere, like some kind of modern art painting, forming anarchistic splotches on tile and wall and window. A few poor students, bruised and bashed, still tried to crawl out, and now and then a policeman would kick them in the ribs.

'Wow,' said Frankie.

'It's a good thing, generally, to teach youth that it must show respect for authority. This place is a fountain of revolution. It produces treason and sedition and liberalism with boring monotony. These young people, they think they are entitled to so much, they think so much should be changed, they have no respect for the lives their parents have built for them. I would be even harsher than El Presidente. I would shoot ten every month, regular as clockwork.'

They went through torn-up office after torn-up office, at last finding the inner sanctum of record-keeping where, industriously, the two men pillaged first the C's and then the many

Castros who had, over the years, applied to the university for admission. It didn't take a long time, for there were very helpful photos, and, as it turned out, Latavistada had an attribute ever so valuable to a secret policeman: a photographic memory.

'Ah, here, I think. Frankie, this? Does this seem right?'

'I ain't ever seen the guy.'

'No, this would be him.'

He handed over a photograph, while he studied the file. What Frankie saw made almost no impression on him, as images seldom did. He drifted a little, then made an effort to concentrate and saw an oval face not without its appeal, the eyes dark and sharp, under a crop of dense black hair. The nose was strong; the guy almost looked Italian, or Sicilian even. Yet the face also was so young. It had no lines, no strength, no passion to it, only a voluptuary's indolence.

'He looks rich.'

'What an excellent observation. He is. It says here he comes from Biran, above Santiago, almost in the Sierras. His father has an estate and works, or worked, for many years for United Fruit. You see, it's always the same, this business. It's always about fathers and sons. This little prick wants to show his papa he's a bigger man, that he will amount to something. So where papa controls a thousand acres, sonny will someday control the nation.'

Frankie had no idea what the Cuban was talking about.

But then he said, 'And here is where he will flee. Back to Oriente and the mountains, where he is son of the favored lord, out of reach of the law. Well, Frankie, we shall reach him, no?'

30

'And another thing wrong with you,' Papa said, 'you're lazy. You're evilly lazy. You lie around all day dreaming. You are incapable of doing a man's work. Additionally, your bathing habits are the source of much laughter. I labored so hard for so long to produce *this?* What a sorry specimen you are. Are you a *cabrone?* You are not a homosexual, are you?'

'Papa,' he said, 'I am not a homosexual. I am a masculine man.'

'You are not masculine at all. A masculine man is dynamic. He makes things happen by will and effort — '

'And by licking the boot of the North Americans of United Fruit.'

'Yes, it's true, I worked for them, but only to acquire money to buy land and build this place and marry and bring all you worthless children into the world. And to borrow tractors from. Without their tractors, where would we be? Señor Jennings, he smiled when the tractors disappeared and he never took them back until the plowing was done.'

'The generosity of the Americans is wonderful. They come to our island and steal and degrade us and you are grateful they let you borrow a tractor now and then!'

'Bah! A man knows gratitude. He feels it. He is not ignorant and petty and selfish and vain.

You are all of them. I should have worked you harder. That was my mistake, to my shame. You never had chores. I should have worked you like a dog and made you into a man. Instead, you are womanly.'

'I am not womanly. I am between opportunities, but I swear to you, I am a man of destiny.'

The house was large but crude. It was full of dogs and guns and cats and chickens and dirty boots and crumpled clothes and books and blankets and horse tack. It was really a barn with rooms and beds, and it suited Angel the father perfectly, for it is exactly what he'd wanted to build in the world, from the raw jungle, and he had done so. Animals more or less roamed through it, and its shabbiness was worn proudly, as if to say, true people of the earth live here. Savagery was everywhere; even his wife wore a gun and when she called the younger children to dinner, it was with a gunshot.

Outside, not everywhere but in a certain direction, the jungle loomed, and beyond the jungle the peaks of the Sierra Maestra penetrated the clouds, remote and forbidden. You could hide an army up there and no one could get you out.

'What did you do today?' Papa demanded. Papa loved to fight. It was his amusement. He worked, he fought, he made children and then ignored them. That was his way.

'Papa, I told you, it's a vacation. I relaxed.'

'You could have helped the boys weed around the cane.'

234

'I am a lawyer and a thinker. I am not a sugarcane worker.'

'Your mother says you swam in the morning and played *beisbol* in the afternoon.'

'I am a superb baseball player. Why should I not do what pleases me? The children love me.'

'You tell them lies, and you are always the hero in those tales but in no other.'

'I will be the hero, father.'

'Bah, heroes.'

'Tomorrow I will fish and in the afternoon, I will borrow a rifle and hunt. Tomas tells me there are boar by the Sierra de Mayari.'

'Meanwhile, I worry about the price of sugar and the campesinos and the health of their families and whether or not the generator will last another year and what to do if the price of fuel goes up and the North Americans develop a cheaper chemical sugar, and all you do is sleep and hunt and drink! God himself would be ashamed of such a son.'

The old man spat into the fireplace, but missed.

★ ★ ★

He fished, he hunted. He caught sixteen sea bass with the old campesino Jose, who'd been there so long he claimed to have witnessed the Americans running off of San Juan Hill and used to amuse the kids with those stories when they'd been young. In the afternoon, he hunted, and the dogs drove a boar into a bog and he shot it with an old cowboy rifle. It squawked and shivered

235

and shat while it died, but die it did, and rather swiftly too, for the young man did most things with casual elegant precision, and shooting was but one of them.

The boar butchered by he himself: knifing and peeling, and reaching into the bloated guts and pulling them out with his fingers so they oozed with shit and food and blood and filled his fingernails as he yanked. The gutpile abandoned for others in the jungle, he brought the hollowed thing home slung over his shoulder, like a cape that oozed blood down his body. He was a magnificent red god, man as savage, gone to jungle, killed in jungle, and returned with meat. His papa did not look twice at him as he trudged with the animal's carcass into the farmyard. But that meat fed the family one night and the fish another, not that there was any shortage in the larder, because Angel Ruiz Castro was a man of importance and substance, even if he browbeat anyone who came within his range, unless they were North American.

And then the boy took a trip. His destination was Cueto, the railroad town that ran up to Antilla and was larger than the muddy shanties of Biran. He knew a certain lady in this town. If she was not there, he would visit her sister. It wasn't that he wanted to do this thing, it was that he had to. A man has certain needs and they can't be satisfied always in matrimony. What is a man to do when he is far from his home and waiting for the clarification to set in?

She was not there; nor was her sister. But a neighbor was. He was big and handsome with

236

that Spanish nose and those imperial ways that all commented upon. He moved gracefully, and had once been elected the greatest high school athlete in Cuba. Had not a war and then a political awakening occurred, he might have been a great *beisbol* player. He could use the money to finance a fight against the North Americans who paid him; what a wonderful idea!

Anyhow, this lady's husband was away in Santiago for his American-owned company, Dumois-Nipe, a subsidiary of United Fruit, and so the young man's dalliance had a double-meaning: he was screwing her and he was therefore screwing Dumois-Nipe. In bed, he was magnificent, a tiger, an athlete again, and the sheets grew heavy with the sweat of his labor and the woman sang, and the birds fluttered and the clouds parted. Like a matador, he worked her slowly, turning her this way, then that, encouraging her, partaking in her power, until the two were joined in a dance that was both spectacular and tragic. He rammed in for the kill.

'Oh,' she said afterwards, 'I had forgotten what a young man can do. You look so tender with those warm eyes and that soulful smile, and yet you are so strong. What a man you are!'

He sat back, lit a cigar and loved the wonderful warm wash of afternoon light, the smell of sex and sweat and cigars, the nearness of the jungle with all its savagery, the farness of the Sierras, cool and remote and vast and beckoning, as if they knew secrets.

'Will I see you again?'

'Of course. But only for a while. Soon I must go back to Havana where a destiny awaits me.'

'I assume you will marry a rich girl and join the country club and learn to play golf and drink with the Americans.'

'That is where you are wrong. I will take the rich girl's money and give it to many poor girls, I will turn all the golf courses into agricultural collectives and I will frighten the Americans back to America.'

'Don't let them hear you talk like that, my hero. They don't like it, and they have their ways.'

'I have my ways, too,' he promised.

And that is how he waited for his clarification. He played the *beisbol* with the youngsters in the morning and fished or hunted in the afternoon. Then he wandered to Cueto and had a coffee and read the Havana papers. The furor over the violence of El Colorado and the swiftness of the justice had worn down somewhat, he determined, and he wondered how soon he could head back, with his many new ideas. He was ready for action.

Then, being ready for action, he went and found that action at the Señora Fugolensia's, and a good time was had by all. If the neighbors knew, they never told, for that is not the Cuban way. And if Señor Fugolensia, the assistant district manager for Dumois-Nipe, ever found out, there was no drama, no gossip, no fury. Everything was pleasant and relaxed, because everyone understood how it was in these matters. So the young man had a wonderful time, really, growing fat and sleek and lazy, until Havana seemed just a bad dream. He knew he would go back but, well . . . maybe not tomorrow. Maybe not until next week or the next, and when it came to pass that he was discovered, the agent of his betrayal was not a spy or a snitch or a traitor or an American gofer, but simple chance. One day the next week, Captain Latavistada and Frankie Carbine happened to be driving through Cueto, as they had been driving through all the dusty towns around Mayari, including Guaro and Alto Cedro and Felton and Antillas, and it was Frankie who happened to be looking a certain direction. He saw the young man sitting in a cafe.

They followed him.

Who could have predicted it? And the young man was laughing and tickling his older lady and wondering also when all this would be finished, and he didn't even notice the captain getting the Mendoza 7mm light machine gun out of the trunk of his car, while Frankie checked the magazine in the Star machine pistol. The young man was too busy thinking of love and destiny.

31

It took a while, going through several operators and various connections and then, finally, she was not there. So he waited up in his room, feeling unpleasant about all this. He knew it was both right and wrong at once and that's what he hated so much about it. He knew this was an opportunity, that it could lead them to a better life, a life undreamed of, seen only in magazines. Yet he did not trust these men at all, not even a little bit. They wanted something too much. He hated that sense of the pressure against him, their wills, expressing themselves in small ways. It wasn't like the service. In the service you had orders, in the highway patrol you had procedures, and everything was what it was and no other thing, not really. This was different. Maybe what one boy said was the right move and maybe what another said, and if you guess wrong it all blew up in your face. It was all part of a world he'd never quite trusted, expressed in a secret language of gesture and pause and hint that he never quite understood. He didn't see how he could be comfortable in such a place. But there was the issue of family, too: if he could make a certain kind of success for himself and for them, if he could give his son opportunities, didn't he owe it to the boy? His old man had never given him shit for opportunities, and he wouldn't be like that. He'd die before he was like that. If nothing else, he would give the boy some opportunities.

He tried again, though it was too soon. Back in Arkansas it would have been about 6:00 P.M.; she should be back home now, making supper for herself and the boy. But it was summer. The boy was out of school. He'd been in school when all this had begun, now he was out, as it was getting into late June. Who knew where they'd gone? Maybe they'd gone out for a little picnic or over to the Blue Eye drive-in, where the boy had the hot dogs and root beer that he loved so much. Maybe it was a church gathering or a —

But she answered.

The operator explained to her that it was long-distance from overseas and clicking and snapping filled the wire and then it was just the two of them.

'Oh, hi,' he said, 'it's me,' as if it could be anyone else.

'Good lord, Earl, I jump six feet every time the phone rings. I was in the garden the last time and couldn't get here in time.'

'I'm sorry. It's these operators. She hung up too fast.'

'How are you? They called from the congressman's office and said you'd been hurt a little, but they didn't have any details. They said you were a hero and would get another medal. But they didn't say anything else. So I called Colonel Jenks and he didn't know either.'

'Sorry, I should have called. Yes, I was hurt some, but it wasn't a thing. I'm fine. I'm out of the hosp — '

'The hospital!'

'It's all better. I have a limp, but it'll go away.'

'Good lord, Earl, what happened?'

'Oh, it was a law-enforcement situation, there was a little shooting, and I got nicked. It's nothing.'

'Earl, you never learn. Now you are risking your life for less than nothing, meaning that braying toad Harry Etheridge, whom I wouldn't trust any further than I could throw the Frigidaire.'

'Boss Harry is nothing to take home, you are right on that score.'

'Earl, you get back here. Your boy misses you terribly. He just looks out the window like a sad sack. I can't get him to play ball or anything. The last time you were gone for so long, he was so young he didn't really understand. Now he knows you're gone and I can see him hurting inside. He's getting quieter and quieter.'

'Well, see, that's the thing. As you know, Congressman Harry's gone home. But see, I have an opportunity here.'

'Oh, lord.'

'It's with the government. There's some work they think I can do for them. They like me, they've made me what looks like a right fine offer.'

'Earl, you are happy in Arkansas and so am I. You don't need anything from the government. Last time you worked for the government, you were shot seven times, all over the Pacific. I thought that was over, but now you're with the government and you've been shot again. And all

242

so soon after the last time you were away — and it took a full year before you were fully yourself on that one, and God knows what you did, and not even Sam will tell me a word about it. You just say, as you always say, 'It was nothing.' '

'Junie, it's the boy I'm thinking about. If I got a big job in Washington we could live in a much nicer place, he could go to better schools and have a life we can't dream of.'

'Yes, that's wonderful, it's all for Bob Lee, but it involves some kind of helling around and there'll be more shooting and in your heart of hearts that's what you love. You're an old dog so used to blood sport you still go all slobbery at the thought. I know you, Earl, but I also know that as big a hero as you are, you will run dry on luck one time out. Maybe the next time out. That boy doesn't need a hero, he needs a father. No boy can live up to a hero. He'll die trying and you'll already have died being one.'

'Junie, I have to take this chance. I'd be no good to myself if I didn't, honey. I won't wait so long to call the next time.'

'Oh, Earl,' she said, 'you never change. Not a bit, not in all these years. I love you.'

'I love you too, Junie.'

She hung up and the click sounded loud and far-off at once.

He looked around, trying to chase the black dogs that nipped at him and made him hunger for a drink, because that was the sure thing that would chase them off. Only then they'd come back, meaner than ever. He knew he couldn't stay in the room, since it was still early and he

243

could feel Havana somehow happening outside the walls.

So he told himself he needed some air. He took the elevator down, just a big crewcut American in an old khaki suit and a white shirt and old Marine Corps brogues, and walked through the lobby, filled up with louder duplicates of himself, and out into the streets. Across the way, the Parque Central was jammed up with people who mingled this way and that or argued baseball or drank beer. They sure seemed happy. The Cubans loved to talk and drink and hug and smoke. He never saw a people that knew how to have a better time. He wandered a bit through the crowds and under the trees, thinking he might mosey over there to that Hotel Inglaterra where a party seemed to be going on, but then the crowd seemed to push him in a different direction, he left the park, he wandered down busy streets drawn by the sound of the jivey, fast-stepping Cuban music. Who could deny the magic of that stuff? All kinds of little bars and clubs seemed jammed up and swinging hard, full of revelers, and he tried to pick a one that he'd feel comfortable in. He wandered along cobblestones and didn't feel like going as far as the Bodeguita del Medio, and after a while he found a clean, well-lighted place called La Floridita that looked less Cuban than the other places, more big-city America.

In he went, finding himself in a dark hall that was all bar at one side and all people everywhere else, while a mambo crew wandered about, paying out that blood rhythm of the Cubano

244

music. Earl took a reading and divined that he liked the place, that it was too crowded for problems and that there were enough Americans here so he would feel pretty much at home. He slipped through crowds of merrymakers until he found space at the bar. Some kind of party was going on and the place was full of action; he could feel whatever it was pounding in the air, loud as the music, a hum of drama. It was as if ballplayers were here, but they couldn't be, because it was the end of June, the season had been running near to three full months. Maybe movie people, but Earl didn't know anything about movie people, so none of the faces were recognizable to him. He turned his back on it, and when the barkeeper came up, in his red jacket and black tie, so fancy, Earl tried out his brothel Spanish to get a gin and tonic with no gin, but plenty of tonic. The cooling of the liquid helped some, and he had another pretend-drink, just minding his own business. Everyone seemed to be drinking milkshakes in cocktail glasses and behind the curved bar there was some kind of highly idealized view of the harbor as it must have looked from a conqueror's ship heading inward. It was somewhere along in here when he became aware that a new person was next to him, and that she was staring at him.

He looked over.

Well, sometimes it happens. She was what the boys would call a knockout. She was dark and brown, and he saw not Cuban, but some sort of Asian — Filipina, maybe. But she had white in her too, and something fierce in her eyes that

245

he'd only seen in Japanese field-grade officers, a kind of bravado and swagger that just drew you in.

'You're a big one,' she said.

'I happen to be, yes, ma'am.'

'Are you tough?'

'What?'

'I said, are you tough?'

'Not really.'

'Damn.'

'What's the problem.'

'I've got this big guy pawing me. He won't take no for an answer. Coming here was a big mistake, but I can't seem to get away.'

'Ma'am, I can't fight him for you. It doesn't work that way. I don't need the trouble and people get hurt bad in fights. Best bet is call a cab and walk fast for it and he's probably too drunk to come after. Or have the barkeep call the cops.'

'You're a cop yourself, I can tell.'

'That's true. But I'm not on any kind of duty here. I'm just telling you what I think would work for you.'

'Yes, that would work in Manhattan. But this is Havana and this guy's a god around here. These cops and the barkeepers all love him.'

'Well, I could walk you out and get you a cab a block away. Don't want no trouble.'

But trouble, alas, was already there.

Earl felt a hand on his arm, and he was spun around with just enough force to imply the possibility of violence, and he found himself staring into the square, handsome face of a large

246

American male. The fellow looked like some kind of Viking, bronze and broad and incredibly alive with hostility, a gristle of white beard clinging to but not quite obscuring his pugnacious jaw.

'Say, bub,' the man said to him, 'what the hell is going on here? Is he bothering you, Jean-Marie?'

'No, he is not bothering me. *You* are bothering me. Please, I just want to get out of here.'

'You hear that, mister?' the man said. 'You've upset the gal and she wants to leave. Who do you think you are, anyway?'

Earl was aware immediately that this was a strange situation. Everybody was staring at him. A semicircle had formed around them, the music had stopped, even the clink of the glasses landing on the marble tabletops had stopped.

'Sir, the lady asked me to call her a cab, that's all. I think I'll just go ahead and do that, if you don't mind.'

'Well, pal, it seems I do mind. Hmmm, don't we have a problem here though. It's called face. I'm bracing you so *I* can't back down, and you don't look like you've got much back-down in you either.'

'Sir, I don't want any trouble.'

A broad grin spread across the man's face, as if he'd just drawn better cards against good cards.

'Do you know who I am?'

'No, sir.'

'Sure you don't. You know, this happens to me

all the time. Guys get lit up when they see me and they get all scratchy because they want to be the lion. So they come up to me. Oh, and when I don't back down, then all of a sudden they *don't* want to be the lion anymore. That's all right. I'm going to go easy on you. I'll just walk away with my female friend here and you go back to your little soda pop and it'll be — '

'That'd be fine, sir, if that's what she wants.'

'I don't want to go away with you, Mr. Hemingway,' said the Asian woman, Jean-Marie. 'I want to stay here.'

'Well,' said Earl, 'there you have it.'

The big man looked Earl up and down.

'I'm a boxer,' he said.

'Done some of that myself,' said Earl.

'I could flatten you in two seconds.'

'I don't think so.'

'Oh, well, I guess you showed *me*. Look, pal, let's part friends, okay?'

And with that the man threw his punch. It was absurdly telegraphed, as he pivoted just a bit, cocked his right shoulder, cocked his arm, and set his right foot before launch. The big fist flew at Earl like some sort of softball pitch from a woman, and as it swept toward him, Earl almost cracked a smile.

He ducked under it easily enough, then slipped an equally slow and oafish thing thrown with the left, where the man was not nearly as coordinated, and then Earl kicked hard, and both the man's legs flew out from under him and he hit the tiles with a crash. His arms and legs flew akimbo as he rolled, breathing hard, then he drew himself together as if to make another rush at Earl.

Earl bent close.

'Now, sir, I'd stay down. You could get hurt. I can use either my left or my right to work jabs into your middle and then knock you into 1965 with the other. I'll kill your guts so your hands quit and when they die, I'll kill your head. I don't want to go to no prison for breaking your jaw or nothing. You just stay put, and have a good laugh along with the rest of the folks.'

The man just glared at him, but made no move to get up.

Earl stood, turned to the exotic woman and said, 'You know, let's get you that cab.'

'Excellent idea,' she said.

They walked out hastily, pushing through the crowd that parted to let them by, turned left at the sidewalk, and soon separated entirely from La Floridita, down another nameless street, also choked with bars and people.

'Who are you?' she said.

'You wouldn't know the name. I'm nobody. Earl Swagger,' he replied.

'Oh!' She leaned back and appraised him. 'The bodyguard. Yes, that's who you'd be, all right. You're the big hero. Everybody says you're joining the bright young men on the third floor.'

'I don't know what that means,' Earl said.

'Oh, you can't keep secrets here, in a little town like this one. Really, I'd have thought you're a little straight-ahead for those boys. They think they're really clever. I wouldn't get too close to them. Roger's all right, but that creepy little assistant of his? I hate the way he pretends like he's not paying attention but you can see him writing everything down in his subconscious.'

'Thank you for the advice.'

'And I have to know. You really didn't know who that man was?'

'No.'

'Mr. Swagger, you are priceless. Really, I love it. Served him right, the blowhard. Hemingway. The writer. Famous, rich. He's a big fisherman and game hunter.'

'Seems I've heard the name,' said Earl, trying to place it, 'but I can't say where. Shotguns, is that it? He's some kind of shotgun expert.'

'I'm sure he is. Well, you made him look foolish.'

'I can't worry about that. He made himself look foolish.' Earl scanned the street for a cab. 'Look, there's one. Cab! *Cabbie!*'

His command voice got through the babble and the cab pulled over.

Earl escorted her to it, opened the rear door.

'There you go,' he said.

'You're not even going to buy me a drink or wait for me to invite you over?'

'Ma'am, I probably got myself in enough trouble back there. I don't need no other tonight.'

'No, I think the little boys you play with will think you're really cool. Not that you care. That's what I like about you, Mr. Swagger. You really don't care what people think, do you?'

'To be honest, no, I guess I don't, ma'am.'

She reached in her purse, and pulled out a card.

'Please don't call me ma'am. I'm not your great aunt. I'm Jean-Marie Augustine. I manage the TWA office here in town; my husband's a pilot, not that he's ever here. Anyway, this is a dangerous town, Mr. Swagger. I'm giving you my card. If you need a friend, you give me a call. I know people, I can make phone calls, I speak Spanish like it's my own language, because it is my own language. I can help you.'

'Thank you,' he said, 'but I'm not planning on staying around long.'

She laughed.

'That's what I said when I got here ten years ago. Good night, Mr. Swagger.'

'Goodnight, Mrs. Augustine.'

'By the way, you belong on this street. This is the street where you live.'

'My street?'

'Yes, look.'

She gestured to a painted sign on a building front right at the corner that identified the thoroughfare: Calle Virtudes, it said.

'Kai-yay Ver-tude-ez,' she said hard and fast, with a particularly forceful roll to the R's of Verrr-tude-ez.

'What?'

'It's the street where you live. I can tell.'

'I don't get it.'

'In English, it's Virtue Street.'

She smiled, closed the door and the taxi rolled away.

32

'You go in back. If you see him, kill him. Shoot him many times. Stand over him and fill him with bullets. I will do the same from here.'

'Uh, you want signals or anything, Ramon?'

'We don't need no fucking signals. Come on, my friend, let's go kill something big.'

In hunting frenzy, Captain Latavistada seemed to change character entirely. His brow sweated, his skin radiated heat and sweat, he trembled with anticipation. It was not at all that he was scared; it was that he was so happy. He seemed about to slide into a state of slaughter glee so intense that all other things were closed out. It was as if he didn't really remember who Frankie was. He just wanted to close on the prey and kill it hard.

'Vamos, amigo!' he barked at Frankie, who had never heard that tone of voice from his new colleague before, but recognized it as something rare and valuable. It meant Ramon was more than a mere torturer; he was the rare man who loved battle.

Frankie looked at the Star machine pistol in his hands, not that he had any idea how to run it. As machine pistols go, it seemed to have more knurled knobs and levers than it needed. But weren't they all pretty much the same? You point, you squeeze, you squirt, and something has a whole lot of holes in it fast. He'd done the same work in the French bookstore in Times Square, with a gun just as strange, so he felt loaded for bear, his own heart going thump-athump, as he headed alongside the house just as Captain Latavistada, with the big light machine gun, headed up the walk.

Frankie got around back, and thank god there were no kids, no dog, no maid — no horse. Shit like that got in the way. He climbed up on a patio, unsure what to do, and squatted for just a second under the canopy of a lush palm, amid ornate wrought-iron furniture, aware of the sun, the heat, the perfume of the flowers, the buzz of insects. Before him were two screen doors which led into separate sections of the house. He tried to decide which to go through when choice was taken from him and he jumped in surprise. For whatever reason, Captain Latavistada suddenly opened up, and the roar of the gun, even on the other side of the house, was deafening.

★   ★   ★

Castro enjoyed the second half of the cigar more than the first half; that's where the buzz was, and it loosened tiny vibrations in his head. He lay back, naked, and watched the smoke drift and curl above him. It was the smoke of history, drifting this way or that, and only a strong man could make it obey him. He had that strength. He had known for some time. It was evident in the way others respected him and yearned for his attention and his command authority. It was evident when he spoke, and the words magically appeared in front of him, and he had the crowd and could mold it to his wishes, make it a violent animal or a weeping mother. It was evident in the way that he always won his debates and could ever so quickly assemble facts into an argument with an iron will, unassailable, imperturbable, as solid as a force of nature. It was evident in the way he saw swiftly into the heart of things, to their absolute center, and could master complex systems like Marxism in mere hours, sharpening them to the chisel point of their truth, and then seeing exactly how they would be applied in practical situations. He had never met anyone like himself, or anyone who could stand up to him or *mother of Jesus have mercy on your poor sinner lord Jesus look after me for I have sinned please dear lord do not end my days on earth here in this place though I am unworthy and* —

The thunder of explosions, so loud it paralyzed him, became the dominant feature in his universe. There was nothing else. As he prayed, he lay frozen while the percussions intermingled with the roar of carnage as the atmosphere of the house was savaged, and filled with chaos and fear. His fear. He quaked, he froze, he whimpered, he prayed, he almost shit. Then it was silent. He heard clicks, scrapings, the heavy breathing of physical effort. He sensed his enemy, his would-be assassin, very close. Then the wall above his head exploded, spraying him with plaster dust and wood scraps, like the blast of a high-pressure hose. And the noise at that precise moment was momentous. In fact the whole world was turning monstrously unstable, as across the room, where Señora Fugolensia had pictures of the Holy Mother as well as herself, her husband and assorted relatives, that too began to dissolve or dance, pulverized into a mist of plaster dust, torn wood, what have you.

He knew enough to know he was being fired upon by someone with a large automatic gun. He wanted to be far away and hiding his face in his mother's bosom. But then his reflexes took over, he rolled to the floor and began to crawl for the far exit as another raking burst sawed its rough way through the room.

★   ★   ★

The captain kicked open the doorway. The gun was like a mystical lance in his hand, yearning to express his contempt for the soft bourgeoisie world that hadn't the spine to do what must be done, which sentimentalized revolution and found it fascinating, which adored the deviant, the non-pious, the arriviste. All his pathologies were gloriously astir and his loins burned with fervor. He needed to crush, to kill, to obliterate, to establish his primacy. He desperately needed an enemy.

What he found was a dumpy naked woman whose titties sagged, who had a plump belly above her bush, who ate a piece of toast in the kitchen and looked at him with utter bewilderment. Had she shown fear he might have let her live but it angered him that she did not immediately yield to his magnificence, so he cut

255

her in half with the Mendoza 7mm, emptying a whole magazine into her. Blood flew everywhere, a hurricane of the stuff, spraying wall and kitchen appliances and tabletops and floor with equal disdain.

Amazing how quickly a twenty-round box will use itself up. Quickly, he ejected the spent magazine from the top of the weapon, pulled another out of his pocket, slammed it home, and pivoted with the heavy weapon — eighteen pounds, its bipod wavering as it swung — and fired another magazine into the center of the house.

The destruction was magnificent. The gun was a god. Wherever he pointed it, the world erupted as if by a volcano's fury, and things disintegrated or danced or simply vaporized. The atmosphere filled with dust and smoke. A pipe shattered and water spurted out of the walls. It was as if the house itself were bleeding. Empty shells cascaded out of the hot gun, littering the floor. It was a profound experience for the captain to be the humble bringer of such grief to a world.

Jesus Cristo, no more ammo. Again, the thing was like a wet dog, that just shook itself empty in one spasm. Laboriously, he dropped to one knee — his shoulder ached — opened the latch that ran along the top of the receiver next to the magazine well, popped out the magazine, pulled another from his pocket, inserted it till the latch clicked, then reached forward along the barrel and pulled and released the bolt with a snappity-snap-snap.

He rose. Now where was this *cabrone*, eh?

Where had this little puppy fled to? Come to papa, little boy. Papa has a present for you. Come ahead, my son. I have a nice surprise for you.

★ ★ ★

God, is he done shooting? wondered Frankie. He had no desire to get nailed by his good friend the captain, who seemed to have gone a little screwball with the machine gun. He was blasting *everything*. That's how these people did it, they just waded in and started whacking. But Frankie saw himself catching a stitch of eleven or so slugs up the gut and bleeding out under palm trees, far from New York's grit, him with all his big plans and new possibilities. That he did not want.

So he hung back, content to let the captain do the massacring, allowing himself the responsibility of the mop-up. The captain fired again.

★ ★ ★

Castro found refuge in the bathtub. He endured bombardment by pulverization and thunder, as whoever was shooting expended a whole magazine into the bathroom. A bullet ricocheted off the tub with a gong of death, and veered who knew where. He lay naked and vulnerable, aware that he shared the tub with pieces of glass and wood, with chunks of metal, with a significant accrual of dust and debris. He knew also that he was dead. How long before they found him?

257

The captain looked at the adulteress's bed. Its sheets were rumpled and sweaty and the stains of sexual exchange were smeared here and there. He smelled a lover's cigar as well. He had just finished a hose-job on the bathroom and the closet, riddling both. But the bed insulted his Cuban manhood. It reeked of illicit pleasure, so it was in direct competition both with his brothels and with his intense Catholic faith. Something atavistic rose in him, and instead of looking for the man he had come to kill, he decided to punish the bed.

This was an event of incredible carnage. The bullets tore into pillows and sent puffs of feathers exploding into the air, to fill the room with snow, while at the same time the mattress itself leapt as if in great animal pain as bullets buckled it. As the magazine wore itself out, the bed gave up the ghost, so to speak: it tilted crazily as rounds tore away the two far-side legs, a spring popped from the mattress like a dying snake, dust flew, empty shell casings flew, the whole a drama of extraordinary sensual pleasure.

Then the gun was dry.

Mother of God!

He knelt, pulled the old mag out, and was reaching into his pocket for another when a naked man flew out of the bathroom with a look of abject terror on his face, eyes bugged like fried eggs, flaccid body so white and pale with fear it was almost a comical scene from a movie. To make it more ridiculous, this naked figure had

258

shod himself with his mistress's slippers to protect his feet from the glass, so there he was, immense, white, terrified, naked, his equipment flopping, running like a bunny rabbit and poor Captain Latavistada could only watch him go, for he could not get the magazine into the gun fast enough.

'Frankie!' he screamed.

★　★　★

The doors blew open and Frankie stared into the terrified, scrambled face of his quarry.

This was it. The Star machine pistol came up, the range was five feet, six at the outside, the mark was jaybird naked and terrified to see another gunman, and Frankie fired.

Except he didn't.

Fungool, it didn't work.

He looked at it in his hands, saw various knobs set this way and not that, jiggered them and then the gun fired but did not stop. It ate a magazine in two seconds, and the bullets just rose on the house, cutting a stitchery of dust and then flying off into space.

But the naked man, meanwhile, threw himself off the balcony and ran amazingly fast, pink slippers flying from his feet as he disappeared into some jungle shrubbery. Frankie had his .45 out by this time and sent seven pills into the weeds after him, maybe hitting him, maybe not. The captain was next to him, and clearly he was not yet done shooting, for he heaved the machine gun upwards and unleashed another

259

whole, jolting, jackhammering magazine that more or less chewed up the area into which the man had disappeared.

'Ha!' said the captain, his face aglow with sweat. 'It's wonderful, eh? Such fun! Hunting men, god, what sensual pleasure! How alive one feels!'

'Uh, he seems to have gotten away.'

'Possibly. But he is naked and wounded and in a jungle. I do not think he will get far.'

Frankie nevertheless had a sense of great disturbance in the world. He knew a bad thing had happened, and he would have some explaining to do to Mr. Lansky. Then he peered back into the house and saw nothing but devastation; it had been shot to pieces.

'Ramon,' he asked nervously, 'shouldn't we get out of here before the police come?'

Ramon looked at him, incredulous.

'Señor Frankie, you forget. We are the police.'

33

He lay naked in thornbushes. Every bit of him hurt. His heart would not stop hammering. It was now dark. His mind was still scattered. He was in jungle. He had run naked through jungle for what seemed hours. He had no idea what to do. He yearned for guidance and courage, but none came.

And then a lot came.

He had a moment of perfect clarity. It all fell together: the government had tracked him here. Those were members of the Secret Police. They had come to kill him, so that El Presidente could sleep without fear of his throat being cut in the night.

At last he knew what to do, and what came next, and where his destiny lay. It was not in strikes or speeches or elections.

I shall, he thought, now make a war.

34

'Well?' said Pashin.

'Well, *what?*' said Speshnev.

'Well, where is he?'

'Where it is safe.'

'Where it is safe. But do you know where it is safe?'

'Actually, I do not.'

They sat in José Martí square in the old town, two men, one elegant in his western banker's clothes, the other rather bohemian, in floppy linens, with a red bandanna about his head and well-worn espadrilles on his crusty feet. This one also wore sunglasses, circular and aesthetic, protecting the poet's delicate eyes from the sun. One might consider it a meeting between T. S. Eliot and Ezra Pound, if one were so given.

Speshnev took a banana out of his pocket, peeled it, and began to eat it.

'He has run away. He has broken contact,' Pashin explained to him. 'You were sent here to manage him and control him, and then to kill a man sent to kill him. Instead, you save that killer — twice, *twice!* — and now the subject has fled your ministrations and I am left to explain all this to Moscow. Possibly he has given up politics altogether, bought a farm and is busy raising babies in the countryside.'

'The banana: fountain of potassium. Have one, Pashin.'

'I am not a monkey. Bananas are for monkeys.'

'Two propositions, both debatable. Anyhow, this one will never give up politics. He's too idiotic. He actually believes in the mumbo-jumbo of destiny. Besides, he loves to practice speeches in the mirror and admire his fabulous heroism and beauty. No, I sent him because after the murder of El Colorado, I feared a general purge. It's how these fascisto-imperialists always work. Relax. Have a banana. Fuck your secretary.'

'Ah! You are so disrespectful. We have a mission and you take better care of an American gangster who was sent here to kill the man you were sent here to protect than you do of the man you are to protect.'

'Actually, I believe I have protected him very well.'

'You are so arrogant, Speshnev. You think you know so much more than we younger men.' Pashin looked away, pinching the bridge of his nose in pain. It was clear he was getting pretty much roasted on a daily basis by blistering memos from Moscow.

Speshnev enjoyed the young bastard's pain. 'Have you thought of antacids for that stomach queasiness, Pashin?'

Pashin sighed mightily, with the air of a man resigned to the Roman legionnaires driving in the spikes. It was an unpleasant necessity to be gotten over. But then he turned and stared directly at the older man.

'It may interest you to learn yours is not the only operation in Cuba, and that I believe mine will yield far more bountiful benefits than yours. Mine is professional, disciplined, carefully managed. This shit of yours was dreamed up by some old romantic on the upper floors of Dzerzhinsky Square and it's all very melodramatic, very old Comintern, but utterly useless in a world of jet planes and atom bombs. Mine will be the far greater contribution.'

'And if not, your uncles and brothers and cousins will say so anyway, so what difference does it make?'

'You must find the young man, you must bring him under control, you must reestablish your influence. That is not a romantic quest, that is a hard order, direct from the top. And, you must do it soon, do you understand? Let us say toward the end of the month, by, say, the last week of July. Do you understand?'

'I do.'

'I want progress.'

Speshnev swallowed the last third of the banana, mashing its sweetness between his teeth, enjoying the rush of pleasure as both flavor and aroma toasted his palate, then tossed the banana peel into the garbage can.

Of course he knew where Castro was. He knew where he would go exactly but what bothered him he would not say to Pashin. In fact, as he was summoned to the meeting, he had already purchased bus fare to Santiago.

The reason was that he knew Castro would head home to Oriente, where he was a prince. He would not go somewhere he was not known and loved. He wasn't strong enough for

264

anonymity. His vanity was too overwhelming. It would never be a part of his way to disappear quietly. He was too weak for it.

But Speshnev had read an account in that morning's *Havana Post* that upset him profoundly. Police 'thwarted a bandit attack in the town of Cueto,' the press reported, and a woman was killed in the gun battle. That was what the newspaper report said, and Speshnev had no doubt it was all lies. Nevertheless, whatever it was, such action was uncomfortably near Castro's home, and it signified that possibly others undreamed of had noted the boy's presence and sought to eliminate him.

Now he reasoned that even if he weren't involved, the shooting so close would spook the boy. But the trip back to Havana would seem too far; he would instead hide in the closest city, that city being Santiago.

But the fear of Castro somehow being caught — he had as yet committed no crimes — wasn't Speshnev's main fear. His main fear could be summed up in one sentence: What will this crazy young asshole do next?

35

Lansky hated the theater of it. It ate up time for no good reason, when he had a million things to do. It was all so unnecessary, for who down here was really paying much attention?

But the Important Man insisted. The Important Man laid out the rules and Lansky, who always played by the rules until he saw a way to bust them, and the bank too, obeyed.

His driver took him from his apartment in the Sevilla-Biltmore just off the Prado, into the old city, down winding, crowded roads, past houses built by the Spanish and the Creoles. Then the car curved around to the west, passed through grimy industrial neighborhoods, down busy streets, twisting now and then through smaller streets, then found a main concourse around Centro and soon plunged toward Santo Suarez.

While he was in the car, Lansky changed from his well-tailored suit into something awful and cheesy: a loud Hawaiian shirt, a pair of ill-fitting lemon slacks and, most annoying to a man who loved the leather of fine shoes, some ridiculous sandals that exposed his toes to the world. A man of Lansky's dignity and probity should never face the world with his toes exposed. Then, to top it off, a porkpie and a pair of rattly sunglasses. A sleek business executive had gotten into the car, a man of sharp intelligence and subtle tastes, and a low-rent whore-chaser climbed out. It made him quite annoyed.

He was let out near the bus station, where he caught a no. 4 bus all the way out past Santo Suarez, and then got off. He walked among negroes out there, past dives and joints and pool halls all bleached white in the sun, past bodegas and farmacias and lottery agencies, until at last he came to a cheap negro hotel, went in without talking, passed the desk without talking, and took the ancient lift without talking to the fourth floor.

There was a door ajar. Sometimes it was this room, sometimes that, depending, but the door ajar signified which. He approached, knocked, entered without hearing a thing, closed and locked the door behind him. The Important Man sat on the bed or in a chair, again depending on what was available in the room.

This time he was in a shabby chair by a dirty window, in semi-darkness, looking out on Santo Suarez. He barely acknowledged Lansky.

Lansky sat next to him.

There was never any ceremony, as with the old men, no elaborate ritual of politeness and asking after family, not at all. He would remain silent for hours if Lansky didn't, by habit, just get to it.

'What is it this time?' Lansky asked.

'You know what it is,' said the Important Man.

'I don't have any idea.'

'Then your intelligence is very poor. Three days ago in the rural province of Oriente, some cops shot the hell out of a house, killing a woman. She was naked in her own house, they blew the living hell out of her, and shot the

267

house to tatters. I've seen the reports, of course.'

'An American woman?'

'A Cuban woman.'

'What has this to do with me or my enterprise? What has it to do with yours? Why is this important?'

'Because it wasn't a raid, as everyone is saying too loud, but a hit.'

'Hmmm,' said Lansky.

'Yes, hmmm,' said the other. 'It was a botched, pathetic, out of control screw-up of a hit. It was bullets flying, the wrong person killed, the neighbors in hysteria, rumors flying, the Secret Police Political Section in a frenzy, and when they go nuts, we hear about it, we have to file reports to Washington, Washington goes nuts and asks more questions, the business climate suffers, the whole goddamned apparatus gets shaky.'

'I don't know a thing about it.'

'Of course you do. You ordered it.'

Lansky didn't say a thing.

'I have sources. I know things. I *told* you to clear anything through me.'

'I was under some pressure from my people after that congressman almost got clipped. They have a lot of money invested down here and more set to come. They don't want to lose it.'

'We don't want them to lose it either. We don't want AT&T or Hilton Hotels or United Fruit or Hershey or Domino Sugar to lose. We cannot allow that to happen.'

'There is a threat. Nobody was doing a thing. We acted.'

'You acted ridiculously and poorly. Was it that

268

weasel New York guy who made a scene at the party? He's more volatile than the usual cheap thugs New York sends down. He'll scare these businesspeople. We don't like that.'

'He has his uses. He is supposedly very good.'

'Well, here's what he accomplished. He failed to hit the target because the whole thing was poorly planned and pitifully executed. He drove the target underground. *Completely* underground. Political Section has no idea where he is. Worse, we have no idea what he'll do now that someone has tried to kill him.'

'He has no organization.'

'But he has leadership skills. He will get an organization fast, and that upsets us a great deal. He can start things that can't be stopped. That's the way it happens sometimes. Now he's beyond reach, unless we turn the island upside down.'

'Nobody was doing a thing!'

'Again, you are misinformed. In fact, the opposite is true. We are very much doing something. We've brought a man down. An excellent, tested, experienced man, not some screwball New York eyetie button. We're tracking it all very carefully, manipulating it quite smoothly, building for the moment. Our man won't miss.'

'I did not know this.'

'You don't have to know it. You have to clear initiatives through me, so I can ascertain whether or not we are working at cross-purposes. If we are working at cross-purposes, as we now are, it happens as it has now happened, with each move making it harder, not easier, on the other's move.'

'All right,' said Lansky.

'Yes, all right. So you back way off. You put this New York gunman on the shelf, do you understand?'

'Yes.'

'Let's be clear: your team, off the field. Our team has operating room. It will happen, and everybody will prosper.'

'For a certain amount of time. You people have to move quickly, as I am under pressure. Pick a date. I give you a month. Say, by late July. You must do this job by then, or I will let my people go at it again. After that time, my man is back on the case, and he may not be tidy, but he will be successful.'

'I will — '

'This happened because you were sleeping and it got too far. So now we may have to clean up after you. My advice: do your job, so that we don't have to do it. It's much better for all of us that way.'

'We will do the job. It's in the cards. We have an expert.'

'Excellent. I'd offer to buy you a drink, but it appears to me you're too young to drink.'

'I look younger than I am,' said Frenchy Short, 'but I think older than I am, too.'

36

For the longest time, nothing happened. A week passed, then another. It seemed Roger and Frenchy were busy each day, coordinating with sources, making plans, contacting Washington, reading reports. That left little for Earl to do, so he just wandered Old Havana most days, enjoying the denseness of it, staying out of bars, sitting on benches, learning the town. It always helped to know the town. He watched the cops too, with their dark green uniforms and their tommy guns carried everywhere, sloppily but meaningfully. He could tell, just by reading bodies: everybody hated the cops.

Then one day it changed. Suddenly, action. Roger and Frenchy acquired a boy's aura of spy mystery in their behavior, telling him what they'd set up was absolutely necessary. It turned out to be a trip to the airport, but not the one Earl had imagined. Instead of catching the Air Cubana Connie for New York and then home, he encountered a deep blue Navy Neptune, diverted from sea patrol, its props spinning brightly in the sun. It had landed at one of the lesser strips, far from the big bright commercial jobs that brought the johns to Cuba by the thousands. He climbed aboard without anything by way of ceremony, though with some difficulty, as the pain in his hip was still present and when he wormed up that ladder under the plastic

271

bubble nose, he felt it but good. The flight to Guantanamo lasted two hours, as opposed to the twelve-hour ordeal by car of the original journey. Everyone involved was polite, almost deferential, but professionally discreet. He had been stamped with both the mystery and the glamour of the Agency, which meant that the young crewman, even the two young pilots of the Lockheed, regarded him with a certain necessary awe, just a step or two down from trembling in his presence.

This was funny to Earl, who had professionally hated the navy second only to the Japanese for all those years in the Pacific. In fact, his hatred of the navy dated back further than that, to a certain forgotten episode at Norfolk in 1934. But that was nineteen years ago; no need to think of it now.

Instead, he sat back as Cuba rushed by beneath him. It was green and dense, cut by mountains humped up toward the eastern extremes, a kind of endless Guadalcanal.

The plane vectored in through mountains unlike anything he'd seen on the island's jungly flatness, and it came to rest on an airstrip that seemed to be in the middle of America. America was everywhere he looked. Officers awaited him. They were from what he guessed would be called Naval Intelligence, and they took him once again to blank but comfortable officer's quarters in the little America that was the Gitmo. He settled in to a steady barrage of the respect his mystery earned him, had a nice lunch with the two fellows in the Officer's Club, where he was waited on by a marine. Everybody called him Mr. Jones.

One of them, the one called 'Dan,' seemed especially curious about Roger Evans. How was Roger? Was Roger all right? Did Mr. Jones know Roger at Harvard? Oh, he knew Mr. Jones couldn't answer that, it's just that at Harvard after the war, Roger was such a piece of work, what with his medals, his war record, his ferocious tennis and his mysterious connections. Dan hoped Mr. Jones would say hello to Roger for him. Dan kept meaning to get to Havana to have a drink with Roger, but his duties — the Cold War, you know — kept him pinned here at Guantanamo.

After lunch, he was issued fatigues, and the two fellows drove him over hills and through glades until at last he was at a place where he knew he'd be home: the sign simply read COL. MERLE EDSON RIFLE RANGE, USMC. He knew who Colonel Edson was too, though had never met him: he was called 'Red Mike,' was a Nicaragua marine like Earl, and had led Edson's Raiders during the war. He was under a marker somewhere on Hawaii with most of the friends Earl ever made.

But what awaited him was only a gunny and a couple of lance corporals at one shooting pit. Far off, three hundred yards distant in the butts, a single target had been raised like a postage stamp on a pool table.

'Mr. Jones, the sergeant here will take care of you. We'll be back in two hours.'

'Thank you, Lieutenant Benning,' he said.

273

'Dan, please call me Dan, Mr. Jones.'

'Dan, then. Thanks, you've been very helpful.'

'We try to do our part.'

With that the officer smiled mysteriously, climbed back into the Navy Ford, and drove off.

Earl turned to face the gunny.

'Well, Earl, I won't ask how come that boy is calling you 'Mr. Jones'.'

'Hello, Ray. I thought that was you. Damn, it's good to see you.'

They shook hands with the warmth of men who'd shed and lost blood together in hard places.

'You too, Earl.'

'Last time I saw you was in the triage station on Saipan, right?'

'That's the one. I heard about you on Iwo. I was still in sick bay.'

'You were lucky to miss Iwo, Ray. Wasn't no place for human beings, I'll tell you. So what have you got for me?'

'Well, we were told to get a good rifle ready for a man from Washington.'

'Hell, I'm from Arkansas.'

'Earl, I just know I got orders and so I follow 'em. This has 'very important' ticketed all over it. They wanted us to mount up a sniper rifle and to take it out of inventory as if it never existed. That ain't no easy thing in the Marine Corps, where we got to watch every last damn penny.'

'Sorry for the trouble, Ray. These boys do business their own way. Can't say I like it much, but I signed on to something and I have to ride it out.'

'Well, I'm glad it's you getting this here rifle, Earl.'

'Ray, I'll get it back to you if I ain't damned dead.'

'Believe you, Earl.'

By this time they'd reached the cover just ahead of the shooting pits, where hundreds of marines gathered each day to zero or practice with their M1s. All training canceled today, of course.

Earl saw a rifle lying on one of the tables, almost like a religious icon presented during high mass.

'It's a Model 70, Earl, a Winchester.'

'Yes, I have one back in the rack at home,' he said. 'The barrel on mine is narrower.'

'The Marine Corps rifle team bought a mess of heavy-barreled target models back in the thirties for team high-power. Did right well with them, too. Major Schultz won the Wimbledon Cup in 1938, some big shooting match, very important. Our armorers bedded and adjusted the rifles and put a Unertl 8x scope on. Somehow we ended up with six of them for our rifle team down here. This here's the most accurate.'

Earl looked at the sleek tool, blued steel, wood brightly burnished, the whole dark thing much loved and tended after. It specialized in hitting black paper circles at a thousand yards.

'Well, let's see if it still remembers where the black is,' said Ray.

'Hell,' said Earl, 'let's see if *I* still remember where the black is.'

He got into a good prone, and the two lance corporals, evidently armorers, bent to fit the rifle to him. The sling had to be let out some so that he could get it cinched up tight. They coached him, for the intricacies of shooting cinched were something that, once drilled in him, hadn't stuck around. He'd never shot with a sling in combat, but then all his killing had been done up close.

Then there was the issue of getting the scope properly focused so that the crossed wires of the reticule stood out black and precise, yet what lay beyond them was still clear as well. This took some diddling, and the bad news was that Earl's vision had deteriorated some, so that he had to place his eye in a certain way for maximum efficiency of the system.

'You hunt any, Earl?' Ray asked, as Earl cracked a box of 173-grain brown-box ammo from the Frankford Arsenal and threaded the shells in behind the bolt, down into the magazine well.

'I do, and dearly love it. Took my son after his first whitetail this spring, but he decided not to take it.'

'I know he'll be a sure shot like his daddy.'

'I hope he don't never have to fire a rifle at a man,' said Earl.

He shoved the bolt forward and down where it locked like a vault door closing, then squirmed into position to find the rifle after a time — after his muscles quit ticking and stretching — pointing naturally so that the crosshairs bisected the black dot of the target three hundred yards out.

'Any time, Earl.'

Earl settled in, until it was only himself and the rifle, and then the himself part went away and only the rifle existed. He forced all his concentration on the intersection of the two dark lines in the dark of the spot that was the target, waiting for it all to settle. It never would, he knew, but he knew also that you had to read and feel your own breathing, so when the crosshairs fell through absolute center, you were already into your trigger press.

The gun snapped, jerked, rose an inch or two and settled back down. He watched as the target disappeared into the butts and anonymous men put a spindle through the hole. When it popped back into view he saw a white marker, lower left hand quadrant of the circle.

'Good shot. Fire again please, sir,' said the lance corporal hunched on the spotting scope.

Earl sent four more downrange, clustering his hits in that lower left area. Then he relaxed as the rifle was taken from him and the other lance corporal clicked the scope the prescribed amount of windage to the right.

Earl received the corrected rifle back and fired another cluster of five, this over to the right, but still under the bull. The lance corporal worked over the rifle again, and when it was returned with the new corrections, it put the cluster into three inches at the center of the bull.

'That's a good three hundred-yard combat zero. You still shoot a bushel, Earl.'

'I ain't forgot as much as I'd thought.'

For the next hour or so, they diddled. The young men coached Earl through his positions, and he forced reluctant muscles into positions they hadn't assumed in years. He practiced sitting, kneeling and offhand, the latter at a shorter range for snap shots.

'Trigger feel fine, sir?' asked one of the boys.

'Could let off a little more lightly,' Earl said, 'but not too lightly.'

'Yes, sir.'

The rifle was taken from him, broken down from its stock, and the tiny twin screws in the mechanism manipulated. Reassembled, a few ounces had vanished from the press. He requested more and it was done and measured to be a two-pound trigger, and was then slopped with shellac to keep the tiny screws from slipping under the pounding of recoil.

'We've made you a sniper, Earl.'

'Next thing you know, you'll be painting my old face green like a bush. Wouldn't that be a thing.'

'Earl, green. What a sight that would be.'

And then at four the Navy Ford returned with its two crisp officers in their tropic khakis, neatly pressed and ironed, a far cry from the sweaty marines who'd been working hard in the sun all afternoon.

The two didn't approach the marines directly. They parked and waited.

Earl waited as the two lance corporals quickly and effectively cleaned and greased the rifle, restoring it to a condition of maximum accuracy. Then after their nod, he placed the rifle and two boxes of the Frankford 173-grain brown-box ammo into a civilian gun case that had been thoughtfully provided, took it, shook hands and turned to go meet his sponsors.

'Earl,' said Ray, behind him, 'I hope you know what you're doing, getting mixed up with these birds.'

'I hope I do too,' said Earl.

★ ★ ★

Earl took a shower, changed into his suit and a fresh shirt, and went with the two officers to the Officer's Club, where as 'Mr. Jones' he felt himself the secret celebrity of a dull room full of dull naval officers and their dull wives. He saw the odd marine officer here and there, including an old-breed fellow here and there, and felt a longing to go over and say, 'Hey, I'm Earl Swagger, USMC, wonder if you'd mind if I joined you.' He knew they'd say, 'Hell no, Mr. Swagger, set yourself down and we'll listen to your sea stories and we'll tell you some of our own.' But that didn't happen, couldn't happen, wouldn't happen.

He had good steak and salad and passed on the drinks, though the two officers each belted back a couple of martinis apiece, and, loosened up, began to yap idiotically about 'it,' by which he took it they meant the Agency. They didn't say, but their curiosity was overwhelming. 'What's it like,' they wanted to know. 'How secret is it? How tough to get in?'

He knew the answers to none of their questions and really didn't give a damn about either of them, the kind of dandy, fancy,

279

educated boys who somehow didn't end up in the lines but always wangled intelligence or communications or staff. No, that wasn't true. There were a few who —

But a seaman, clutching his cap, came in and whispered something in Lieutenant Dan's ear, which sobered the young fellow up instantly.

'We heard from Roger,' he said. 'Finish up. You aren't getting another night on the navy. They want you in town but fast.'

'Okay,' Earl said. 'Havana?'

'No, Santiago. It's only an hour away. We'll get you there by staff car. They say something's about to happen in Santiago.'

'What would that be?' Earl wondered.

'Maybe there's a war about to break out,' Lieutenant Dan said.

'Hell,' said the younger officer, 'it's more like an orgy. Hey, Mr. Jones, take me along.'

'Jerry, what the hell are you babbling about?'

The answer, from Jerry, was one lascivious word: 'Carnival.'

37

Speshnev worked the streets, but it was difficult to get people to pay attention. It was carnival week in Santiago and those not yet drunk thought only of becoming drunk, and at night with the music, the beat of the drums, the running of the blood, who could tell? What adventures lurked, what possibilities beckoned?

He began at the Plaza de Armas, the plush green square that was the center of Santiago's red roofs and riotous streets that careened out of control toward the harbor. He started in the lobby of Hotel Casa Grande but wandered in wider and wider circles, avoiding the billy goats pulling children in the square — he doubted either goats or children knew much — then moseyed through the great Cathedral of Santa Ifigenia, where the devoted lit candles and the priests muttered like conspirators but dried up when a stranger approached. It was the one place where the air was not filled with love and pleasure and cigar smoke; only the muttering priests were there, and those hungry to confess so that their consciences would be free to accumulate yet more sin over the weekend of paganism, thus to be purged again with time in the booth.

He drifted by the oldest house in Cuba — a conqueror built it in 1516 and now, in 1953, conquerors were here still — and eventually wandered over to the heart of the city, Calle Herrera, locus of bars and tourists, the latter who had tired of Havana's commercial vulgarities and come in search of a more refined style of debauchery in the night. Perhaps they wouldn't have to pay as much for their pleasure; it might even be free. There was so much excitement that it reminded him of Catalonia in 1936, where the war was fought for real and people's passion — for revolution, bread and freedom, not sex — was so intense the desire reached out to embrace death itself. There were no tourists in Barcelona in 1936 and too many in Santiago in 1953.

He kept moving. He strode by police stations and military installations, he got his hair cut at one barber's and his chin shaved at two others, and his shoes shined three times. He bought seven bolita tickets and four cigars. At every stop he paid attention, asking an outsider's bland questions, hoping for interesting answers. He located the biggest newspaper, and followed a fellow with a notebook to the bar where all the reporters hung out — reporters, especially the stupid American ones, had been a source of much information in Spain — and jostled among them, again listening, drinking for camouflage. He had too many beers, most of which he poured down pissholes in the men's.

What?

Well, nothing. It's carnival time, my friend. Relax, enjoy, perhaps a pretty woman will take notice of you.

Not that. The other thing.

282

Oh, that. Just rumors. Nonsense, stupidity. Nothing definite. Nothing sure.

There was nothing about a leader, about a plan or a conspiracy, about strikes or demonstrations or speeches or mass movements. No name was magic, no name was spoken. But still . . .

Someone had heard that someone had been collecting Cuban army uniforms from ex-soldiers, or from bums on the street, offering them rum for the old green shirts. Someone else said he had heard that someone had seen someone buying as much .22 ammunition and as many shotgun shells as possible in a variety of sporting goods stores. Someone else said that certain men had not been seen in a few weeks, men of good standing, shopkeepers, carpenters, factory workers, not students or ex-soldiers. Where were these men? Where had they gone? What did it mean?

No one could say. Alas, Speshnev did not have sources in the police Political Section or, other than the overheard buzz of gossip in the restaurant, in the press. He had no support here in this far city, no networks, no informants, no enthusiastic believers to be manipulated. He had nothing except his wits and his legs and his impatience at the carnival madness.

He walked, he walked, he walked, finally trying to figure out if there were targets of opportunity for the ambitious young man whose ill-discipline, whose temper, he feared was behind all this. The police station was too big, as was the army base, which was garrisoned at some monstrosity called the Moncada Barracks north of Martí Square, fronting on Calle Carlos Aponte. With its crenellated walls it loomed above its own parade ground, almost a castle. A thousand men were quartered there. What would the point be, other than suicide? Only a fool would try such a thing. That left the post offices (unlikely), the radio stations, the municipal government. But those were direct targets, that would strike hard at the president, make him lose face but not really any power. A subtler man might try to discredit him before his sponsors or clients, possibly by aiming at some symbolic target, like an American building, say the mansions owned by executives of the United Fruit Company. Yet that would bring marines by the boatload, hellbent and righteous with fury. It would turn Cuba into the forty-ninth state even faster than it now seemed to be heading. Would this young man do such an insane thing? Even Speshnev couldn't believe he'd be that stupid.

Another thought: the docks. Here the big American ships — the sugar vessels, the fruit carriers — put in to load up on Cuba's wealth, which was fated to become American wealth. If you sank a ship full of sugar, it would have a certain mythic resonance, no? It would echo back to the battleship *Maine* blown up in Havana harbor so many years ago, but with a comic twist. Better still if the bomb killed no one, but just forced the ship to settle into the cold water. And if he also did the same on a Bacardi rum tanker? It could be accomplished quite easily by surprise. All that sugar, all that rum, turning Santiago de Cuba's harbor into the biggest mojito the world had ever seen! What a magnificent gesture.

But then he realized that's what he, Speshnev, Speshnev of Spain who'd learned at the toe of Levitsky, the master, that's what *he* would do. Castro would not. Castro was too vain for cleverness, too narcissistic for the oblique. He wanted simply to blow something up and make himself famous, that's how limited his poor imagination was. Never trust a man who can't play a good variation on the Ruy-Lopez defense.

Nevertheless, Speshnev spent a day down there, finding only sweating men and tough foremen and American bosses, plus plenty of armed guards. The Americans were taking no chances with their property, however ill-gotten it was, carnival or no carnival; men with guns lurked everywhere. Nobody would attempt anything there. Not even the maniac Castro.

★   ★   ★

Roger and Frenchy had better contacts. They met with the political department of Domino. They dined with the head of security at United Fruit, and key executives. They met with representatives of Bacardi in the Bacardi mansion. They consulted with their sources at Cuban Military Intelligence, in the castle-like barracks called Moncada.

Everywhere, they received the same news, if it was news at all under the blare of carnival. It was nothing definite. It could never be sourced or tracked. It didn't come from snitches or

285

networks. It was more a feeling that the pagan revelry would make a wonderful cover for an angry strike. Everyone would be drunk, everyone stupid, everyone (or most everyone) sexually spent and in that state of listless bliss that follows the act. Maybe it was pure intuition, or pure superstition. Maybe it was sunspots acting up far out in dark space, causing men of earth to act madly. Maybe it was summer, getting hotter by the moment, and people began to fabricate to escape the heavy press of air under the influence of rum and the bare flesh of women's shoulders, the beauty of their legs, the smoothness of their skins.

But still: someone overheard someone saying it was coming.

Yes, carnival.

No. Something else.

It. It! You idiot, *it!*

When?

In carnival.

Who is the leader?

You know who.

Say his name!

The name is forbidden. I cannot say. Everywhere ears are listening, so I cannot say. But nevertheless it is coming . . .

One night after dinner with the same Bill and Ted whom they had vanquished on the tennis court so many months ago, the four men sat on the terrace of one of the United Fruit mansions up in Vista Alegre, on a hill above the town. They sipped mojitos, drawing on immense and zesty cigars from the nearby Fabrica de Tabaco Cesar

Escalante, enjoying the cool shimmer of a summer night in the Antilles, the spray of stars, the soft sea breeze, the sounds, from far off on the Calle Herrera of mambo beat-beat-beating of a jungle tom-tom as the revelers tuned up for the real letting-go yet another night down the pike.

'I hope you boys are up to this,' Ted said.

'We are,' said Roger.

'Roger, you and Walter play a mean game of tennis, that I know. But . . . this is a bigger game. The company has millions tied up. Its entire posture on the market is based on the political stability of our operations down here. I suppose we can reconfigure to Panama or someplace in Central eventually, but, Roger . . . I just hope you're up to snuff on this one.'

'Sir,' said Roger, 'we saw this one coming months ago. We've been moving actively to counter it. We're ready. We can't preempt because our mandate won't allow it but it won't be Pearl Harbor either, where we're caught with our thumb up our ass. If anything happens, you can bet we'll be in operational mode fast. We know where it's coming from, we have put some extraordinary measures in place. Your bananas are safe. Your pineapples will be untouched. Your sugarcane will go unburned.'

'Here,' said Bill. 'I'll drink to the empire of the banana. I'll drink to bananas forever in the U.S. of A. And I'll drink to these two young guys, who I'm sure will be as tough on the playing fields of politics as they are on the tennis court.'

Walter — everyone still called him this, though 'Frenchy' was beginning to catch on with a

287

certain soignée crowd — sat quietly through Roger's report. He had been doing the journeyman's labor, liaising with cops and spooks and gangsters, calling plantation foremen and simpatico college professors and the like while Roger toured, lobbied, represented, looked glamorous and savvy and cool. Walter had not slept in three days, and he yearned for a good night's sleep.

'What do we know?' Ted asked. 'Not the bullshit you give the papers or the ambassador, but the inside stuff, the skinny.'

The funny part was that poor Roger didn't know either. He had no head for details.

'Walter, can you brief the boys?'

'Sure, Roger. We know that a certain fiery radical leader, who had already attracted a large if unorganized following for his astute publicity ability and talent for speechifying, was nearly killed by the Secret Police about a month ago, not far from here. He escaped. It appears to have been a botched operation set up clumsily by the Secret Police Political Section, without authorization from anybody. He disappeared, presumably into the slums of Santiago or possibly one of the neighboring towns or farms. We had been watching him some time.'

'You know where he is now?'

'Er, not really. He's smart, he's clever, he's treacherous, he's now supremely motivated and presumably mentally destabilized. He was never the coolest cucumber in the fridge and something like this could turn him cuckoo. But we're not trying to prevent him from acting;

we're not praying we skate by this time. Oh, no. Our hope is that he *does* try something. And we think he will. He lacks patience. For all his talent, he's a rather shallow man. If he does this thing, whatever it is, we are positioned to deal with it swiftly.'

'How, Mr. Short?'

'Sorry, sir. Can't tell you. Top secret.'

'Not even a hint?'

'No, sir.'

'Well,' said Roger, 'we have a man who's a specialist in these matters. You might call him our *numero uno* manhunter. If there's a trail, he'll follow it. If there's a shot, he'll make it. And there will be a shot.'

You fucking idiot! Frenchy thought behind a face as bland as a nickel. *You have just given up everything to impress two schmoes from a banana company.*

'Here, here!' said Ted. 'Here's to the shooter.'

'Here's to the man who gets it done for keeps,' said Bill.

'Here's to an American hero,' said Roger.

'Here's to a professional,' said Frenchy. They all raised their glasses, drank deeply, and sat back to enjoy the night and the unperturbable future.

38

The crowds were everywhere, just getting warmed up for Sunday night's craziness. Poking its way through them, the car was stopped at least twice by outlaw mambo bands and their followers, who surged into the streets to provide the atmosphere of anarchy necessary to lubricate the proceedings.

'Mr. Jones, I hope you can keep your mind on your work with all those babes around,' said the younger officer, eyeing the flesh jiggling by, loosely packed into brief dresses.

'Mr. Jones knows what he's doing. Roger wouldn't have picked him otherwise,' Lieutenant Dan said, with an obsequious look back at Earl, who felt involved as a go-between in some strange ritual between Dan and Roger he couldn't begin to understand.

The two naval officers ultimately delivered Earl to the Hotel Casa Grande. It looked like a white wedding cake turned upside down, all square and creamy and shuttered up tight but with a vast marble-floored porch fronting the green square in central Santiago, whose space had been seized by the entire human race preparing to lose its soul.

He waited in line for twenty minutes because the place was so crammed, and he worried there'd be no room for him. But there was; and he was led upstairs. It was an extremely nice room, maybe the nicest he'd ever been in. He tried not to be impressed; he tried not to think, *Wish Junie were here now.* He took a shower, ignored the music, grabbed a night's sleep, and the next morning went looking for field gear, on the sound principle you can't go manhunting in street clothes.

He had a checkbook issued by Frenchy, and could use it to pick up anything he wanted. That was one of the perks of working for the best outfit, Frenchy had assured him. No questions asked. If you need it, if it makes you happy, then you buy it.

Carnival was everywhere, but he pushed his way through the crowds, roamed across the Plaza de Armes, and found that most places were still open. At a sporting goods store better than anything in Blue Eye — or Fort Smith or even Little Rock, for that matter — he found a pair of very fine Abercrombie & Fitch hunting boots that cost more than most suits he'd ever bought. They were thick, sinewy leather, dense and soft, and protective. Jesus Christ, $75 for boots! He held them, smelled their supple leather, their weight, the waxy waterproofing that ran across the welt. They were quality, no doubt about it.

Go ahead. What differences does it make?

But something held him back. Instead, he bought the much cheaper Stoeger boots, the six-inch size, for only $5.95. They were fine. They were okay. There was no trouble with them, though the leather was duller and darker.

Then he went to the clothing department and

acquired quickly a pair of Filson tin cloth bloused trousers in a dark green, a Filson shirt of the same cloth in the same shade, and a brush-brown waterproofed duck hat with a ventilated opening above the brim to let the air circulate. A canteen, a day-pack, a poncho and a pair of binoculars completed the wardrobe. He added gear: a waterproof flashlight, a compass, a good Buck knife, a plastic cigarette pack carrier, mosquito repellent, a first-aid kit and six pair of socks.

'Oh, a hunting trip, señor?'

'Yes, that's right.'

'In the Sierras, the boar are very active this time of year. Big brutes, they go three hundred pounds. Their tusks are like razors and they are very violent, valiant animals. They do not surrender. I have seen them charge with two legs broken. They are like a fine bull. It will be a good hunt, I know.'

'I expect so.'

'Ammunition? We have extensive ammunition. Oh, except for .22 and 12-gauge. For some reason there's been a run recently and we are sold out until the new shipment. But you wouldn't hunt boar with .22.'

'No, I wouldn't. But I'm all set in that department.'

'I wish you luck, señor. You will have a wonderful time. Carnival this week, hunting the next. The best of all manly pleasures, hunting in both its manifestation. The pleasures of the flesh and of harvesting the flesh. What could please a man more?'

292

'Well, you make a good point, sir. I do hope I enjoy myself.'

Even without the extravagance of the Abercrombie & Fitch boots, it still came to more than a hundred bucks! He wrote the check, feeling somewhat larcenous and compromised in the process. He expected some trouble too, as a stranger in a strange town who barely spoke the language. But there was no trouble. This was a well-to-do place, used to catering to wealthy American executives who fished or hunted dove or boar for their leisure, who paid by checks that never bounced. So it was not a problem.

Next stop was a laundry where he had all the new gear washed, to get the stiffness and the wrapped-in-a-factory smell out of it.

'You still open?'

'Yes, señor. Till seven, like any day. We must work before we play.'

'Ain't that the truth. So, can you do this new stuff for me? Get the smell out?'

'The hat too, señor?'

'Yeah, the hat. It's like a derby. Make it soft like I've worn it a hundred times.'

'Si, señor.'

'And you have a big dryer out back, right?'

'Yes, señor.'

'Here's what I want you to do. Put these boots in a laundry bag. You have some change in the register?'

'Si,' said the man, looking at him quizzically. He'd obviously never been asked to dry boots, then if he had change, in the same breath.

'Good. Throw all the change in the laundry

bag with the boots. Let it run the whole time I'm gone. And I know it'll be loud. But I'll pay, believe me, whatever you want. I want the boots banged up and the leather softened by the action of the coins. I may have to wear 'em tomorrow, and I want them as soft as possible. Okay?'

The two Cubans exchanged a look that expressed the universal befuddlement in the presence of the insane, but Earl didn't care.

'Be back in couple of hours. Is that enough time?'

'Yes.'

He went for lunch, wandered a few blocks, getting shoved this way and that by the crowds, finally wandered into a lunchroom. Was he in Cuba? He had a hamburger and a Coke and some french fries. Everybody in the lunch room was an American, except the help.

Then he walked a bit, picked up the washed and folded clothes, no longer new, and the softened boots, went back to the hotel, laid everything out, took the rifle from its case, ran the bolt several times to feel its smoothness and solidity, checked the security of the sling, checked the scope settings, wiped the lenses with lens tissue, and tried to relax.

Impossible.

He put a call in to America, to Junie, because it had been some time and he felt restless and unsure. Something far inside was unsettled, as if he had a gripe and didn't want to be far from a john. But it wasn't that, it was just a little something.

Someone picked up.

'Hello?' It was the boy's voice.

'Bobby! Oh, Bobby, it's Daddy!'

The boy's voice, dullish in the answer, suddenly lit up with pleasure.

'Daddy! Hi, Daddy!'

And so Earl talked with his son. Except he could not. At key moments, he found words often difficult to produce.

'So, how are you?'

'I'm fine, Daddy. Seen lotsa deer. Them woods is full of deer.'

'I'll get you one this fall, you bet on it.'

'Yes, sir. Daddy, you aren't mad at me 'cause I din't shoot that one in the spring?'

He saw that the kid had assembled the two phenomena in his mind: his inability to shoot the springtime deer and his father's immediate disappearance.

'No, sir. Not one bit. No, I am not. You'll be fine, young man. We'll get you a nice one in the fall, if that's what you want. Now, is Mommy there?'

'No, sir. She's over to the church.'

'Well, you tell her I miss her. I miss you, too. Bob Lee, Daddy loves you very much. You know that, don't you.'

It was the only time he had ever used the word love with the boy.

'Yes, sir.'

'I think I can polish this off soon. I'll be home. Bob Lee, I'm going to bring you a nice present, you'll see. And then it'll be like I was never gone, and I won't go nowhere no more, okay?'

'Okay.'

'Now tell Mommy I called.'

'Yes, sir.'

'Bye now.'

'Bye.'

He hung up, feeling like he'd just failed some test. He'd meant to say so much. But he'd said nothing.

Lord, he needed a drink. Just one damn little one, a splash of gin against the cold ice, leavened by the tonic, almost a soda pop with just the softest little buzz to it. But that way was the road to hell, with no way back.

Instead he went to the window to observe the full spectacle of carnival. And there was a lot to be enjoyed: the music seemed everywhere and everywhere there was music there were the crowds. He could sense that the gaslit plaza across the way was jammed with them, and there were neon-lit amusement rides, temporarily erected across the way, as well as vendors selling all manner of drinks, the whole thing a great ocean of human want and need in the warm dark. The gaslamps flickered, giving the whole thing even more sense of life. It was like one huge parade.

Just watching it all, he didn't feel so cut off. He wasn't the killer. He wasn't the one man among them designated to put the crosshairs on a living being and press the trigger. This one was different from combat. He'd killed, too many times, but always an armed man trying to or planning to kill him, or his men. He'd never shot a prisoner, he'd never shot a wounded Jap. He shot what would hurt him and his and nothing else.

And now?

What am I? Dear lord, who have I become and in whose service am I prepared to do this deed? Why is this what you have to do to get a nice house in Washington and pretty clothes for your wife and a good school and college education for your son?

He had no answers and the questions hurt. He decided to go down to the restaurant, have some dinner, and turn in early.

★　★　★

The bar on the porch of the Casa Grande was jammed. A variety of smaller carnival parties had somehow collected into a single one, and two or three competing mambo quintets wandered the floor, issuing manifestos of pleasure and rhythm. Everybody was smoking, everybody was touching, everybody was shaking. It was an orgy of human groping. It overlooked the park and all the tables were crowded.

He headed toward the bar with his usual routine in mind, which was to enjoy the sense of celebration, the closeness of other if strange human beings, but not to drink and lose himself. He slid through the throng, dodging dancers, slipped through darkness, found a relatively isolated spot at the bar at the end of the long porch, and parked on a stool.

'Señor?'

'Ah, rum and Coke. Charge me the whole

ticket, but no rum. Put an umbrella in it. Okay?'

'Of course, señor.'

Soon enough it came, soon enough he was sipping, looking out to the square where the real action was, where the life of the city at play really took off. The smoke seethed, the bar was strung with lights, the music rose and jiggled.

He smoked, had another drink, enjoyed a brief if debilitating fantasy about bringing Junie and the boy down here, hoping they'd enjoy what was so special about it, yet knowing they wouldn't. An hour or so dragged itself by, and he thought enough time had passed so that he could get to sleep.

Instead he saw someone waving at him from a busy table of Americans, all of whom were staring at him with equal parts adoration and passion. She detached herself and he recognized her immediately: the woman Jean-Marie Augustine, the Filipina, rapturously beautiful tonight in a low-cut tropical dress that showed her smooth mahogany shoulders, her cleavage, and the tightness of her body through hips and legs, down to pretty red toes in some kind of high-heeled sandals. She had a flower in her hair and as she approached, he tried not to feel excited at her attraction to him and his to her, and he tried not to be intoxicated by the intensity of her sweet perfume, and he wondered, near panic, what the best way to get out of here fast would be.

'Well, hello,' she said.

'Hi, there. I thought you were a Havana gal.'

'Oh, I am, definitely. But carnival. I mean, you

have to come. It's the best show on earth.'

'These folks know how to throw a party, that's for sure.'

'Oh, and this year, they say the fireworks might be on the ground as well as in the sky. I had to come up and get a look at it.'

'I wouldn't pay too much attention to rumors. They're always wrong.'

'Except that what would the famous Sergeant Swagger be doing up here if there weren't something big going on? You don't seem the type to come up for a big party.'

'I just do what these young kids tell me.'

'You're quite the celebrity. The man who bested the mighty Hemingway. Now they say you're up here on some secret mission for the boys on the third floor, to defend our interests. The bodyguard who became a government agent and saved the banana for America. God bless the banana, staff of life.'

'I don't even *like* bananas, not a bit. But between you and me, I don't think these boys could find the sky if they didn't have a sign marked 'up'.'

She laughed.

'Look, why don't you join us? It's some businesspeople, all wealthy and connected. The Bacardi crowd. They know who you are. They'd like to bask in your glamour. It would be like John Wayne or Joe DiMaggio coming over and sitting with them. You'd find it pretty amusing, I think. Most of them are worthless.'

'Once they saw what a down-home buckra I was, they'd go back to yakking about the stock market. I really ought to head upstairs. I don't think there's a chance in hell of a thing happening here, because nothing on this island happens on time, but I ought to be ready just in case.'

'So mysterious. But that's what I'd expect from the manhunter.'

'You are well informed, I have to say.'

'Down here, everybody talks, everybody gossips. You can't keep a secret. All right, Sergeant Swagger, mystery man of the Caribbean, I'll go away and let you do your duty, as all marines must. You still have my card, right?'

'Yes I do, Mrs. Augustine.'

'Please call me Jean. Everybody does. I'm just Jean, the famous Jean of the Havana smart set.'

'Jean, then.'

'So if you need help and these young kids you're working for, even though you detest them, can't do a thing for you, you call me.'

'Sure.'

'And thanks for being such a good guy that night with that big jerk. You were terrific. Guys like you, always married, always decent. Always. Just my luck.'

She gave him a kiss on the cheek, squeezed his arm and slipped away through the crowd.

He finished the rumless-and-Coke, threw down too much money on the bar, and found a quiet way out.

★ ★ ★

300

He showered but could not sleep. He lay in the darkness, waiting for it to come but it didn't. He tossed, turned, tried to quell his mind. The smell of the woman was still in his mind, and possibly what she represented: a whole world of unimagined possibility. And this business too, with its promise of the fancy job in Washington, some idea of a big house, a fine school for the boy, a sense of becoming something so far beyond what he was supposed to become it disturbed him.

Somewhere in there he actually drifted off. But it was a shallow, restless sleep, broken by dreams. In one of these he was back in the water off Tarawa, that moment of the war's darkest horror, where the Higgins boats had gotten caught on the reef and they had a whole thousand-yard walk in neck-deep water under heavy Jap fire. The tracers were white-blue, like snakes or whips that lashed or struck across the water, and it was so deep and heavy you could hardly move and there were times when the island ahead disappeared behind swells and the ships behind disappeared too, and there you were, one man, neck-deep in water, defenseless — alone, it seemed, on the face of a watery planet.

Gunfire.

Then he realized the gunfire wasn't in his brain.

He snapped awake and listened as the shots rang through the night.

He got up, raced to the westward-facing window and opened the curtain, pushed the shutters open wide.

Facing the square, he saw nothing but the flicker of gas lamps in the park, but he knew the gunfire came from behind, to the east.

Frenchy called three minutes later.

'It's happening. The idiot attacked the Moncada Barracks. There's a gunfight going on there now. We can get him. How soon can you be set?'

'I'm ready now,' said Earl. He hung up the phone, picked up the rifle case and headed downstairs.

39

The mulatto Cartaya stood before them all and once again sang his song, a catchy tune that bore an embarrassing similarity to a famous English seaside rhythm.

Marching towards an idea
Knowing very well we are going to win
More than peace and prosperity
We will fight for liberty.

Onwards Cubans!
Let Cuba give you a prize for heroism.
For we are soldiers
Going to free the country.

Cleansing with fire
Which will destroy this infernal plague
Of bad governments
And insatiable tyrants
Who have plunged Cuba
into evil.

On and on it went, through several more verses, and by the end, most of the men were weeping. They felt it so profoundly. It stirred them, deep in their Cuban souls.

They were not radical students or intellectuals, members of any elite or vanguard. They were just men. Most were factory workers, agricultural workers, shop assistants. There was a watch-maker, a teacher, a taxi-driver, a doctor, a dentist, a bookshop assistant, a chimney sweep, three carpenters, a butcher, an oyster seller and a nurse.

They came not because of him, but because of *it*. It was Cuba. They felt it. He was only the instrument of will. He made it happen by conceptualizing it, by focusing on plans much discussed but always lacking behind them the necessary force, and by supplying that force. What he stood for, they didn't know; what his programs were, they didn't care. He may not have stood for anything. He was just the one who had appointed himself the leader, and by reputation he gathered them. They didn't even know him, they didn't care about him; he was just the man who'd made it happen over the past month.

Having talked this over a thousand nights in coffeehouses and over chessboards and cigars and after rallies, he knew who to call. He had begun to make phone calls — thank you, Mr. President, for the wonderful Cuban phone system, the best in the Caribbean — from the town of Artemisa, ten miles east of Santiago, on the plain that separated the mountains from the seas, as was this farmhouse where they were now meeting. He made phone calls to men he knew and trusted, who in turn made phone calls to men they knew and trusted, who then . . . and so forth and so on, and now there were eighty or so of them, gathered here in their shabby khaki uniforms, with their shabby weapons, a few

American M1s or carbines, a Winchester .44 lever rifle, but mostly .22 hunting rifles or old double-barreled shotguns used for doves. They followed him because there was no one else to follow. They followed him because whatever was said of him, this much was true: he had a big set of balls.

'Companions,' he said, 'fellow crusaders. Tonight is the night of nights. Perhaps we die, perhaps we triumph. But we will not pass without having made the ultimate attempt. Companions, brothers, long live freedom! Long live Cuba!'

He was best at moments like that. Perhaps his true gift was the ability to put into simple, rugged language those things they all felt, and by doing that, become the vessel of their emotions.

They raised their rifles and cheered by the light of campfires in the barnyard, and then there was nothing left to say. They went to their cars, twenty-six in all, rickety old vehicles, some barely drivable, and climbed in three or four to each one, and off they went.

He was in the second car. He drove. Nobody talked, though some men smoked. The convoy, obeying rules of traffic, not politics, accordioned this way and that, expanding and contracting as it went over the dusty roads, found the slope, passed through the outskirts of Cuba's second largest city, rotated around the traffic circle, and headed down the Victoriano Garzon for Avenue Moncada and the future, whatever it might bring.

He worried that the man ahead would lose his

way. He worried that the cars would lose contact with each other and wander, the whole unit breaking down into nothingness. He worried that he would be a coward. He worried that nothing would go as planned, that he would be captured and the legendary Ojos Bellos, whom all knew of and all feared, might cut his eyes out and make him sing a song of defeat and surrender and betrayal. He worried that he would die a forgotten nobody, and all his dreams and all his convictions of destiny and change and power would disappear for naught.

They drove through streets sleepy but not as sleepy as he had imagined. He thought that by now everybody would be drunk or in bed with a new partner. Yet it was still surprisingly crowded. Now and then a soul would notice this strange parade of beat-up old vehicles rumbling through the streets and watch, wide-mouthed, wondering at meanings. Still, no alarm was given, no commotion created. If the assemblage confirmed certain rumors, the cars outraced them to their destination.

They rolled onward into the night.

★ ★ ★

In the way that time collapses when that which is anticipated and seems forever away is suddenly upon you, they turned right off of the central thoroughfare of Victoriano Garzon and down the Avenue Moncada, passing the military hospital on the left, then a number of small wooden officers' houses, buried in trees, and finally, at

306

the intersection, arrived at Checkpoint 3, access to the barracks. The building itself loomed ahead at the oblique, the castellated ramparts visible in the night, so that it looked like something the great Don Quixote himself would charge, lance ready, heart athrob. Its yellow-and-white color scheme stood out in lighting from the porch that ran along its front. A low wall surrounded it, a parade ground lay to one side of it, and only a gatehouse marked it off from the rest of the world. It housed a thousand men, but tonight, or so the plan assumed, they would all be drunk.

The plan was simple, and at least it was a plan. The first car sped ahead, opening a distance between itself and the rest of the column. As it went, Castro prayed to God in his heaven that the advantage of surprise — his only advantage — was to be protected.

He slowed to a creep, the speed of a man walking, as ahead, the first car reached the checkpoint, and six men leapt out in the best of the uniforms.

'Make way for the general!' shouted Guitart, their leader, 'open the gate for the general.'

It worked, almost magically. The three guards snapped into a present-arms in honor of the general and as they froze, their old rifles locked in place vertically against their chests, they were overcome and disarmed. Guitart and his party shoved them ahead and went inside to open the gate.

And then, just as magically, it fell apart. Castro saw chaos and disaster emerge in the form of three men, two soldiers with American submachine guns and a sergeant with a pistol at his belt. They shouldn't have been there, but they were, and so it goes in the affairs of men and revolutions. They were evidently on some sort of perimeter patrol, and stopped abruptly and just stared at what they could see and no one else could: a line of twenty-five cars creeping along, lights out, jammed with men.

He had no choice but an act of sudden, stunning violence. He had no hesitation. He veered savagely, running up onto the pavement, bouncing over the curb, turning on his headlights and pinning the three in the glare. They panicked, but it was too late, and he rammed into them, knocking them asunder, felt the ragged jolt as the car crushed against them. Weapons flew, bodies flew.

But not the sergeant. He alone was quick enough or sober enough to react, and rolled to the right, just a hair, and the charging vehicle did not hit him.

Castro leapt out; the sergeant had to be stopped.

But he was gone, except for the sounds of his pistol, which he had drawn as he fled, firing off seven rounds as fast as he could and screaming 'Assalto! Assalto!'

He was the hero, not Castro, for in that moment the entire complexion of the event changed.

Castro, out of the car, saw that he was too late, but still thought that if the column moved quickly it could penetrate the barracks, bring fire on the soldiers, overwhelm them with fear, cajole them into dropping their arms, and therefore take over the city.

But he turned now and saw chaos. When he leapt from his car, that was the signal — he had forgotten. All the other cars halted, and the men now poured from them, rifles and shotguns at the ready, hungry for the battle that now seemed destined not to occur in the barracks itself, but here on the Avenue Moncada at a kind of forty-five-degree angle to the barracks.

'The cars!' he screamed. 'You must get back into the cars!'

It began slowly. A shot spanged off the hood of a car, and then another, and then another. The noise was almost more terrifying than the prospect of death, for when the bullets fired, their noise filled the air and beat against the eardrums, and in the next second, they smacked into automobile metal with a vibratory clang.

Castro saw that now was the only moment he would have.

'Attack!' he cried. 'Open fire! Kill the bastards.'

With that he ran to the front of his own wrecked vehicle, seized a machine pistol from the ground where one of the two now moaning soldiers had tossed it in the moment of his ugly smashing, turned and pointed it at the windows and doors looming ahead to the left, and unleashed a roar as he emptied the magazine in one shuddering, lurching burst.

A few men raced past him, rushed through the checkpoint, and began to move in on the barracks. But a blast of fire from the windows drove them back or pinned them down.

All along the line, the rebels retreated to their vehicles and fired, their .22 and shotgun blasts filling the air. The whole side of the corner of Moncada seemed to dance as the rebel rounds tore against it, blowing out windows, pulverizing the façade. And then, as if a storm had spent itself, the men stopped shooting, all reaching the end of their magazines in the same second.

The soldiers by this time were fully awakened. An officer inside must have realized what was happening and rallied them. By whatever presence, at each window and doorway it seemed three men appeared, each with a rifle, and each shooting as fast as he could.

Now it was a torrent of fire from the building, and it was the cars that shuddered when hit by the fusillade. Windows smeared, then shattered, tires flattened, shocks gave up. The cars, like dying animals, settled brokenly toward the pavement, screams arose from the hit, a man or two fell limp and dead.

Castro struggled with the machine gun, got another magazine from the soldier's belt into it, and again sprayed the building. He watched his bullets dance along, and for a moment was buoyed by the power he unleashed, having in his mind a recent event where the power of the guns was directed only at him.

But then the soldiers above opened fire, and he dropped in a blizzard of detonations, as rifle rounds from a hundred weapons sought him out.

'What do we do?' someone asked.

'We must be strong! We must be brave. We

must hold. Guitart is inside. He will attack them from the rear.'

But at that moment a squad of soldiers broke from the barracks, headed across the street and began to work their way along the wall, where they had another angle from which to fire at the gaggle of revolutionaries. Shots began to bang this way and that off the cars. From somewhere farther out in the parade ground, a machine gun post jumped to life. A fusillade of bullets chopped into the ground and the cars, bringing up clouds of dust where it struck.

They fired tracers, and the flickering of the illuminated rounds filled the street with light. Then, a car exploded, its tank punctured by one of the burning bullets. A plume of feathery flame rose, tumbling, revealing the carnage.

The parade of wrecked vehicles lay in the street, all tattered from gunfire. Among them, the rebels cowered, rising now and again for a shot with the little .22 rifles, which sounded like twigs breaking against the shovel-poundings of the heavier battle weapons inside.

Feeling insanely untouchable, Castro walked along the line, screaming imprecations at his men.

'Fire on them! Mow them down! Give them a taste of lead! Show them no mercy!'

But his screams seemed to have no effect on the crouching men.

Finally, one looked over at him from the shelter of the car he cowered behind.

'It's finished. We are running out of ammunition. There are too many of them.'

'No,' he said, 'you must stay and fight till the end. Cuba demands it.'

'Cuba doesn't demand my death,' said the man.

'Guitart and his men are inside. They will bring fire on them from behind and we will move into the courtyard. Have faith, my broth — '

'Guitart is dead. I saw him shot down.'

'No, my brother, he — '

'We are doomed!' screamed the man. 'Order a retreat! We have failed.'

Castro looked up and down the line; some men returned fire, but for each shot a rebel fired, a storm of rifle and machine gun bullets answered. Two cars burned. Guitart and his people were dead. Across the street, he could see soldiers creeping among the line of officers' houses, moving closer under fire-and-advance maneuvers. It meant that he would soon be under direct fire from three sides. And behind the soldiers would be the torturers.

'Fall back!' he screamed. 'Retreat and regroup for another night, my brothers. I will cover you.'

He watched them melt into the night, those that could. They scampered off, drawing fire. Some fell and died. Some fell and crawled. Some made it and disappeared into the houses down the road.

At last he was quite alone except for the wounded and the dead, in the flickering of the firelight. Most of the shooting from the barracks had stopped and he saw why. Soldiers on either end of the column of wrecked cars slithered along, dipping in and dipping out. A grenade went into a car and detonated with a flash. A soldier bayoneted a man on the ground, dead or not.

He fired at them with the submachine gun, driving them back, but then he was out of ammunition.

He tossed the gun away and picked up the other one.

'You will not take me alive, you bastards!' he screamed. 'You are the milk of pigs, and you defile Cuba.'

He stood up, fired quickly, still driving them back, but then that gun too, was out of ammunition.

'Are you quite done?' someone said.

He turned.

'You!'

A man stood in the ragged linens of a peasant, under a straw hat pulled low. But it was the Russian.

'Yes, me, you idiot.'

'How did you get here?'

'What a ridiculous question. Not as ridiculous as this travesty, but still ridiculous. The question is: how am I going to get you out of here.'

'They are — '

'Not yet. Not quite yet.'

He smiled. He pulled two amazements from the pockets of his baggy trousers. Grenades.

'Best drop under cover, you brainless young idiot. Do I have to tell you *everything?*'

Castro knelt between two cars, and the Russian quickly pulled the pin from each grenade and tossed them into the Avenue

313

Moncada. The two blasts occurred simultaneously.

And with that they were off, dashing between two houses, cutting down an alley, then down another one. Soldiers followed, but they dipped down another alley. Ahead, Castro could see an old farmer's truck pulled by the side of the road, its engine idling.

'What is — '

'Never mind. Your luck hasn't quite run out, but it will if you delay.'

They ran to it, climbed in, and pulled themselves under a tarpaulin, where Castro discovered to his horror the truck's cargo was manure.

'Oh, Christ!' he said.

'If you are too pretty for shit, my friend,' said the Russian, 'then you are too pretty for revolution.'

He smiled, banged on the back of the cab, and with a lurch the ancient vehicle took off.

The Russian looked over.

'I think we've made it, for now. The glorious socialist future awaits your next brilliant decision.'

40

First the long passage of shot-up, burned-out automobiles. Already children scampered upon them in the wash of morning light, while crowds fought to get closer to look at the ruination, but were held back by soldiers. The signs of battle were everywhere, in the pools of blood that lay coagulating on the Avenue Moncada, in the smell of burned powder and gasoline and raw, ripped metal, in the debris upon the street. A few small fires still burned, so the smoke was in the air too, and the odor of the blood. Ahead, where the corner of the barracks loomed yellow and white in the sunlight, the ratholes of gunfire riddled the pretend medievalism of the structure. Most of the windows were shot out.

Frenchy and Earl sat in their station wagon on the street near Guardhouse 3, waiting as a major spoke on the radio headset to a headquarters somewhere, checking their credentials before allowing them to pass.

The Cuban soldiers were full of themselves, their juices all aflow, their eyes bulging with drama, self-importance, pride of victory and machismo. Every one of them swaggered, carried or wore his weapon at a rakish angle, smoked cigars or cigarettes or drank from an extra rum ration released by Major Morales, the hero of the day, who had rallied the men inside, killed the first invaders, then poured fusillade after fusillade down on the rebels crouching behind their automobiles. The major was almost certainly drunk himself by this time — on victory and praise, but also on rum, a shield against his pain: his younger brother, a lieutenant, was officer of the day and had been shot down by Guitart in the first seconds of the fight.

Earl could read the battle from what he saw, as he and Frenchy waited. He saw how it really hadn't been a battle at all, which meant there'd been no real victory either. The attackers never got inside and the defenders just blasted them from the relative safety of the barracks windows or the wall along the parade ground. Worse still, the attackers had no support, no artillery or mortars, not even grenades or much in the way of automatic weapons. It was more a gesture than anything, and it had produced nothing but failure.

'Whoever dreamed this one up ought to be busted back to recruit,' he said bitterly to Frenchy, for it offended him to see something done so stupidly, and to see so much blood spread across the pavement because of it.

'It wasn't exactly von Clausewitz, was it?' said Frenchy.

'Well, I don't know who von Klauzerwittz is, or was, but it wasn't even Dugout Doug, that's how bad it was.'

'Roger wilco,' said Frenchy, then turned to a major who had just hung up the radio headset, 'Are we clear now? Have you called your headquarters?'

The major turned, instantly transformed by

316

whatever message he had gotten at the other end, and began to backpedal pathetically.

'I am so sorry, Señor Short, I did not know, I have only this minute learned, and I have been ordered to assist in any way possible.'

'No problem, mac,' said Frenchy. 'Just let us inside so we can see what's what and get a message off to my headquarters as soon as possible.'

'Yes, sir, yes, sir,' and with that he turned, made signals of urgency and importance to all the soldiers lounging arrogantly about and pretending to be war heroes, and they parted, pushed back the crowd and opened a path. Frenchy drove the black Ford forward, through the checkpoint, and into the courtyard of the barracks, where only a few rebels had penetrated.

'Are you ready for this?' Frenchy said to Earl. 'You thought you saw it all in the Pacific, Earl. But just like the man says, you ain't seen nothing yet. This'll clear your sinuses.'

They pulled over, and got out.

The screaming was general.

By this time, the military had captured at least sixty men in various places around Santiago, some just blocks away, some in the military hospital where they'd gone for medical assistance, some in the Hotel Rex down the street, some a far distance gone. They were in the process of running the interrogations there in the yard.

Most had been beaten in the capture, and some now were being beaten even more savagely.

Yet this was not torture. This was simply how things happened and as Earl looked about he saw a dozen or so brutal dramas playing out. In one corner, two soldiers held a rebel down or against a wall while two others beat him with rifle butts — not so hard as to knock him out, but just hard enough to deliver maximum pain. All over the yard it was the same: rifle butts smashing the nose or shattering the teeth, or breaking the knee, the ankle, the instep. The prisoners didn't scream much, as most were beyond it. One man's face was lost in a mass of blood, and was so seriously injured, by Earl's reckoning, that he could not possibly survive.

'See, these guys don't mess around, do they?' said Frenchy.

'That's just the warm-up,' said Earl, and nodded toward a tent erected a little farther down the Avenue Moncada, in front of the central entrance to the barracks. That was the source of the screams. That was where security guards formed a cordon around machine gun positions, the whole area already marked off from the general traffic by a wall of barbed wire.

'They do the hard work in there, I'm betting.'

'You're right,' said Frenchy.

'Let's mosey over and take a lookie-see,' Earl said. 'I want to get a good sense of whose side I'm on.'

'Yeah, sure. We can get a header on where he is.'

'If he's the guy at all.'

'Oh, he's the guy.'

They moseyed over, and of course a lieutenant

warned them away, but Frenchy whispered the magic three letters of the outfit, flashed a credential, and the lieutenant looked nervously about to the major from outside, who nodded, and the man let them pass.

No one interfered. They walked forward but stopped as a man was led outside. Bandages covered both eyes, but they had been sloppily applied, and from underneath each a river of blood flowed jaggedly down his face. The man could hardly walk. He was babbling pathetically, and then he went down to his knees, sobbing.

'Watch yourself,' said an officer. He pulled a Star automatic from a holster, thumbed back the hammer and leaned over and quickly shot the man in the back of his neck. The victim pitched forward, his skull hitting the asphalt with a thud. He was still, yet more blood coursed from the head wound, to mingle with the blood from his eyes.

The officer holstered his pistol, yelled and two men came over and dragged the corpse away.

'That was,' the officer said to the two Americans, 'the traitor bastard Santamaria. Oh, he thought he was so clever, but look how he ended up. That is the way we handle treason in Cuba.'

'We could learn a lesson from you,' said Frenchy.

'You could indeed.'

'What are you finding out?'

'See the intelligence officer inside. Latavistada. He is in charge. He has all the answers. He does the cutting.'

'It's the man we think it is? This is what I have heard.'

'That is the name given up from the lips of the condemned.'

'Does anybody know where he has gone?'

'They had no plan. There are no escape routes. He fled, that is all, the coward. We will catch him, and then Ojos Bellos will have a conversation with him and then he will be shot, like that dog Santamaria.'

'Thanks,' said Frenchy.

'Of course. We are partners in this, your country and mine.'

Through this exchange, Earl stood mute, as if paralyzed. His face had gone dull and it showed nothing, not horror, not repugnance, not judgment. He had seen so many bodies in his time and so much killing that nothing here was worth reacting to; it was only to be remembered.

He and Frenchy ducked inside.

There Ojos Bellos, Captain Ramon Latavistada, his uniform smeared with blood like a butcher's, worked his magic. The screams were intense, the pain horrific, and the man chained before him writhed and shivered and begged. For his part, the captain was not frenzied or excited in the least. He worked slowly and precisely, with a doctor's delicate touch. He cut, he whispered a question, he listened gravely, he consulted with staff, he checked this information against other information, he cross-checked, he indexed, he made certain good notes were being taken, and then he went back to work. He affected the anguish of a country doctor telling a

320

longtime patient the news was bad. He pretended that what he had to do was hurting him as much as them, and he begged them to cooperate, and then he cut them, cut them some more and cut them yet again.

'You're the Americans we were told to expect?' asked a young SIM staff lieutenant.

'That's us. What have you got?'

'It is this Castro, as we suspected. He seems to have invented this thing quickly. A month ago most of these men were dream revolutionaries, fantasists, pretenders. Then the call came, and it is amazing how quickly they gave up normal lives to assist the man. He has a gift, that is for certain. Of course by now they thought they'd be sipping champagne in the presidential palace, not dangling on a chain while Ojos Bellos worked upon them. We will get him, though.'

'How did he get away?' Frenchy asked.

'He fought till the end. Most left before he did. Most recall him there, shouting, giving fire. He has balls, that one. It must be said. That is why he is dangerous. He has the conquistador blood. That is why he must be hunted and shot.'

'So nobody saw him leave.'

'Ojos Bellos is working under the following theory: that it is logical that a man wounded earlier in the fight and not able to flee, he alone would have been there and seen what happened. So we are checking and cross-checking, and attempting to come up with a prisoner who was taken there at the site, after a wounding. Alas, many of those men did not survive the wrath of the soldiery.'

'They were shot on the spot?'

'A mistake, I admit it. But if such a man exists, Ojos Bellos will find him. Nobody can hide a thing from Ojos Bellos. He learns everything, eventually.'

'We'll wait. I want the latest intel to flash to Washington. You can imagine how upset they are.'

'Yes, of course.'

'I'm going to duck out for a cigarette,' Earl said.

'No,' Frenchy said, 'you should — '

But Earl hit him with a look that told him coldly to back way the fuck off, and Frenchy melted in the power of that glare.

'I'll, um, stay here, and um, maybe I can — '

But Earl was already out.

He breathed deeply, even if the air was shot with gasoline, burned powder and blood, moved away from the torture factory and found a tree to squat under, facing only the green parade ground and, miles beyond it, the high mountains of the Sierra Maestra. They looked somehow clean from this distance. He swiftly opened a pack of cigarettes and fired up a Camel, drawing deeply as if the smoke had some salutary effect, some abrasive, scouring cleanliness. But there was no cleanliness here, and overhead, hawks or vultures, birds of carrion whatever, reeled and fluted in the pale, cool early morning sunlight.

But he had no chance to settle down, for as birds of carrion whirled overhead, one in human form approached on foot, fast, bent, dark, near apoplexy.

'Hey,' he shouted, and Earl looked over to see that he had been followed from the tent by a familiar figure that he could not place in time or memory, until at last the man's sheer aggression imprinted itself, and he recognized him from his previous anger at the fancy embassy party some weeks ago.

'The fuck?' said the dark furious man. 'You just fuckin' walk out on Captain Latavistada like you're some kind of fuckin' *better* than him? Who the fuck are you, a prince, a nancy, a fuckin' Mr. Too Fuckin' Good for everybody?'

Earl rose quickly and it occurred to him to punch the prick bloody under the banyan tree on the parade ground, and how much pleasure would be had in the feeling of the flattened nose and the broken teeth and the spew of blood, but instead he just stared at him hard.

'Yeah, you. You fuckin' goofball, this is the shit that has to be done down here to keep it all from going blooie in our faces and Captain Latavistada is a *great* man who gets that while some fancy dick like you, you like to cold-cock guys in train stations and ambush 'em while they're reading the newspaper on their sofas, but you ain't got the fuckin' hubcaps for this sort of thing. You yellow piece of shit, I ought to — '

'You shut that yap, mister, and shut it hard, or I will shut it for you, and all these Cubans can watch me pound the snot out of you ounce by ounce.'

Whoever he was, he was taken aback by Earl's defiance, but the surprise instantly transmuted into rage, his face flashed the dead white of

323

assault, and he waded in. His first blow, a wide, circular notification by wire, was easily evaded, and Earl instead snared the second one, only slightly less telegraphed, transformed its power by the primitive alchemy of judo back onto his attacker, and rammed the guy's noggin hard against the trunk of the tree.

He did it a couple more times, taking satisfaction in the gash he opened in the hairline and the spurt of blood. Then he dropped the man, hard, on the ground.

'Ow, fuck,' spat Frankie Carbine, 'you fucking — '

'You piece of shit, you get up now and in one second I will beat the side of your head in and fertilize this shithole with your brains. I am not your kidding type, so you listen now or you die in five seconds.'

The man stayed down. He put his hand to his hairline, now producing copious blood, that before swelling and turning purple-yellow like a rotted grapefruit.

'You got me with a trick.'

'Yeah, a trick called faster and tougher, you fucking human blister. I ought to pop you and drain all that pus out now, you New York grease factory.'

He dared the man to rise; the man, though still deep full of aggression, was not stupid; he stayed down, but the look in his feral eyes and his ugly knitted features suggested that the next time he saw Earl would be over the sights of a pistol.

'Earl, Earl,' Frenchy suddenly crooned,

breaking though the small knot of Cubans who'd gathered to watch the amusing spectacle of a big man crushing a smaller one, a sure laugh-getter in most of the world's precincts, 'it's all right, ignore him.'

He turned to the man.

'Sport, Lansky would have you shipped back to the States in a straw basket if he knew what you'd just pulled. We are trying to stay on top of a fluid situation and get it done, and we don't need showboat New York thugs going screwball on us. You get back to Havana or I will make a phone call and you will not see Manhattan again in a dream.'

Sullenly the battered man rose, scuffed insolently at the dirt, and launched a gob that wasn't aimed east enough to strike Earl but not west enough to avoid insult. He slumped off.

'Who's that jaybird?'

'He's a mob guy. He hangs out with the secret police and reports to some big people who run the casinos in Havana. He's nobody, really. He's a worm, that's all. He's not worth beating up.'

'Son, if you call that 'beating up', you don't know much about beating up.'

'Well, yeah. Anyhow, we have something. Something good. We have to move.'

'What is it?'

'Latavistada broke the witness. It was all in Spanish but I understood. Beautiful Eyes is making sure and dotting all the i's. But the gist of it is that someone saw Castro being led off right at the end by some kind of peasant. But a weird kind of peasant. Some tall, lanky, scrawny guy, with bristly gray hair. The description was, 'like a poet'. He looked like a poet, by which I take to mean slightly bohemian, or intellectual, what we might call a beatnik. Mean anything to you?'

Earl thought for a second.

'Yeah,' he finally said. 'It's somebody who knows what he's doing. These clowns will never find this guy, believe me. He's too good for them.'

'Is he too good for you, Earl? You'll have to hunt him down, too. You have to be better than he is.'

41

At one point, the Russian moved into the cab with the old man who was driving, and gave directions. He seemed to sense ambush and roadblock and sudden troop appearances as if he had a radar in his brain for such things. He always knew which street to turn down, how the alleys connected, and following these methods, he got them to the outskirts of a town abuzz with police activity.

Next came the river, where he cleansed himself and felt somehow repaired, or at least improved in spirit. By then it was the middle of the day.

'Time to rest, my friend,' said the Russian.

'Where? We need shelter.'

'If we seek shelter, we alert someone who in turn mutters something to someone else and before you know it, you're before the wall, only this time, I'm standing beside you. Oh, and neither of us has any eyes. No thank you. You rest here, by the river. You keep low. Sleep if you can. We have a long journey ahead of us.'

'To where? I should be with my men.'

'Your men are dead. Your task is to survive and consecrate their sacrifice. We won't comment on the stupidity of it all, and if you win in the end, you can order the historians to portray last night as a triumph instead of a folly. If they refuse, shoot them and find new historians. Now rest.'

Speshnev thanked the truck driver, and bid him off, and when he had gone, led the young revolutionary down closer to the river. Here, he was invisible yet had a view across the water to the city, and a view down the dirt road that ran atop the crest. In the distance lay some peasant *bohios*, thatched-roof huts, surrounded by broken fencing, donkeys and chickens.

'You wait. Go nowhere. Shit in your pants. You don't need to tell anyone about your heroism. You wait here. I have arrangements to make.'

'You can get me there,' Castro said, gesturing to the beckoning mountains that seemed to be just yards away but were still miles off.

'To do what, live in a cave? Just wait.'

And with that, he vanished so quickly that Castro had a sense that he was magical. Could he be an angel? Castro didn't believe in God, but he believed in God's angels, paradoxical or not. Possibly this man was such an angel. Whoever he was, he was a capable fellow. He certainly knew a lot of things. He had a gift for suddenness, either in the appearance or the disappearance department.

The young man lay and tried to sleep. But he was too agitated. He kept seeing bodies shot and sloppy, arms and legs flung out, blood spattering everywhere. He kept hearing the sound of the bullets ripping into the car. He kept feeling the spray of glass whizzing at him as a bullet shattered a windshield. He kept thinking of what he could have done that he had not or what he had done that he wished he hadn't.

He turned his vision to the city across the

328

muddy river. One could tell that El Presidente was quite upset by the little adventure of the night, as police squad cars, the unmarked black cars of the secret police, and the jeeps of the military were everywhere, stopping cars at road-blocks, yanking occupants out to examine their documents. He watched them from across the water, nestled down deep, close to the bank. Even some airplanes buzzed overhead, old Mustangs the Americans had given their little Cuban brothers. But the planes stayed high and seemed to be merely for show; the police cars never came close, all in all; it was quite comfortable by the river, as the noon elongated into afternoon. He found a comfortable way of wedging himself into the vegetation so that crushed rushes cushioned his backside; it was like a very nice bed. He wished he had a cigar. But he saw that a cigar would be of no help in his current predicament.

A few hours later, near nightfall, an old peasant wandered the road. He seemed in no particular hurry to get anywhere and no one would pay him the slightest attention. But at a certain moment, he disappeared into the bushes. And when Castro next saw him, he was quite close; but he had taken his old hat off, and Castro saw that he was the Russian.

'Say, you are a tricky fellow.'

'I may know a thing or two. Here, I bring you some treats.'

He had food and a bag of clothes, for Castro a short-sleeved shirt to wear over his army pants. The young man took off and squirreled away his army fatigue shirt. He drew the cream-colored shirt around him, buttoned it, and it hung over his belt, partially obscuring the military nature of his pants. It wasn't much of a disguise but it certainly was better than the sergeant's uniform, which all of Cuba was hunting.

He wolfed the food ravenously, for he felt as if he hadn't eaten in days. It was a cold pork sandwich and a bottle of warm beer, but still delicious.

'What is the word? What have they done to the men?'

'I told you. Forget the men. The men are gone. They rounded them up and took them to the barracks and Ojos Bellos cut their eyes out and they were shot. Such is life. Such is war.'

'All of them?'

'Most, it is said.'

'It shouldn't have turned out like this. We didn't even make it into the barracks. We were hung up outside and — '

'I saw. Someday I will teach you how to plan and administer an attack on a fortification. You don't just drive up to it, you idiot. What did you think would happen?'

'I thought the soldiers would be drunk. And I did not think they would fight for Batista.'

'They were drunk but not drunk enough. And they don't give a shit about Batista. These are bored country boys in dull garrison duty. Give them a chance to shoot something and you make them happy. You gave them the best day of their lives. They will tell stories of the heroic defense of the one thousand against the one

330

hundred for a century.'

'They were lucky. I — '

'No, you were stupid. Now stop it. Don't argue with me. You don't know enough to argue. You need your rest. We will move in a while.'

'The mountains?'

'You didn't have a plan for this?'

'No. I thought we'd succeed.'

'You are truly an idiot child. You should have yourself neutered so that you don't pass your simpleness on.'

'I already have a son.'

'Not that you've seen him in months.'

'Where are we going?'

'It's all arranged.'

'Havana! Yes, Havana!'

'Let's survive Santiago first.'

'But the future is — '

'The future is the next three days, or there is no future. I've made arrangements with certain people. We'll get you out. You will go into exile. You will learn, read, study, master tactics and training, absorb organization and administration, broaden your mind and meet people.'

'I could have done that before. Why now such a generous scholarship offer?'

'You don't know, do you?'

'No.'

'You're famous.'

'What?'

'Right now, you're the most famous man in Cuba. Your picture is in all the papers.'

'I am famous?'

'Absolutely, though for differing reasons. To

the police and the military and El Presidente, you are a monster. To the Americans you are a threat. To the people you are a hero.'

This genuinely pleased the young man. A broad smile crossed his face, unbidden; he seemed to glow in the knowledge of this new thing. He was no longer a street-corner orator, a voice occasionally on the radio, an essayist for little radical papers like *Alerta*. No, he was famous. He forgot to ask about his wife and child, his parents, his men. All no longer existed.

'What do they say of me?'

'Vain boy! What, do you think this is going to get you a movie contract?'

'No, I care only for my country and my people. I have no need of this fame except as a tool to save my country. But . . . '

'But is it a good picture?'

'Well, yes.'

'Yes, it's a good picture. It happens to be your wedding picture. You and Mirta. They've cut her out of it, of course, so all the girls will like it. But it means that if you are seen, you are a phone call away from losing your eyes and getting a bullet in the skull. So we must move quickly.'

'Off, then. But . . . where? How? They are everywhere.'

'You leave it to me, sonny. This is what I do.'

★   ★   ★

''*The Blue Mountain / And River Cauto! / Sinews of the eternity which begat us. / The mountain warms us with its great heart, /*

Splendid son of excellence and infinity.' There, what do you think of that?'

'It's quite awful.'

'You are truly not a Cuban. That is the poem of Manuel Navarro Luna, 'Poemas Mambises'. It is a great work and it expresses that which is before us.'

'You may not be terribly fond of romantic mountain poetry after you've spent time being hunted by men in mountains. Believe me, they don't write poems about that kind of an experience.'

But Castro could not be denied, for before them lay the Sierra Maestra, the blue crest of mountains that dominated the coast around Santiago. They had trooped for hours in darkness, through brush, around farms, through chicken coops, avoiding the main roads, moving ever onward, going to rest in daylight — and now, in light, had at last emerged from the city so that there was nothing ahead of them except . . . mountains.

They could see the mountains, green and lush in the high summer of late July. It was like no other part of Cuba, looking more like the American West than anywhere, with woods clinging to the elevation. Beyond the crests, the mountains plunged precipitously to the sea.

'Will we make it?'

'We have a good lead. I do not know if they have changed their tactics yet, and turned to the countryside. I see no indication. But we will make it or not depending not on ourselves, but upon their skill. Do they track well? How well

333

trained are the dogs? Are the trackers smart in the way they follow us, or do they lumber about with a battalion and stop to smoke twice an hour? Do they know the roads? Can they follow spoor? What is their instinct for landform? How badly do they want it?'

'These are soldiers and policemen. I do not think they will enjoy the deep forest a bit.'

'That is true. But another question: Are the Americans involved? If the Americans put good men on the job — or even one good man — then we could be in trouble. A shame, but that's the way it goes.'

'Would they have such a man?'

'Actually, yes. He's here. I've met him. I know him slightly.'

'You should have killed him.'

'Actually, I killed somebody who was about to kill him. Twice even! They seemed such good decisions at the time. Now, I must admit, I have doubts about my own judgment.'

And it seemed to work so well for such a long time. Almost gaily, they took a road through the sugarcane fields of the coastal plain, and workers nodded at them and the young man waved back enthusiastically. He was not recognized, and they stopped for lunch in a little group of huts in the lee of the mountains, where nobody paid them much attention.

There was a last field to negotiate before the forestation of the slopes took over, then they were gone, happily, invisibly. But it was a raw patch where the cane had already been cut, and nothing but brown stubble remained. A smarter way might have been to travel the dirt road another few miles, and cut into the hills where the fields were thicker. But Speshnev decided the speed was worth the risk, and it was of course the wrong decision.

Speshnev heard a faint buzz and looked upward and saw the plane. He had a hope that it had either missed them or thought of them as just two more peasants wandering this way and that across the landscape, but the plane did not miss them and it did not think they were peasants, for it banked around, vectoring lower to get a better look at them, and if there was a moment when they might still have gotten away with it on bluff, that disappeared, for the young man panicked and took off running madly for the treeline.

Fool, Speshnev thought, but then he worried that the plane had snipers aboard, and so he too took off at a run.

42

A night of screaming had passed and then another morning. And then things began to happen. Earl watched it. Captain Latavistada and some aides came out of the torture tent, much agitated. They began shouting. Ripples spread through the assembly on the barracks' parade grounds. The soldiers formed up into loose squads, and someone began signaling a fleet of parked trucks to rev up and maneuver into a column. The captain was not quite an idiot; he knew this job could be done better with fifty men than with five hundred so he only took a hundred and fifty, ten trucks full. It took some time to get the trucks loaded, and while all this was going on, Earl sat and smoked a cigarette.

In time he smoked another and another, and then there was still a further delay as the dogs were brought up, and one of them got away, attacked a soldier, and had to be shot, and there was a scene between the civilian dog handler and the officer in charge. Earl had smoked almost a whole pack of cigarettes by the time Frenchy returned.

'Okay,' he said, 'they think they have him. A patrol plane spotted two guys heading for the mountains east of here, maybe ten miles. When the plane came around, the guys broke and ran. It's got to be him, right? Who else would be headed into the mountains and take off like that when spotted? And he's one of the few who hasn't been accounted for.'

'Two men,' said Earl. 'The Russian is still with him.'

Frenchy nodded.

'So we ought to get going. We can tag along with the convoy, then break off and move faster on our own.'

'Nope,' said Earl.

'What?'

'I said 'Nope'. Meaning, no, negative, zero, nothing, no, nope.'

'I — '

'See, he knows where he's going, that parade of fools has no idea, and the whole thing just ain't going to work. We throw in with them, we are plumb flat busted before we get going. Okay?'

'Earl, this is not a time to be playing games.'

'I ain't playing no games. We ain't going to get a shot at him if we go with these boys. The old fellow running our guy is too smart for that. Tracking won't work. The only thing that will work is interception.'

'I don't — '

'You get on that phone to your friend Roger St. Whatever-the-Fuck Evans. You get him on the phone to some prissy-ass boy at Guantanamo named Lieutenant Dan Benning. Dan loves Roger. He thinks Roger's going to get him into your outfit, so he wants to impress Roger. Here's what we want. A U.S. Navy helicopter out of Guantanamo to pick us up in Santiago. Pick a close-by spot, I don't know the town well

337

enough. Tell 'em to bring their best maps of the area — that is, the best *nautical* maps, with offshore depths indicated. Even our navy's smart enough to have 'em.'

'What do you need depths for?'

'Because I'm looking for a spot on the coast where the deep water runs in close to shore.'

'Whoa. I am so lost. I am — '

'He ain't just running this boy to noplace. He's got a plan. Best way out is by boat. It's probably set up. They'll go out where it's deepest, because the boat can get in close. It means they don't have to use no dinghy and they won't be hung up on the surface for an hour while they're rowing out.'

'How the hell will you know which way they're coming from? They could come through those hills in a hundred different ways.'

'I'll probably read it from the maps. But when I get there, we'll take a look-see of the area from the air. We'll figure out how he'll come through. That's where we'll set up. Those Cuban bastards will march him right to us. And we'll do the job they sent us to do and become big heroes and live in nice houses in Washington, D.C. Now get on that phone, sonny. Get on it fast.'

★ ★ ★

There was only a small problem, and that was that Roger wasn't immediately reachable by phone. He wasn't in the office or at the club, or on any of the courts that Frenchy knew about. So, goddammit, where was he?

338

'That's your job,' said Earl. 'I'll find the guy. You find your boss. Which one do you think is harder?'

'It's hard to guess where he is. He . . . he does things, meets people, that's his job. It's unpredictable.'

'Fine. It's your goddamn future going up in smoke, not mine. I can always go back to Arkansas and hand out speeding tickets.'

But finally Frenchy reached Roger, who neither explained nor apologized. The request was made. The flight was arranged. The pickup took place as planned.

After clearing the city, zipping over the harbor, sliding beyond the ever-thinning slums, the chopper at last broke free to the wild coast east of Santiago. Off to the left, the mountains bulked up cool and green, but here, as they raced along the coast, the land was just hilly, crusted with scrub vegetation, thorn, sawgrass. It was emerald green, but the green of green hell. It must have been 100 degrees out.

The sand of the beach blazed white, the blue Caribbean lapped gently against it. Vibrations, the odor of gasoline, and the roar of the engine filled the air. The bird was a Sikorsky S-55, just the newest thing. It looked like a double-decker Cadillac with a rotor and a boom attached, yet was as agile as a dragonfly, and even built up a good head of speed as it raced east down the coastline.

Earl worked the maps with the young ensign copilot while the crew chief and Frenchy waited below and the pilot kept the bird running hot and straight. Earl and the ensign designated a spot a few miles east of El Brujo, but not quite yet to Siboney, a beach town; that's where the bulge of dark map blue indicating navigable waters arched closest to shore. The chopper eased out of the air, kicking up sand and water as it hovered just beyond to drop off its cargo.

Earl rolled out, the Winchester slung on his back. Frenchy followed. He'd picked up a little M1 carbine somewhere and had a Government Model .45 in a tanker's holster. The two scrunched in the sand and watched as the helicopter rose to altitude, dipped its nose and rotor and headed back to Gitmo, fifty miles farther east. The beach was deserted.

'Now what?' Frenchy asked.

'Now we walk and climb.'

'Where?'

'Up there,' he said, and pointed. The hills rose steeply, though blanketed in forest. Earl consulted the map, upon which he'd made many notes, read the lines of the peaks a mile beyond and several thousand feet up, made further examinations through binoculars, wiped the sweat out of his eyes with his arm, pulled the hat back low over his eyes.

'There, I'd say,' he said, pointing to a certain gap in the crests that seemed no different from any other gap.

'Okay.'

'We shoot a compass reading and take off.'

'He'll come that way?'

'That's the gamble.'

340

'But just so I can explain to the board that ends my career, why? I mean, they'll need a good laugh.'

'Well, he's looking at the same hills right now, but from about six miles inland. And he's probably seen the trucks arrive by this time, seen them soldiers get out and form up and move out. So he knows he's being pursued. He'll track a way over the crest, but it won't be the most obvious, the lowest. He's too smart for that. He'll stay away. But he won't do the highest either, 'cause he'd lose too much time and he's got a schedule to meet. He's already made his arrangements. They can't be changed at this time, 'cause he don't have no walkie-talkie. Whatever they set up, that's what they're committed to.'

'Yeah, well, fine, but still I count at least five gaps up there, and that's discounting the highest and the lowest. So it'll be one of those gaps? And you know which one.'

'Yeah. See, he has no recon, so he doesn't know what's on this side. You have to see it as he sees it, and interpret it from the knowledge that he has. He has no idea that one, over there, leads to a natural fold in the earth, and that going down it would be much easier. The vegetation ain't so heavy either. No, way he's looking, he'll take the one that's the closest thing to a straight line from where he is, yet ain't obviously, outstandingly low. So that would be the one I have selected.'

'Man, I hope you're right.'

'Oh, I'm right. The question is, are you tough

enough to make it? We've got a climb to make, double-time.'

'Yeah, I'm fine. You know why? All that goddamn tennis. I'm in the best shape of my life. Boola-boola. Let's go make a big noise.'

43

First came the difficulty of unloading. It seemed that several of the sergeants had not recovered from drunken celebration after the attack on the barracks, and had disappeared, which left the squads in command of corporals. But the men resented the corporals, who had no power to grant leaves or promotions, and who therefore need not be obeyed. So the unloading went slowly and imperfectly. Upon at last exiting the vehicles, the men would not stay formed up in squad units. Instead, this fellow saw a friend from that squad and that fellow saw a friend from this squad, and soon it wasn't a formation at all, it was just a large group of men standing around in a sugarcane field near a village, a crowd actually, with no place to go.

Captain Latavistada screamed himself hoarse trying to get them to obey his orders. But he was not regular army; he was the ranking Servicio Intelligencio Militar officer on the spot, and so he had inherited command by virtue of SIM's predominence over the regular army. Its officers, in protest, had refused to accompany the men in the field. Not even Latavistada's threats of investigations could move the aristocratic officers — one of them, Morales, was after all the hero of the attack! — to cooperate with the differently connected and cultured Latavistada, more of a middle-class striver who had succeeded merely by excellence at torture, which was any fool's path to the top.

But ultimately, Latavistada bullied the men into some kind of rough obedience, primarily by finding the largest of them and beating him severely with a riding crop. Latavistada was many things, most of them horrible, but he was not and never would be a coward.

At last, hammered into some semblance of order, the men began to trudge out in the hot sun, across the sugarcane fields, to the Sierra Maestra that loomed ahead, led by a squad of barking, yapping dogs and their handlers. In a short time they came to the village, where several elders were rounded up and questioned.

No, they had seen no fleeing men.

No, they knew nothing about tracks.

No, they had no food to share.

A sergeant looked to Captain Latavistada in frustration. This was going nowhere and the men were losing interest, beginning to peel off in twos and threes to find a shady spot in which to rest, laying down their rifles, drinking too much from their canteens. The operational edifice of the thing was on the verge of teetering into chaos.

It was at this moment, fortunately, that the dogs picked up a scent. Latavistada could tell by the changed pitch in the barking, and his enthusiasm inspired most of the men to reassemble. In time a corporal came running over.

'Sir, we have a good spoor. The dog man, he says the dogs have the scent of the wild one, Greaseball, and we've found tracks and broken foliage; we can track them.'

'Excellent.'

He turned, gave a quick burst of orders to his corporals, and the men reassembled sluggishly. But he sensed it was time to get a little respect from all of them.

He gestured and an old man was brought over.

'I thought, old sir, you said no one had been through here.'

'No, sir,' said the man. 'What I said was, I had not seen anyone come through here. I cannot be held responsible for what I have not seen. Such would not be fair at all.'

'But then,' said the captain, 'life itself is not always fair, is it?'

He pulled out his Star automatic and shot the old fellow squarely between the eyes. It was a magnificent shot, and the old man collapsed into a pile in a split second, dead long before he hit the ground.

Captain Latavistada felt the need to further explain the day's lesson to the villagers.

'Do you now understand? When an important official requests your cooperation in the pursuance of his duties, it is the duty of all Cubans to help immediately. We do not have time for cleverness and games. I understand you easterners far out here in the provinces are backwards in your ways, but that is not an excuse. We require immediate obedience. That is what we do in Havana and that is what you owe your country and your president.'

The villagers quavered in the fiery presence of such a man, and could not meet his gaze. It occurred to Latavistada to order his men to burn the village, for they would certainly love that, most of them being from villages just like it and therefore hating it passionately, but he elected instead to move out to track the fugitives, believing he had accomplished enough of an educational nature that day.

★ ★ ★

'What was that?' said Castro.

They were halfway up a hill, thistly and brambly, ten miles east of Santiago; the hill was the only thing that lay between themselves and the sea. But it was not an easy climb; they had a long way yet to go.

'I suspect they have just shot somebody,' said the Russian.

'Oh, god. They got here so fast.'

'Not actually. In any decent police state, they'd be a lot more efficient. In Red Spain, for example, toward the end, the discipline we had achieved was phenomenal. The Spaniards made excellent secret policemen. They had a gift, though I must say it surprises me to find it so lacking in you or in any of the president's crew.'

The closeness of danger increased his loquacity exponentially, while the wild fear in the young man annoyed him. He could not help but notice it. A twitch about the dry lips had started up, really repellent. Ugh, the whole left side of the mouth jerked upward spastically. The eyes were unable to focus, the face had turned gray, the breathing shallow, the sweat clammy on his pale, oval face. For some reason, this brought out the monster in Speshnev.

He felt like sitting the young man down and lecturing him for several hours on all the things he did not know, on the sentimentality of his dreams, the vagueness of his plans, the suicidal nature of his operations. This fellow had so much to learn! He had learned nothing yet! He was unformed, like some sort of retarded child who with his pretty face and incredible luck bobbed this way and that on the tides of history.

They had found a path through the forest, which essentially trended upwards, broken up here and there by knots of rock. The skyline was invisible given the heavy canopy and the only penetrating light came from behind, not above, where it reflected off what could be seen of the sugarcane field where it was still visible between the knitted tree trunks a half mile or so down the slope.

'We had better be going, no?' asked the young man.

'Not quite. Let's see how he's going to run this little drama. Look about for a tree, straight, with good stout branches.'

'Do we have — '

'Yes, yes, yes. Find one! Do something helpful for a change!'

The boy found one; Speshnev, of course, found a better one. He commanded the boy to lean against its trunk, his legs splayed for support, his arms wrapped securely about the center shaft. That posture established, Speshnev used him as a kind of stepladder, pulling himself up till at last he stood on the braced shoulders and therefore was able to gain leverage on a thick branch at shoulder level. From there, he scampered like a monkey up the trunk and when he was high enough, locked himself against it, pivoted, drew his binoculars, and fixed on his pursuers.

In time, he came down.

'What did you see?'

'What I expected, mostly. Amateurism. He moved the troops out from the village, but raggedly, at the half-step. He was smart enough to break one team of athletes — fast movers — off to the right, where evidently the foliage is thinner. They're the blockers. They're going to race us to the top and cut us off, and drive us back to the main body.'

'Oh, Christ.'

'He probably has only one or two good platoon-level leaders. That would be par for this pitiful army. His best man he clearly put in charge of the fast movers, for that's the key to his operation.'

'Will we beat them?'

'Well, no. But we don't have to. He didn't send enough. They will reach the crest ahead of us, but they will be hot and angry and sloppy. And, there aren't enough of them to form a line. They'll stagger, lose contact, look for the easiest ways through the thorns. At a certain moment, we'll go to ground. We assume they'll pass us by. They'll run into the main body. There'll be a scene, recriminations, threats of punishment. Under that distraction, we'll make it to the crest at one of its lowest points, but not its lowest, because once they realize they have missed us, they will go immediately for the lowest one. Do you see?'

'How do you know all this for certain?'

'One just knows certain things. Come on, now. We have to get as close to the fast movers as possible, for the further they come down, the more they will recover and the less sloppy they will become. The higher up we encounter them, the better for us.'

'I hope you know what you're doing.'

'So do I. These are the only eyes I own.'

★   ★   ★

Earl saw the execution. He was in the gap at the crest of the hill and the village was a full mile away. But the 10x Leica binoculars resolved it well enough: he saw the pistol come up and jump, and the old man go instantly limp, and fall hopelessly to the earth. From so far away the sound of the shot only reached him seven seconds later and it was dry crack, not like a shot at all, but windblown and hollow.

Something in him recoiled at the ugly nakedness of it. He fixed his binocs on the officer, now busy giving orders, and saw without surprise that it was the fellow with the scalpel who worked on eyes. He spat into the dust, slipped back a little, lit a cigarette.

In time, Frenchy caught up. He was limping badly.

'Goddamn boots,' he said. 'I have a blister.'

Earl looked and saw the young man had the Abercrombie & Fitch luxury items, creamy dark leather.

'You'd think for all I paid for them,' Frenchy said, 'they wouldn't be bad.'

'You didn't break 'em in good. Say, where'd you get that pistol?'

'Earl, it's just like yours. A Colt Super .38. I saw the guys you put down. Man, I had to have one.'

'Don't shoot yourself. Or me.' Earl pulled his pack around, pulled out the first-aid kit, and got out a bandage.

'Here. Patch it up. You've got a lot of walking left today.'

Frenchy set about to repair himself while Earl peered over the crest, watching the officer make his dispositions. He watched as a designated crew stripped off helmets and packs and left rifles behind, taking only canteens and pistols, and began to assault the mountainside in a single line, on the double quick. He broke the remaining troops into three other elements, and each set off to find a different way up the mountain.

Frenchy asked him what happened.

'He shot an old man,' Earl said. 'Then he split his troop up into four elements. He's sending one, stripped, to block the hill. The others will maneuver and pursue.'

'So where do you think they are?' Frenchy said, fiddling with his own binoculars.

'Somewhere about halfway down. Probably less than a thousand yards from where we now sit. Somewhere down in that forest. I'd guess they're in the brush, because they might be visible from the trails. If the officer can spot them, he can bring fire on them and pin them. Then it's over.'

'Maybe the officer will do our job for us.'

'I don't think so. I think they'll get up close to the crest and try and hide from the boys coming up fast. They think they can evade, get over the crest, and get down before the officer can reassemble his people and get them onto this side in some kind of order.'

'So where will our boy go over the crest?'

'He'll go over where it's brush so that nobody can get a fix on him. Then he'll beeline down, but not where it's easiest. I make it halfway down there — ' he pointed to a fold in the side of the mountain, ' — and that gets him to the beach, not as fast as where it's clearer but under better cover.'

'So that's it.'

'That's it. And he'll make it, too. This has been figured nicely, I think. Very good job. This guy is a professional.'

'You know how it's got to be, Earl,' said Frenchy. 'Castro, then the other guy. Kill them both, Earl, and send the message we came here to deliver. The Big Noise. Then we can go home heroes.'

'Oh, boy,' said Earl, 'that's just what I want to be.'

44

Roger thought he would be seedy. In his mind, all Russians were pitiful little men in suits cut by drunken chimpanzees, with bad haircuts, bad manicures, bad teeth. But this fellow was well equipped, even splendidly equipped, in all the important areas: the linen suit was British, his hair was well trimmed and Brylcreemed back smoothly, he had glossy fingernails and his teeth were white and flawless.

'You look surprised, Mr. Evans. You have never spoken with one of us, I take it.'

'No, I haven't,' said Roger. 'I have never felt it necessary. I know my task. Now see here, uh, Mr. Pashin, this was your idea. Let's not turn it into an ordeal, let's get on with it.'

'But a drink, surely.'

He raised his hand, snapped his fingers with authority and instantly, obeying the mandates of the cosmopolitan culture, a waiter hurried over.

'Señor Pashin?'

'Ah, I shall have the '48 St. Emilion, as usual, Rodgrigo.'

'Si, Señor Pashin. I should have known.'

'And you, Mr. Evans?'

Roger almost made a big deal. You don't drink with the enemy. It just isn't done. Nobody would understand. But he felt considerable stress from a variety of difficulties, and so, what the hell?

'Gin and tonic. Tanqueray. Large slice of lime,

352

but don't squeeze it. I'll squeeze it myself.'

'Si, señor.'

They sat, the two of them, in the elegant bar of a restaurant called the Salon Miami on the Malecon. Across the way, just beyond the traffic, the blue Caribbean stretched to the horizon, under lowering clouds. A single palm was visible, blowing. It looked like some weather was coming in.

'Well,' said Roger, 'you're probably not one for chitchat. Nor am I. You sent me this message. Here I am. You said a proposition. I am here to listen. I must warn you, I will almost certainly say no. We have very strict rules. I will also make a report on this to my headquarters, as I am required to do.'

'Well, that's fine, if you want to. Anyhow, yes, I do have an offer for you. Think it over. You may find it to your advantage. I am not a salesman and this isn't a sale. It's just that we find ourselves, or so I am led to believe, in somewhat parallel circumstances.'

The drinks arrived; Roger had his, quickly ordered another. The Russian, meanwhile, was making quite a show of his, sniffing it, sloshing it, taking a small taste, then a larger, then giving his okay.

'Not to be rude,' said Roger, 'but what could you hope to offer me? And how could we possibly be in a 'parallel' situation.'

'Assistants. Mine is an older fellow. He has supporters in Moscow and they have an interest in having him succeed. I cannot discipline him as I feel is necessary because he'll crybaby to them

353

and I'll get snotty cables from home. Very annoying.'

'And mine?'

'Same problem, different situation. Yours is younger, very ambitious. He has a mind full of schemes. You don't quite trust him, nor should you. You're not sure quite where his loyalties lie.'

Roger made a not very successful attempt to hide his annoyance that the Russian knew so damned much.

'Oh, you think I have a spy in your office, Mr. Evans? I assure you I do not. But it's a small diplomatic community, and people talk and I listen. So I know you are not sure where your assistant's loyalties lie.'

'They lie with me, Mr. Pashin. I am the Agency, as far as he is concerned.' But even as he spoke it and radiated belief as if it were deep religious faith, a certain anger flared deeply within his interior landscape. Who really knew about Walter 'Frenchy' Short. Who *was* Walter 'Frenchy' Short? Where the hell did this 'Frenchy' stuff come from anyhow?

'Well, if that is so, then I have wasted both our times and I apologize. I will leave you now, if you prefer. Or we may have a pleasant visit, gossiping about embassy society. I hear you are a very fine athlete. That is helpful; I'm sure it helps you. I wish I had a gift like that. I'm just a grind, trying to — '

'All right,' Roger said. 'It's true. One could have a better assistant than Walter. I'm not certain how his mind works. It disturbs me a little. There are people who just belong, and

354

people who don't. I am of the former. I am liked, I am noticed. He is not. No one would select him. He is expendable, I am confident to say, and therefore possibly bitter and treacherous.'

'Well, you have been frank, so I will be frank. Let me express my situation freely. Unlike you, I am crippled in fear. If this Speshnev brings off something spectacular, it could ruin me. I must be honest with myself: I cannot let this man, this Jew, this Bolshevik, this romantic, this old dog, this grotesque figure out of *A Coffin for Demetrios* have a great success and attract attention. I must stop it now or I will regret it forever.'

Roger didn't say a thing. He didn't have to. In his way, the Russian had just precisely articulated his own terrors, now that Frenchy and his cowboy chum were out in the bush. If Frenchy succeeded, he profited, and now that everyone knew about Castro, now that he was famous, the ante was upped considerably.

'I want nothing from you,' said Pashin. 'This isn't a deal or an alliance. I just want to pass some information to you. It will help you profit. You will triumph. Your triumph will be Speshnev's downfall. Do you understand? I will tell you, pay the bill, and depart. You may do what you wish with the information. If you can use it to rein in your supposed underling and his wild schemes and at the same time advance yourself, so be it. Check it out any way you please; you will see that it is accurate, I guarantee you.'

Roger said nothing.

'All right, then. Speshnev is, as you have suspected, with Castro. I spoke to him only a day ago, by phone, and have spent the ensuing time making the arrangements he requested. What you have not suspected is that he isn't just helping him flee into the mountains to hide indefinitely. No, far more is planned for young Castro. Speshnev is to get him to the coast by late this afternoon. There a Jamaican trawler lurks offshore. It is actually an NKVD radio vessel, equipped with some of our most sophisticated equipment. It is a tribute to just how intensely certain of our intelligence executives believe in this Castro that Speshnev has set up, through me, his rescue, a rather elaborate thing, quite expensive even by your standards. Castro will be taken offshore and disappear for a while. He will actually be in Moscow, where he will undergo rigorous training in various political and guerilla arts. At a propitious time in the future, so trained, his talent honed, his mind made supple and aggressive by education, his motivations laid out in black and white, he will be infiltrated to begin a war against El Presidente. Through it all, Speshnev will be his mentor, his guide, his spiritual leader, his confessor. Both will prosper. You will not. Your country will not. Alas, I will not either.'

'We have a man there to block.'

'Let us hope he is good. As good as Speshnev. But few are, so, sadly, this fellow probably isn't. I know the one. Beefy, a police type. I've seen pictures.'

356

'Yes, that's him.'

'So if this American gets the Cuban, so be it. I hope he gets the Jew too, but if he does not, it doesn't matter, for he has destroyed him just the same. You are happy, I am happy. But if the American doesn't get him, then I advise you to advise your navy to intercept the vessel — it is called the *Day's End* — and board it. Remove the two of them. Speshnev actually doesn't know much, as he has been on vacation in our winter wonderland. But still, he will amuse your debriefers. As for the Cuban, shoot him and feed his body to the sharks. The *Day's End*. Registered in Negril Harbor. The boat number is NC554. That's the one. There's your treasure. Now, you are a hero, I am a traitor, but a safe one, and that is that.'

He threw down the last of his wine, rose, and walked off.

Roger watched him go, a man sure of himself and now of his future. Roger signalled his two bodyguards to draw close, and as they approached, he thought about how quickly he could get to the embassy, how quickly he could report to headquarters, how quickly the navy could intercept the *Day's End*, and where he would end up living in Berlin.

45

There was nothing to be done. They would die or they would not die. What could be done had been done.

Speshnev, with his strong wrists and fingers, kept the boy's face buried in the vegetation. With his knee locked into the boy's buttocks, he pinned him to the earth. They lay in the brush, in stickers and thorns, amid snakes and scorpions, under a fiery sun on an airless day. They lay as intimately as inverted lovers, though no sexual tension was felt by either. There was too much fear for that. A slight rush of wind moved leaves against each other, a dry, crackly rubbing.

Speshnev had the discipline himself not to look, but he knew the boy lacked it, which is why he pinioned him so. You could never tell. Some men, for some reason, have a special sensitivity to another's eyes upon them. When hiding or sneaking or crawling or penetrating, a key rule: never, ever look at the man you're trying to evade or fool. To do that is to risk alerting him and if he's alerted, you are dead.

They lay deep in the brambles, which snarled about them, scraping and cutting. They were surrounded in vegetation, in so far and so tight no one could believe a man, much less two, could penetrate that deep. Speshnev's clothes were dark enough and, with his body, he covered

358

the creamy lightness of the boy's thin shirt. Hours seemed to pass. He would not allow the boy any movement at all, and he himself had acquired a stillness that was unto death. Many men can't be still for very long. The blood courses, the muscles tighten, and, moreover, any impingement on the flesh increases thunderously in its sensation. Many cannot endure such a willful torture.

Speshnev could and he didn't care if the boy could or couldn't, the little monster wasn't going to give himself or anyone else up.

Something stung him. Something crawled up him. Some sweat — or was it blood? — ran down from the dark bandanna about his head, tickling him as it went. He took an ascetic's pleasure in tracking each of these discomforts. Locked savagely beneath him, the boy squeaked somehow, shuddered a bit, but could not escape the clench that bound the two together.

The soldiers were only fifty feet away now. Speshnev hadn't looked at them for an hour, but he'd registered them in detail earlier. They had no rifles, no packs, and they had sweated wholly through their khakis in the long, fast, demanding climb upwards. Some had pistols, others had machetes. None had hats. They seemed to have recovered quickly, more quickly than he had anticipated. Possibly the officer beneath, Ojos Bellos, had chosen only athletes for this mission. The man was not quite a fool. Athletes would find their breath faster, focus their vision more sharply, commit more assiduously to the physical demands of the ordeal.

'All right,' an officer screamed in Spanish. 'Another ten feet, and halt. Do not rush yourselves. Look very carefully and methodically, if I catch anyone not paying attention, I will beat him myself, do you understand?'

The line of soldiers edged forward through the heavy brush, wading through a sea of thorns.

'Lieutenant, it hurts and my feet are so delicate,' mocked a man, to much laughter.

'Lopez, you I will personally humiliate with a horsewhip. Now shut that fat mouth of yours, and do your duty.'

More laughter, but still, these boys were professional. Speshnev guessed that it was three-to-two against.

He pressed harder against the boy. A mosquito hummed in his ear. A fly bit him. A new track of sweat or blood coursed down his face.

★   ★   ★

'So what are we looking for?' asked Frenchy.

'I don't know,' said Earl. 'If I see it, I will know.'

They were about three hundred feet back down the mountain, on the sea side, having backed off the crest as the soldiers came up and established their blocking positions. Earl was locked against a tree trunk, the heaviness of the wood supporting his binoculars as he scanned, steadily, left to right.

'Suppose they don't come this way.'

'They'll come this way. It's the only way.'

'How do you know?'

'Because now he has to come over under cover. So you look at the covered areas. Some are so dense a man couldn't get through. Some are so light, a man, especially two, could easily be seen. So he's got to come over in one of three zones, where the brush is thick enough to cover him but not so thick as to slow him down.'

'It all looks the same to me,' said Frenchy, a few trees away, arranged similarly to Earl, staring into binocs as well.

'I *know* that,' said Earl. 'That's why *I'm* doing the looking.'

Frenchy said nothing. He had nothing to say. It was hard for him to pay close attention to the monotony of the crest of the mountain where it was tangled in brush. It was green twisted into a kind of matting atop the spine of the mountain, of unvarying density and coloration.

'How the hell can you see so *much?*' he complained.

Earl didn't reply. He was too busy looking.

'Maybe he won't even come this way. Maybe he'll go parallel along the mountain to some other spot, and maybe go over tonight. He saw those troops, too. Maybe he had time to get the hell out.'

'Then what's he do?'

'Well, I don't know. Works his way to Havana.'

'Havana's four hundred miles away.'

'Goes back to Santiago.'

'Filled with soldiers and people who'd sell him out in a second.'

'Maybe he just hunkers down in a cave.'

'This kid? With his sense of importance, his

361

conviction of specialness? He's going to hide in a goddamn cave?'

'Well, what's *here* for him?'

'The boat.'

'Well, we're still not sure there is a boat.'

'No,' said Earl, '*you're* the only one who isn't sure there's a boat.'

After a bit Frenchy turned around to regard the deep blue Caribbean, cupped in the arms of a bay, but from this height also yielding a vision of horizon. A tawdry wooden craft seemed to be meandering about, with dirty sails, dragging some fishing netting. A negro crew struggled to look lively on its raggedy, narrow deck.

'Oh,' said Frenchy. 'I hadn't noticed it.'

'Yeah, well, no fishing boat runs that deep in the water and it don't head in to shore, particularly on the one place the map shows is deep enough for it to get in real close by accident. That's the 4 P.M. bus out of here.'

★ ★ ★

The boot was American. He had seen them in the war, toward the end, in the false peace before he was re-arrested, that one strange month of May 1945, when Americans and Russians mingled freely in the rubble of the Third Reich, and one world seemed gone forever and a new one, a better one, aborning from the destruction and the vodka.

The Americans made fine boots. Unlike Russian boots, which were simply bags of unfinished leather sewn brutally to a sole in the approximately appropriate shape, the American boot was designed exactly to the contours of the foot, it was drawn tight by a netting of laces, it never slipped off or grew wobbly and if lost would be replaced in minutes. Pity the poor Soviet soldier who lost a boot; he'd go without until . . . well, until.

Speshnev had ample opportunity to study this boot, particularly. It was seven inches from his eyes. It was planted firmly against the rocky ground by a private in the Cuban infantry, presumably a stout farm lad, judging by the evident stockiness of his ankle and the length and breadth of the foot. He put it where he put it, which was just in front of Speshnev's face and that was, actually, quite a lucky thing. Had he placed it closer, he might have stepped on Speshnev's face, felt the give of flesh beneath, and blasted away with the Star pistol he brandished. Had he been farther, he might have had a good angle through the dense thickets of bramble and thorn and caught a glimpse of the non-organic, and done the same ugly deed with his pistol.

But as it was he was simply set against the earth, and Speshnev, on top of his frozen ward, lay concentrating on his boot because he could look no other place. What he could hear sounded like an ax blade whizzing close by, hungry for his scrawny neck. But it was actually the blade of the machete the young soldier wielded as he probed and flicked and stabbed, searching for the bodies of hiding men, unaware utterly, for now, that those men were literally at his feet.

The whisper of the blade waved magically through the brush, and Speshnev felt its breeze, and particles of leaf and branch its edge liberated, as they drifted down upon him.

Then silence.

Then the sound of rush, as an artillery shell comes in, the one that gets you — he knew this, having been blown up twice, once in Spain, once outside Novograd — and the blade struck earth savagely but two inches from the end of his nose, and vibrated ever so gently. The soldier was stabbing randomly into the brush about his feet.

Beneath, the boy squirmed; but Speshnev had iron fingers about his mouth, crushing his lips to deadness, so he could not involuntarily give a coward's squeak and reveal them.

The blade probed, came closer, and withdrew.

'All right,' the sergeant called. 'Move forward another ten feet. He's got to be here somewhere.'

'I think this greaseball has shit himself to nothingness,' came a jeer, followed by laughter.

'If so, you'd smell the shit. I think he's somewhere down the hill and he's put a bullet in his greaseball head.'

The soldiers moved onward. It would be another hour before they were far enough away for Speshnev to move, and then he'd only have a few minutes before the main body of troops got up here, with the dogs, and picked up the trail ahead.

'Are we safe?' muttered the boy, when at last Speshnev released his iron grip.

'Hardly,' said the Russian.

'They're over,' said Earl.

'How do you know? I didn't see a thing.'

'The birds. A flock of 'em just blew out of the brush, fast and sudden.'

'Earl, birds fly out of the jungle all the time.'

'When they take off on their own, the head Johnny goes first, his lieutenants follow, then come the privates and then the gals. When they all blow out at once, they've been startled.'

'Maybe it was a boar or a coyote.'

'Ain't much moving about a forest during daylight, and with all them soldiers over there, there'd be even less. No, it's them.'

Earl slipped the binoculars back into their case. He picked up the rifle, ran a last check over it, unlocking and easing back the bolt to double-check that a .30-06 nested comfortably in the chamber, then quietly relocked it, rechecked the safety. By this time, Frenchy had come over and kneeled next to him with his carbine at the ready.

'Okay,' said Earl, 'he's got to go left because it's thinnest there. He's got to get down fast because that boat is getting in close and his meet-up is probably scheduled for 1600 hours and that boat just can't linger there forever, not with all the naval activity this close to Gitmo. He'll go down left, there's a natural fold he'll be in, then they have to avoid that open field, so they'll have to detour around that before they reach a last line of trees. I'm betting there's a creek over that way, 'cause you can see the trees are greener, they're getting more water.'

'I didn't see that.'

'No, you didn't. Anyhow, I have no way of knowing which way they'll go around that field, but I do know they won't walk down the middle of it. I'm betting men racing down a hill ahead of dogs and troops are going to be hellish thirsty and the temptation of that water will be too much, since they have to go that way anyhows. So that's where they'll head. And that's why we have to be there first. He'll pick up we're on him if we're still moving into place as he gets there.'

'Sounds good to me,' Frenchy said sportily.

'It don't matter how it sounds to you,' Earl replied. 'That's how we'll do it.'

★   ★   ★

In many ways, coming down is worse than going up, especially if speed is an issue.

Speed was an issue.

Speshnev could see the trawler just a few hundred yards off the beach, yet it was still half a mile away — downhill — and the craft couldn't linger there forever. He knew he had to move them quickly.

But that meant his muscles and the boy's had to work against gravity and momentum, always on the tippy, tippy edge of disaster, their legs buckling in pain as the fibers clenched in exactly the opposite way as they'd clenched when climbing.

He heard the boy huffing and puffing beneath, and there was an edge of panic to all that labored breath. Once, already, the boy had lost control, and gone shooting by him, hellbent on destruction, on a broken leg or shattered ankle, and Speshnev had grabbed him and a chunk of brush simultaneously and guided them to a slow-down and then a stop.

'I can't go any further.'

'If you value your eyes, you'll stop complaining and start moving.'

'Oh, Christ,' said the boy.

'Yes, call to Christ, but whomever you call to, get going.'

'I am so thirsty. I have dust in my throat.'

'There's a whole ocean out there for you.'

Speshnev looked back. As yet no dogs had crested the hill, but it could happen at any second, and here, where the forest was thin and rocky, where their feet kicked up puffs of dust and shale, they'd be easily spotted and brought under fire. And under fire, there'd be no escape. The Cubans weren't any kind of shooters, but there were enough of them, and their fusillade would either bring down the runners dead and wounded, or pin them for more leisurely fates.

'Go, go.'

Off they ran, trying to control the wildness that built in their limbs as they rushed down, fast but not too fast, close to the edge but not over it.

The boy gasped in agony, and even the mighty Speshnev, escape artist and ambush master, assassin and agent, guerilla and infantry commander, had to admit this was the most difficult moment in his long war against the forces of darkness. His ankles ached in the effort and the body's fear undercut everything. He didn't think they'd make it, not without a bad fall and if the fall were bad enough, it could end them. And the boat was so close.

The boy collapsed, heaving.

'I can't go on. I'm spent. Leave me.'

'Stop it. I don't have that choice.'

'I'm gone, blown, finished. I have no — '

'Look, ahead, beyond the meadow. Do you see it?'

'The boat? It could be miles away, that's how little chance I have of — '

The dogs barked. Speshnev looked up and saw three of them, unleashed, against the crest. They howled to indicate they'd picked up the scent and waited patiently for their masters and permission to bound down the hill.

The boy was beyond caring.

'Not the boat,' Speshnev said. 'No, look down there, just beyond the field. See where the trees are so much greener? Water. There's a creek bed there. We'll head there, we can make it before the men get over the top. Water, Castro, it'll revive you. Once you get the water, you'll recover instantly. You're simply dehydrated, that's all. Come on — '

And he lifted the boy up, feeling the tremors of surrender in the lax musculature and the heart beating desperately, the lungs sucking over dried lips for oxygen, and never quite getting enough. 'Come on, now, just fight it another two hundred yards, and there's salvation!'

★　★　★

Frenchy had never believed in it. Not for a second. It seemed some fantasy to him, some improbable crusade that this Davy Crockett from Arkansas were pulling on him. But then he saw them: two men, one of them demonstrably the young political leader Castro, rushing helter-skelter downhill exactly where Earl had said they'd come, their arms windmilling for balance as they fought the pull of gravity, both ashen and desperate, both craven with thirst.

If he felt any triumph, Earl didn't show it. His manner was glum, matter-of-fact, professional. Now was time for the shooting.

Earl unslung the rifle. They were about two hundred yards out, on a slight ridge, and Earl had sited them so they had a good line of fire straight onto the widest part of the creek, where a beaten man could drown his face in sweet green water and suck it down, and cool his weary, booted feet. No limbs, no brush, nothing interceded to deflect the bullet. It was a simple matter for someone as sure a shot as Earl.

'You can make it?' Frenchy nevertheless asked, nervous. 'Should I cover and lay fire on in case you miss?'

'Shut up,' said Earl.

Earl squirmed some, found a good shooting position and drew the rifle to him as, now three hundred yards away, the men rushed toward the water. They'd drink and rest for a minute, then hurry onward. Frenchy turned and saw that the trawler had gotten within fifty yards of the beach; it would be an easy slosh, and its cargo safely aboard, the boat would set fair wind for

Jamaica and be gone in minutes.

Earl locked his knee and rose and hunched simultaneously behind the rifle, feeling his way into a solid shooting position. Frenchy squatted next to him, watching the prey through binoculars as they approached.

He had a moment's study of Castro, familiar from the picture but weirdly different here, in the flesh. Frenchy thought of a big baby at one of his prep schools, sent there by an overmanly father for some toughening up, a boy who cried each night and was too fat for sports. The boy disappeared one night, actually beating Frenchy out of the school, though Frenchy's crime wasn't melancholy and self-loathing but simple cheating. Castro had the same gray look of defeat, and the flesh through his face trembled at each step, loose and slack. His lips rose like a wave under the vibration as the foot struck the ground, and Frenchy saw not heroic intensity or worker's will to endure but simple, abject fear, a face bathed in sweat, a shirt translucent with the moisture it had captured, everywhere baby fat and terror at play on the big, clumsy, boy's body. He was infantile, a class goat picked on by the football captain.

Frenchy let the binocs slide left to see this mysterious Mr. X who was running the show. What he saw was a wiry European in a dark bandanna like a peasant, and a peasant's dirty smock and sandals, but something no peasant could ever have: intense and impenetrable dignity.

It occurred to Frenchy that here was the real

370

thing, so rarely glimpsed, almost mythological in Agency culture: a high-ranking, superbly trained and motivated true Red agent. He couldn't help but be impressed, for even as he watched, he could tell the boy was lost in panic but the old goat was still clever and making shrewd decisions even as they reached the water.

'That guy looks like a Russian,' he hissed, so excited he could hardly stand it. A victory of immense proportions was just before him. Kill Castro, as Plans had decreed, and capture this guy! What a coup! What secrets he could unlock! Why, you could build a whole career out of one afternoon's work and bask in sheer glory forever.

'Kill the Cuban,' he said, 'wound the Russian. Hit him in the leg, the knee. We'll take him. He's unarmed. Jesus Christ, what a catch.'

★ ★ ★

The boy collapsed in the pond, and thrust his head into the water. But Speshnev grabbed him before he could gulp in the gallons.

'No. Don't lose control. Small, easy sips, wet your lips, let it hydrate your body. If you swallow everything, you'll bloat and your internal temperature will go out of balance and you'll collapse. I'm not carrying you.'

The boy fought him for just a second, bucking like a horse to get his snout into the wet, but then yielded. He dipped in demurely, and sipped.

'Excellent,' said Speshnev.

He himself at last bent to the surface and

371

admitted the water, and felt the miracle of it as it spread hope through his body. The sheer pleasure of it was better than anything sexual.

But in a second he was back in the game, pulling the boy from the water, letting him rest on the bank, but at the same time looking around.

The boat was so close now. A line of trees cut the beach off from the creek, and then it was but a hundred yards or so until they cut across the nakedness of the sands. Speshnev looked back, at the crest of the hill. The dogs were still baying; the soldiers had not arrived yet and as the distance was over a half a mile, he knew he was too far for any kind of accurate shooting.

He took a quick scan about, and his senses saw nothing except the blend of forest and jungle that was Cuba, the palms jutting out among the pines, the odd bright flower, the singing of birds, the bright sun above, behind some clouds.

'Here, wrap this around your head, it'll keep you fresh for this last little bit. Hurry.'

He pulled off his dark bandanna, soaked it in the water, then handed it over.

Then he heard the shot.

★ ★ ★

Earl didn't like it. The problem was the intimacy. In battle, over iron sights, the enemy was a blur. You pressed, the gun fired, and down he went and you moved on. If you were close enough to see the bullets hit and blow holes in him, then the fight was desperate and crazed and horribly dangerous, so there was no time for thought, you operated on instinct alone. But the sniper's curse is his intimacy and now, the magnifications of the eight-power scope blew up the faces of the men who lay before him.

He saw not a Red politico but a fat boy with greasy hair and an unmolded, unformed look to his face. And he saw the man who'd twice saved his life, crafty and professional, almost on the verge of what appeared to be a great coup. This man was the enemy, he told himself, and tried to believe it desperately.

Earl had always followed his orders. That was the compass heading of his life.

The Winchester was set solid against his shoulder, supported by bone not muscle, his body itself solid against the ground, helped by the cupping effect of the slight rise against which he curled.

'You can hit one guy, throw the bolt and hit the other, say, in the knee?' Frenchy implored.

He didn't say a word.

'You want me to get set to move down there with the carbine? If you hit the old guy in the leg, I *know* we can take him alive. He's no dummy. If he doesn't go with us, the Cubans will pick his bones clean in a torture chamber. He'll see it.'

There was no waver in the crosshairs, so solidly was the instrument supported. He had examined each face and now set the reticule on the boy's neck, under his ear, in the softness just behind the jaw; the shot would blow out his spinal column and he would be a footnote in

Cuban history. Earl knew the arc to target two was short and that he could flick the bolt in a second. He thought the Russian would be quick, but how quick? He guessed he'd roll right, and Earl could hit him in the fat part of the thigh, hoping to miss the femoral which would bleed him out in minutes. He had an image of the man squawking, his hands flown to the wound in his leg, trying to stanch the flow. He would know exactly who shot him.

He felt the trigger come back against the urging of his fingertip, as it drained the ounces out of the mechanism.

He put the rifle down.

'You know what? I ain't pulling your trigger.'

Frenchy looked at him.

'What?'

'Forget it. I don't do this kind of thing. It ain't my way. Do your own killing, junior.'

'I — You *have* to. For God's sake, Earl, this isn't a *joke*. This isn't a *game*. This is what it is, what we do, what our country needs. You *have* to, for God's sake.'

Earl just spat into the dust.

When he looked back, Frenchy had raised the carbine and pointed it at him.

'Earl, you will do what I say. You *will* do it. Do you get it? You don't have a choice. Now, fast, before they get away.'

Earl chuckled.

'There's another trigger ain't getting pulled, kid. Don't make me laugh.'

And Frenchy didn't. The rifle came down.

'This is so *wrong*,' he said.

'Let's let the Cubans decide what to do with this boy.'

He went back to the scope and put the crosshairs into the exact center of the distance between Castro and the Russian, on the shimmering surface of the water, so that each would feel the shockwave of the bullet as it roared past, and each would know that they were taken, and saw the Russian's hand dip into the water and come out with a soaked handkerchief. The boy reached to touch it and in that instant, as each man was connected to the handkerchief between them, he pressed the trigger.

When the scope cleared recoil and came back down, mist still hung in the air from the bullet smashing into the water, and the Cuban was running crazily toward the beach.

The Russian had disappeared already.

46

Lieutenant Sarria dreamed of caramel-skinned beauties, with white teeth and flowers in their hair. He was fifty-four years old and much darker than caramel. His hair was salt and pepper, his body long and sinewy and his eyes sad. He dreamed of young ladies often. The way they walked, with music in their steps. The jiggle of their breasts under their blouses. Their behinds, proud and sassy. The magic in their smiles, their eyes. Their toes, long and slender and pink below, caramel atop, their —

He was jerked awake by a noise.

'What was that?' said Corporal De Guama, making coffee.

'It sounded like a shot,' said Private Morales.

All three men wore the green-brown uniforms of the Cuban national police, though without ties and much in need of cleaning and pressing. They were normally stationed at Sevilla, just a few miles inland, but with all this madness of the insurrection at Moncada, they had been sent out to set up an outpost on the outskirts of Siboney, the beach town. When they got to the beach town, though, the lieutenant decided it was unlikely the fleeing man would come this way, where it was so populated. So he had moved west down the beach by jeep and been unable to locate quite the perfect place until, well beyond Siboney, they came upon an old planter's shack, where they'd been for a day, out of radio contact or telephone contact, but ready to defend Cuba and the president with their lives, meanwhile catching up on much-needed sleep. Sarria would never rise above lieutenant — high enough for a negro — and the other two were men whose ambitions had been ground into indifference by the rigors of avoiding duty. All three men were armed, but two of the three revolvers carried between them were empty. Only the lieutenant's held ammunition, though as it had held that same ammunition since 1934, he wasn't entirely certain that it would fire.

'Well,' said the lieutenant, 'I suppose we'd better go do something.'

'I suppose,' said De Guama, sadly. It seemed that something *always* interrupted his coffee. 'May I finish my coffee first?'

'He always wants the coffee,' said the corporal. 'He lives for the coffee.'

'Well, De Guama, actually, no, I'd prefer if you just went along this time. Would that be all right?'

Sarria wasn't being sarcastic. He wore the mantle of command somewhat unsurely. He genuinely wished to know if it was all right with the private.

'No, no, it's fine,' De Guama said.

The three men rose. Morales could not find his cap, and De Guama had taken his boots off.

'I'll have to stay in the sand, where it's soft.'

'Yes, yes, that's fine,' said Sarria.

They stepped out and saw only what they had seen for two days: the blinding brightness of the

377

beach, the blinding blue of the bay, the blinding though lighter blue of the sky, and the dark green of the forest here where the Sierra Maestra plunged so precipitously into the water. The sun was hot, the wind was still. Prickly sweat came at their hairlines immediately and began to run down their cheeks. The air had been superheated by the sun and to breathe was not pleasant. It was July, after all.

'I think it came from there.'

'Is this dangerous? A man with a gun? Maybe I'd better run back to town and call for reinforcements.' De Guama was not the bravest of policemen.

'It's just a hunter,' said the private, Morales. 'He's cornered a boar, he's finished him, that's all.'

'The boar don't usually come down this far,' said Lieutenant Sarria. 'They like it up the mountains, where it's cooler.'

The three walked along the beach for a while, but could see nothing of consequence. Birds, flowers, the sand, the floating gulls, a trawler of some sort fishing close in.

'I've never seen them come in that far,' said Morales.

'Maybe they were the ones who fired?'

'A gun on that old tub? I doubt it. It certainly is low in the water, though. Maybe it's taking sea.'

'We should inquire.'

They walked ahead and though they would later argue about it, it actually was Morales and not De Guama who saw a flash of movement off to the right, in the trees, and alerted the others.

★ ★ ★

Speshnev had squirmed into the trees and gone to dead, still calm. He waited and waited. No soldiers appeared. None at all.

He tried to reconstruct the last several seconds in his brain. He and the boy, kneeling in the water, letting it soak, drinking slowly, not glugging like fools. The boat a few hundred yards away. No soldiers yet at the crest. No noise, no sense of approaching men, no nothing.

He soaks his handkerchief, hands it across and at that moment feels the whisper of hot air as a bullet roars by. Simultaneously, his handkerchief is torn from his hand to flutter across the pond, and at the same second the surface of the pond explodes in a bright plume of water.

The size of the blast, the noise of the shot, the force by which the handkerchief was ripped from his grip all indicated a heavy-caliber military bullet. Yet why had the bullet not struck head, his or the boy's? He realized the handkerchief was shot from his hand on purpose, for a shooter gifted enough to put his round into it could have just as easily shot either through the eye or the ear.

But that mystery was quickly enough forgotten. What had to be done now was more exact and specific. Find the boy. Get the boy to the boat. Yet how could he do so with a marksman about, possibly hunting him, possibly playing tricks on him. And why would a marksman play a trick on him?

And then of course he knew. It could only be one man. And the message was: you must fail. Fail and live, attempt to succeed and you die. I will have to kill you. But this time, I only make you fail.

Well, he thought, you are a clever man, a brave man, but I have a duty to do as well, and if I have a chance, then I will kill you, too.

He realized with perfect clarity the man wouldn't shoot him. He just wouldn't, he knew, at least not to kill him. He would watch from his perfect hide and if Speshnev seemed about to do it, then he would shoot.

Speshnev realized that —

But then movement caught his eye. Through the screen of trees, he saw three policemen. Where the hell had they come from? From the sloppiness of their clothes and the indifference of their postures, he determined that they were not the army troops being driven forward by Captain Latavistada. In fact, they moved so tentatively upon the beach it was as if they'd prefer to be anywhere else. The sound of the shot could not have delighted them.

Yet here was the comical part. The manhunt was run by the best of Cuban intelligence with advice from the CIA, and it had failed completely. These three idiots had succeeded.

For he now saw that they approached a clump of rags hunched trembling behind a knot of trees, and that clump of rags could only be Fidel Castro.

                    ★   ★   ★

'Is it a man?' De Guama asked.

'I think it is. A bum. He is sleeping.'

'*You!*' cried the lieutenant. '*You!* Wake up!'

The figure, indeed a man and not a clump of rags behind a glade of palms, stirred. Eventually a raggedy mop of hair came up, a pair of wet brown eyes, a broad axe of a nose, a pinched mouth, a whole face.

'It is him!' said De Guama. 'Good Christ, it is Fidel!'

The young man assembled himself slowly, then got up, his hands raised.

'I thought you would be a negro,' said Lieutenant Sarria. 'I thought only a negro would have the strength to fight the president.'

'I am fighting for the negroes as well as all other Cubans,' said Fidel. 'I fight for you all.'

A whistle sounded far off.

All four of them looked up the hill. There, at its crestline, troops were assembling, an officer was shouting orders smartly, dogs were barking, and then the unit started to move.

'They will kill me,' said Castro. 'Please don't give me to them. The man in charge, he has cut the eyes out of many of my friends. He will cut my eyes out and then shoot me.'

'Yes,' said Lieutenant Sarria, 'Ojos Bellos, of SIM. I know his reputation. De Guama, Morales, you run back and bring the jeep. We will transport this bad boy into Siboney.'

The two turned and ran off.

'You may as well sit down,' said Sarria. 'It'll

381

be a few minutes yet.'

'Thank you,' said Fidel.

The two sat. Sarria held his pistol in his hand, but did not point with it or gesture with it dramatically. Frankly, it scared him a little.

'You won't try anything, young man? I'd hate to have to shoot you. In twenty-seven years as a policeman, I have hurt nobody. I would hate this to be the day I had to kill a man.'

'I'm too tired,' said Castro. 'I've been running forever. I need to sleep and eat. They will kill me eventually, I know, but I am beyond caring.'

★ ★ ★

Kill him! Speshnev ordered himself.

He had finished a long squirm through the brush, reached a creek and loped along, leaving the shooter far behind but keeping a bearing on the three policemen and Castro. Three: too many. Pray for a miracle.

He crawled forward, sliding through the earth itself, the floor of jungle rot, feeling the coolness just beneath the surface. He'd shimmied up an embankment, low-crawled some feet, and now was just ten feet away from them.

Then the officer sent the two men off. Now there were just the two of them, the boy and the old negro.

He looked back, and could see the soldiers easing their way down the mountainside, still forty minutes away.

He thought: kill him. Kill the old man.

Work back through the brush, staying out of

the sunlight, the open. Reach the boat. It can still be done. The shooter cannot see me, he will not track us.

Kill him!

He reached into his pocket and withdrew a flick knife. With a snap of his wrist, three inches of naked blade spurted out like a lizard's tongue, and locked in place.

Kill him!

At this point it was so easy. The old negro policeman had his gun out, but it rested easily against his thigh, the finger not even on the trigger. Speshnev recognized it as an old Colt revolver, but so beaten and ancient it was clearly not the gun of a pistolero. The man held it so sloppily and with so little tension that it seemed strange to him.

Speshnev looked at him. He was in his fifties, with a face much ravaged by a hard life. Yet his eyes were milky with moisture and depth, surely the sign of a humane man. The men with feelings, they all had eyes like that unless they were insane, and Speshnev had really met few who were completely insane.

He saw how it would happen. He would be upon the old dog so fast, the man would not have time to look up. The knife would flick out, go to the throat, probe and cut the carotid, and the old man would bleed out in seconds.

Then grab the boy, hold him in the treeline, and race along it till their waving and screaming caught the attention of the men in the trawler. Then they could race into the surf, swim outward, and the boat would pick them up.

383

Do it, he commanded himself.

Yet the old man was so relaxed and without aggression in his body, Speshnev could not find it in himself.

Do it! he commanded again, trying to find the energy for this last, horrible thing.

★   ★   ★

He was so damned good. God, he was good.

'Shoot him, for Christ sakes,' said Frenchy. 'Shoot *someone*.'

'If he moves on the cop, I'll shoot him, Junior. Then and only then.'

'He's a Red agent.'

'He's a man doing a job. We'll see how hard he does it. If I have to, I will. You shut up and keep on the glass.'

Through the scope Earl could see the little drama playing out. The sitting policeman with the revolver, the failed, beaten revolutionary, and the Russian agent crouching in the shadows. Earl had picked him up moving west just inside the treeline, a shape flitting through shadows. It took a great game eye to pick up prey like that, through a scope, but Earl had read the land and knew how he'd have to travel to close on the fleeing boy.

He and Frenchy had moved a few hundred yards down the shoreline. They'd gone inland just a bit, where the land rose, and now were two hundred feet up and three hundred yards to the rear. They could see the two men sitting on the beach, and the shadow that had moved into

384

place not long ago, crouching, gathering his strength.

Don't go, Earl thought. I will kill you if you move on him.

He held the rifle just over the head, so if the Russian lurched, he'd rise into the crosshairs, and Earl would fire and the bullet would take him in the spine. He didn't want to, but he also knew that he would.

'You could kill them both, still,' Frenchy said. 'Do you know what this could mean? It could mean everything for us. It could — '

'Shut up,' Earl said.

'Earl, if you don't do this, I can't protect you. You know that. You are on your own. There will be consequences. There are always consequences. Oh, wait, he's getting ready to move.'

But Earl had caught it. He watched as the form of the crouching man seemed to settle as if coiling to gather strength. Earl saw one hand low, the other high, and guessed that with one he would block and with the other, he would cut.

But it wouldn't come to that.

I will kill you, Earl thought.

★   ★   ★

Now. The policeman rose. He leaned over the boy and gave him a touch on the shoulder as if to cheer him up. His defenses were completely relaxed. His mind was far away. He was reaching out in his compassion to settle the boy, who had begun to sob, out of delayed reaction to the events of the last few days.

385

'There, there,' said the old negro lieutenant. 'It'll be all right. You are so young. You have plenty of time left.'

Do it, Speshnev compelled himself.

He gathered his strength for the spring and the kill and the race to the boat, he drew the knife hand back, he studied the three steps it would take him to close the distance, he took his breath, he calmed himself, he —

He saw the ships.

Two white vessels, closing fast on the trawler, each bearing the flag of the United States of America. Coast Guard cutters.

Speshnev knew he had been betrayed, that killing the policeman to free the boy was pointless. He knew there was no exit. He knew it was over. The cutters surged toward the trawler, blocking its escape.

Speshnev faded back.

Not today, he thought.

47

By the time the soldiers got them back to Santiago, and Frenchy had made his report to headquarters, another day had passed. Moncada still bore signs of the gunfight waged there almost a week before, except that by now the burned cars had been removed and the shot-out windows boarded up. From there, they caught a cab to go back to the hotel.

It was a time of much revelry, as if carnival had been extended magically. On all the newspapers, the headlines screamed: FIDEL FINITO. There was a famous picture, taken at the village of Sevilla, of the hangdog young revolutionary and his humane captor, the negro lieutenant named Sarria, now as famous as Fidel himself. The radios blared with official announcements from the president stating his pride in the security forces of Cuba, and saying that after the Cuban way, the bad son Fidel would receive a fair trial — this to counteract all the terrible news of the torture and murder of the revolutionaries. Meanwhile the communists, the laborites, the socialists, the ortodoxos all denounced Castro as a putschist, unwilling to apply the principles of democracy to the process of change, and demanded excessive punishment. Everybody hated him, except of course the people.

Maybe that is why the streets were so full and

the music so loud, maybe that is why the rum flowed so freely and the fireworks detonated so brightly. Whatever, it was a slow journey through the packed streets to the great Hotel Casa Grande at the Plaza de Armas. Both men were exhausted and dirty and wrung out from what had passed. But finally it was Frenchy who spoke.

'I just want you to know what you threw away. You threw away any chance of succeeding with the Agency, of rising in it. Do you understand that, Earl? You are a very great man, a hero, but you are a stubborn son of a bitch and you have betrayed me and made me look foolish.'

Earl let him blare on.

'Do you realize that this means no move to Washington? No big house in McLean? No good school for your — '

'Are you done yet? I'm tired.'

They reached the hotel.

'Earl, I'm very sorry. I tried to help you. I still can't believe you did this to me. Earl, I can't help you any more.'

'You see this rifle gets back to the marines at Gitmo, right?'

'Fuck the rifle. There's more important issues than the rifle.'

'Not to me. You see this rifle gets back or I'll take it personally.'

Frenchy swallowed at Earl's hard glare and the implied threat, and said nothing.

Earl turned, left the car, and climbed up the stairs to the porch. He needed a shower and a night's rest before heading back to Havana, by what means he was not yet sure. He just knew that's where the airport was.

'Señor?'

'Yeah?'

Three Cuban state policemen in those brown-green uniforms were waiting up there for him.

'You have a visa?'

'What?'

'A visa, señor?'

'I came in with a congressman. It was an official — '

'You have no visa, señor, you must come with us. This is against the law.'

'What the hell are you talking about?'

'It is the law, señor. In Cuba we always obey the law.'

Then two other policemen joined the three, then three more. Swarming him, they moved him to the black paddy wagon that had just arrived, and took him away.

48

The cab dropped Frenchy at the United Fruit Company executive mansion up in Vista Alegre, above the hot and fetid city, where he was staying in a VIP suite. He walked in, dragging the carbine and the sniper rifle, the Super .38 hanging in his tanker's holster in plain sight, hot, sweaty, dirty, his young face covered with stubble, aware exactly of how glamorous he was.

People looked, people gasped, people pointed. He seemed to have become the man he had always dreamed of being: cool, elegant, wary, tough, savvy, capable. A hero. There were several young American women staying there, various daughters or mistresses or new young wives of important United Fruit execs, and he could tell that at least two or three of them watched him as he sauntered into the bar and ordered a quick beer, the two rifles leaning against the next stool. He knocked back the cold drink and settled in for a moment or two of reflection. What he was thinking, however, was: They think I'm such a cool customer!

God, he enjoyed his little performance!

He knocked down the last of the beer, picked up the rifles, sauntered back through the lobby to the concierge and said, 'Luis, don't wake me. I'm going to sleep for the next six years.'

Luis nodded, but alas also had something himself to present Frenchy. The Medal of

Honor, like Earl's? Not quite. No, it was a yellow telegraph message. He looked at it.

HELO FLIGHT SET GITMO 0900 HRS STOP MEETING AMBASSADORS OFFICE HAVANA 1500 HRS STOP MANDATORY YOU ATTEND STOP EVANS

Shit.

Already it was beginning. How would he explain? Was it a failure with total catastrophic ramifications or was it just a setback of some sort? He didn't know. He'd been out of the America House so long he'd picked up no gossip or context. He had no idea what was going on, what was being said, what he could expect.

He went upstairs, peeled off the dank jungle clothes, and climbed into the shower. The water, piercing and furious, restored in him the illusion of good health, and he dried.

He thought he ought to call Roger. He didn't like the tone. MANDATORY YOU ATTEND. Roger almost never spoke harshly or gave direct orders, so it bugged Frenchy that he was taking such an attitude. He picked up the phone, dialed the number and waited. And waited. And waited. Nobody picked up.

All right. He dialed Roger's apartment. No answer there either.

He checked his watch. It was about four. There was no reason for Roger not to be there, unless he was off at a match somewhere, and it seemed unlikely he'd be playing tennis so soon after the Moncada business, but you never knew.

391

He dialed a secretary he knew.

'Hey, Shirley, what is — '

'Walter,' she hissed. 'What are you *doing*? You can't call me.' The phone clicked as she hung up.

He dialed back.

'What the hell is — '

'If I get caught talking to you, I'm screwed, too.'

'What?'

'Call me tonight at my place.'

The line went to dial tone again.

★ ★ ★

Frenchy slept for a few hours, went out for a late dinner, ate alone in the nicest restaurant he could find, and then thought about, but decided against, a whore. He finally got back in around eleven. He dialed Shirley at her apartment.

'What is going on?'

'There's a big flap. The word is, you're out.'

He didn't say a thing for a while. It did happen: a big screw-up, a blown assignment, especially if you weren't one of the old boys with the Harvard/OSS pedigree, could spell the end. They didn't like it when other people failed. They were allowed to fail, but nobody else was.

'Who says?'

'Walter, *everybody* says.'

'Shit.'

'There's a guy here.'

'A guy?'

'Yeah, he's thrown the whole place for a loop. He's one of your guys. Nobody will say his name. I only know he's here and he's got everybody scared to death.'

'Tall guy. Real undistinguished looking. Could be a salesman. Nothing special about him, except the way people scurry and defer, as if he's some kind of great man.'

'That's the customer.'

'And bald?'

'Yeah, bald.'

Shit thought Frenchy. The man called Plans was back in town and he smelled blood.

49

Nobody could ever accuse Speshnev of missing a boat. He hid in the jungles for the rest of the day, and as he supposed, at twilight, when all was deserted, the old trawler *Day's End* ventured close to shore again, just in case. Its officer was just being thorough. Speshnev signaled him, and ventured out to the craft. There were no Americans about this time, and the voyage back, under motor, took two days, during which he and the young officer, Lieutenant Orlov of Soviet Naval Intelligence, had a great time, as Orlov had not heard his own language spoken in a year.

Upon his return to Havana and his little room behind a barber shop in the old part of the city, Speshnev showered and shaved, took the last of his cached funds and went to a casino. He ran $600 into $6,000, then went to two more casinos where, at each, he ran a thousand into four thousand. Then he checked into the Nacional, the biggest suite available, and slept and slept and slept. Then he made certain calls, monitoring certain situations, bought a new suit (white linen), a straw hat, and a very fine pair of British shoes. He smoked a cigar, had a fine lunch, and then went to see Pashin.

The man kept him waiting in the trade legation's outer office for quite some time, and then at last admitted him. Pashin didn't look up; he was busily writing some document with a fountain pen, clearly purchased from a nice store.

Speshnev sat down.

Pashin looked up.

'Did I tell you to sit?'

'No, but I decided to do so anyway. It's more disrespectful that way.'

'Do you know what I'm writing?'

'Yes, I suppose I do. You really should let me edit it. I can improve it. I can make it sing. Do you know that I have published two novels and in certain circles am considered a master?'

'What am I writing?'

'The report to Moscow Control, with copies to all fathers, uncles, cousins, brothers and hangabouts of the Pashin clan. About the feckless Speshnev and his multiple failures. How the heroic Pashin tried desperately to rein him in, to keep him headed in the right direction, but the old goat simply insisted on going his own way, and how his mission has collapsed into total failure. How he should be recalled immediately, *immediately*. Is that not right?'

'You make a joke of everything.'

'Actually, no, I make a joke of nothing, except young snots with party connections who get in my way and make my life difficult. Defeating the Americans was difficult enough; now I also have to defeat you, Pashin.'

'There are men outside waiting to escort you to the tanker *Black Sea*, currently awaiting your arrival. Does that improve your mood?'

'It has no relevance to my mood whatsoever.'

Pashin said, 'I'll just go straight to my favorite

part: 'Entrusted with the political responsibility of guiding the subject, Comrade Speshnev instead guided him into a foolhardy and premature adventure, which resulted in catastrophic results for our cause, which has been set back many years, if not forever. Then entrusted with the responsibility of rescuing the subject from the mess that he himself had created, Comrade Speshnev instead guided him into capture, where he currently resides, utterly useless to us and quite possibly soon to be executed. In all his responsibilities has Comrade Speshnev failed, and all his enterprises have achieved humiliating failure.' '

'Why do you bureaucrats like so many big words? You call the knucklehead a 'subject'. He is a foolish boy who will be much improved by his time in prison. Oh, and you fail to mention that I had nothing to do with the adventure in Moncada, as I had just saved his life from an adventure in Havana. And that had I not saved his life from his idiocy at Moncada, he would have been killed in the frenzy of death and torture. Through my efforts, he is alive and safe. In a year or so, we can get him out. This place is so insane, they may even pardon him at some future date. And he will remember who helped him. And he will know where his future lies.'

'Save it for your barracks-mates, Speshnev. You came, you failed, and now you must return. That is the law. Old romantics like you, coming into a modern operation like mine, with the support of other old dreamers. It sickened me, but I just let you destroy yourself as I knew you would.'

Speshnev said nothing, but reached into his suit pocket, extracted a photo, and pushed it across the desk.

'I must say,' he said, 'you do take a pretty picture. When your mouth is closed, you actually have quite a handsome face. I think you'll agree that it's a good photo and the old fellows at Control will find it so *amusant*.'

Pashin just stared at it, hard. A vein in his head twitched a little. He swallowed.

'That does look like an excellent choice of wines. A St. Emilion, eh? My, haven't you turned aristo in the west? Say, the American is a handsome chap, too. You two boys aren't, ha ha, a *little too friendly*, are you? The handsome ones so frequently are, I don't know why, it's very mysterious. Still, that may not hurt you in the service, as many of our senior members have peculiar tastes. But I wouldn't think you — '

'*Silence!*' bellowed Pashin. 'I will have none of this. Who do you think you are? What do you think you're doing? You were not authorized to — '

He ran out of words.

'Havana,' Speshnev explained, 'is quite the city of sin in the western imagination. Many American husbands come here to philander. Thus many American wives have need of a skilled corps of private detectives, able followers and discreet photographers. Fortunes change hands in that way every day, and so I just hired one with some of my casino winnings. You seemed not to like me so I thought I'd best protect myself. But I must say, you even surprised *me* in your rush to self-destruction.'

'You are a bastard,' said Pashin. 'A Jew bastard. You Jews, you are the origin of all our misfortunes, with your — '

'If they give you a choice — unlikely, but still one can never tell how these things change — take the 9mm over the 7.62 Tokarev. The nine is larger and is guaranteed to finish the job in one shot. I've seen it happen many times. We used them in the war and they never failed. The Tok, because it is so small and its velocity so high, often sails through, simply blowing out a few ounces of vital brain matter. You can't start speaking or stop shitting or drooling. Very annoying.'

'No one will believe this picture is authentic. You have no case. You have this stupid forged — '

'Oh, it's not forged. The private detective who took it is highly skilled. And our laboratory people will examine the negative and be able to tell that it's not forged.'

'It proves nothing.'

'No, but my good friend Lieutenant Orlov of the Naval Intelligence Service radio trawler *Day's End* has tape recordings of the American Coast Guard cutters *O'Ryan* and *Philip Morgan* receiving their instructions late on the afternoon of the 27th. The Americans are very sloppy about procedural matters. You should never trust them. They don't even bother with encipherment. It's on the tape and it goes like this: 'We have an intelligence contact from the American embassy in Havana on high authority from a Soviet source stating that the known

398

revolutionary Castro will be off-loaded from the beach west of Siboney at approximately 1600 hours today. You are authorized to intercept, but advised not to come over the horizon until 1530 hours.' Imagine, talking in the open like that.'

Pashin stared at him, sweat prickling his hairline.

'They'll be able to put it together. It's not that difficult and even the people at Control aren't that stupid. You hated me, you were afraid I'd succeed, you betrayed me to the American. It all fits: the date, the timeline, the photograph, the recording. No, I'm afraid it's curtains for you, young man.'

'You are a monster, Speshnev.'

'Of course I am. Now throw away that report you were writing.'

Pashin paused just a second, then realized that in doing so he was simply prolonging his antagonist's pleasure. He ripped the report up, dispensed with the pieces in his wastebasket.

'Now I shall dictate your report. It will be much better than the one you were writing. It will reflect well upon the both of us, how we removed the boy from the killing frenzy after the attack but then how wise we were, when we saw the change in mood, to engineer his capture, the one sure guarantee of his survival. We both have a rosy future, comrade. And of course, you may keep the picture as a reminder of our time together, since I retain the negative. And as we go our separate ways, I'll know that I always have a friend and ally in the brilliant young Pashin.'

He smiled and began to dictate.

50

He arrived at 2:45 and nodded at the duty marine, who only barely nodded back. Inside, people he'd known for months, whom he'd laughed with and drunk with, girls he'd tried to date, men who'd admired his closeness to the fabulous Roger, all looked away, as if whatever he had might be catching.

It was of course all around the building that he'd been leading a hunter-killer team after the revolutionary, and that he'd failed, and been lucky that some old Cuban cop was there to save his bacon. It made the Agency look so bad. They hadn't seen Moncada coming, and never caught up to it, and the business community was expecting some action, and instead they just got Boy Scout stuff in the mountains, to no consequence.

He tried to be lighthearted about it, and he was dressed surprisingly casually for such an important meeting, in old blue jeans, a knit shirt for polo playing — as if he'd ever played polo! — and a blazer. He wore his Bass Weejuns and no socks, and looked as if he'd just stepped off the quad at Princeton. If they were going to hang him — and they were — he'd be comfortable, dammit.

Frenchy climbed the steps and went back to his office on the third floor, but it was empty. Soon enough, Shirley, a Vassar girl of famously high spunk quotient, leaned in. She and she alone had the guts to face him, and to speak civilly, and possibly risk all for it.

'Don't you remember, Walter? It's in the ambassador's office.'

'Yeah, I just thought — ' he said, and trailed off.

'Walter,' she said, 'for what it's worth, I always thought you were a good guy. I'm sorry you had to bury your light under that prick Roger. It's too bad when this stuff happens. Good luck.'

That seemed to be it: Shirley knew the score, it was all over except the part where the negro help washes the blood off the walls.

'A little late for luck, I think,' he said, smiling. 'But who knows what's up the old Short sleeve?'

He left for the ambassador's office, which took up the whole east wing of the second floor and had to be accessed through a series of increasingly lavish offices, and as he passed through each, people scurried to look the other way or suddenly found the files or documents before them utterly fascinating.

When he at last reached the big office, he heard laughter. It seemed the old boys — the ambassador himself, who probably didn't really know Frenchy's name, and Roger and Plans — were sharing a giggle. Something had amused them.

The door was open. Frenchy leaned in sheepishly.

'Uh, hi,' he said.

'Well, well, well,' said Plans, looking amused, 'our last team member is here. I was all set to

401

bawl you out for being late, but I see it's exactly 3 P.M. sharp.'

'Yes, sir,' said Frenchy.

'Well, do come in.'

'Dick,' said the ambassador, 'since you boys are going to go all skull-and-bones, I think I'll absent myself. I have many things to attend to and I don't want to hear anything I can't tell my wife.'

'Thanks, Jack. Your cooperation is noted and I will whisper your name in many ears.'

'Thanks, Dick.' He smiled facilely, made deeply insincere eye-contact with each of them, and sauntered out, as if he weren't totally nonplussed at being evicted from his own office.

'Short, do come in, and sit down. Understand you ran a hell of a race in those mountains,' said Plans.

Frenchy went over and sat in an overstuffed chair. He felt awkward. The ambassador was some kind of big-game hunter, so animal heads hung everywhere in the office, which was done up like a Russian-Jewish set designer's Metro-Goldwyn-Mayer version of a Harvard eating club. It was heavy on flags, ships in bottles or too big for bottles, eighteenth century battle paintings, beautifully bound books in red leather, and a big eagle symbol embossed on a disk in bas relief, painted richly. Frenchy had never been in here, he realized.

Plans smiled sadly. 'Now, Short, suppose you just run through what exactly it was that happened up there, just for the record, and so I know what sort of a situation I'm facing.'

'Yes, sir,' said Frenchy.

He told, as quickly as he could, in measured terms though colloquially, how he and Earl had come in from the other side of the mountains, how Earl had read the land brilliantly and understood exactly where the target would be led, how when they'd made the intercept, Earl had it all before him and wouldn't pull the trigger.

'Hmmm,' said Plans. 'I've seen this man's record. He killed many, many times in the war. I don't understand his refusal.'

'I don't understand it either,' said Roger. 'It was his willingness to kill, as evinced by his war record, that made us bring him in in the first place.'

'Well,' said Frenchy, 'you don't get much in the way of explanations out of Earl. He does what he does by his own standards, without doubt. All the career offers, the possibility of a better life for his family, the ideas of helping the Agency and the country, all that meant nothing. His mind works in very strange ways. He just wouldn't do it.'

'You *said* you could — ' Roger began, but Plans cut him off with a gesture, then asked, 'Where is he now?'

'The Cubans have him detained on our suggestion. We haven't figured out what to do with him.'

'Excellent, as I haven't yet figured out what to do with *you*.'

'Sir,' said Frenchy, 'not to discount a failure, but could I point out that in the end this may work out to the good. If we'd actually killed the revolutionary, he'd be a martyr. Who knows what mischief that would unleash? Now he's just another convict in the Cuban prison system. Anything can happen to him if he's not executed, though he still may be. So the same thing has been accomplished, but there's no trace of our connection. And in fact Earl *did* essentially stage-manage the capture.'

'Yes, all that may be true, Short. But it's irrelevant. As I recall, you were given an exact and specific assignment. The point, need I remind you, was to send a message. Remember the Big Noise? We were going to make a big noise. 'We will not be trifled with'. That was the message we meant to send, and that was the message that did not get sent. So you see, there is a problem here.'

Both young men looked at the floor.

'Well?' Plans said. 'Someone has to answer. That is the way of the organization. Will one of you please speak? Let's not mince words. I want to know exactly whose fault this was. Where does the blame go? Someone has to pay. Which of you will it be? Who gets the ax?'

It was Roger who finally spoke.

'I have to be frank here, Dick. It was Frenchy — *Walter* — who ran this mission, it was Walter who found and pushed Earl, it was Walter who swore for weeks that Earl could be brought under discipline. I think the record will show that I had severe doubts about Earl Swagger and raised questions many times. When I raised questions, it was Walter who downplayed them,

404

who minimized them, who invested totally in Earl. I blame myself, of course, for not monitoring the situation more aggressively, but as you know, you sometimes have to take a certain level of staff performance on trust. I trusted. My trust did not bear fruit. Now, I like Walter very much, but I do wonder if he's a shrewd enough judge of character for this kind of work. It takes a certain I-don't-know-what, a certain sophistication to get certain things accomplished, and the honest truth is that while there are many things Walter can do and do well, this may not be an area where his capabilities come to the fore. Walter, I'm only telling the truth, painful as it is for me.'

Frenchy nodded.

'Sure, Roge. Tell it the way you see it.'

'Mr. Short, possibly you have a counterpoint to make. You'd best make it now or the situation will have gotten away from you.'

'I only know that I did my best.'

'Ah. Well, one cannot ask for more. But sometimes even that isn't enough. And so I suppose that a judgment has been reached, that — '

'Oh, one thing, sir,' Frenchy said, 'should I give you the report for counterintelligence and you'll see they get it, or should I just send it through normal channels? I'm not sure what's best and, gosh, I'd hate to make another darned mistake.'

★   ★   ★

Earl was taken to the same prison in Santiago that now housed Castro, and indeed found himself in a cell three down from the young revolutionary leader. Not that anyone paid any attention to him: eager to show its humanity to the world, the administration of Presidente Batista had ordered the revolutionary shown to any and all, so for nights and days on end, a parade of newspaper, news magazine and radio and television reporters flooded through to ask the young Cuban questions tinged with admiration. No one realized that the man three cells away had so recently had him in his sights, with his finger on the trigger.

Earl went largely unnoticed. His demands — to see a lawyer, to make some calls, to reach an official at the embassy, to speak to any other American — were routinely ignored, but otherwise he was not ill-treated. He was able to shower daily, was fed well, exercised in the yard, and soon made friends with a few other prisoners, with whom he shared cigarettes and rough humor, most of it directed at the young man who was the special guest and carried on like a movie star, quickly attracting a host of hangers-on and factotums, quickly adjusting to his celebrity and his wisdom, coming to be on first-name terms with the American reporters especially, who seemed to find him so admirable.

'That one, he'll wake up with his throat cut,' one man said to a crowd that included Earl, smoking cigarettes in the sun as, across the way, the young man spoke earnestly to a young Frenchwoman, braless under her blouse, who wrote down his wisdom with relentless diligence.

'Watch his head grow,' another said. 'When he got here, he was a failure. But they all treat him like a hero, and now he believes it.'

'They say he is a secret *communista*. He'll have us all dancing to the red jig if he gets his way, you watch.'

'You, *norteamericano*, what do you make of such a young fool?'

'He does carry on, don't he? He reminds me of a movie star. They get famous too young and they never recover. They always think they're important.'

'He has much learning to do, that is true.'

Once it even passed that Castro and the man who'd hunted him at gunpoint stood next to each other in the food line, though Castro didn't realize such. He was engaged in intense political conversation with two companions, and if he even knew Earl was an American, he never acknowledged it.

A moment came when their eyes happened to lock, and Castro gave him a politico's warm nod, and Earl nodded back, and the transaction was complete. Castro went back to his dialectics, having thought up several more important points to make.

Then one night, Earl was moved. He was not chained or brutalized, but was taken at a decent hour to a paddy wagon, locked in its rear — again, without the binding chains of a dangerous man — and driven to Havana. It took a full day, but the driver and guard were decent and joked with him, bought him cigarettes and beer and a fine lunch, pointed out beautiful girls as they passed, and were it not for the lock in the back, it would not have been an uncomfortable experience.

In Havana, finally, he was taken not to the gloomy and distressing Morro Fortress but to a substation far from downtown, and again ensconced in comfort. The cell was roomy, he was the only prisoner in this wing, and he could read, smoke, drink or sleep as he wished. One night a guard even asked if he desired a woman. He said no.

Finally, after four days, a man from the embassy showed up.

'Oh, hope it wasn't too much trouble for you to come down here, sir. Don't rush or nothing,' asked Earl.

'Now Mr. Swagger, a sarcastic attitude won't be of any help here.'

'Look, just get me out of here. I never want to see this goddamned island again.'

'Well, we are trying to get it sorted out. The Cubans are very forgiving on many issues, especially where Americans are involved, but they do have a few rules. You never got a visa. Usually it's just a formality, but for some reason they are adopting a hard line on this one.'

'Well, you go on up to the third floor, Office 311, where Evans and his little pal Short hang out, and that's the source of your hard line.'

'I'm sure I don't know what you're talking about. I believe you accompanied Congressman Etheridge and you whisked through Cuban Customs on the strength of his VIP protection, but someone in the embassy should have gotten you an entry permit and no one seems to have done it. Whoever made the mistake, it will take some sorting out, and we are working on it.'

'Swell,' Earl said. 'I know you'll do your best.'

So he sat. And sat. And sat.

* * *

Frenchy enjoyed the silence.

Finally, Plans spoke.

'Are you sure you want to play it this way, Short? This isn't the attitude I was looking for from you and I will be honest with you, I can be very nasty.'

'Hmm,' said Frenchy, 'I don't have any career left to protect. If I understood, and I believe I did, you just decided to end my career. Fine. No problem. You and Roger can go on and on. But I do have a duty to do. Not to either of you, but to the Agency. I intend to do it.'

He smiled brightly.

'Short, I — '

'Sir. If you look at the mission statement for this station, you'll see that way down the list of my responsibilities, I am counterintelligence officer. It's a joke, of course, but it's there, and I have every right to pursue my responsibilities and take them where they lead. So, on a random basis, I have hired a Cuban private detective to tail certain embassy types, and to photograph them if they have meetings or make contact with unknown people, just as a precaution. My, my, my, what have we here?'

He reached into his pocket, removed a manilla envelope.

He looked over at Roger.

'Roge, you've been a great supervisor. But I'm only telling the truth, painful as it is to me.'

He slid the envelope to Roger, who opened it contemptuously.

'Oh, come on!' he said. 'What the hell is this? Jesus Christ, what the fuck is this? Really, this is meaningless. What do you think this is going to get you, Walter? This is so ridiculous.'

Plans took the photo.

'Pashin, Roger. You and Pashin,' said Frenchy.

'Look, sir, I meet many people, some of them enemy agents. You have to have contacts, that's the way the game is played. So meeting with a Sov is simply a routine part of my duties and — '

'But by charter,' Frenchy said, 'you are formally obligated to report to counterintelligence all contacts with known or suspected enemy agents. Since I am counterintelligence, and you did not report to me, you have formally broken regulations in a highly sensitive area.'

'This is ridiculous! This is insane! Damn you, Short, I never, *ever* should have trusted you. Dick, he's simply obfuscating, trying to make a big deal over a tiny infraction to get the spotlight off his inability to do the job in the Sierras with that cornpone cowboy gunslinger.'

But Plans didn't say a thing. He looked at the photo, read the accompanying report, then looked back to Frenchy.

'This meet took place at the Salon Miami restaurant on the Malecon, July 28,' Frenchy said. 'It can be verified easily enough. On that day at 1400 hours, Roger sent an eyes-only hot flash to 8th Fleet Intel at Guantanamo, requesting urgent interception of a Jamaican vessel named *Day's End*, code-named 'Billy', off Siboney, east of Santiago. The two closest vessels were Coast Guard cutters that in fact blocked the vessel but made no attempt to board after they heard that a certain revolutionary had been captured by Cuban police. *Day's End* was the Sovbloc escape engine. So Roger got a big chunk of info from Pashin and acted on it very quickly. He almost became a hero — that is, if Earl Swagger hadn't outfoxed him and managed to get the target arrested. But Roger never reported his contact with Pashin to counterintelligence and never divulged the source of his information. Discreet? Possibly. But possibly he also knew that the Russians just don't give information away. So if he *got* something, he had to *give* something. What would that be? Very curious.'

He sat back.

'Really, Dick,' said Roger, 'it doesn't mean a damned thing. The Russian had some kind of internal situation he was dealing with and this was his solution. I didn't give up a thing. You have to trust me on this one. My record is perfect, you've known my dad for years, I was in the war, I'm one of the — '

'All right, Roger.' He turned to Frenchy. 'Short, I don't want you to send this.'

'Frankly, 'Dick', I don't give a fuck what you want.'

Plans turned back to Roger.

'You moron. You *idiot*. You fool.'

'Dick, what possible difference could it make? I will simply explain — '

'Don't you see? When this hits CI, they will be on me like cats on a bleeding mouse. This gives them license to pore through *every* operation I've got running. It in essence screws me to the wall and sets me back *years*. And they'll leak to Congress, to the press, to some red-hunting senator.'

'Roge, I think what Dick is saying is that CI is run by someone who doesn't like him and wants to thwart him. Someone with ambitions as big as Dick's. And you've played into this august gentleman's hand. A few leaks, a few phone calls, a few indiscreet Washington cocktail party comments, and Dick will no longer have the ear of the Director and the president and our kind of senator. Isn't that right, 'Dick'? Oh, may I call you 'Dick', because you know Dad and I rowed crew at *Hahvahd* with your nephew Teddy or Skip or Butch and your sister Biffy fucked your son Tad on the front porch of Dad's cottage in Naragansett one night after the crew finals.'

'All right, Short, that's enough. Roger, I'm going to ask you to leave now.'

'Sure, I — Dick, just a second. I don't think I should leave. He's going to fill your head with — '

'Roger, I said get out. You run along now.'

★   ★   ★

It was astonishing. Walter Short! How incredible! Why, the gall of the man. And after all Roger had tried to do for him. It's odd, isn't it, how some people just have no sense of obligation or appreciation.

He thought — in fact he wanted — to linger outside the ambassador's office and catch Dick after he dismissed Short. That way it would be settled, and it seemed clear to him that Short would have to be moved somewhere — that is, if he didn't Take the Hint (people like him never did) and offer his resignation. Some people just can't fit in, even when you bend over backward to accommodate them. They just don't get it. They haven't a clue.

Roger glanced at his watch and saw that it was now 5 P.M. Dan Benning was coming in from Gitmo that night and Roger had hoped to set up a meet between him and Plans over drinks. Dan, now there was a fellow who got it! Dan would certainly impress Plans, what with his background, his family, his Naval Intelligence experience, his Harvard degree, and Roger saw how he and Dan could make a team that he and Short never could have. Dan lacked Short's deviousness, his narrow hunger for self-advancement, his crudity. That had always upset Roger about Walter, but one did the best one could with what one was granted.

So he was at loose ends. He thought he ought to go upstairs to his office and see if anything new had shown up in the in-basket, plus he had a batch of reports to file and a few phone calls to make. None of this was particularly important, but nevertheless it had to be done, and he assumed moreover that he was coming up now on a period when he'd be working alone in Havana station, until a suitable replacement for Walter Short could be located. So he didn't want to get behind, with so much responsibility resting on him in the weeks and months ahead.

He walked upstairs to his office, nodding at people who nodded back gravely at him. They could sense the blood in the air too, he knew; they knew that the destruction of Walter Short was proceeding, and although so necessary, it made them all a little nervous. That is why they looked at him with such an odd sense of disturbance on their faces.

He reached his office, turned the doorknob and —

Say, what the hell?

He must have locked it before he left. Yes, that's it, probably subconsciously he'd sealed up, so as to impress Plans with his security arrangements. Of course. He'd locked it.

He got out his keys and —

Say, what the hell?

For some damned reason or another, his key didn't fit. He tried to force it, but then worried that he'd break it off. Damnedest thing! What on earth was going on? Locked out of his own office! Well, doesn't that take the cake! What a joke! And what a time to have it happen, with Plans in the building!

★ ★ ★

'All right, Short,' said Plans. 'Let's see what you've got.'

'What I have is: I win. If I don't win, you lose. It's pretty straightforward.'

He smiled.

Plans glowered at him. And then he laughed.

'Not bad. I could see three other ways to have played it, but I like your instinct for the jugular and your decision not to go against Roger, but to come at me. Pretty good. I like it.'

'Roger is — '

'Forget Roger. Roger is finished. Roger is on his way to an associate professorship at Iowa State. This was never about Roger. This was always about you. Always.'

'I don't understand.'

'I know all about China, Short. I know how well you did there. I know you were disappointed to be dumped here, working for a moron. But you had been discovered, Short. You know why? You shot three prisoners in China. I like that in a man and I've been watching you ever since. Do you know how rare that is, what a treasure that is? Handsome and adorable, well-schooled, polite, and an ice-cold killer, all in the same package? Amazing.'

'You didn't care about Castro?'

'Oh, a little. It doesn't matter. He'll be taken care of, eventually. He's not going anywhere. No, it was about Walter H. Short, of Williamsport, Pa., who was kicked out of seven prep schools for cheating or drinking, who was kicked out of Princeton for cheating, who became a nothing cop and scared everybody in his department so

415

much they sent him to Hot Springs, Arkansas, to get rid of him. There, he shot and killed at least three people, found a mysterious and not-yet-understood way into the Agency, impressed his trainers and ended up in China, where he did better than anybody before or since.'

Frenchy said nothing.

'You had talent, Short. But did you have discipline, character, steel? Could you work with a Harvard idiot who got all the glory, whom everybody loved because he had a great serve? Could you be his little buddy? Could you play along, secure that you were the real thing and he never could be? Could you flourish in Cuba with gangsters, secret policemen, torturers? How tough were you, under the veneer?'

'I can do it,' said Frenchy. 'I think I've proven that.'

'Almost. Maybe more than almost. I loved the way when you were cornered, you fought back balls to the wall, and Roger never knew what hit him. He's wandering around now, wondering why his office keys don't fit the lock. It'll be a week before he has a clue. Feel good, Short? Triumph, revenge, justification?'

'It feels okay.'

'Don't give me that, Short. I've been there. It feels *great*.'

Frenchy had to admit. It felt *great*.

'You're almost there, Short. In Plans, full-time. No more embassy shit. The hard work of empire: clandestine guerilla work, extortion, hard dark ops, the odd arranged accident here or there. Only the cream get in, but my kind of

416

cream, nobody else's kind of cream. Hard dark boys, for hard dark work. You're in the elite. They'll whisper your name at cocktail parties, the women will flock like hens, men will somehow *know* that you're special, you're an elect, and they'll defer to the man who's actually fighting the Cold War. Everybody respects the warrior, Short. We're wired up that way, deep in the snake part of our brains. Do you want it, Short?'

Frenchy knew the answer: yes.

He nodded. 'What do I have to do?' he asked. 'What else is there?'

'You've shown one weakness throughout this. Only one, but it's significant. A sentimental indulgence.'

'Tell me what it is, and I'll correct it.'

'Earl Swagger.'

Frenchy sat back. It was true. He loved Earl. He could never say that, but Earl was the best, the strongest, the truest. Nobody was like Earl and being with Earl was a privilege.

'He's your ideal man. He's very attractive. Incredibly brave, sublimely competent, utterly capable. What a player for our side he'd make.'

'You want me to recruit him? I don't think he's comfortable with the indirection that — '

But then he saw where this was going. It wasn't going to recruitment, or to some cozy little world where he and Earl would be buddies, neighbors, they'd live in MacLean and go to the Agency every day and laugh and joke and watch their kids get older and older and in some far-off Valhalla they'd have a drink and a smoke and look back on fabulous, adventurous lives.

'He's a loose end,' said Plans.

'He's Earl Swagger, a Medal of Honor winner.'

'We can't have a man who's not under discipline or influence running around. He knows too much. If he's one of us, that's fine; if he's from a world where we're important and can bring influence, that's fine, too. But he's none of those things. He's out of our reach and he knows too much. He was the triggerman on Big Noise. He's fine now, you say, but what if he changes in the next few years, grows bitter, feels ignored, has a political or a psychological change of heart? Maybe he's pissed at the marines for kicking him out or at the VA for not sending his pension and medical benefits. It could be anything. You have to think of these things, Short. They're part of the game, too.'

'I was afraid of that.'

'You brought us Earl Swagger. You made Earl Swagger. He's your creation. Now you must deal with it.'

'Jesus.'

'Don't curse. I don't like cursing. Can you handle it?'

And the terrible thing, of course, is that not only could he handle it in the abstract, but he knew how, exactly, whom to speak to, what buttons to push, what leverage to employ, how it would all work out, so perfectly.

418

51

Again with the secrecy. It was so tedious. He thought all this nonsense was over. But the signal came, and when it came it had to be obeyed, by certain protocols.

And so: again. The elegant businessman in tropical worsted, the sort of man who'd look comfy with a doll on one hand and a satchel with $200,000 in the other, this man gets into his air-conditioned limo. It ducks this way and that, up streets and down them, through alleyways, up hills, around garbage dumps, and finally it deposits another man, not so elegant. Instead the shlump. Bermudas, striped, a panama with too broad a brim, a Hawaiian shirt, cheap big sunglasses, and gym shoes. Any low-rent tourist, a low-roller in the lowest houses, the kind of visiting Jew who came to Havana not for action but for the illusion of action.

That man wandered the streets for a bit, until he was convinced that no one could have stayed with him, then took the bus, the no. 4, until only the shvartzers were still aboard, finally getting off far from the glories of Centro, way west in Santo Saurez, the tough black place, and finding the hotel.

Up he went, the fourth floor, and found the door to a new room slightly ajar.

The important boy was there. He too was undercover. With him it was Bermuda shorts

419

lime green, high socks, those white shoes the British wore, and kind of shirt you rode ponies on. He looked so college boy it was a joke. Not that he wouldn't be noticed; he would. But he'd be dismissed instantly by anybody watching as a dumb kid searching for poontang who took the wrong bus.

'So what now, genius? We're done, no? That bad boy, he's finished.'

'Sorry for the inconvenience. I set this up because I thought there should be some thanks. Your people may have almost gummed it up, but in the end, they kept discipline and let us work it out. You cooperated. That's a great start.'

'You were there? Give me a break, you guys were lucky that old cop came along when he did. Otherwise our boy is fat and happy in Mexico, setting up his next run.'

'No, Mr. Lansky, let me inform you. We did what we said we would; we were there, we pulled strings, we made sure the guy was caught and he'll be convicted and he'll disappear.'

'Maybe so. You're happy, I'm happy, now let's go our separate ways and hope nothing like this ever happens again.'

'An excellent idea. But our cooperation with each other would be very helpful in that eventuality.'

'So it would.'

'So I want to give you a gift. A gift of appreciation. For Meyer Lansky personally, that only Meyer Lansky would appreciate.'

The older man's eyes narrowed. He leaned forward. Then he reached into his pocket, took out an elegant Cuban already trimmed, made a show of licking it just so, fired it up, and exhaled a pile of smoke.

'What could you possibly have for me? A bag of money? An idea of who's tapped and who's not? Inside dope on who's ratting us out while drinking our booze, screwing our women and spending our money under our protection?'

'Can't help you with any of that. It's new business. I can only help with old business.'

The older man regarded the chutzpah of this youngster with considerable scorn. His eyes narrowed. He didn't like this a bit. Was there some tap going? Was this some plot against him and the old men? He looked the boy up and down and saw only a fraternity boy, guileless and silly.

'What do you want?'

'I don't want a thing. I just want you to get what you want.'

'And what would that be?'

'Justice. Revenge. Old scores settled. Retribution. Order in your world.'

'What are you talking about?'

'I know the story. It's said there was a boy who was a son to you. He was a visionary. He got things done. But when he got greedy out in the desert, you had him dealt out of the game.'

'What the fuck!' said Meyer, who hated cursing. 'Who the fuck are you, sonny? That's libel, blood libel. You can't talk to me that way. You don't know who you're dealing with.'

'I only say what's said.'

'I loved Bennie Siegel like a son. Never, never,

421

never would I have him hit. I am not a hitter. I don't kill people. I think, I figure, I see angles. I'm proud that I don't have to kill. I'm too smart to kill.'

'The man who killed Bennie Siegel is here, in Havana.'

Old Meyer sat back, regarding the bland youngster in the ridiculous outfit sitting across from him. His eyes narrowed. Up and down he looked, hunting for some sign of weakness. He studied the pleasant, unmemorable face, the clear eyes, the close-cut hair. He looked for the lick of lips, the swallow, the involuntary look off into make-up land where lies are invented. Nothing. The boy just looked back, completely calm.

'Let's say you have my attention.'

'We brought him in. He was our triggerman, and he's the best in the world at that kind of work. You don't have a man who can touch him.'

'It would take someone highly skilled to slab Ben.'

'He's that, in aces and spades. You've seen him. Your crazy New York torpedo smelled it on him, and nearly went after him twice. Good thing you held him back, because if he went man to man with Earl, he'd have been crushed like an insect.'

'I don't like this,' said Meyer Lansky. 'Why are you telling me this?'

'I want you to know how much we appreciate what you did, how you held back, how you let us operate. In return, I give you this. Earl Swagger, that cowboy, he killed Bennie Siegel. Shot him

422

eight times in the head in 1947 in Beverly Hills. Blew his face off with a carbine and walked away laughing. Bennie'd said he'd get him for a sucker punch Earl threw in Hot Springs in 1946. Earl worried that Bennie would do what he said, so he struck first. Earl is a killer. Ask the Japs. He killed a bucket of them.'

'Says you. How do I tell if this is some thing you're spinning like a web. It's what you guys do.'

'True enough. But Earl told me in the mountains, when we were alone. You doubt it? Then I'll tell you what Earl told me, what nobody could know except the man who killed Bugsy Siegel, and the cops. Only the shooter would know. A little tidbit that was never publicized, that never got out. You check it out, and you will see that I am telling the truth.'

Meyer stared at him hard, trying to see inside.

'It's this,' the important boy said. 'After he'd shot him seven times, he walked up close to the window. Ben Siegel is already dead, his head punched full of holes. He's on the sofa. Blood is everywhere on his nice Glenn plaid suit. His legs are crossed, the *L.A. Times* is in his lap. But that wasn't enough for Earl. Earl takes his time, aims perfectly — ' the young man mimicked the aiming of a light rifle as if he had done so himself, the closing of one eye, the steady press on a trigger, ' — and *pow!* drills the last carbine slug into the eye. He aims, blows the eye out. He could do it, he's such a good shot. The eye sails across the room and lands on the carpet. Right? Do you know that?'

Meyer knew it. All the old men knew it. They had paid good money for it. But nobody else knew it, except the man who killed Ben Siegel.

'Earl is in a prison outside of Havana,' said the young man. 'He will be moved tomorrow at 4 P.M. to the airport. The car will travel through Cerro down the Avenue Mangiari before bringing him to the airport for deportation. It'll be a single car driven by two plainclothes policemen, a black 1948 Buick Roadmaster. Swagger will be in back, handcuffed. They'll be on that road about 4.15 P.M. Tell me, Mr. Lansky, will it still be said after tomorrow that Meyer never killed?'

Lansky just looked at him, but he was thinking how fast he could get hold of Frankie Carbine, and at the same time seeing at last exactly why it had been ordained that Frankie would come to him.

52

'Well, Mr. Swagger,' said the man from the embassy, 'the Cubans have finally seen the light. You'll be relieved to know this is your last day in Cuba.'

He'd been here close to a week. In truth, it had been all right. The Cubans in this small place treated him well, and in a funny way it was a pleasure to be in a world where things made sense. No one whispered bad advice, no one tried to manipulate him against his own best instincts. They just fed him well and left him alone.

'Swell,' he said. 'I'm flying out of here?'

'You'll catch the 5.30 Air Cubana back to Miami. Courtesy of the State Department, you will then be flown back to St. Louis. From there you are on your own. Of course the Cubans have made it clear, you are never to return.'

'Wasn't planning to.'

'Well, that's fine. Your belongings were picked up from the hotel, though the clothing you bought on the government expense account is of course government property and has been remanded to government inventory.'

'Wouldn't have it any other way.'

'We had your suit cleaned.'

'Ain't you boys going out of the way, or what?' Earl said.

'Do I detect some sarcasm in your voice, sir?

You have been in violation of the law and we have worked very hard to make this as pleasant as possible for you. Cuban justice can be extremely brutal, and you have been treated quite gently.'

Earl just smiled.

'You will be released at 4:00 into the custody of two Cuban police officers. You will be handcuffed. Those handcuffs will not be removed until you are at the gangway to the aircraft. You will then board the aircraft and that will be that.'

'Fine by me.'

'I want your assurances you will cause no trouble. You have already been an embarrassment. You are to make no scene with the policemen. You will willingly allow the handcuffs until you reach the plane. You are to get on that aircraft and be gone. Is that clear? The deal we worked out with the Cuban State Police is dependent upon it.'

'Yeah, sure.'

'Thank you, Mr. Swagger. Now this interview is at an end. I suggest you clean up. Your clothes will be brought to you and you will be on your way.'

The man rose officiously, and without ceremony turned and left. Even the Cuban guard in the interview room, an amiable English-speaker named Tony, seemed baffled by the coldness. He was a good guy who'd buddied up to Earl a little bit, even gone and gotten him extra cigarettes.

'Earl, that man, he's got a pickle up his ass.'

'Don't he, though?'

Tony led him to his cell in the deserted place. No locking was necessary; it was run more like a hotel. Earl waited until another guard brought him his suit on a hanger, with shoes, socks, underdrawers and a shirt. Then he wandered down to the shower room, took a nice one, dried, came back and got dressed. Looking at his watch, he saw it was close to 4:00.

Out of here, he thought.

Finally. What a goddamned waste!

★　★　★

In the '38 Buick parked down the street from the jail, Frankie Carbine sat in the front seat with the binoculars, next to a darker guy from SIM who was guaranteed reliable and was running the car that day for Captain Latavistada, who sat in back. He could see the place just fine, blown up ten times, a stairway out of a blocky municipal structure that had long since lost its polish. A heavy-gauge locked cyclone fence ran the perimeter, wearing a gnarled tangle of barbed wire. A couple of cops in their dark uniforms were stationed outside, but in the Cuban way both men were relaxed behind sunglasses on chairs, smoking and paying little enough attention to anything.

Frankie looked at his watch.

It was almost 4:00.

He felt like screaming. It was so close. He tried to keep his pulse and his heart calm, but all he could think about was putting a full magazine

427

into the *strunza* that killed Ben Siegel. He'd smelled it on him the first second, that stink of death. The guy was a stone killer; he had to be paid back in kind for what he'd done.

Frankie hoped he just riddled his guts. Then, he'd walk around and the guy would be lying there, bleeding and crying for mercy, and Frankie saw himself taking out his Colt .45, leaning over, and pressing it against the man's eye.

'Familiar, *strunza?* Like you done to Bennie.'

BLAM!

He'd blow that eye clean out of its socket and the world would see what happened when you went against the outfit. Mr. L would be so proud; all the old men of New York, they would be proud too, and Frankie could come back anytime he wanted. But he wouldn't. He and Ramon, they would take over —

'Frankie, are you all right?' asked Latavistada from the backseat.

'Yeah, fine.'

'Frankie, you should relax. Don't get too excited. It's going to be fine. It's going to be easy,' said Ramon, who had the Mendoza 7mm machine gun and a batch of clips.

'It's almost time, Ramon,' Frankie said.

'Yes it is, my friend. We will do this thing and then the world will be ours.'

'You let me do it,' said Frankie, patting the machine pistol that lay across his knees. 'This guy and I, we had words. We had problems. He's a big guy, he smacked my head at Moncada. Today he learns what a mistake that was.'

428

'Yes, Frankie. The privilege of the first shots goes to you. You shoot him good, Frankie. Nothing fancy, just a burst into him, and watch his head as the bullets destroy it, and then I finish with the heavier gun, the two policemen, any witnesses. Then we pull our pistols and make certain. It is a very good plan.'

'Oh, fuck, here they come.'

Ramon spoke briefly in Spanish to the driver, who started the car.

And here they came indeed. It was a big Roadmaster, another Buick, dead black, with four pissholes on the side, driven by two plainclothes men from the state police. One puffed a big cigar. Both wore sunglasses and Panamas and guayabera shirts, burly men in their thirties, handsome after the dark Cuban fashion, one a negro, the other white. Both looked comfortable, settled, on the way to a meaningless detail.

Frankie stroked the Star machine pistol on his knees. He was ready. Christ, was he ready.

★ ★ ★

Frenchy watched from a bodega across the way. He hid behind two bunches of bananas and looked through a dirty pane of glass to the station. For some reason he knew he ought to be there. He wasn't sure why, he just felt obligated.

The transaction unfolded without drama. How could there be drama? Frenchy just watched as Earl came out, in his suit, his hands behind him where they'd been manacled. There

429

was no tension in him, as everybody seemed to be buddies. The two cops led him down the stairs to the car, and a third walked behind, talking to Earl, laughing with him.

He watched Earl. He was the same as he'd been when Frenchy first laid eyes upon him seven years ago, perhaps more etched with age, perhaps a few pounds heavier, but essentially the same man, the eternal noncommissioned officer, blessed in battle, narrow otherwise in vision, the salt of the earth, the man who's made it happen for four thousand years of war. Now he, Frenchy, little Walter who'd been so mischievous in prep school, was planning his execution.

Frenchy tried to feel something but one of his talents was the way in which he disconnected himself from events he planned or executed. He didn't really have a conscience, though flashes of regret would occasionally pass through him. He'd once imagined something better for Earl, and maybe part of getting him down here was a way of making something up to the man for the way Hot Springs had ended, though he'd tried to make up for it in other ways, too. But it hadn't worked out. You couldn't save an Earl Swagger from his own nature. You couldn't make him see the point, you couldn't get him to bend. He wasn't a bender.

The car passed and sped down the road.

Frenchy made the sign of the cross. Not that he believed in such hocus-pocus; it just seemed appropriate somehow.

Via con dios, amigo, he thought, and turned back to buy a banana.

430

★ ★ ★

The policeman next to Earl was talkative, as the car picked up some speed and headed out into traffic.

'So, you're a cop, right?'

'Back in the States, yeah. State cop.'

'Ah, we are state policemen, too. It's a good job, is it not, señor? People show you respect.'

'Well, I agree that it's a good job, but there's been days when I've wished I got a little more respect.'

The man in the backseat with him laughed.

'Oh, yes, the bad ones, they have to be instructed. That is why all policemen must have big hands so that when they strike a bad one, he knows he has been struck and therefore he shows respect and feels fear.'

'That's pretty much my theory, too,' said Earl.

The driver barked something at Earl's seatmate, and watched Earl in the rearview mirror briefly.

'He doesn't like it?' Earl asked.

'He thinks I talk too much.'

'You do talk too much, Davido,' said the driver. 'You always talk too much. A policeman should not talk so much.'

'So, I like to enjoy myself. Anyhow, this man is not a criminal but an American policeman, a man very like ourselves.'

'That's fine, but do your duty.'

They drove now through a slum, and the traffic grew heavy. The streets were full, and now

431

and then the cars jammed up, sometimes even halting.

'I don't want to miss my plane,' Earl said. 'It's a great country, but I have had a better run of luck in my time.'

'Look,' said Davido, 'he's a policeman too, and my cousin Tony vouches for him. We can take his cuffs off. A policeman shouldn't be in no cuffs.'

They broke free of the traffic as the buildings dropped away, yielding to fields and huts. The car speeded up.

'Well, I think you should put them back on when we get to the airport,' said the driver. 'Who knows who is watching.'

'I don't want to get you boys in any trouble,' said Earl.

'No, it's no trouble — ' but then Davido laughed as Earl withdrew his hands, uncuffed, from behind him.

'Did you see that? Jaime, did you see that? He slipped the cuffs! Amazing! How did you do that?'

'I've worked a lot with these here old-style cuffs. There's tricks to shake 'em a boss con once showed me. You didn't set 'em tight enough. I was able to shift my wrist and bring some pressure in a certain spot. You need to have a lot of strength in your fingers. I'll show you how to set 'em up so no bad guy ever does the same to you, okay? Maybe save you getting your throat cut one fine night.'

'See, this is a very helpful man,' said Davido, and it was only because Earl had rotated toward him, was not sitting back with his hands locked

432

behind him, that he was able to see the black car scoot out from behind, accelerate to equal their speed, and the barrel of the gun rise, behind it the grim and determined face of Frankie Carbine.

* * *

'*Faster! Faster!*' barked Frankie.

'No, no, not here,' corrected Ramon from the backseat.

But Frankie could hardly control himself. His whole body shook in fury and hunger. He leaned forward, his eyes bugging, his breathing hard.

'It's too crowded ahead,' Ramon warned. 'We'd never get away. Wait till the road is clear, and we are out of the traffic. Then we pass him and *bzzzzzzt!*, it is finished, and off we go.'

Frankie settled back, but some incredible fever gripped his brain. He wanted to get in close, open up, watch the death and be done with it. Ahead the unmarked police car poked along, completely oblivious to the executioners so close behind. Frankie could see Earl and the cop in the rear, talking, even laughing now and then. They all seemed to be having a pretty good time. It filled him with rage. It was so wrong. Blowing out Ben Siegel's eye, then having a wonderful time in Cuba. His breath came harshly, through a dry nose and mouth, almost hurting as he sucked at the air, as if there weren't quite enough air available.

'Frankie, this is hunting. You must be patient for your shot. We wait for the ideal moment and it will come when it comes. To rush is to fail. Corporal, you are doing an excellent job of driving. Frankie, see how the corporal is doing. He is smooth, relaxed, in command. He has perfect control. He knows exactly when the moment will be, and he will spurt ahead. *Bzzzzzzzt!*'

The corporal, some kind of Indian with a dark though not negro face, laughed, showing white teeth. His eyes glittered like another true killer's; this was extreme pleasure for him.

The car ahead slowed, tangled in traffic. The corporal pulled expertly to the side of the road, let two cars glide by, then slid back in line. He didn't want to get too close, but just to stay in contact, to be close enough to spring when the moment arrived.

But whatever was holding up the progression suddenly vanished, and the traffic lurched into motion. For a while, they drove through dense city streets, sometimes coming close to their prey, sometimes sliding back inconspicuously.

Then their quarry turned, found a broader road, and accelerated. The corporal adjusted accordingly, and the buildings on either side fell away, giving way to peasant shacks, small shops, unused, scraggly plots of land and the odd bar or so. Overhead, the scream of a multi-engined plane at a low altitude suggested they were approaching the airport.

And then, suddenly, a car between them and the police car pulled over. Ahead beckoned open road, no oncoming traffic, and the opportunity for the clean kill.

'*Vamos!*' said Ramon, for this was the moment, but the corporal had read it too, and was already accelerating. Frankie twisted sideways and back, lifting the machine pistol, vaguely aware of Ramon in back bringing his heavier gun up to rest on the window frame. It was now, it was happening.

Almost in slow motion, the cars closed distance, and in even slower motion the corporal began to drift to the left, floating out in the oncoming traffic lane, not lurching as if in attack, but in a fluid, controlled maneuver that could not be read as aggression until too late.

The black Roadmaster seemed to be standing still as the corporal closed with it, and the back window came into range. Frankie saw Earl leaning slightly forward, around the man on his left. He saw this over the barrel of his gun.

But at that moment came the squeal of brakes as ahead a school bus lurched into view, pulling out from behind a stand of trees into the oncoming lane. The car heaved, shuddered and the corporal braked through deceleration and slipped back just in time to miss the head-on.

The bus flashed by.

'Now go, *go!*' screamed Latavistada, and the corporal punched it hard, this time overtaking the car.

But Frankie knew: he'd been seen.

★   ★   ★

Earl smiled at his new policeman friend, and twisted his arm as if to show him the trick with

435

the cuff — though actually coiling that arm and tensing. He knew what he had to do. He suddenly uncoiled, driving the point of his elbow with a sick thud into the hinge of the jaw on the right side of the man's face, a clean, pure, knockout blow if ever there was one. The echo of the thud filled the car but Earl was almost faster than its meaning, for he was up, leaning forward into the front seat as the driver looked up at him, eyes wide in fear but way behind in the reaction.

Earl uncoiled another blow to the head and felt the solid, shuddering jolt, but this man was quicker by a bit, and tougher too, and he didn't go out but just went back, moaning. His foot reflexively hit the brake and the car skewed sideways, pulling up a screen of dust, its tires screaming against the pavement and then the dust of the shoulder until all purchase was lost and it lurched into a gully. Earl hit the man again and he sat back, in a fog.

One second passed as Earl forgot who he was and why he was there. Then it all came back to him. He hit the door of the car, pulled it open, rolled out, and scrambled up the embankment. He saw the black car of the two gunmen slewed over as well. The gun barrels swept toward him and he went down, slid into some bushes.

No fire came. He'd been too fast. He crawled desperately away, and thorns and burrs and sharp leaves tore at him, but no pain could halt him. When he thought he was far enough away, he rose and ran blindly, to put as much distance as he could between himself and his hunters.

53

Frenchy had taken down all the Harvard crap. Out went the tennis rackets, the pennants, the photos of the '47 tennis squad clustered smiling and blond around that stupid trophy. He threw out all messages from Roger, who wanted his personal goods back. He had a certain police detective visit Roger and suggest, unsubtly, that Roger get the hell out of Cuba. Word reached him that Roger had obeyed his order.

Frenchy no longer wore boola-boola blue blazers and tennis flannels but instead dark tropical suits, bespeaking a man of gravitas and intensity. He fired Roger's secretary in an ungentle fashion, and promoted a new girl from the pool who would be loyal entirely and absolutely to him. To make sure of that, he proposed that night, and the next started screwing her hard. He changed the locks on all the file cabinets and the security vault. He had the carpenters nail down the windows. He forbade the janitor to come in unannounced. He directed that all correspondence to Roger St. John Evans be destroyed immediately.

Frenchy was now on the move. He at last had a budget he controlled, an agenda he believed in and no one to suck up to — people, including the ambassador, now sucked up to him. He could give free rein to all his impulses toward destruction and conquest. He had wasted no time, and, using as leverage his ability to arrange extremely profitable grants from the Agency to various factotums in the Cuban security apparatus, directed a general closing down of all radical elements of society. Several newspapers and magazines were raided, their staff members carried off to unforgettably rough treatment in cells in the Morro Fortress. All reports on interrogations were forwarded to Frenchy, and he read them with concentration, looking for connections and cross-links, points of weakness, methods of attack. In very short order he developed a superior working knowledge of the Cuban radical underground. And, of course, he ordered surveillance of the Soviet Trade Legation doubled.

And, again in astonishingly short order, he became beloved and feared. The businessmen were not used to directness, instantaneous results and the pure aggression that was Frenchy's style. But they were practical men, and they got it; secretly, they'd been sick of Roger's airy, aristocratic manner and offhanded laziness, and had long since caught on he didn't know or do a goddamned thing. Frenchy came to each corporation, made an intimate pact with its security officers, and provided a special gift of intelligence to each powerful executive, all without destroying anyone's ego on the tennis court.

But now he had the first crisis of his young career.

He had no time for rage or recriminations. He simply marked it down as a bad operating

438

principle, using ill-disciplined, untrained workers, while at the same time realizing that he was more or less committed to them.

'You find him again, you kill him. That's what those two bozos have to do now, and if they fail, Mr. Lansky, it will upset me. Believe me, you do not want to upset me, do you understand?'

Lansky, who had faced some of the most brazen gangsters of all time, was contrite in the face of Frenchy's newly emergent power personality. He was a shrewd enough judge to realize that this was who Frenchy had been all along, and that his true essence was simply coming out. And of course, it was true: his men had blown it.

'They'll succeed this time. I am as upset as you.'

'I'm not upset, Mr. Lansky.'

'Meyer.'

'I'm not upset, Mr. Lansky. I don't get upset; I get things done. Now I need answers. Can these two find him on their own?'

'Truth is: probably not. Give them guns or knives, let them loose, and they'll get a job done. This New York fellow once sprayed a cop in Times Square. He even killed a police horse. The Cuban is known as a torturer.'

'I know Captain Latavistada's reputation. I saw him operate at Moncada after the attack. Even the other men in SIM fear him. But the question is: are they clever enough to find Earl Swagger, for your sake and mine? You say no.'

'The Cuban has formerly worked out of Santiago. He knows that city. Here, he's like an

439

Iowa boy in New York. As for Frankie Carbine, a smart one he's never been. He was used in New York for jobs with guns or fists. He was a soldier. He never would have become more than a soldier.'

'All right. I will find Earl. You get these clowns off the street. Right now, they're doing more harm than good. When I find Swagger, you have them ready to move. I want them hot and loaded for bear with a full tank of gas. I'll give you an address, and they will do the thing. And they will succeed this time. This is a very dangerous man, but on aggression alone they will succeed. Even this man is made of flesh, not steel.'

'I will set it up.'

'Thank you. Now I have some calls to make.'

★   ★   ★

He quickly arranged to meet the heads of the Cuban Internal Security Ministry and its action arm, the Cuban Secret Police, at the well-appointed Internal Security headquarters in the beautiful Capitolio building, that mock version of the U.S. Capitol set amid gardens in Old Havana.

'Gentlemen,' he said gravely, 'I want you to understand that a lie has been told. It is a good lie, a lie in obedience to noble principles. I told it.'

The two man stared at him, surrounded by their staff members. Cigar smoke hung heavy in the air. Old campaigners and battlers, formed in the *gangsterismo* politics of the thirties and forties, believers in the presidente who had rejoiced in his return in 1952, the two weren't quite sure what to make of this supremely confident young American who was said to be so highly connected to American power that the ambassador himself feared him. They would wait and see what the young fellow had to say.

Frenchy blazed ahead.

'The lie was that the American who escaped yesterday from two state policemen was a simple tourist with a visa problem. We told you this. We lied.'

'And, what,' asked the chief of the secret police, 'was he then?'

'He was a spy. He was a traitor. We had caught on to his activities, had him arrested on a technicality and were in the process, with the help of your state police, of returning him to America for interrogation.'

'If this is such a dangerous man, why weren't we informed, Señor Short?'

'I could tell you another lie, but I won't. The lying is no good. It was my decision. Everything was meant to be low-key, unnoticed. He himself did not even understand that we were on to him, or so we thought. But he was far cleverer than I gave him credit for, and he understood what fate awaited him. Thus he assaulted your men and managed to escape.'

'Well, then, we must begin a manhunt. He is almost certainly still in Havana. Why, we can blanket the city with his picture. We can put it on

441

the television. We can describe him on the radio. Our Cubans are patriots and they will hunt for him if so instructed. He won't be able to move ten feet without being spotted. Our departments stand at the ready to prevent the spread of the communist plague.'

'Yes, I knew you'd say that, and that I could count on you. And I request your efforts in helping me locate him. I request your intelligence networks, your spies, your connections in the underworld. But I would prefer nothing of a large public nature to happen. We don't need more outrages of the sort that scare our businessmen and harm the investment climate. If your people can locate this man, I'd prefer if they hold off once they spot him. I have a team, a very special team, well trained and highly experienced, who will handle the actual details of the arrest. So I want no all-points bulletins and no television or radio announcements and no posters. No, I want it done on the hush-hush; that is, by word of mouth, by description, by interrogation, by observation — but not with a raid. I will handle the raid.'

'This is a very unique situation,' said the secret police chief.

'Yes, it is,' said Frenchy. 'And if it helps, I'd be happy to tell certain people how cooperative you've been. I'm sure that if I whispered certain things in certain ears, certain forms of aid could be forthcoming to each of your departments. Our budgets for fighting subversion are quite large. I have no problem citing the names of

442

those men and departments who have shown special zeal in their duties. Those who hurt my enemies become my friends and I pay my friends in generous ways.'

'Then tell us what you require.'

54

He found the card and a nickel, got the operator, gave the number, heard it ring, and waited for it to be answered. It wasn't and the nickel came back.

Earl looked around. He wasn't sure where he was. He'd raced through woods, followed a filthy stream until it led to some broken-down houses, cut over to something of a main drag. He moved quickly, keeping his eyes down, and nobody seemed to notice him. He spied a bus, ran after it, and gave the driver a buck. Then he waited for change. The driver would remember someone who hadn't picked up his change.

He rode till the end of the line, through the fall of night, to what seemed like the outskirts of the city. In the dark, he felt a little better, and he wondered what the hell to do. Go to the airport on his own? That seemed like a good way to end up dead. Call the embassy? But whatever Frankie Carbine's motives were, the intelligence that had made it happen had to come from the embassy. They were trying to get rid of him, not help him. Should he just try and get a boat out on his own? The U.S. was only ninety miles away by sea, a night's trip. Some fisherman could get him there. But what would he pay with? And whoever *they* were, wouldn't they be watching the docks?

He walked about, secretly aimless, but

seeming possessed of sense and destination. He knew that aimlessness would be recognizable and memorable, whereas a sense of destination would not. He walked, walked, walked.

This was a swell mess, all right. Gangsters trying to kill him in a foreign country where he didn't know the language or the rules, or where to go, or who to turn to. He just wanted to get home and put this island behind him, one more island he'd survived. He wanted no triumph, no vengeance, no —

Then he remembered the woman. Yes, he had her card, yes it had her number. He went into a hotel, found a phone booth and thanked God for AT&T, which had wired Cuba from one end to the other, pretty as you please.

He got the operator, gave the number, waited for the ring and —

'Hello.'

'Thank God you're there. Do you recognize my voice?'

'Of course. I'd heard they kicked you out.'

'They did but then someone else tried to kill me. So I'm on the run. And you are the only person in this town I trust.'

'God, you have a talent for trouble. I never met a man with a talent for trouble like yours.'

'I won't argue with you there, Mrs. Augustine.'

'Jean. I told you, Sergeant Swagger, Jean. Where are you?'

'I have no idea.'

'Well, that's kind of silly, isn't it? How can I help if I don't know where you are?'

It was true, and here it was: trust or die. Or,

possibly, trust *and* die.

'I seem to be across from a church. It's Catholic, and the sign says Santa Maria — '

'Do you have any idea how many churches of Santa Maria there are in Havana?'

'Well, this one is Santa Maria de la Marbella.'

'Of the beautiful sea. You are not far off the Malecon at its most eastern end. Go there. Go to a place — let's see, it would be called the Bodeguita San Juan. I don't think it's far. I'll be there inside an hour.'

'What will you be driving?'

'A Pontiac convert — no, no, I'll take Juanita's car. It's a prewar thing, a Dodge I think.'

'I'll look for you in an hour.'

★　★　★

He watched her from across the street, in the shadows. She pulled up directly out front, and waited, then finally pulled away after ten minutes. Nobody followed. She swung around again, slowed but didn't stop, then pulled away. Again, there seemed to be no cars in pursuit and, looking up and down the street, he made out no lurkers or observers. And she of course gave it another try, slowing then stopping.

He dashed across the street, opened the rear door behind the driver side, scooted in and sank to the floor.

'I hope that's you,' she said.

'It is me. Just pull out, no need to hurry, and go about two blocks and pull over. Then check and see if anybody behind you pulls over, too.'

446

'Wow,' she said, 'this is just like a mystery.'

'It ain't nowhere as much fun.'

She did as he directed, and then, that last security precaution passed, pulled out.

'I thought I'd missed you.'

'No, I was watching you. Sorry for the delay, but I wanted to make sure.'

'This is very exciting.'

He didn't say anything.

'You can stay at my place. My girl won't tell anybody. It's safe there. Out in Miramar. All I have to do is hit the out-of-town highway and — '

'No, please don't. I'd like you to take me downtown. To a place called Zanja Street.'

'Zanja Street? Near Chinatown. That's where the prostitutes are.'

'I know. There's one there I helped some weeks back. Esmeralda. I believe that she'll hide me.'

'Earl, there's plenty of room at my place. You'll be safe there.'

'No, I won't. And neither will you. You think you know about gangsters because of the movies. You think they dress funny and talk funny and wear carnations and funny hats. I've seen some of them movies, too. But let me tell you, they're trash. That's all. Trash. They will bust in and kill me and if you're there they'll kill you and that's that.'

'What about the embassy? That would at least make some sense.'

'I don't trust that fellow Roger.'

'Well, Roger's gone. Unceremoniously. He was dumped mysteriously in the night. The younger man, Walter, he's in charge now. Maybe he's not as bad as Roger.'

Earl didn't say a thing until he came up with, 'Well, there's too many people paying attention in an embassy. The woman on Zanja Street is my best bet.'

The car stopped and started in traffic. Jean turned on the radio, and soft mambo music poured tinnily from the box. She rolled the windows down and the smell of sea came in, and the smell of flowers and the smell of rum.

'You're not planning some cowboy thing, are you?'

'No, I am not planning nothing except to get the hell off this place. It was a mistake ever coming. I have been shot at in too many hard places to die in a gutter in a city I don't know, for reasons I don't understand.'

'Do you have money? I have some money for you and I can get you more.'

'Thanks, I'm fine. You've done enough.'

'Earl, I know people.'

'I'd just get them in trouble.'

'Okay, we're almost there.'

Earl sat up. He saw the bars and bodegas of Zanja Street. He saw arches and cafes and girls lounging and smoking, showing too much flesh. The cobblestones and neon signs and banks of lottery numbers. He saw pimps and grifters and knife fighters. He saw sailors and mid-western dentists and palm trees and fruit stands and cigar rollers.

'I should be fine here.'

'I will say, you are a piece of work, mister. I

448

never met a piece of work like you.'

'I ain't all that much fun, once you get to know me.'

'Please, let me help. I know I can help.'

Earl had thought this out pretty carefully. Now he gave it to her.

'You say you know people. There's a fellow in this town, some kind of European, maybe Russian, I don't know. But he's the sort people will have noticed. Wiry, salt-and-pepper hair like steel wool, full of electricity. He's always laughing. Funny guy. Funny in his comments, funny in his beliefs. I think he's a Red, but he knows what he's doing like nobody's business. I think he'd help me.'

'Does this genius have a name? A place? I will find him if you give them to me.'

'When I met him, he called himself Vurmoldt. He said he sold vacuum cleaners from Omaha, Nebraska. Atom powered, or some such foolishness. But later he laughed at what a phony lie that was, and what a lame thing it was to come up with. I never got the real name. But believe me, people will know him. And if you ask for Mr. Vurmoldt the vacuum salesman, he will hear and know you came from me. When you meet him, ask him if he's gotten a new handkerchief yet. He will know what that means. Ask around. Ask people who do business with the Russians. Or who watch the Russians.'

'I know a couple of Brits who are in that trade, I think.'

'They will have noticed him. You must get word to him.'

'Suppose he betrays you for some communist purpose? I don't like communists.'

'I don't like them neither. But I think this one is okay. It's a risk, but it makes some sort of sense.'

'What should I tell him?'

'Tell him I'm with Esmerelda. That's enough. He'll find me.'

'Not that it matters to you, but will I ever see you again?'

'No.'

'Oh. Well, thanks for the truth.'

'Look, I didn't plan this world, I just live in it. If I didn't have responsibilities and I saw you in that bar and you smiled at me like that, I'd have fought the Pacific all over again for you. But that can't happen. You know it, I know it. Knowing you has been the best thing about this trip by far. I wish there was more. But there ain't. That's the truth.'

'You always tell the truth,' she said. 'What a terrible, terrible gift.'

He leaned close and kissed her and smelled her, and didn't want to leave her, but if he didn't now, he never would. And so he did, stepping out into the shadows of Zanja Street.

55

The pimp was sullen. The pimp was nervous. The pimp was upset because he paid good money and this sort of thing was not supposed to happen. It never would have happened until recently, but now that El Colorado was gone, things were *muy loco*. Nobody ran the business, no one knew who to pay, who to call, and the *policia* were getting more and more greedy in their demands on poor working men such as him.

Then the officer hit him in the mouth with a sap. He went down, spitting teeth and blood, and the Indian kicked him savagely in the guts, twice. He curled in pain, whimpering. He could do nothing. There were three of them: the officer Latavistada, the Indian, and a *norteamericano*.

Latavistada leaned over.

'Friend, you know my reputation. I am the one they call 'Beautiful Eyes' for a certain skill with a scalpel. You will get used to me, as I am soon to be very important down here. So now would be a good time to impress me and get a head start on our relationship. We are looking for someone. A big man, *norteamericano*, short hair, thatchy, iron gray. Moves like a cat, always watching. You would not mix with this man, amigo; he carries that meaning. You know where he is, don't you?'

'Sir, I swear it. I have only seen the usual

Americans. They want to get fucked, they want to get drunk, they want a virgin, they want a negro, they want a yellow woman, they want all three, or they want all three in one, but for all of that they don't want to pay so much. That is all I know.'

This conference was taking place in an alley off of Virtue Street, in Centro. It was one of many such conferences Captain Latavistada and his two cohorts had engineered over the past few days, all up and down Virtue, up a few blocks on Zanja, in many of the buildings with the doors with the hatchways, near the rail station, down the twisty pathways of Old Havana.

'Should I kill him?' asked the Indian.

'I don't know. Should he kill you, señor?'

'Please, sir, I just want to make an honest peso.'

The captain spoke in English to the American. The American said something briefly.

'Even my American friend thinks you should be killed. We don't feel your hunger to do your duty to your nation, as exemplified by me.'

'I swear I know nothing.'

'How many women work for you?'

'Five.'

'Five! A lie! It must be ten at least. Your teeth are gold, that switch knife had an ivory handle, the chain you wear around your neck, it too is gold. Your dying Jesus is gold. A man could not accumulate such wealth on five whores. That is ten-whore wealth if ever I saw it.'

'I don't know. My gut hurts so bad I can't think straight.'

'Get him up, Corporal,' said the captain.

The Indian, immensely strong, lifted the pimp and rammed him against the wall. He put his forearm heavily into the sweating man's throat, so that the pimp felt death but seconds away if the Indian so decided.

'I will come back tomorrow,' said the captain. 'I had better see ten whores with black eyes and swollen heads and big blue lips, so that I know their master has spoken to them thoroughly and that they have held nothing back. The whores talk among themselves, they know things.'

'Yes, sir,' said the pimp.

'Now go do the necessary,' he said, nodding to the corporal, who released the pimp and shoved him roughly on his way.

'Well, sooner or later,' Latavistada said in English to Frankie, 'one of these fellows will talk. Meanwhile you and I, we are establishing our bona fides down here.'

'This is good, but I ain't getting rid of the buzz in my head until I see that fucking guy in a gutter with his fucking face blown off. Oh, I want that fucker,' said Frankie.

'We will get him. You'll see. Havana is really a village, and everybody talks. He's down here, where else could he go? And some whore or pimp will give him up rather than face Beautiful Eyes and his American friend.'

'I hope you're right. I'd hate to bring more bad news to Mr. L.'

They walked back to the car. There wasn't much point in getting into it. They'd spent the evening cruising. They only took one break when

Frankie felt a sudden need to drill three Chinese hookers on the third floor of the Pacifico, a few blocks down Zanja from the Shanghai Theater, but that only lasted a few minutes.

'I should call,' said Frankie. 'My boss will want to hear what is going on.'

'Yes, of course.'

And so he did, walking across the street to a pay booth, inserting a nickel, ordering the operator to connect with Meyer's private number, knowing the old man would be up at this hour, totaling the house's take on this night as on all others, and watching as the courier left for the airport with the checks so that he'd get to the Miami bank at opening hour, 10 A.M.

But Meyer wasn't interested in a report.

'What the devil took you so long? I have been waiting for hours for you to call.'

'What is it, Meyer?'

'Ah, some other people are interested in helping us find this fellow. And they've put the word out, and now there's a report.'

'I'm all ears.'

'There's a whore who works a brothel just across from the dirty movie place — '

'The Shanghai. On Zanja. We were just in that neighborhood.'

'Yes. Some months ago, when the congressman was in town, he kicked the hell out of her, and our man pulled him off. He saved her life. But the afternoon he escaped, she disappeared. She hasn't been to work since.'

'You think he's there?'

'Frankie, go slow. Don't go busting in all in a

454

rush, like you did the last time. Take it slow. Make sure he's there. Be thorough, be careful, be precise. You have to do it this time.'

'I won't fail you, Meyer. Not this time.'

'Her place is on Zanja Street. No. 165 Zanja. The apartment is 204.'

Frankie committed it to memory.

'We're on our way.'

'Go end it on Zanja Street,' said Meyer.

56

There was no way to sleep. The orange burn of the lamps at the marquee of the Shanghai flooded through the window of the small apartment across Zanja Street; its flickery intensity was unstoppable. You could not escape it. In the room, it penetrated everywhere, not only on sheer power but also by its imperfect wiring, which filled the air with crackle and hum and the on-again, off-again buzz of the ever-pulsing middle letter 'g.'

He curled away from it and hallucinated sleep, but sooner or later that buzz cut the darkness, his eyes popped open, and he saw the fireglow on the wall. Once so disturbed, he could not recover unconsciousness. He'd rise, and turn, and there she'd be.

Esmerelda didn't talk. She didn't sleep. She just looked at him worshipfully, as if adoring a saint. By the second day it had begun to weigh heavily upon him. If she'd spoken his language, he'd have screamed: *What do you want? Why are you staring at me? Are you crazy? It's not right to stare at anyone like that.*

But she just stared, dumb and adoring. She was hefty, he now saw, and without makeup quite appalling. The beauty and body that Congressman Harry Etheridge had tumbled for and tried to capture didn't really exist; they were the delusions of an old man who thought of sex

456

too often and hunted it everywhere.

Her skin was pockmarked. Her teeth were false. Sometime back in a terrible past, someone had cut her badly and the lacework of scars embraced her throat, ran down her chest to the dark hollow between her immense breasts. Not that they were beautiful breasts — not like the plush, streamlined ones on the long-gammed, flouncy-skirt babes pilots painted on their bombers during the war. No, unsupported, they flattened like sacks of flour, slapping this way and that under her blouse. Her hair was black and greasy. She had a mole next to her left nostril. Her nose had a blunt, hard-busted quality. Her fingers were stubs, her arms were sheathed in flesh, and her behind was a hemisphere all its own.

On the first night, she'd been all tarted up, open for business. On that occasion, her cheeks were artificially red, her lips swollen also with red. Makeup caked her face, pinkish on the cheeks, crusted black above her eyes. Earl thought: Only a bosun's mate at sea a year could harden up for this poor old woman.

She had to be forty, well used, much saddled, much infected and reinfected, much rotted. She was in her knowledge of what men want and do beyond surprise, but for one: her love of Earl.

He had in some inadvertent way pried open the gates that held back her emotions, that had been hammered shut by twenty-five years of pimps cutting and beating her, johns screwing her or demanding yet more recondite pleasures, mamasitas treating her like meat, her pay for all that agony and debasement a few dreary pesos, a dollar now and then, and then back in daylight to her little chamber across from the Shanghai, to be alone with her fears and doubts.

Now she had only Saint Earl to worship. Jesus didn't do the trick any more, though he still hung in agony two or three times in each tiny room of the tiny apartment.

Sweetie, he thought, you sure as hell could have done better than this old man.

But not by her lights. She gazed at him adoringly. She touched him sexually the first night, as if to say, whatever, *whatever* you want.

He shook his head no, and it only made her love him more. He took his wallet out and showed her a picture of Junie, the one taken at the USO party at Southeast Missouri State Teachers College, when he'd been on bond tour in January of 1945, where he'd fallen in love with Junie, and one day after the picture was taken they'd gotten married, and one week after the marriage he'd left to rejoin the battalion for the invasion of Iwo Jima.

'My wife,' he'd said loudly, 'my *wife*,' not knowing the Spanish for it, but hoping that she'd see in Junie's delicate beauty, the upturn of her nose, the flaxen quality of her hair, the perfection of her lips, the warmth in her gray eyes why he loved his wife so, even if, truly, he thought she now had disengaged from him and all his damned adventuring.

But Esmerelda didn't understand. Oh, she understood the wife part, but she didn't see how that equaled chastity. She seemed to believe that

458

yes, he loved his wife, wasn't that wonderful, now let's cuddle and fuck.

'No,' he said, seeing the hurt it administered, wishing he didn't have to hurt her. 'No.' And he wondered, how do I explain? I have to stay true to this woman. It's all I have left in this world.

Esmerelda had touched him on the inside of the thigh.

'No,' he said, 'my wife. My *wife.*'

* * *

That was three days ago. Now it was only waiting. Esmerelda didn't leave in the night. She was his sentinel. In daylight, she went out with some money he gave her and came back with food: egg sandwiches, rice and beans, a pint of milk, some banana-like chips fried as if they were potatoes, and on that he subsisted.

He was scared.

Earl was scared.

Not like this. Really, no, there had to be a better way. He looked around for a weapon and only a paring knife was capable of taking human life, or possibly an old chair could be broken up and yield a club. But of course what he wanted was a gun. Without a gun, up against heavily armed men, he knew he was lost.

He thought about sneaking out in the night, conking a cop and taking one of those 9mm Stars they had, that looked just like .45s. Or maybe he'd be even luckier and come across the one in three officers who toted a tommy gun.

He obsessed on it. Just a good roundhouse to

the side of the head, not too hard, and the guy would be down and out for an hour. You grab the gun, and you feel the dense solidity of it, the purposefulness of it. Nothing feels better than a gun to a man who's hunted or hated or been oppressed or beaten. He can lose his imagination in it, because he knows that no matter what they do to him, if he uses it well, they will remember that night, their widows will cry and their orphans will beg. That is something to a man who has no other thing. God, he wanted a gun.

But he knew if he conked a cop, it would get to his hunters and they'd know the neighborhood, and they'd start busting down doors and smacking people around, and once they did, someone, *someone*, would talk. Someone had seen something. Someone always does.

So there was nothing. He, in the tiny apartment, Esmerelda staring intently at him, as if he were religious.

I ain't no saint, honey, he thought.

Time crept by, harshly. It seemed to crawl up stairs littered with broken glass. It took many a break to catch its breath. It was not a busy little worker. He finally took his damned watch off, because he kept checking it, and it would not move.

It was late, yet still the traffic ran up and down Zanja Street. Men went into and out of the Shanghai Theater or gathered laughingly and drunkenly at the Cafe Bambu a couple doors down from it. All glowed orange intermittently.

He watched the smoking men, the strutting women, the prowling cars; he heard the hoots, the whistles, the shouts, the clash of a dozen languages — but he saw nothing, not now.

He withdrew from the window, turned, and there was Esmerelda staring at him, her dumb eyes filled with love.

He smiled back, uneasily, wishing he had something to do, and then he heard men on the steps. They were trying to be quiet but they were approaching steadily.

★   ★   ★

Walter was having dinner with the head of United Fruit's marketing division, his wife, his daughter and his son. They were at the Tropicana, the world's most beautiful nightclub, and the meal was fabulous, even if now the waiters scurried to clear it, and deliver a last round of drinks before the floor show.

Stew Grant was a terrific guy and his wife, Sam — Sam! — was one of those eastern horsewomen types Frenchy loved so, but could never speak to. And the kids, Tim and Julie, were wonderful, the best American teenagers anyone could hope for. The subjects had ranged from Korea to Senator McCarthy — Stew thought he was a great man — to this new star Rock Hudson to United Fruit's prospects in its business arrangement with General Foods and this idea for dehydrating fruit to package in cereals, which looked very promising. But Frenchy couldn't take his eyes off the tanned, thin and aristocratic Sam, and she couldn't take her eyes off him. After all, he was . . . well, he

461

was the government's man in Havana, and —

'Señor Short?'

'Yes?'

'A phone call. Urgent.'

'Jesus Christ. I am — '

'It's from Mr. Lansky.'

'Ah.'

Frenchy excused himself, followed the waiter back through tables to a house phone, and picked it up.

'What's up? News?'

'They have him.'

'What?'

'They have him. They're moving in now.'

Frenchy's heart danced.

'You're sure.'

'I am. Someone saw something and told someone and one of your snitches got it to the cops who got it to me. We're dealing with it now.'

'It's a great night,' said Frenchy.

Then he checked himself. Great night: Earl dead. Same thing. And in the next second, by his special gift, he denied the flood of regret that came over him, and hastened back to the table. The floor show was about to begin.

★　★　★

Now it was happening. It would happen here, in this little room, with no toilet. Men with guns were coming for him and they would kill him. It couldn't be a whore with her trick, for they'd be talking bravely. It couldn't be an old lady, for she wouldn't be creeping, she'd be walking brazenly.

462

No, it was men, moving silently, maneuvering for position, trying to set up for a swift, brutal assault.

I will make a good fight, he told himself.

He gathered her up, soothingly, and slid her along the wall to a closet, gently pressed her into it and urged her down, into a ball. The bullets would be sprayed if he knew these boys, and they'd find her too, but that was the way it went.

He slid back, edging along the wall silently, because he knew they'd be listening for him. In his left hand he held the paring knife, and he'd taken a belt from one of her pitiful dresses and tied it around the hand, so that if he were hit or stabbed, and in pain opened his hand, his only weapon wouldn't fly away, irrecoverable.

I can get at least one, he thought. I can cut the first man through bad, and maybe I can get his gun from him, and maybe I can get it into play fast enough and maybe I can get another couple. Maybe I can get that goddamned New York boy, that rat, and maybe he's with the captain who cuts out the eyes and I can get him, too. If you're going out, you want to take some bad'uns with you.

Now it was silent.

He knew they were there and he knew there were at least three, because he'd heard the cracking of floorboards simultaneously from different spots as they crept along, which meant it wasn't his Russian pal, who always worked alone. Three would be about right to kill one man, unarmed, by surprise. Two would do it, but three was right, and that would be Frankie, the

463

captain and whomever was driving the car.

It was three.

The room was filled with flickering orange from the dirty window. Honks and squeals from outside filled the air. No sound came from nearby, but under the blade of light admitted by the crack beneath the door, he saw a shape move, then another. Two men had passed in front of the door to get to the other side.

He tensed.

He watched as someone gently tested the knob. It was locked, though there was no deadbolt. It was quiet, then a thin blade appeared, sliding through the crack in the door and up to the lock, where it rested, steadied itself, began to hunt for leverage, and quickly enough got the lock released.

Earl tensed, feeling his own little knife, which could slash but not reach deep enough to get a good, blood-filled organ.

Not here, he thought.

The door opened, gently. He heard scuffling, then a voice.

'Anyone in there care to buy a vacuum cleaner?'

57

Captain Latavistada set it up very nicely. He stationed men for blockade duty at each end of the block on Zanja Street. He infiltrated four more men around back of the whore's building and even got two on the roof. He himself, with Frankie and the Indian, waited down the street, out of the glare of the Shanghai's orange lamps, beyond the Bambu, as these brave young men maneuvered into position.

He watched, ever the military commander, through binoculars, over the hood of the car.

'He's not so smart,' he said.

'I never said he was smart,' said Frankie, who was next to him. Before them at the angle, its façade caught and made shadowy in the orange glow, lay the apartment building at 162 Zanja, pastel green, a kind of standard Havana structure fallen into bad repair, over-ornate in the Spanish fashion, of stucco, around a courtyard onto which it opened, proud yet at the same time a dump.

'Look, it's no place to hide,' said Latavistada, pointing to the window known to be apartment 205, Esmerelda's. 'It's too far to jump to the street. There's no balcony, so he can't swing to another apartment or climb to the roof. There is only the one door as a way in or out, and the one little window. He should have done better.'

Frankie was tense. This guy was slippery, he

had to be crushed. Tonight would end it for good.

'You sure this information is fresh? I don't see nothing going on in there.'

'No, that is it. That is where both mamasita and her girls from down the street say Esmerelda lives. Number 162, Calle Zanja, 205, second floor. That's it. He's there, he has to be.'

'Shouldn't we just do this goddamn thing? He knows he can't be there forever. Sooner or later he's going to make a move and we don't want to lose him. Not in this mob.'

Taxis, old cars, even the odd Cadillac wandered up and down Zanja Street. The whores lingered on the street corners. Men crowded into the Shanghai, and also at various loud arcades along that side of the street. There was the Bambu as well, next to the Shanghai, and its tables were full of smokers and drinkers and laughers. It was the human race, gathered to fuck for just a few pesos, here on Zanja Street.

'They start a new movie soon. The crowd will die. Then we move.'

He leaned forward, peering hard into his binoculars.

'Yes, two men are on the roof. Yes, they are in position. Yes, let me check, down the street, yes, down the street the other way. Yes. Frankie, are you ready?'

Frankie made sure his tie was tight, his hat was low. He had the Star machine pistol and this time he knew how to run it good. He'd practiced. It was locked and loaded. A little twitch of the trigger and it was jitterbug time.

466

Plus, he had his two .45 Colts.

The captain made a last check on the Mendoza 7mm, then hefted it. The corporal had a sledgehammer; there was nothing to check. Being methodical, he checked it anyway.

The captain rose from behind the car and nodded to the man at the nearest traffic blockade. That fellow spoke into a radiophone to the other car at the other end of the block, and then he and his partner hauled the sawhorse into the street and halted traffic.

Latavistada led. The three men crossed the street and loped along it, each festooned with his heavy weaponry. They stayed steady with the last knot of cars emptying the street. But then they reached the building and ducked inside, down a central corridor that smelled of garbage.

That passageway yielded to the courtyard, which was encircled by the building's two levels of balconies. They headed up the wooden steps to the first, turned left and went three doors to no. 205.

That was all. There was no ceremony or ritual of preparation. They reached the door, the corporal recoiled with the sledge, then put his massive strength behind it and unleashed a blow: the door blasted open, its locking mechanism shattered.

Frankie was in first, knowing exactly that he owned whatever lay beyond. He moved like a ranger, remembering stuff. He remembered to pinch off the safety so the machine pistol was alive, like a dangerous snake. He remembered to move swiftly in a straight line, as he hunted. He knocked over chairs, he ducked around corners, with the gun always pointing, ready instantly to unleash a burst.

But there were no targets. Or, rather, there was no Earl Swagger. No, there was only a fat gal swaddled in blankets, on her knees in a devotional position before a candle which itself was under a painting of the Virgin. She looked up in horror as Frankie bore down on her with his war face on, his mouth clamped tight in savagery, and she made no attempt to evade or cower as he kicked her in the face, knocking her to the floor so as to continue in his crusade.

But then he realized it was pointless: other than the praying gal, the apartment was empty.

He remembered to put the safety back on the Star so he wouldn't drill himself, set the gun down and returned to the central drama, which had already begun: Captain Latavistada and the woman.

She cowered. The captain yelled at her in Spanish, the full force of his magnificent manhood engaged. He was like a vulture, his wings spread and flapping, his eyes glaring, the beak hungry for blood. When she would not answer, he struck her hard, in the face, knocking out her teeth, which Frankie saw were dentures. The Indian righted her by her hair, and she spat at Captain Latavistada, though he was quick enough to avoid the slow-moving gob, and he repaid her with a terrible blow to the face. He beat her methodically for a few minutes, asking no questions, while the other policemen gathered in the doorway, watching the master at work. He worked her body, her nerve endings, her spine for maximum pain. She bucked spastically in the grip of the Indian as the captain had his way. Finally, he stood back, and the Indian dropped her. She fell in a heap to the floor.

Gently the captain knelt. He cushioned her and drew her upright, soothing her pain and fear, cooing to her.

Esmeralda faced him and spoke.

She spoke in pride and love. She spoke in nobility and triumph.

Latavistada looked over at him.

'We are too late, my friend, I am sorry to say. Half an hour ago, a man and three negro sailors came. The *norteamericano* went with them. Esmeralda understood that their destination had to be the harbor. If he is there, he is lost. Alas, if he is on a boat, he has escaped.'

The frustration rose like a steam in Frankie's mind, scalding him. He wanted to crumple in agony, the pain was so intense. So close, yet so far. Not quite fast enough. Never had a chance. That fucking guy was always ahead of him. He was a slippery motherfucker, he was —

'Wait,' said Frankie, as inspiration struck. 'I have an idea.'

'It's too late.'

'For most men. Most men'd get on that boat and take off and not look back. Not this one. I know what'll bring him back.'

'Frankie, my friend, you speak in riddles.'

'Come on. And bring the woman,' Frankie said. 'And your scalpel.'

58

With each step, each turn, each new smell, his sense of lightness grew more intense. They walked, tightly knotted, down Zanja Street toward the Capitolio, and no one paid them any attention. They were just another knot of men, five of them, two whites and three negroes, tightly clustered, pushing their way through the throng under the gaudy bright lights of the clubs and the bars.

'You see, two men hurrying along together, people might notice. So I brought these fine negro men and we are a crowd, a mob, tribal and instinctive in our lust for pleasure and freedom, sailors or tourists or soldiers, who would notice?'

Skirting El Capitolio, they entered the crazy streets of Old Havana, with its latticework of vivid neon overarching the narrowness, its grottos of tiny bars and bodeguitas, its cobblestones and crowds. They plunged down Lamparilla, straight toward the harbor, and soon a breeze full of sea smells reached them.

They ducked under an arch, and broke out of buildings proper, and the docks were before them. Tankers floated serenely, and huge freighters, like skyscrapers on their sides. Cranes towered above, reminding Earl even in the dark of preying birds, their hungry wings out-stretched. Garbage was everywhere; nobody cleaned up the docks.

'Up here. It's not far.'

And it wasn't. In a gap between ships there was a smaller dockage for smaller craft, and they headed toward it. Dozens of fishing boats and pleasure craft — some spiffy, some old wrecks — bobbed at the ends of spidery piers that shot out into the serene harbor. It didn't take long to find a scow called the *Day's End*, with its one mast, its twists of netting, its low waterline.

'I can't let you belowdecks. There's sensitive equipment there. You understand.'

'I don't give a shit what you have aboard. You can listen to the squids all day long, for all I care.'

Two more blacks lounged aboard the *Day's End*, and waved as their comrades approached. A white officer with a grave face came on deck. He didn't look happy.

'He don't like Americans, that one,' Earl said.

'It's his training, that's all. He'll do what I say. He admires me. He thinks I'm a hero, the young fool.'

'Dumb kids.'

'We'll drop you at Key West by tomorrow afternoon. Then you're on your own.'

'Much appreciated.'

'Don't mention it. Though I must say, you owe me for one perfectly fine handkerchief. That was one of my favorites.'

'I'm a little short on cash. You'll take a check, won't you?'

'Cash, check, pesos, rubles, pounds, lira, I'll take anything, old man. A fabulous shot, by the way.'

471

'I was to kill him and wound you.'

'Why didn't you do it, Swagger? Look at the trouble it's caused you.'

Earl merely smiled.

They reached the craft, and leapt the foot of space between it and the dock. Earl landed, felt a tremble as the craft vibrated under his weight. He looked back and saw nothing but blackness, in the distance a blaze of light from Old Havana.

'That way, Swagger,' said the Russian, pointing across the water. 'By motor we run that passage out of the harbor, between the Presidential Palace and the Morro Fortress. It's a small thing, and we are done, in open waters. Nobody can stop us. You go home. I guess I'll find a place to go. Too many people have noticed me. Your girlfriend was able to find me, so it's time to move on.'

He wore a linen suit coat over a peasant's white shirt and pants, and a pair of ropey sandals. His face was brown from all that time in the mountains, and he was still sinewy, lithe, quick, peppery and full of laughter. He turned.

'Orlov, let's put out. No point in waiting.'

Orlov nodded and shouted orders. The crew scampered to unlash the mooring lines and the boat floated out, three, four, five, then seven feet from the dock. Orlov started a motor, it coughed, spat the odor of smoke and gasoline, then ever so gently began to propel the boat ahead, gliding across the black water, while the men hurried to this or that task.

No one told him what to do, so alone Earl went up to the prow, settled against some kind of crate padded in netting, and lit a Camel. The craft seemed to pick up speed as the young lieutenant navigated it across the black water, and skillfully followed channel markers until reaching the narrows. At a certain point, two men unfurled the sails, which filled with a breeze, and the boat scooted ahead, knifing the water.

Then Cuba itself closed in around them again, until it was but a hundred yards off on either side. But no one hailed them, no lights came on, no sound arose. The country rushed by in perfect darkness.

Earl looked left and even at this late hour the Presidential Palace blazed brightly, lit up, its columns proclaiming a grandeur that really didn't exist now, if it ever had. More menacing were the forts that guard the harbor entrance and bulked up on either side of the channel, military structures with heavy walls and openings for guns to protect against invasion. The Morro was the most imposing of them.

But then the forts slid past and the open sea beckoned, black against the inky blue of the night sky. The sea was empty, unmarked by lights signifying other ships upon it. The sky vaulted huge above them, smeared with crazed pin-wheels of stars that radiated enough light to glint on the black surface. The bite of air was fresh and cold and nothing tainted filled it, no stench of garbage or fuel or human pathos.

Someone settled next to him; it was, of course, the Russian.

'We'll run hard to Florida, north by northeast.

As I said, by midafternoon. It's a short trip across. Key West, and you're home. What will you do?'

'Nothing. Catch a bus back to my farm. Be with my wife and my boy. Do my job.'

'Don't mix with these fellows or in these matters again. Everybody's clever, nobody believes, nothing's what it seems. It'll be the death of you, I swear.'

'I've learned my lesson, believe me. Smoke?'

'Yes, thanks.'

Earl got out his Camels and snapped out a butt, which the Russian took. Earl pulled out his USMC Zippo and leaned forward, cupping the flame, and the Russian inhaled to draw on it, the flame flared, the cigarette glowed red, and the Russian settled back to enjoy the pleasure of the tobacco.

'You know,' he said, 'you Americans make a good cigarette, that I'll say. English cigarettes, shit. The French, they could learn a thing or two from you but still, not too bad. Cuba for cigars but America for — '

But he saw the American was not listening.

Instead he peered intently over the Russian's shoulder, back to land.

The Russian turned, and saw only the dark escarpment of the Havana seawall, above it the great avenue called the Malecon where a surprising amount of traffic coursed back and forth and all the restaurants and bars still glittered, for the city never really slept.

'What is it?' he asked.

'I walked all over Havana,' Earl said. 'We just

passed Manrique, which intersects Zanja Street just down from the Shanghai Theater.'

'And?'

'And I saw a gumball.'

'What?'

'A police light. Blinking red. Way up Manrique, maybe all the way to Zanja. It's only a few blocks. It had to be at her apartment.'

'Her? Who are you talking about?'

'There was a cop car at Esmerelda's.'

'Oh. The whore.'

'Yes.'

'Police cars go to Chinatown all the night long. It is the nature of police cars to — '

'This boat, it has radio gear? Sophisticated radio gear, for overhearing conversations?'

'Swagger, I — '

'You know it does. You can listen to Havana police frequencies then.'

The Russian looked at him queerly.

'What on earth are you getting at? What possible difference can it make? All that is behind you now. You go to America, Orlov will drop me in Mexico and I'll find the soft route home. It's finished, the Cuban adventure.'

'Mr. Vurmoldt, please. Have the young officer monitor the cop frequencies. This late at night, all the boys chatter. I know, I do it myself. Tell me what you hear. Tell me what is going on.'

'Swagger, you are truly insane.'

'Mr. Vurmoldt, it's important. Please.'

Wearily the Russian rose. Swagger heard conversation behind him, some disagreement, and then the younger man turned the wheel over

475

to a mate, and vanished beneath decks. The
Russian followed.

★ ★ ★

Earl smoked and brooded. He sat alone at the
prow of the boat and watched the horizon pitch
this way and that. Sea spray hit him, and he
wondered what to do.

Then the Russian found him.

'Well, I have the whole story. What do you
want to know?'

'Everything. She helped me. She didn't have
to. I knew I shouldn't have left.'

'One does what one must.'

'What happened?'

'There was a raid. The story is not pretty.'

'She's dead?'

'They shot her.'

'Oh, Christ,' he said.

'Eventually.'

Earl waited a second or two, but he had no
choice in the matter, so he asked the next
question.

'Eventually? What does that mean?'

'It seems her screaming got on their nerves
after a while.'

'What do you mean.'

'He cut her eyes out. The secret police officer
called Ojos Bellos, Beautiful Eyes. And his
American chum. After she ran up and down
Zanja Street screaming, the American shot her.
She's still in the street.'

Earl was surprised how hard it hit him. He

476

wanted to puke, but the pain went red into rage a few seconds later and when he came back to earth everything was clear again.

'Turn around.'

'Swagger, you are a fool.'

Earl yelled past the Russian to the young officer, 'Turn this tub around, goddammit. I have business.' It was his command voice, dead and powerful and undeniable.

'Swagger,' said the Russian, 'I am a man of the people. But I am not a man of persons. This is a person. It is very sad but what happens to persons is of no consequence.'

'I got her killed.'

'She was a whore. Havana is a whore town. Tonight, as on any night, five thousand whores were fucked by twenty thousand men. Fifty of those whores were beaten because men beat whores. Of the fifty, one died. This night it was this whore. Thus is it eternally in the wickedness of the world. The death of one whore? It has nothing to do with the forces that control history and political destiny. It has nothing to do with systems, yours or mine. It has nothing to do with — '

'Fuck all that shit, mister. Do you have a gun?'

'God, Swagger. Truly unbelievable. You would go unarmed otherwise. Against men who wait for you.'

'How do you know?'

'I heard the cops talking. They do not like this Beautiful Eyes very much, but also they fear him. They wonder what game he plays. He would not let them move the body. He sits there with his

American friend and an Indian, heavily armed, waiting at the Bambu. Waiting for what? We know what he is waiting for, don't we, Swagger.'

'It don't matter.'

'And what would it prove?'

'It don't prove a goddamn thing except maybe I still have some gun speed left.'

'Swagger, what a red guerilla you'd have made.'

'Fuck all that shit. Here's where we are: you wouldn't have come across Havana without a gun to help a hunted man. You have a burp gun somewhere too, I know.'

'Back in the hold of the tanker *Black Sea*. The tiny pistol I used in prison was the bribe I used to get *out* of prison.'

'You wouldn't have come across Havana without no gun. You're too careful and too salty. You're an old Texas Ranger in this game and so you're packing big heat, I know you are.'

The Russian turned, nodded to the young officer, who shouted orders, and the boat began to come about.

'Truly amazing,' the Russian said, turning back to Earl. He shucked off his coat and slipped out of something heavy, handing it over to Earl. 'Where would one get a gun in Havana in a hurry?' he asked rhetorically. 'I could only think of one place, a certain museum to imperialism, protected only by the charisma of the American empire. And so yes, I helped myself.'

It was a basket-weave shoulder holster of ancient, much-burnished leather. Earl pulled it on like a coat, sliding a shoulder into each of the loops of the strap, which was held in place by a leather X-piece at the back. Then he tied the holster down tight against his belt, reached up, slipped out the weapon it concealed, feeling how quickly the holster yielded its grip.

It was a Colt Peacemaker, with the short 45/8-inch barrel in the Long Colt .45 caliber. The finish was so well worn from usage that it was a dead gray, the casehardening long since faded away, the gutta-percha stocks smooth from much work. It felt familiar to Earl, reaching out for his hand from a past so dead it hardly existed any more. His old daddy had carried this kind of gun as a sheriff and he, Earl, had cleaned it every day for ten years, or got beaten bad. He and the pistol were therefore on intimate terms. Earl had shot it a lot, so it held no surprises, but a good question was, had the old marshal who'd owned it and brought it to the war of 1898 honored it or ignored it? Earl tested the hammer pull and found it slicker than soap, and knew that sometime in the past the old boy had honed its internal surfaces, maybe planted a little leather ringer where the mainspring mates with the frame, to make it better for man-killing work. He noted that the front sight had been filed way down, again for speed-work out of the holster. He shook each cartridge from the cylinder, then cocked — smooth as glass — touched the trigger on an empty cylinder to see what pull dropped hammer, and discovered a trigger as responsive as a cat with its back up. He reloaded, and the Russian handed over an old box of cartridges, which Earl emptied into his coat pocket. It was a gun that had done some good killing work in its time.

'Swagger, here's the terrible thing,' said the Russian. 'I don't believe I've ever seen you this happy.'

59

It is 4 A.M. on Zanja Street, the hour of Odudua, the dark mistress of the underworld according to the cosmology that is *Santeria*. Odudua is married to Obatala, whose job is to finish creation; hers is to destroy it. As you might imagine, it is not a happy marriage. So she wanders alone at night, deciding whom to take.

The men lounging in the sidewalk cafe in the orange glow of the Teatro Shanghai, sipping coffee and smoking, have no knowledge of Odudua; they don't believe in her or in the system that created her, a fusion of Catholicism and Nigerian pantheism, so they would consider themselves theoretically immune to her predations. Perhaps they are right; perhaps they are not. This is the evening they will find out.

Captain Latavistada has his feet up on a chair and is smoking a very large cigar. He is well pleased with himself. He enjoys torture, destruction and death as necessary pillars of the state, and tonight he has done his duty. He hopes for more duty to do. He feels marvelous, alive, tingly, his vision sharp and precise. He loves to fight and he hopes he gets to fight some more tonight. The coffee is loaded with sugar, so he is all ajangle. Next to him, on the floor, resting on its bipod, is the formidable Mexican 7mm Mendoza light machine gun. It is cocked and ready; its safety is off. He hopes he gets to use this fabulous weapon again tonight, for its novelty has not worn off. It enchants him.

Across from him, more feral and hunched, his ratty eyes dashing this way and that, sits Frankie Carbine. He has taken his sunglasses off. He is drinking beer. His black tie is tight. He wears leather gloves. He wears a narrow-brim fedora. His jacket is buttoned, all three buttons. In shoulder holsters under each armpit are Colt .45 automatics. Across his knee is the Star machine pistol. It too is cocked, safety off, ready to go in a second. Frankie drinks beer but it doesn't numb his senses. They are too sharp for that. He is ready. It should happen. The guy, the fella, whoever the fuck he is, he will have heard what they did to the broad.

Now they wait, and people give them a wide berth, out of respect for the seriousness of their commitment to law and order. Though it is late, Zanja Street is not empty. Here and there a whore still trolls for tricks, for often the gringos would come down to Zanja Street not quite brave enough to be with a woman yet. They'd find a place and drink and nurse their courage, and work themselves into a state where they felt beyond their own moral compass and no longer responsible for their actions; that was when they wanted a dark, heavy woman, with large breasts and a willing mouth, and no capacity to judge, no need to forgive, no common language except the fuck and the suck. That commerce is common still at this late hour.

So Zanja Street is crowded this night. Somewhere a mambo band plays, somewhere a woman laughs, another screams. Knives are carried and used; pimps beat the recalcitrant; whores and tricks eye each other, each waiting to begin the ritual of the barter; sailors drink; the captain and the mobster sip and wait, and the Indian corporal lounges close at hand, silent and watching, not at their table but the one beside it, a loyal servant. They all wait for a man who would be a fool to face their armed might, but they believe he will arrive nevertheless, before dawn.

And Odudua is there, too. She also waits. No one sees her, for she never takes visible form. But she is there and she knows that tonight will be a good night for her and that she will have many to take with her back to the underground in the minutes before dawn.

★   ★   ★

Earl is of a killing mind. But it's not rage, with rage's sloppiness, its rush, its phony bravado, its capacity to deflate, then disappear abruptly. Rather, it's focus. He knows certain realities: this fight will be short and violent and close. Who shoots first wins. Who's got the stronger will wins. Speed helps, courage is a plus, righteousness a treat, but this one comes down to who gets closest fastest.

He knows the area, having studied it out the window of Esmerelda's over those long two days, when there was nothing else to do. He sure isn't going to walk down Zanja Street like some damned fairy cowboy and announce himself with a cowboy line crafted in a bungalow in the San Fernando Valley. No, instead he'll slither through the Bambu from the alley side, enter through the kitchen, get in close, and of a sudden start shooting. One first to each gut, then back again higher to the chest, which ought to kill them both; if there's time and it ain't gone all to crazy, then put one under each boy's eye or into his mouth or ear: blow them brains everywhere. Close and fast, at muzzle-scorch range.

He is not particularly scared. He has done a lot of this work. He's killed in lots of places, in lots of ways. It's something he knows he's good at. It only bothers him afterwards, but up front, he's so intent on getting the job done, there's no fear or regret. His mind is narrow as a tunnel, and as dark. He thinks only of killing techniques and tactical possibilities; no other impulses flutter in his brain. Son, wife, history, father, mother, sex, money, all that is forgotten utterly. He is so ready to kill.

He gets to Zanja, circles around, sliding through the mob. A dark alley leads to the rear of the Bambu, and he studies it, seeing the door by the garbage cans. A cop lounges there, a rear guard so the boys won't get taken by surprise. Earl studies on it, then slides back to the street, finds a gal, grabs her hard. She looks at him in fear. With his hand he guides hers to the Colt under his shoulder and with his mean glare he communicates only that she must obey. It's certainly not polite but Earl doesn't care or know. He embraces her, whispers, 'Drunk,

drunk!' and himself begins to wobble this way and that.

They careen down the alley, and the cop watches them approach.

'Hey,' he finally calls, 'you can no come this way, señor. No, you must go,' and speaks quickly to the woman in Spanish, in a far more threatening tone, and is so convinced of his moral authority that he doesn't even see the short, brutal arc of the Colt barrel as it slices through the air and thuds viciously into his jaw at the hinge, instantly blotting out his consciousness. He slips, falls like a sack of shot to the pavement. Earl shoves the girl away, and she ceases to exist for him.

He touches the door, finds it locked; a pocketknife springs the lock and he thinks to fold it before stepping into the kitchen, now largely empty, but there are two Cubans in the corner, talking of love, smoking. One sees him, makes as if to rise but is stopped by the four oily clicks of a Colt hammer ratcheting back. This man sees the snout of the gun and shrinks in its presence; he may be brave or a coward, but clearly there's killing about to happen and he wants no part of it.

In the cafe itself a few sit at tables, arguing politics or pussy, or possibly even movies or sports, full of the intensity of the moment. A waiter eyes him, notes it as strange that a *norteamericano* in an abused khaki suit and no tie is walking forcefully from a door that should disclose no *norteamericanos*, but then sees the blunt nose of the *pistola* and he too thinks little of his chances to stop what's coming — and turns instead to his own issue of survival, which he ensures by dropping swiftly to the ground, gesturing to his colleague to join him. In fact, as Earl walks, many people drop silently to the floor, as if he is a black death spirit, as if Odudua walks with him. And they are right: she does.

Earl steps out. Their backs are to him as they concentrate on the street. He walks silently, paying no attention to the other people sitting on the sidewalk, and when he's close enough he raises the gun and —

It happens so fast.

The gun comes up and neither Latavistada nor Frankie Carbine sees and the range is but ten feet, but someone does see, the Indian, who happens to look over from his table of watchfulness close by. He is as naturally fast and aggressive as Earl, his reflexes maybe even faster, and he comes up from his seat screaming 'Arma! Arma! Arma!,' drawing his own automatic from the flapped holster at his waist and in a moment of blind, nearly insane heroism steps between Earl and his targets. And of course Earl must take him first. The heavy Colt leaps against his hand, its old powder flashing brightly in the night, and Earl blows a huge 250-grainer through the Indian's chest, evacuating ounces of lung tissue and oxygenated blood. A fog erupts from the man as if he's a balloon full of liquid atomized by the power of the bullet. But no bones have been hit and though fatally wounded, the Indian is not dissuaded from his own mission, and his automatic rises toward Earl, who must then thumb fast into another shot and another, the last of which hits spine dead-on and pegs the dead Indian backward, where he falls and spills Frankie's table to the ground in a clatter of breaking glass. This takes maybe one full second, but that is enough for both Frankie and Latavistada to overcome their utterly stupefied shock, go to the floor, roll and draw and fire.

They don't aim. It's all too close and fast for aiming and that's why gunfights always involve a lot more shooting than hitting. It's a part of human nature to shoot and shoot, to lose oneself in the thunder of the gun. This is exactly what the literature of such events tells us: that at such close ranges in such frenzies of adrenaline-crazed trigger-jacking, misses happen with extraordinary regularity. The gunshots rise as one noise, so loud, their reports echoing back and forth in the narrow congress of Zanja. Frankie's machine pistol has fallen away, so with one hand he pulls a .45 and starts spraying bullets into the night. Latavistada is also shooting, slightly more directionally. He hits a woman in the knee and a man in the arm, both behind Earl, but it doesn't matter; he can't stop shooting.

Some of these bullets fly to the street, ripping into windows or autos. A car twists and crashes against curb, then lurches onto sidewalk, slamming finally against Esmerelda's apartment building. People flee in the orange light but no one in the fight notices, for those without weapons and an enemy are as insubstantial and meaningless as ghosts.

487

As Earl scrambles sideways to the low wall that marks the cafe from the sidewalk, he throws out three more shots, thumbing them off fast and uncontrollably. Moving, shooting, knowing that moving makes him a hard target, especially for men who are not aiming. Everyone is shooting from instinct. He too misses because that is the way of the gunfight; there's too much chemistry in his blood and his eyes are swollen, his heart is pumping, his muscles are super in their strength but now clumsy, and he is inured from fear or noise or pain. He gets to the wall, and throws himself over.

The inadequacy of the classic single-action sixgun is at this point exposed. To reload is a good thirty seconds of work, during which time either of his antagonists may approach and shoot him. But both their guns are empty, too. There's a brief intermission, a strange quietude where not a sound is heard except the scuffle of the men on the cobblestone ground, the tinny ping of still-bouncing shell casings, the slide and scrape of the reloading process as bullets are shoved into guns or magazines, cylinder rotated in a whirr of clicks, magazines inserted with a slam and a clang of heavy metal hitting heavy metal, with a slight vibration into it.

Then, almost simultaneously, the guns are all loaded again.

Earl has meanwhile decided to abandon plan one and move on to plan two. The problem is, there is no plan two. He simply looks around for a place to retreat into, sees that the street is death, forward is death, and the only possible

488

destination lies forty feet away, a doorway lit by the orange lamps of the Shanghai, with Chinese characters running up each side. Without willing it he's off, running full-out toward the entrance, ducking behind a line of cars which may or may not contain human beings, but certainly aren't going anywhere soon.

Latavistada recovers first. He sees the running man behind the cars and knows a pistol hit on a runner at that range simply isn't in the cards, so he diverts to the big Mendoza next to him on the ground, seizes it, locks it under his arm, pivots, braces and fires. However, the weapon is too heavy and Latavistada can't quite catch up. The gun pounds, the muzzle flashes, the empty shells spin in the air, the bullets trace their stitchery across the automobiles. Bullets pierce glass, or atomize it, tossing geysers skyward, smearing windshields with a blur of hazed webbing. They sing through steel with a whang, they deflate tires, they shred roofs, they pop doors, they make the cars shiver and rattle and then settle. They don't touch the running man, for Latavistada is too slow, and then they stop.

He has run dry. He kneels, pulls a big magazine out of his coat pocket, runs through a fast reload and sees Earl as he darts toward the theater. Up he comes, and *bzzzzzzzt* goes the gun again, and a stitch of geysers pulling yet more debris and dust into the air flies across the building, but the bullets don't quite intercept as Earl ducks into a doorway whose depth provides enough angle to survive the burst.

The door is locked. Earl leans against it once.

It does not give. He blows apart the lock with his .45 and slides through.

Latavistada groans as his prey disappears into the doorwell.

Now he is again out of ammunition. Laboriously he pulls another Mendoza magazine out and slaps it into the magwell up top, throwing bolt so that with a quiver the gun comes alive again. He is aware that Frankie is shooting his guns at the doorway, blowing out quarts of brick dust but accomplishing nothing else. Stupid.

'Frankie, stop, he is inside. We must root him out like a pig.'

When Frankie turns, Latavistada sees his eyes are wild, his lips tight, his face drippy with sweat.

'Calm down, my friend. We have him.'

Frankie gets control of himself and reloads. He looks around for his machine pistol but can't locate it in the welter of upturned tables, broken glasses and plates, knives, forks and napkins, and groaning, squirming citizens that litter the cafe floor.

Both guns reloaded, he turns to Latavistada for guidance.

'You go, my friend, in the door through which he went, the side entrance. I'll go in the main. We'll pinch him and kill him inside.'

'But aren't there other people there?' Frankie wonders.

'What of it?' asks Latavistada. 'Such is the cruelty of life. Let's go.' He laughs madly. 'Isn't this fun! *Jesu Cristo!* is this fun!'

Frankie squirrels away fast, all urgency. Latavistada is more lumbering, less mobile; after all, he has eighteen pounds of light machine gun in his hands, plus three more magazines, each filled to brimming with ammunition. He has to pick his way around the automobiles, two or three of which are now disgorging wounded or terrified people.

'*Vamos!*' he cries, 'out of the way, fools.'

On top of that, he hurts in a dozen places, he suddenly realizes, bruised and scraped and bumped where he'd hit the ground, where he'd rolled hard, where he'd squirmed or crawled on the stone floor. His knee aches; he seems to have skinned it badly.

He hears a crackle, a hiss, and the orangeness of the universe flickers off then back on. He realizes it's the blinking orange lamp that casts its fireglow on the Chinese characters at the door of the Shanghai. An impulse strikes him so strongly he cannot deny it. And why should he deny it? Is he not Latavistada, Beautiful Eyes of the SIM? Is he not the state itself, is he not responsible for all the little children of Cuba? He raises the muzzle of the heavy weapon, getting his arm under it for leverage, and squeezes off a magazine. The bullets sail to his target, the orange neon lamps splatter sparkily into oblivion then slide in an orange sleet to the sidewalk amid a most satisfying tintinnabulation of breaking glass. It is fabulous! But why this gesture of sheer nihilism? He doesn't know. It felt right. It's what had to be done.

He kneels briefly, dumping the magazine,

reloading another. Then he too heads into the theater.

★ ★ ★

Earl crashes into grim brick darkness and sees that he's in some sort of tunnel that must run alongside the theater's auditorium. It must lead to dressing rooms where the G-string gals go to relax between sets. Now it is empty. But he spies down the way just a bit a black curtain marking off an entrance where in an American theater there'd be a door, and some low light creeps around its margins. It's the whitish light of projected imagery, identifiable instantly to any man, woman or child in civilized neighborhoods of this planet.

Earl races to it, ducks through, and finds himself at the head of a jammed auditorium. Yet all there are men, and all are in rapture, their faces lit white by what they see.

Earl doesn't have time to calculate it, he merely drops to his knees and begins to speed-crawl up the side aisle, and after four or five rows squirms rightward, climbing over the feet of men, some of them masturbating. They are too intent on what the screen is showing to pay him attention, though one kicks at him, and he responds by clipping that man hard in the knee with his Colt barrel, causing a sharp cry of pain to echo through the space, competing with the crisp electrical buzz of the soundless film cranking away up top, and the low moans of otherwise occupied gentlemen.

Earl gets so far and stops, crouching under seat level, able to use the little space between the rapt men's shoulders as a spy hole, and sees in that next second Frankie Carbine plunging into the auditorium from the same entrance. Yet he does something Earl didn't do. He stops and looks.

Jesus Christ. She is sucking his . . . Jesus Christ, he is licking her . . . holy fucking shit, he is putting his . . . in her . . .

Earl sees him, face white, eyes open, guns momentarily lowered, transfigured by the imagery. In a second he recovers and is back on the hunt.

Earl rises, his shadow cutting across the light beam — 'Down in front!' comes a cry — cocks and fires once at the illuminated man.

Stricken visibly, Frankie looks over, his eyes even wider, even whiter. A quiver or tremble palsies his limbs. Again the .45 has gone through soft tissue, ripping out chunks of flesh and organ, but no structure has been shattered, so he doesn't collapse to the floor. He is exsanguinating rapidly, but don't tell him that. He isn't interested. He tries to bring his two guns to bear on Earl but can't see him because in that second the flash and sound of Earl's shot has punctured the secret dreams and hopes of the fuck-movie audience, and they rise almost as if in a parade, on command, as the panic of violent death overwhelms their urge to watch naked women.

At that moment precisely, however, catastrophe turns to tragedy for the men of Teatro Shanghai, for the avenging angel that is Señor

Latavistada has arrived at the top of the aisle by means of the front door, having raced through the lobby where a manager will do nothing to stop a crazed secret policeman with a machine gun. What the captain sees is a mass of men coming toward him in panic, lit by the silvery light from the screen.

The captain is not one to hesitate. His philosophy is to attack, attack, attack, and so he simply opens fire on the mob, presuming that one among them would be Earl and what difference would it make if he killed twenty by accident, so long as he also killed the one he intended?

And it is satisfying in its way: the light machine gun rocks in his hands like the sword of god, reaching out to magically punish the world's sinners. He fires a whole magazine, and before him, the gun spits smoke, which rises and is caught into the projector's beam, and its bullets mowing into the surging mob. The bullets are so powerful, the men so packed, that each one penetrates at least three. Some they kill, some they maim, some they cripple, but the crowd is like a giant animal tormented by a man with a whip, and reacting organically, it recoils.

Frankie, slipping badly over on the far side of the theater, the gears of his brain sometimes engaged and sometimes not, sees what Latavistada is doing and, as the men turn to surge toward the exit which he guards from his knees, raises both guns and begins to fire blindly, one, then the other, and sees them fall or flee, and drives them back.

Then Earl, who has squirmed his way back down his row, leans out, waits for the scurrying to clear, and calmly shoots him. The shot was meant for chest and heart, but in the dark, crouching, firing one-handed, how can one be sure? The bullet hits Frankie in the throat, blowing out larynx and spinal cord, and his guns fall to the ground.

By this time Latavistada has reloaded, has heard Earl's shot, has placed it somewhere on the other side of the theater and down toward the front, so he begins to climb over the bodies of those he's shot, oblivious to screams and pleading and protests and shouts of bitter anger, trying to get a glimpse of Earl, who he realizes is hunching beneath seat level.

He locates the sector where Earl would seem to be. He fires a magazine, and the bullets pulverize the theater seats with such force that detonations of shattered wood and upholstery stuffing rise in the piercing silver beam. Surely that would do it. No man could live through such a thing.

But he kneels, quickly reaches for a magazine, and realizes he's out. To pistols then! He dumps the big gun, reaches to his hip and pulls the Star. He clicks back the hammer. Now he's much more mobile. He crouches, looking just over the seat level, looking for his target.

It's quiet, except for the occasional whimpers of men on the edge of death. The air seethes with smoke, illuminated by the silver beam. On the screen, Jose is still fucking Carmen and Carmen still seems to be enjoying it.

Where Earl should be, of course, he is not.

A brush of paranoia pierces the bull-like mental strength of Latavistada. Where is the fucker? Where has he gone? Is he hit? Did I hit him?

He creeps down the aisle, peering down each row for his enemy. He only sees bodies, mangled chairs in the dim light of the screen, all of it flickering as Jose pounds away on Carmen. He has to close. He knows this.

He slides down an aisle and it annoys him to crawl so he climbs to his feet, begins a slow creep until he reaches the halfway point, then hears the scuffle of a determined man. *I have you!* he thinks with a spurt of pleasure so intense it is almost sexual. He leaps up to shoot and drills a runner. The only problem: that running man is not his enemy. Then a strange thing happens. Suddenly he is pinned in light. He is blinded in radiance. It is as though God were addressing him. Ramon, God seems to be saying, time to consider your sins and plan confession.

However it's not God. Possibly it's a trick arranged by that sly bitch Odudua. It seems she has planned things so that the porno reel has run out and no one has stayed in the projection booth to change it, and so the pure beam of light, unfiltered by blasphemous imagery, hits him in his beautiful eyes, and he turns, blinded, and can only barely recognize the form rising from the seats just beyond his, like some creature crawling from a fresh sea. Would this be God?

No, it's Odudua. Next to her, the white guy with the gun, that one is Earl, who shoots him twice in the chest. He slides down, instantly numb. He feels no pain, only immense laziness. As a predator, he feels no fear. Men such as him do not, in any practical sense, experience fear. He feels . . . wonder. How did it come to this?

Earl leans over, presses the gun muzzle against Latavistada's left eye, feels it sink a little under the pressure, and shoots through it into the brain.

Then Earl rises. Somewhere sirens are beginning to wail. Someone begs him to get a doctor. Someone calls for Maria and another for Roselita and one for Mabel-Louise. That one seems to be from Kansas City.

But Earl turns, slips out, for he has no time for the dying. Not any more. He has a boat to catch.

60

At dawn a mist came in. The *Day's End* cruised back and forth just off the Malecon. It was clear that whatever Earl had wrought, it was significant.

The sirens had been blaring for an hour. Ambulances hustled in both directions up and down the Malecon, their flashing lights penetrating the mist that lay heavily on the land and sea.

'By the number of them,' Orlov said in Russian, 'you'd have to say quite a lot of damage was done. This American, he seems to have a special gift for mayhem.'

'It may have cost him his life, however. I see him fighting till his last pint of blood is gone and then, without a pulse, shooting and killing his last enemy before he dies.'

'Possibly you romanticize him, sir. You make him sound like one of their ridiculous cowboys or some legendary cossack. He's a killer, that's all.'

'Orlov, you are very young. I allow myself one illusion per decade. It keeps the world amusing. The true enemy isn't western capitalism, it's boredom. Anyhow, go listen on the radio and tell me.'

The young officer disappeared for a few minutes, leaving Speshnev alone, floating in a netherworld. The mist rolled everywhere, dense and clinging; he felt like a subject in some terrible avant-garde painting, symbolizing existential nothingness, universal ennui, the desolation of the soul.

But then the young man returned.

'Some kind of massacre. Many shot. A high-ranking police officer assassinated. The *policia* are beside themselves. It's quite amusing.'

'But no word on the American?'

'They said some Americans had died and some others been wounded. It's hard to tell. It doesn't sound as if he got away.'

'No.'

'We had better go, Speshnev. At any moment the Coastal Police could come out of the mist and demand that we heave to. We have no business here and I don't want to be nabbed in Cuban territorial waters with this much secret gear aboard. The American intelligence people would have a field day. My career, you know, is not as glorious as yours, but it would die such a death.'

'Just a minute or so longer.'

'Speshnev, you know he's dead. He fought I don't know how many. Clearly he did much killing. But he's gone, he — '

Then they saw him.

He emerged from the mist with his coat tightly wrapped about him. His face was grim and sunken, his eyes bleak and dark. He needed a shave. There was no lightness at all to his step.

'Well, he *is* a cowboy, after all,' said Orlov. 'I give you that.'

Speshnev expected him to falter, to fall and, as in a movie scene, let his coat spread open to reveal the fatal wound, the gush of blood from a shot gut.

But it never happened. Orlov brought the boat in close, and there was not even a need to tie up. The American just sloshed out into the shallow waters until he reached the gunwale, and two negroes pulled him up. Orlov gave the command and they sailed off, into the mist.

★ ★ ★

An hour passed and then another, and all the while the American brooded alone in the bow. At one point, Speshnev directed one of the negroes to bring him a cup of coffee, which he drank while smoking a Camel. Finally the mist broke and revealed them to be alone on an empty blue sea, under a bright sun in an empty blue sky.

The American seemed to relax a bit; he took off his wet coat, rolled up his sleeves, then peeled off the shoulder holster with the old Colt in it. He seemed to contemplate it a bit and then, almost with a sadness in his limbs, he tossed it over the side. In two handfuls, he dispensed with the remaining shells from his pockets

Speshnev approached.

The American looked over to him.

'Hated to do that. A gun gets you through a fight, you feel something for it. Stupid, ain't it? Just a gun. Not like it's a damn dog or anything.'

'I'm certain it went to gun Valhalla, Swagger, where it will drink grog in a great hall filled with wenches.'

'Ain't that a pretty picture.'

'We heard on the radio. They're calling it a guerilla attack. El Presidente will use it as an excuse to crack down on the radical left. Eleven men are dead and twenty-two more seriously wounded. A heroic police officer lost his life.'

'I blew his fucking brains out. Felt damn good too, you know?'

'Yes, I know. It always does. So you succeeded?'

'I got both of 'em. Killed 'em deader than shit. Ain't I a peach? Too bad about them other guys.'

'Don't be upset at the excess, my friend. Progress is made by chaos and tragedy, not by polite chatter. Justice came last night to Cuba, if only for a little while. Possibly it will come again.'

'Maybe so. Now I just want to sleep for a year. How soon can this tub get me home?'

'Swagger, don't go back. They have you marked.'

'It ain't like that's a choice. I've got a job to do. I am the law on Route 71 between Blue Eye and Fort Smith in West Arkansas.'

'You know how it has to end. Not this year, maybe the next. You know what they have to do.'

'No, I don't know nothing about them. I only know what I've got to do. That's the only goddamned thing I have a say in.'

Both men turned. The horizon was flat, the wind strong, the sea empty. In a few hours, America would appear on the horizon.

61

The old men were pleased. Really, there was no bad news, except of course for the tragedy of Frankie Carbine, but Frankie, that boy had always been a hothead, and it was in the cards that sooner or later, someone would blow that hot head off. That was his talent; that was his destiny.

'He lived a soldier, he died a soldier,' said one of the old men in the smokey social club on a completely undistinguished street in Brooklyn. Then he took a sip of his sweet red wine, then a taste of his sweet black coffee, then a puff of his long brown cigar.

'He went out hard,' said another. 'That's to his credit. He done his job, he took his pay, may he rest in well-earned peace.'

But nobody was truly upset over Frankie. What were his prospects, really? It is the duty of some to serve and die so that others may live and prosper. That is the way it has always been; that is the way it will always be. All the men in this room had done their jobs in hard places, all had survived by guile and cruelty and courage and relentless ambition. It was not in them, really, to mourn a fellow who hadn't quite made it up the ladder. And, too, there were other champions to celebrate.

'The Jew, see? He is so smart. I hate to say it, but in some ways this Jew is more valuable than a dozen soldiers. A hundred, even. This Jew, so smart, he presses everything for advantage and he always wins that advantage. He is the house odds twice over. Plus, he only scrapes a little off the top. Not much, just a little.'

The news had just come from Meyer. The scandal of the bloody battle in the Shanghai Theater between guerillas and the police — though of course everyone knew it was between Frankie's men and competing vice lords, fighting for control of Old Havana's theretofore independent brothels, and that Frankie, though dead, had nevertheless won — had scared El Presidente and, frightened, he had decided that his future lay in more cooperation with the old men, not less.

Thus, in private, through discreet emissaries, El Presidente had agreed to certain concessions planned to make the road between him and his American supporters more stable, not less. Instead of taking 20 percent off the top, he was now content with 18 percent. Instead of 10 percent of all heroin moneys, he would accept 8 percent. And as for those very profitable independent brothels in the old town, once under the iron control of that fiery rogue El Colorado and in play ever since his untimely end, he would look the other way if certain Americans of experience took over management. The *policia* had been so informed and would cooperate; the word was now being spread, by various means, to the working men and women of that quarter. Their new masters would soon appear and things would be managed more scientifically, after the modern fashion of the *norteamericanos*.

But best of all, because of a new and very cooperative young man in the intelligence service, pressures against subversives, radicals, students, *communistas* were all to be increased, as in the grand old days of other strongmen. This meant the possibility of unrest and upheaval was much, much smaller, which meant in turn the investment possibilities were much, much more attractive. It was even rumored that Hilton planned to erect a huge hotel near the Nacional!

And that one? The one whose mischief had so scared them a few months ago? Why, he was in prison and would stand trial in the fall and his sentence would be life at least. Our government agents had taken care of it. Wasn't it nice when everybody got along? It was so much better than the old way. If only those *strunzas* of the FBI . . . but that was another matter.

An old man raised a nice glass of Sambuca.

'My friends,' he said, 'I propose a toast. We are secure now. It doesn't matter what Chicago does in Las Vegas. Our island will pour its treasures into our strongboxes forever. Las Vegas can rise or fall, its sponsors can succeed or fail, it doesn't matter, not a bit. The future is ours.'

They all raised their glasses to a wondrous tomorrow, a Cuba forever theirs, untouched, untainted, tamed and perfected. It was the American way.

★　★　★

504

There had been some sickness, but strong as a horse and full of pride and ego, he had survived. Poison? Some would say so. It would be easy to do here in the prison, where certain people could be bribed, certain people controlled. After all, he had many enemies, and many twisted in envy and malice at his name.

There was plenty to hate. He admitted that. Rarely are men given so many gifts as he. He had foresight, wisdom, strength, courage, stubbornness, stamina, and the poet's feeling for the soaring lyric. Women adored him, mothers worshipped him, men followed him.

The trial was but weeks away.

Yet he knew it was but another opportunity.

'History will absolve me,' he had written, and he knew it to be true. History would also celebrate him, then obey him and finally yield to him.

I will show you, papa, he thought. *I will show you.*

62

'And so he escaped,' asked Pashin.

'Yes. He certainly caused a ruckus. What a scandal,' said Frenchy Short, 'and how lucky, really, he got away, or I'd have had some very awkward explaining to do.'

'Remarkable. I'd bet that asshole Speshnev had something to do with it. He has not been seen in days.'

'Old men. Tricky old bastards. Too many tricks.'

'Their day will come, soon enough. Maybe not this year, but certainly the next.'

The two sat at the old bar called the two brothers — *Dos Hermanos* — down by the waterfront, across from the Customs House. The ferry full of cars from Florida was just pulling in. They were drinking mojitos, because for once there was little to do. It was a Saturday, late in the afternoon, and overhead gulls glided and screamed, and out front the traffic roared along.

'And you are off to West Berlin?' Pashin asked.

'Yes. I thought maybe Plans would renege on his promise when the gangsters failed to get Earl, but I suspect he realizes I know too much and have too much talent. And he'd already been telling people what a find I was, how I was the next him. I could be too, you know.'

'I know. You are a formidable young man.'

'Of course all this is possible, my friend,

because you got me that picture of yourself and poor Roger. Saved the Short bacon but good. That was the Big Noise! Boola-boola! What a stroke of genius!'

'Wasn't it. But it wasn't mine. Speshnev used the same photo to blackmail *me*, can you believe it? The audacity of the man. He is a classic technician though, one must say.'

'So I'm a hero. And for you?'

'Well, the old fox has promised to use his influence on my behalf as well. So with your supervisor believing in you and the current man of the hour Speshnev fulfilling his part of our bargain, I do believe I'll be moving ahead shortly to a better posting. Plus, of course there are family allies working for me in Moscow. So this has worked out very well for both of us, I think. Possibly I'll get to Berlin as well.'

'Wouldn't that be a treat! Imagine how much fun we could have!'

'Imagine how far we could go. I'd give you all my colleagues' operations and you'd give me all your colleagues' operations. Yours and mine would flourish, theirs would fail. We'd be chiefs in a year!'

'The future,' said Frenchy Short, 'has never looked better. Progress is our most important product!'

The two young men raised a toast to their brilliant futures.

63

The boy had worked it out, he knew what he had to do, he set about to do it in an orderly fashion. He prepared for the day in the cool blaze of fall when he could fire a rifle and bring down a deer. It wasn't that he wanted to kill the animal for the pleasure of the killing. It wasn't even that the family could use the meat, though of course it could. It was, rather, some sense that in the spring, with his father, he had failed. And that very day his father had vanished, and not come back. So in his mind the two were connected: his failure, his father's disappearance. He solved this problem in a direct fashion: he would bring his father back to him by killing a deer and in some way changing fate.

He'd thought about his failure. He lacked confidence. When he'd brought the rifle up, its heaviness quickly overcame him. He believed he saw a wobble at the front sight and knew he could not yet shoot well enough to slay the creature cleanly, and so he'd panicked. That is how he reasoned.

Therefore salvation lay in the rifle. It was a Winchester .30-30, turned gray, close to purple, for the wear on its once royal-blue finish. It had a steel crescent of a butt plate, and was thin and rattly.

He shot it every morning and every afternoon.

A father should teach a boy these things but he committed to the rifle not with his father but to save his father. He read books on the rifle. He didn't understand the words sometimes, but he labored onward, educating himself, applying his mind and finding what his talents were. He studied ballistics tables, a helter-skelter of numbers that eventually clarified into something hard and clean and truthful. He talked to men who were hunters or known for their shooting ability. He gave himself to the rifle.

'All that boy does is shoot,' his mother would say. 'I'm glad he's doing *something*, because, Lord knows, when Earl was first gone, he just sat around with a long face. But somewhere he decided he would make himself the best shot in the county and surprise his daddy when his daddy comes home, and now it is a full obsession with him.'

The boy drew guns in the margins of his schoolbooks and read the famous writers on guns, Elmer Kaye and Jack O'Brien and even the late Ed McGriffin's great book, *Fast Guns and Trick Shots*. He read *Field and Stream* and *Sports Afield* and *The American Rifleman*. He went to the library and read *A Rifleman Went to War* and *With British Snipers to the Reich* and biographies of Audie Ryan and Alvin York, heroes of the rifle. He read all the Samworth books on firearms and hunting and soon enough knew a Luger from a .45 and a Peacemaker from a Schofield and a Nambu from an Ortgies. The more he read, the more he knew; for some reason, the information just stuck in his mind,

509

and he saw connections and controversies and lessons.

His own shooting abilities grew steadily; it seemed he had a talent, just like his daddy. He could hit things. He knew soon enough to read his own heart, and to shoot between beats. His finger grew subtle and disciplined in the ways it pressed against the trigger, so that it never jerked or hurried, but always came back in the same smooth way, waiting for the trigger on the old 94 to break off, feeling the springs fight him and then snap. He took a hundred dry-fired shots every night and by the second week did it with a penny balanced on the top of the receiver so that in pulling the trigger he didn't disturb the sight picture. He worked all the positions. He built the subtle undermuscles that made him rock-steady in any position.

The hot months of July and August gave way to September. A crispness came to the air, and ever so slowly the lushness of the west Arkansas woods began to suggest the coming of riotous color, a last blast of activity before the snow. So it was fall. So he had worked obsessively for two months. So a spurt of growth had come to him in his obsessiveness and he no longer had a boy's body, but was acquiring what would become a man's body. So now he stood back of the house in a hollow where he had improvised a shooting range. So now he inserted a .30-30 and with easy, steady, practiced fluidity, worked the lever, seating the round. The rifle came up steadily, steadied, and he found his position, the right balance of tightness, looseness, strength, and gentleness. At last the front sight settled in. It would never be dead still, but he knew that the figure-eight it traced would grow smaller and stiller until at last he could anticipate when it was on the target, and when that happened, at some instinctive level, he fired. He didn't hear the report, he didn't feel the recoil.

Far off a puff of dust rose behind a target stand. He called the shot perfect, and knew it was perfect. He opened the action of the rifle, shucked the spent case, picked up his father's binoculars, and indeed saw a cluster of holes in the ten-ring a hundred yards away. He could put bullets there hour after hour.

He turned, feeling good about what he had taught himself to do, seeing some value in it.

My daddy would be proud, he thought.

He picked up the shell, put it in his pocket for later reloading, and climbed from the hollow. It was near dark. A chill sliced the air. He shivered. Somehow time had passed. And then he saw the man.

It looked like a hobo, skinny and bent, shuffling up the long driveway from Route 8 a half-mile away, looking for a handout. The man walked wearily, as if his journey had been long and hard, and nothing in him seemed familiar.

And then of course it seemed all familiar, for the man assembled himself, almost magically, into his father.

'Daddy!' he screamed. His heart jumped, a spasm of pleasure and relief shot through him. He danced, he skipped, he ran, he ran, he ran.

His father, by cruel magic a much older man

now, watched him come, and knelt to absorb the boy in his arms and lift him and hug him.

'Daddy, Daddy, I won't never miss no deer again, I swear to you, I promise, Daddy.'

'That's fine, Bob Lee, it don't matter. I am home to stay and you can bet on that one!'

Acknowledgments

This novel didn't exist until a certain moment in time. I met my editor, the legendary Michael Korda, at a famous New York restaurant. In my pocket were sixteen index cards with sixteen ideas for The Next Book. I knew they pretty much sucked; I wasn't a happy traveler. Most writers will know what I am talking about.

Michael showed up in typical full-Korda fashion: ebullient, cosmopolitan, wickedly amused by the world's folly and full of peppery energy. He declared, 'Steve, I have an idea for you.'

I should tell you, I don't like other people's ideas. I can never seem to make them work; they never feel quite right. But he was paying, for both the lunch and the book, and so I smiled and said, okay, let's hear it, while thinking, *How soon before he forgets this one?*

He said three words: 'Earl in Havana.'

I knew instantly: that was the rest of my life, at least for a year or so.

I don't know if the rest is history, but it certainly was fun. So the first thanks go to Michael Korda for the best other-people idea I ever heard in my life and for a great year in the brothels and casinos of Old Havana and the killing fields of Santiago.

In Cuba, I have to thank my friend and translator Jorge Gonzalez, who trundled me all about the capital city in his thirteen-year-old Lada, explaining things and showing things. He got me to Hemingway's and to the Sevilla-Biltmore and the Nacionale and helped me locate what was once the Teatro Shanghai on Zanja Street and is now an empty field with a sign that says something absurd in that blowy commie rhetoric that is the Fidel style: 'Cubans United for the Revolution.' As if they had a choice.

Jorge was a gentleman and a scholar and I had a great time with him.

In Santiago I stayed atop San Juan Hill and hired two drivers; one, improbably, was named Bryce. I'm sure he went home to his wife Muffy and their two kids, Skip and Holly, where they followed the Harvard crew results. He was a decent man; the find, however, came the next day in the form of a bright green 1956 Chrysler Imperial with those little satellite taillights on the fins. Really a cool car. But the owner of this automobile was a young man named Wenkel as I understood it, and he was a terrific guy. We did Santiago together. The next day, when I flew back to Havana, he drove me to the airport and felt he had to introduce me to his wife and son. I rode in back with the kid, four, shy and beautiful, who finally called me 'Inglis,' just like I was Robert Jordan. How cool is that? I'm hoping for the best for Wenkel and his family; that car alone should be worth seventy-five grand when the thaw finally comes.

Here, the usual merry band helped out. The fabulous Jean Marbella actually hooked me up with Jorge, whom she had met on one of her several trips to the island for *The Baltimore Sun*. At the *Washington Post*, my two immediate supervisors — good old John Pancake and Peter Kaufman — were unperturbably supportive. Gene Robinson, the assistant managing editor for *Style*, is an old Cuba hand (he's writing a book about Cuban music) and he gave me excellent advice. Paul Richard pitched in with reading suggestions and enthusiasm. Retired from the *Post*, Bill Smart, who actually logged time in Cuba in the fifties, helped me recreate the Plaza de Armas in Santiago as it was then, as opposed to the New Socialist Concrete-Gothic monstrosity it's become. Henry Allen made a great, late catch.

My friends Weyman Swagger (also my portraitist), Lenne Miller and Bob Lopez pitched in with keen early readings. Weyman, as I've said before, is a superb natural editor. Mike Clark, the film critic of *USA Today*, loaned me his video copies of three Cuban-set films, most important *Our Man in Havana*, which, among other delights, is the best photographic record of Havana in the fifties available. From Marc Dozal at Noirfilm.com I got another batch of film noirs with Cuban settings or occasional Cuban motifs, including *Miami Expose* and *Affair in Havana*. Marc also found me a copy of *Our Man in Havana* that I didn't have to give back and could study at my leisure. So in some sense my roman noir is set in a film noir. My good friend and hunting partner John Bainbridge gave me a superb proofreading job. And thanks again to

515

Bob Beers, who voluntarily maintains a website at www.stephenhunter.net. Why he does this I have no idea, but he seems to enjoy it.

A few confessions: I am aware that the Earl of *Havana* doesn't connect in perfect joinery with the first Earl, of *Black Light* so many years ago. I trust readers will understand that he's grown in complexity and experience as I've stayed with him over the past few books. Possibly in some better future I'll have a chance to do another pass on *Black Light* — I suppose when Harvard brings out the *Collected Novels of Stephen Hunter* — and reconcile the two Earls into one figure.

I should also say that the pistol I refer to consistently as the Super .38 is now called a .38 Super. I'm not sure when the Super migrated to the rear of the construction, but all the original Colt period documents of the gun call it a Super .38 through the fifties at least. Mine, built in 1949, is stamped 'Colt Super .38' on the slide. I decided to go with Colt. If they don't know, who does?

Finally, as to historicity. The CIA was clearly aware of Castro as early as 1953; the rest I've jiggered to suit my dramatic needs, and had a hell of a good time doing so. For the record, everything is where I say it is in the book and it looks like I say it looks. I make certain adjustments for the sake of simplicity and because I am a novelist, not a historian: other rebel initiatives on the night of July 26, 1953, meant to coincide with the attack on the barracks, I chose to ignore. (By the way, a really good historical narrative on Moncada in English has yet to be written; some brilliant young nonfiction writer out there, get busy.) Fidel was captured a few miles north of where I place him, not on a beach but in a farmhouse while he slept, though his capturer was indeed Lieutenant Sarria; there was an infamous torturer in Santiago named Ojos Bellos, though what became of him I don't know. I hope it wasn't pretty.

Finally, we have no idea when Soviet contact with Castro began. I've enjoyed imagining that it began in 1953. Whatever, History will absolve me.

We do hope that you have enjoyed reading
this large print book.

Did you know that all of our titles
are available for purchase?

We publish a wide range of high quality
large print books including:
Romances, Mysteries, Classics
General Fiction
Non Fiction and Westerns

Special interest titles available in
large print are:
The Little Oxford Dictionary
Music Book
Song Book
Hymn Book
Service Book

Also available from us courtesy of Oxford
University Press:
Young Readers' Dictionary
(large print edition)
Young Readers' Thesaurus
(large print edition)

For further information or a free
brochure, please contact us at:
Ulverscroft Large Print Books Ltd.,
The Green, Bradgate Road, Anstey,
Leicester, LE7 7FU, England.
Tel: (00 44) 0116 236 4325
Fax: (00 44) 0116 234 0205